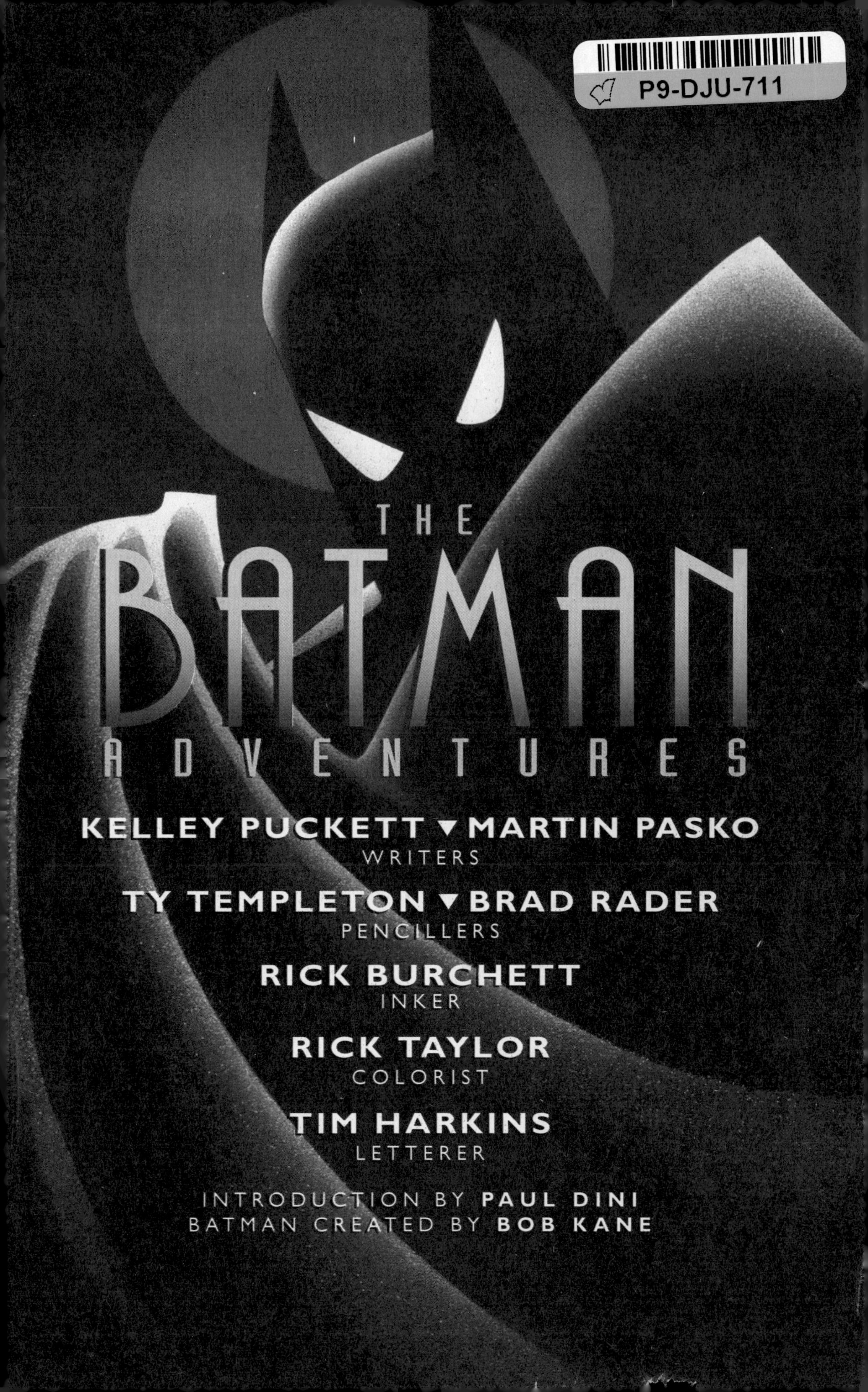

THE BATMAN ADVENTURES

KELLEY PUCKETT ▾ MARTIN PASKO
WRITERS

TY TEMPLETON ▾ BRAD RADER
PENCILLERS

RICK BURCHETT
INKER

RICK TAYLOR
COLORIST

TIM HARKINS
LETTERER

INTRODUCTION BY **PAUL DINI**
BATMAN CREATED BY **BOB KANE**

BATMAN'S MOST ANIMATED ADVENTURES

AN INTRODUCTION BY PAUL DINI

Talk about coming full circle. First there was the BATMAN comic book. Then *BATMAN: THE ANIMATED SERIES*, and finally, THE BATMAN ADVENTURES, the comic book based on the TV show based on the comic book. Of course, it hasn't been a straight shot from point

A to points B and C. Within the fifty-three years between Batman's first appearance in DETECTIVE COMICS #27 and the debut of his current Fox animated series, there have been numerous other additions to the legend and lore of the Caped Crusader. Naturally one thinks of the recent hit feature films, the sixties live-action TV series, the two cliffhanger serials from the forties, Frank Miller's magnificent BATMAN: THE DARK KNIGHT RETURNS, and, does anyone besides me remember

Over the next few pages, we present excerpts from the storyboard art for the promotional reel for BAT-MAN: THE ANIMATED SERIES by Bruce Timm. The film was produced to demonstrate the unique vision Paul Dini and Bruce Timm had in mind. In a slightly altered form, several scenes from this sequence appear in the opening credits for the series.

Batman (along with Robin) as an occasional guest star on Superman's radio series? I thought not, but he was there, trust me.

Blend the best of these elements and you get a remarkably sharp, reasonably consistent image of Batman and his world: Bruce Wayne/Batman, Dick Grayson/ Robin, Alfred, the Batcave, Batmobile, Batboat, Batwing, bat-cetera, Commissioner Gordon, Gotham City, The Joker, Penguin, Catwoman and the rest.

These are the classic elements everyone associates with Batman, and it was to these roots that the production staff at Warner Bros. returned to craft their animated series. The dark, deco look of Gotham City and stylized design of its denizens (by series producers Bruce Timm and Eric Radomski) all hearken back to the simple, yet elegantly rendered look of the early Batman comics. Likewise the stories reflect the straight-ahead action and multilayered characterizations that firmly fixed Batman, Robin, their allies and rogues gallery as enduring members of American popular fiction.

It's a given that as long as there will be animated cartoon characters, there will be spin-off comic books of their adventures. In rare cases (Carl Barks' Duck books, for

example) the comics actually do the animation one better. Mostly, however, an animated character's life in comics seems somewhat tame when compared to that of their screen counterparts. Sequences that are cinematically daring on film lack energy and motion when translated to the printed page. Shadows and muted hues that set the emotional tone of a scene are often reduced to incongruously cheerful four-color brightness. Even visual action, the very soul of animation, seems stilted when laboriously re-rendered (frequently with unnecessary expository dialogue) in comics.

Happily none of these demons can be found within this compilation of THE BATMAN ADVENTURES. Though inspired in design by *BATMAN: THE ANIMATED SERIES*, this book quickly establishes itself as great entertainment in its own right. The stories written by Kelley Puckett (and occasionally by animated series writer/story editor Martin Pasko), and wonderfully illustrated by Ty Templeton and Warner Animation's Brad Rader (aided and abetted by the incredible Rick Burchett and the colorful Rick Taylor), keeps Batman's world dark but not dismal, the villains wicked but not horrific, and the action

thrilling but not brutal.

Be advised right now, this is not "Batman lite," it's Batman Classic: from the macabre black humor of the Joker's TV exposé to the Catwoman's sultry slinkings to a particularly moving glimpse into the Scarecrow's tortured conscience, it's the stuff of bat-legends at their best. And rising above it all is the Dark Knight himself, grim, incorruptible and, with that cape wrapped around him (check out the climax to "The Third Door") looking cool as hell. It's Batman as you've always known him, and will again. Enjoy!

Paul Dini
(Writer/Story Editor,
BATMAN: THE ANIMATED SERIES)

FIRST
ISSUE!

THE
BATMAN
ADVENTURES

1
OCT 92

US $1.25
CAN $1.50
UK 60p

BASED ON
HIT
FOX-TV SH

PENGUIN'S BIG SCORE

ACT ONE: CHARM SCHOOL DROPOUT!

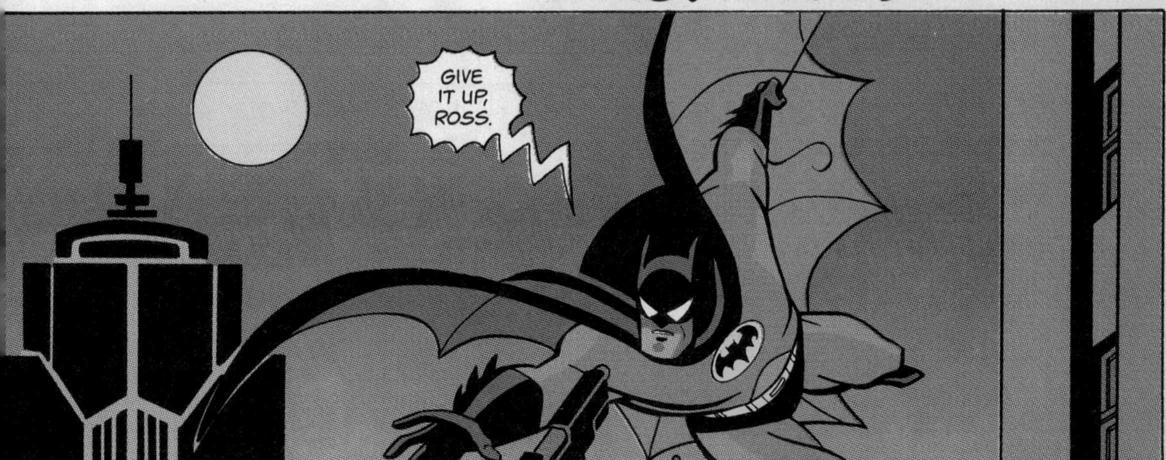
GIVE IT UP, ROSS.
YOU'LL NEVER TAKE ME ALIVE, BATMAN!
SHOOT, ROSS! SHOOT!

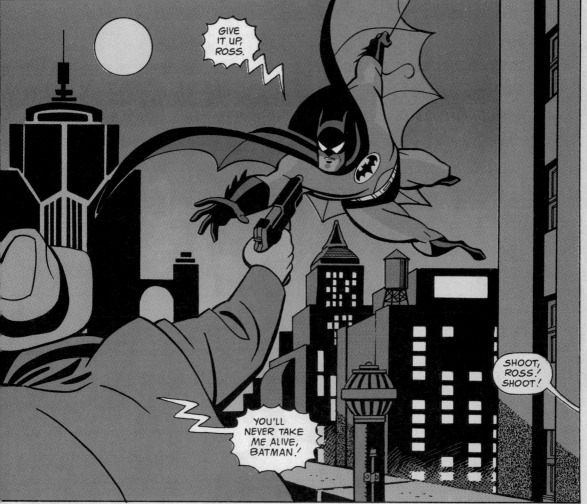

KELLEY PUCKETT ~ WRITER TY TEMPLETON ~ PENCILLER RICK BURCHETT ~ INKER
RICK TAYLOR ~ COLORIST TIM HARKINS ~ LETTERER SCOTT PETERSON ~ EDITOR
BATMAN CREATED BY BOB KANE *WITH SPECIAL THANKS TO SAM ARGO

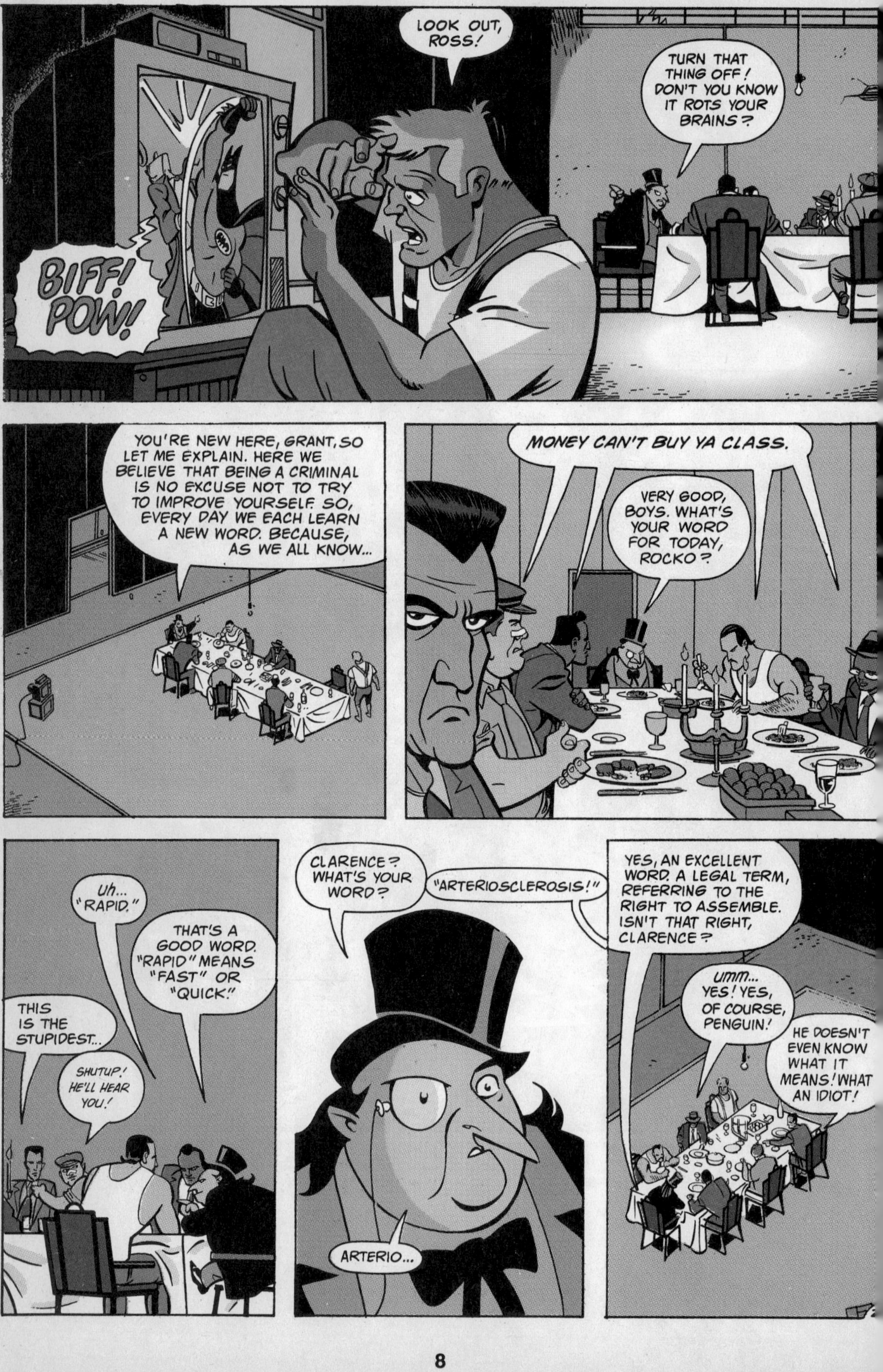
BIFF! POW!
LOOK OUT, ROSS!
TURN THAT THING OFF! DON'T YOU KNOW IT ROTS YOUR BRAINS?
YOU'RE NEW HERE, GRANT, SO LET ME EXPLAIN. HERE WE BELIEVE THAT BEING A CRIMINAL IS NO EXCUSE NOT TO TRY TO IMPROVE YOURSELF. SO, EVERY DAY WE EACH LEARN A NEW WORD. BECAUSE, AS WE ALL KNOW...
MONEY CAN'T BUY YA CLASS.
VERY GOOD, BOYS. WHAT'S YOUR WORD FOR TODAY, ROCKO?
Uh... "RAPID."
THAT'S A GOOD WORD. "RAPID" MEANS "FAST" OR "QUICK."
THIS IS THE STUPIDEST...
SHUTUP! HE'LL HEAR YOU!
CLARENCE? WHAT'S YOUR WORD?
ARTERIO...
"ARTERIOSCLEROSIS!"
YES, AN EXCELLENT WORD. A LEGAL TERM, REFERRING TO THE RIGHT TO ASSEMBLE. ISN'T THAT RIGHT, CLARENCE?
umm... YES! YES, OF COURSE, PENGUIN!
HE DOESN'T EVEN KNOW WHAT IT MEANS! WHAT AN IDIOT!

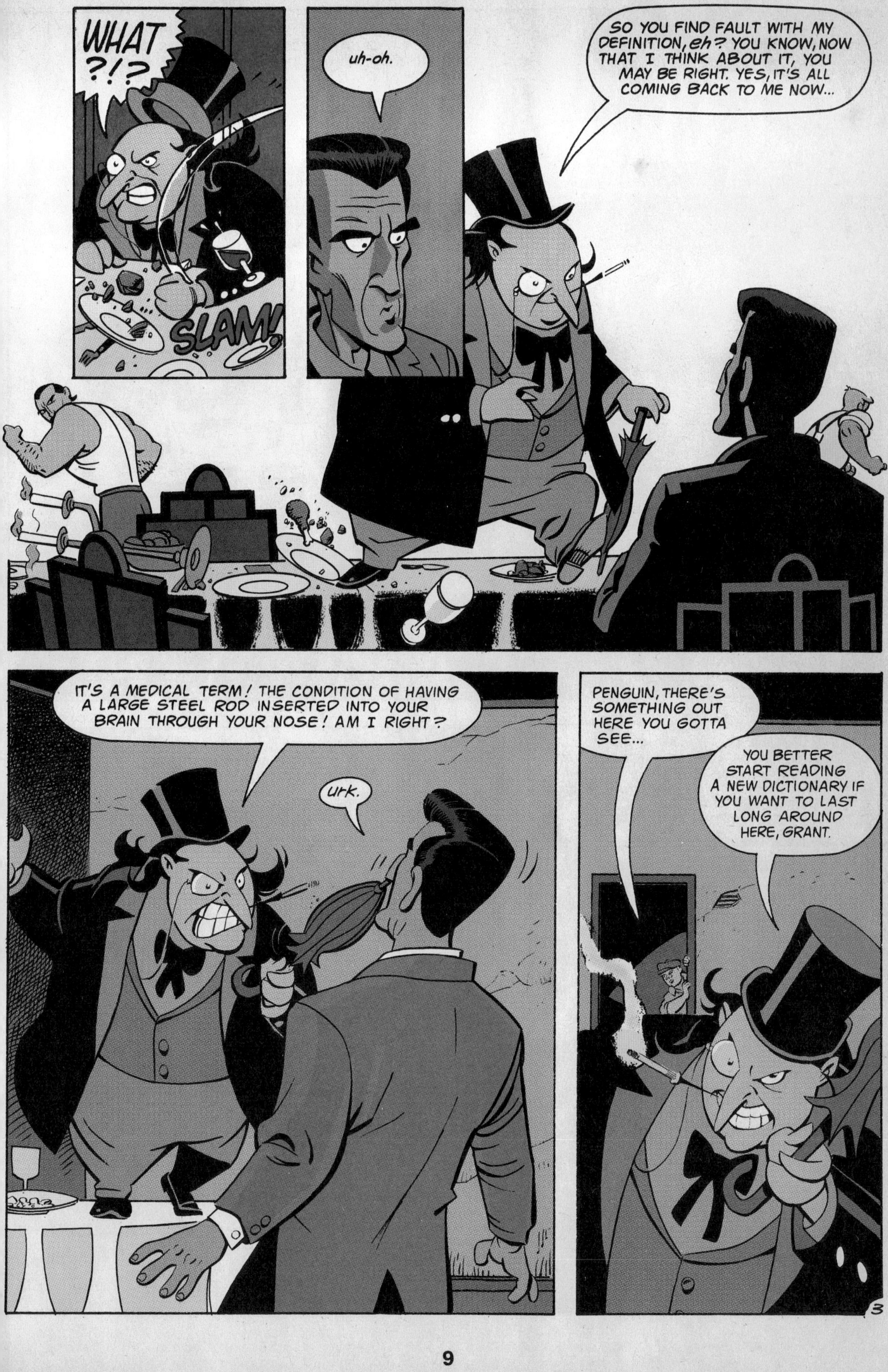
WHAT ?!?
SLAM!
uh-oh.
SO YOU FIND FAULT WITH MY DEFINITION, eh? YOU KNOW, NOW THAT I THINK ABOUT IT, YOU MAY BE RIGHT. YES, IT'S ALL COMING BACK TO ME NOW...
IT'S A MEDICAL TERM! THE CONDITION OF HAVING A LARGE STEEL ROD INSERTED INTO YOUR BRAIN THROUGH YOUR NOSE! AM I RIGHT?
urk.
PENGUIN, THERE'S SOMETHING OUT HERE YOU GOTTA SEE...
YOU BETTER START READING A NEW DICTIONARY IF YOU WANT TO LAST LONG AROUND HERE, GRANT.
3

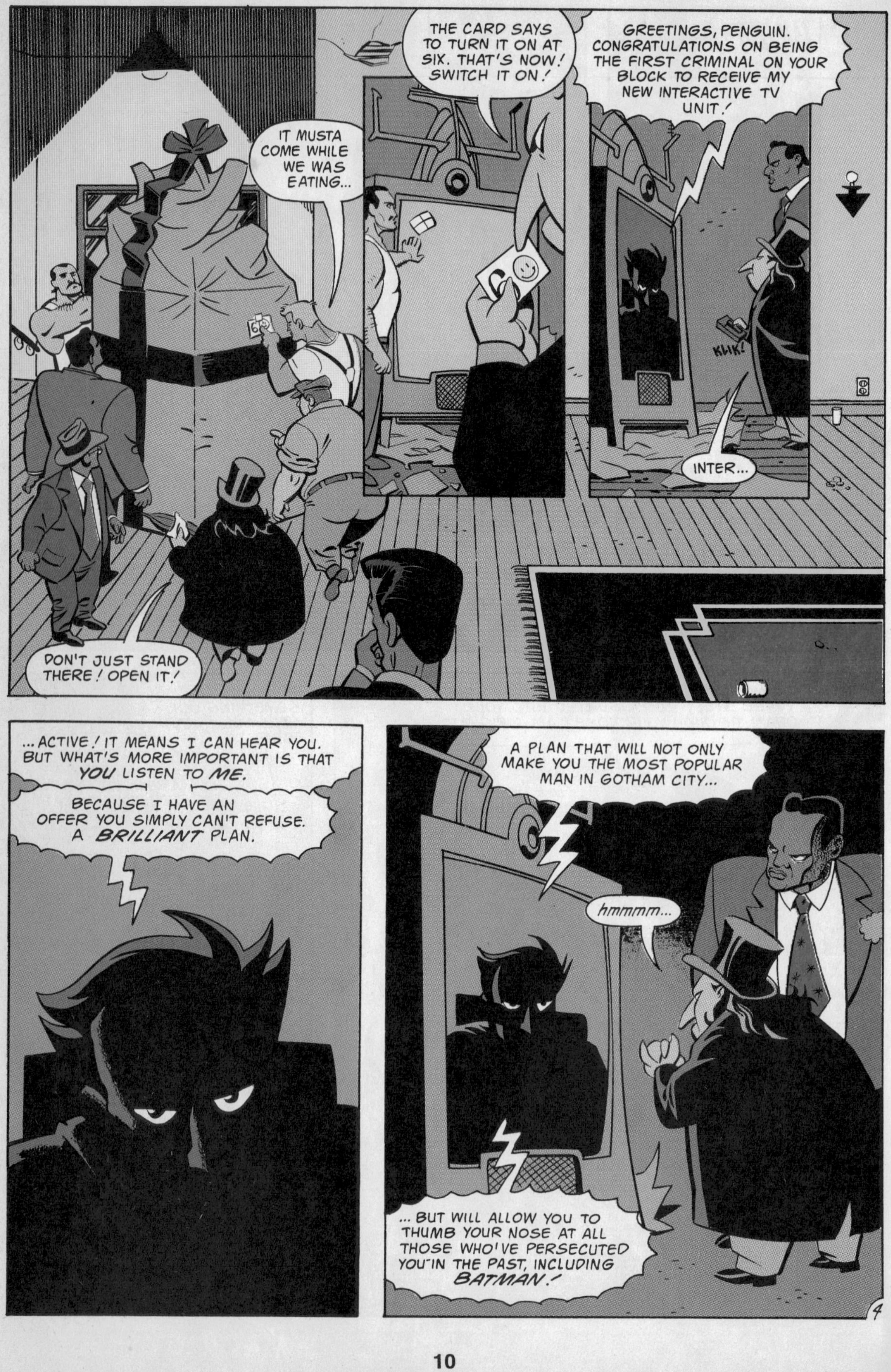
IT MUSTA COME WHILE WE WAS EATING...
DON'T JUST STAND THERE! OPEN IT!
THE CARD SAYS TO TURN IT ON AT SIX. THAT'S NOW! SWITCH IT ON!
GREETINGS, PENGUIN. CONGRATULATIONS ON BEING THE FIRST CRIMINAL ON YOUR BLOCK TO RECEIVE MY NEW INTERACTIVE TV UNIT!
KLIK!
INTER...
...ACTIVE! IT MEANS I CAN HEAR YOU. BUT WHAT'S MORE IMPORTANT IS THAT YOU LISTEN TO ME.
BECAUSE I HAVE AN OFFER YOU SIMPLY CAN'T REFUSE. A BRILLIANT PLAN.
A PLAN THAT WILL NOT ONLY MAKE YOU THE MOST POPULAR MAN IN GOTHAM CITY...
hmmmm...
... BUT WILL ALLOW YOU TO THUMB YOUR NOSE AT ALL THOSE WHO'VE PERSECUTED YOU IN THE PAST, INCLUDING BATMAN!
4

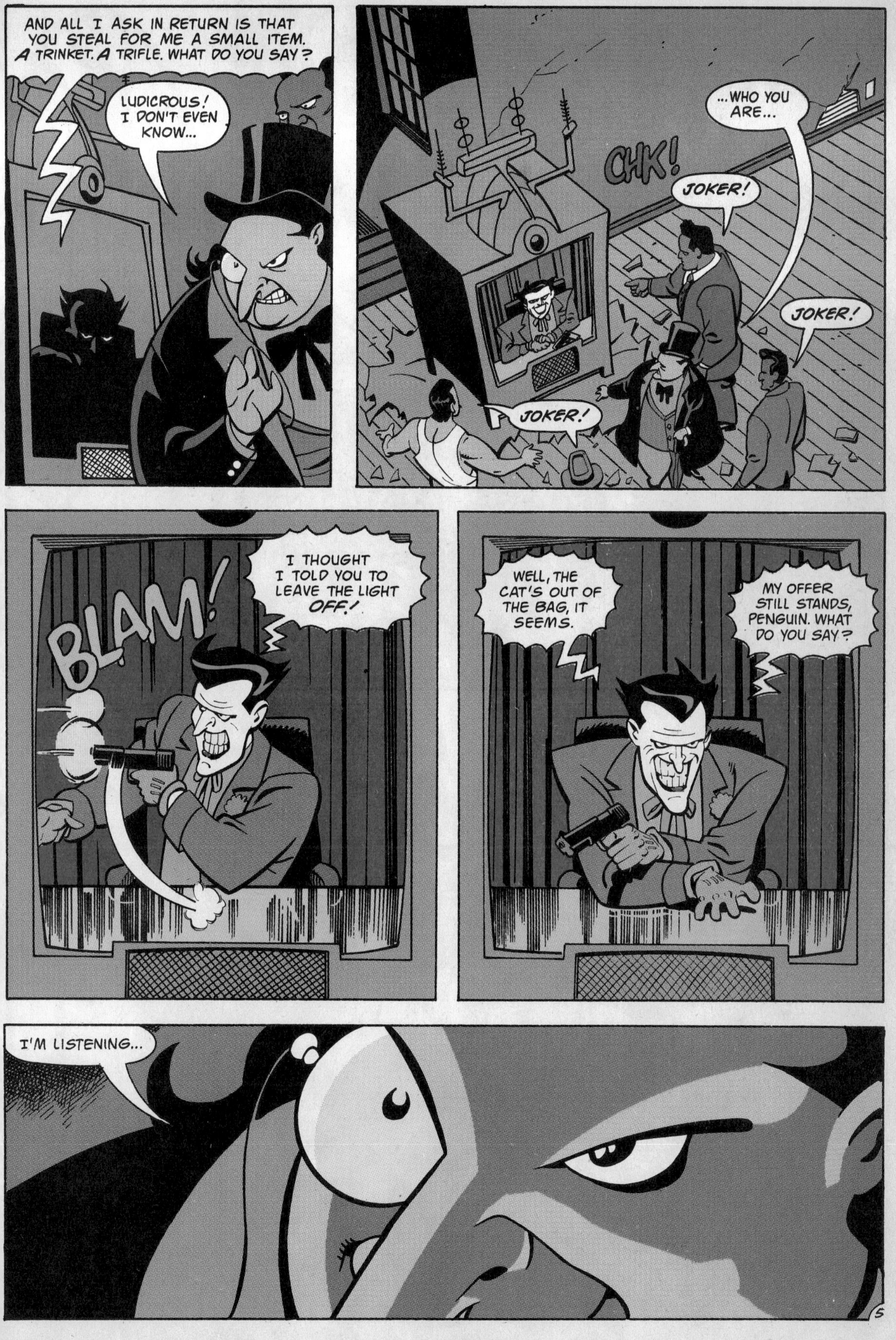
AND ALL I ASK IN RETURN IS THAT YOU STEAL FOR ME A SMALL ITEM. A TRINKET. A TRIFLE. WHAT DO YOU SAY?
LUDICROUS! I DON'T EVEN KNOW...
...WHO YOU ARE...
CHK!
JOKER!
JOKER!
JOKER!
BLAM!
I THOUGHT I TOLD YOU TO LEAVE THE LIGHT OFF!
WELL, THE CAT'S OUT OF THE BAG, IT SEEMS.
MY OFFER STILL STANDS, PENGUIN. WHAT DO YOU SAY?
I'M LISTENING...
5

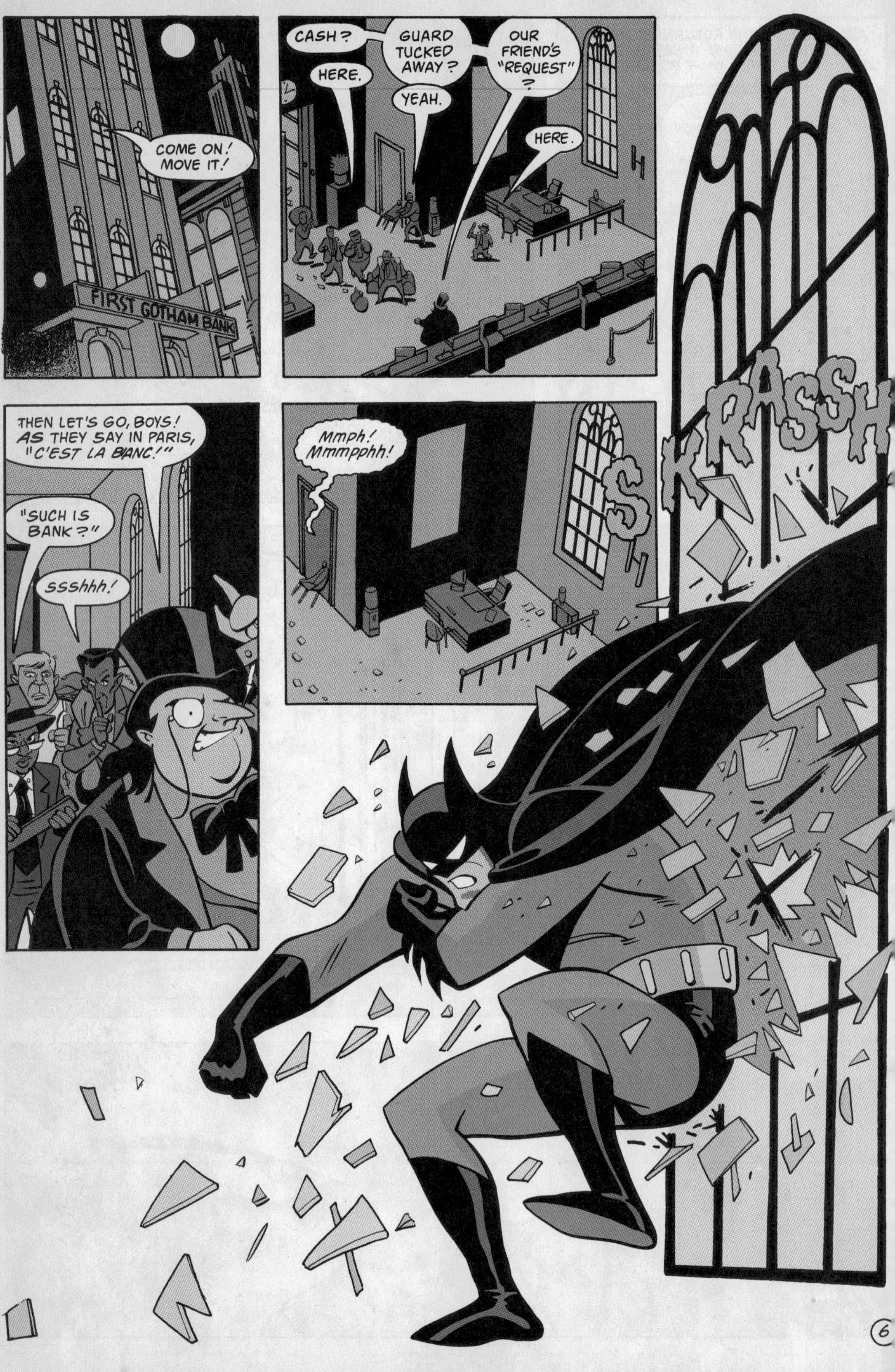

COME ON! MOVE IT!
FIRST GOTHAM BANK
CASH?
HERE.
GUARD TUCKED AWAY?
YEAH.
OUR FRIEND'S "REQUEST"?
HERE.
THEN LET'S GO, BOYS! AS THEY SAY IN PARIS, "C'EST LA BIANC!"
"SUCH IS BANK?"
SSSHHH!
Mmph! Mmmpphh!
KRASSH
6

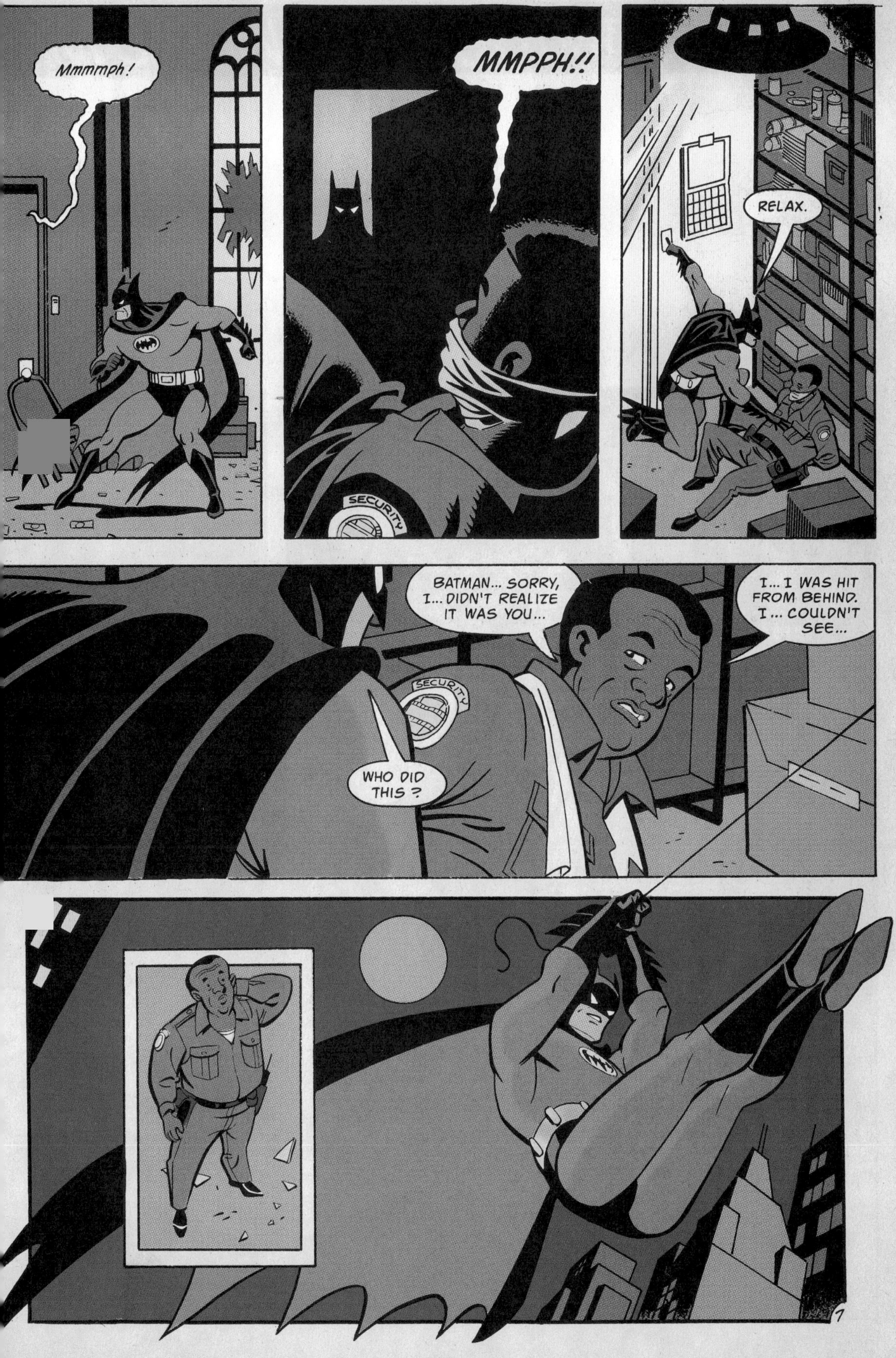
Mmmmph!
MMPPH!!
SECURITY
RELAX.
BATMAN... SORRY, I... DIDN'T REALIZE IT WAS YOU...
I... I WAS HIT FROM BEHIND. I... COULDN'T SEE...
SECURITY
WHO DID THIS?
7

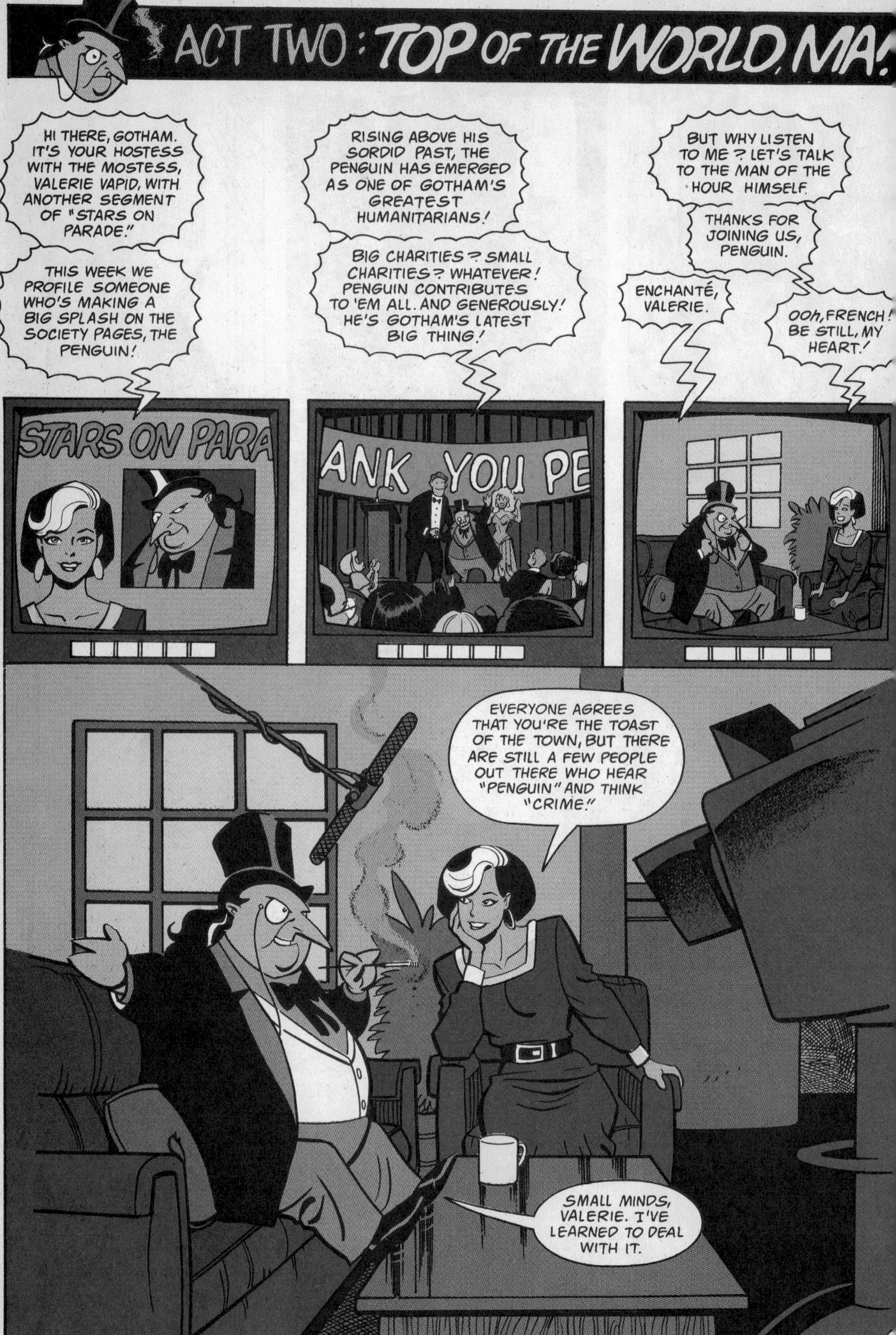
ACT TWO: TOP OF THE WORLD, MA!
HI THERE, GOTHAM. IT'S YOUR HOSTESS WITH THE MOSTESS, VALERIE VAPID, WITH ANOTHER SEGMENT OF "STARS ON PARADE."
THIS WEEK WE PROFILE SOMEONE WHO'S MAKING A BIG SPLASH ON THE SOCIETY PAGES, THE PENGUIN!
STARS ON PARA
RISING ABOVE HIS SORDID PAST, THE PENGUIN HAS EMERGED AS ONE OF GOTHAM'S GREATEST HUMANITARIANS!
BIG CHARITIES? SMALL CHARITIES? WHATEVER! PENGUIN CONTRIBUTES TO 'EM ALL. AND GENEROUSLY! HE'S GOTHAM'S LATEST BIG THING!
ANK YOU PE
BUT WHY LISTEN TO ME? LET'S TALK TO THE MAN OF THE HOUR HIMSELF.
THANKS FOR JOINING US, PENGUIN.
ENCHANTÉ, VALERIE.
OOH, FRENCH! BE STILL, MY HEART!
EVERYONE AGREES THAT YOU'RE THE TOAST OF THE TOWN, BUT THERE ARE STILL A FEW PEOPLE OUT THERE WHO HEAR "PENGUIN" AND THINK "CRIME."
SMALL MINDS, VALERIE. I'VE LEARNED TO DEAL WITH IT.

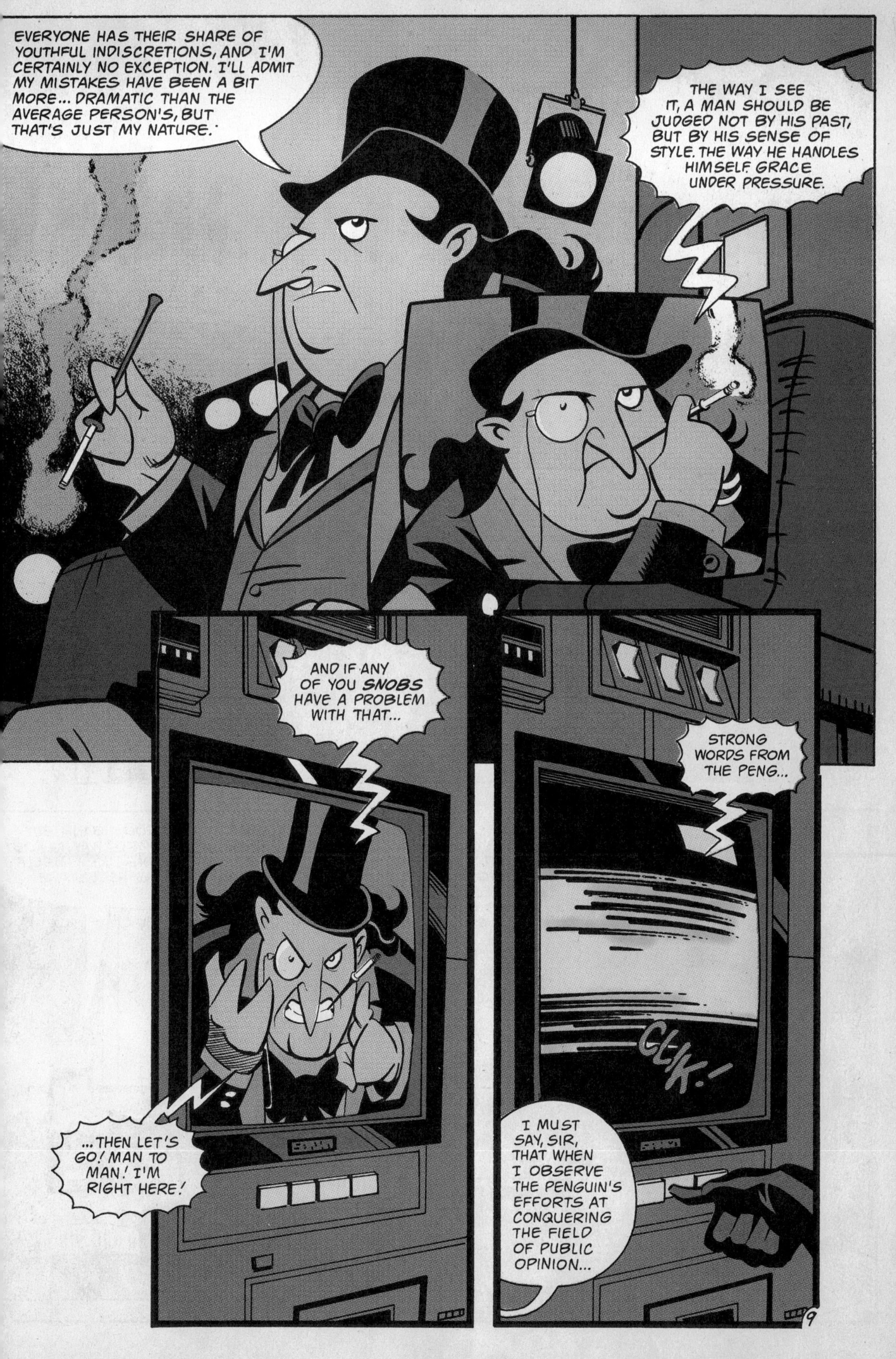
EVERYONE HAS THEIR SHARE OF YOUTHFUL INDISCRETIONS, AND I'M CERTAINLY NO EXCEPTION. I'LL ADMIT MY MISTAKES HAVE BEEN A BIT MORE... DRAMATIC THAN THE AVERAGE PERSON'S, BUT THAT'S JUST MY NATURE.
THE WAY I SEE IT, A MAN SHOULD BE JUDGED NOT BY HIS PAST, BUT BY HIS SENSE OF STYLE. THE WAY HE HANDLES HIMSELF. GRACE UNDER PRESSURE.
AND IF ANY OF YOU SNOBS HAVE A PROBLEM WITH THAT...
...THEN LET'S GO! MAN TO MAN! I'M RIGHT HERE!
STRONG WORDS FROM THE PENG...
CLIK!
I MUST SAY, SIR, THAT WHEN I OBSERVE THE PENGUIN'S EFFORTS AT CONQUERING THE FIELD OF PUBLIC OPINION...
9

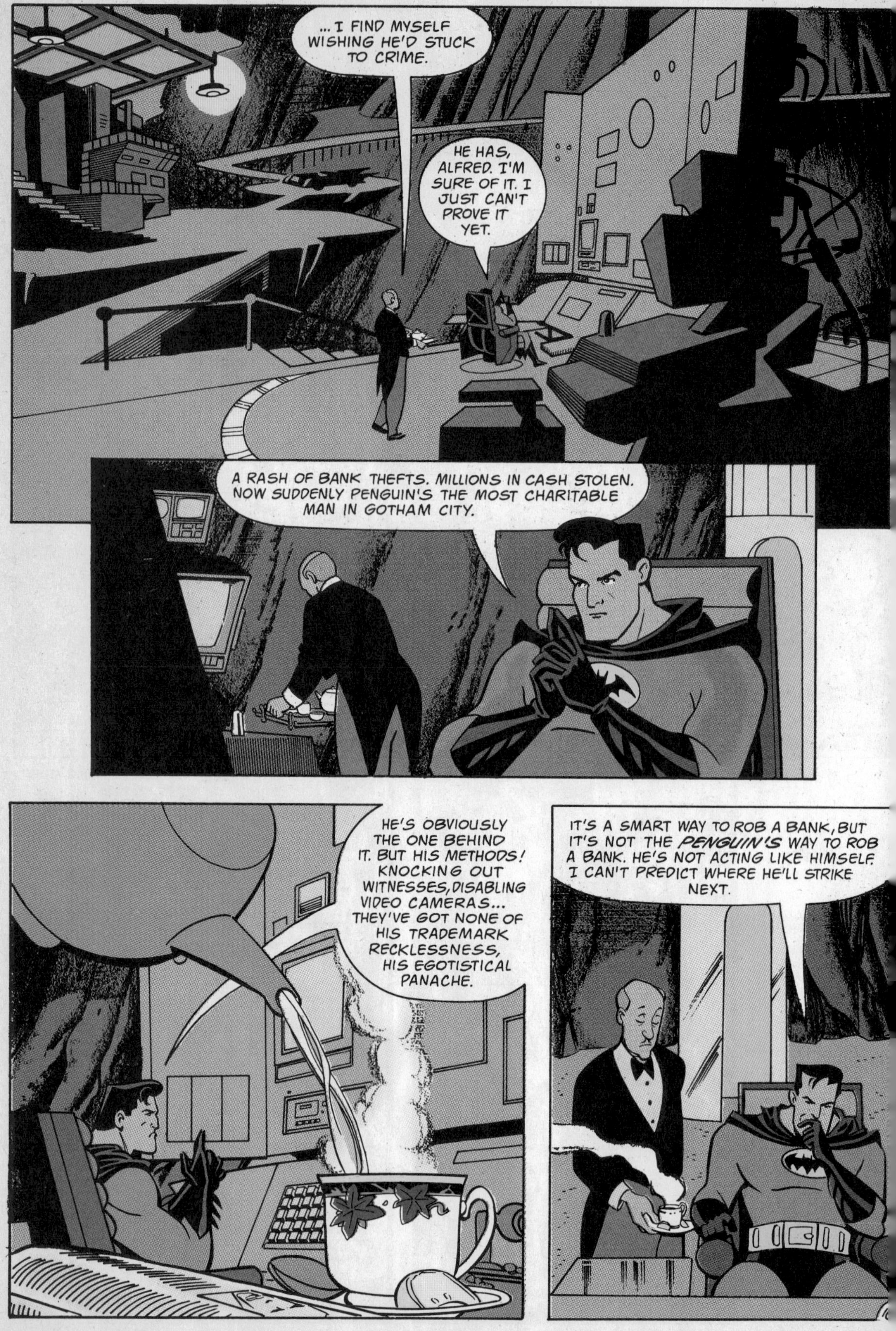
...I FIND MYSELF WISHING HE'D STUCK TO CRIME.
HE HAS, ALFRED. I'M SURE OF IT. I JUST CAN'T PROVE IT YET.
A RASH OF BANK THEFTS. MILLIONS IN CASH STOLEN. NOW SUDDENLY PENGUIN'S THE MOST CHARITABLE MAN IN GOTHAM CITY.
HE'S OBVIOUSLY THE ONE BEHIND IT. BUT HIS METHODS! KNOCKING OUT WITNESSES, DISABLING VIDEO CAMERAS... THEY'VE GOT NONE OF HIS TRADEMARK RECKLESSNESS, HIS EGOTISTICAL PANACHE.
IT'S A SMART WAY TO ROB A BANK, BUT IT'S NOT THE *PENGUIN'S* WAY TO ROB A BANK. HE'S NOT ACTING LIKE HIMSELF. I CAN'T PREDICT WHERE HE'LL STRIKE NEXT.

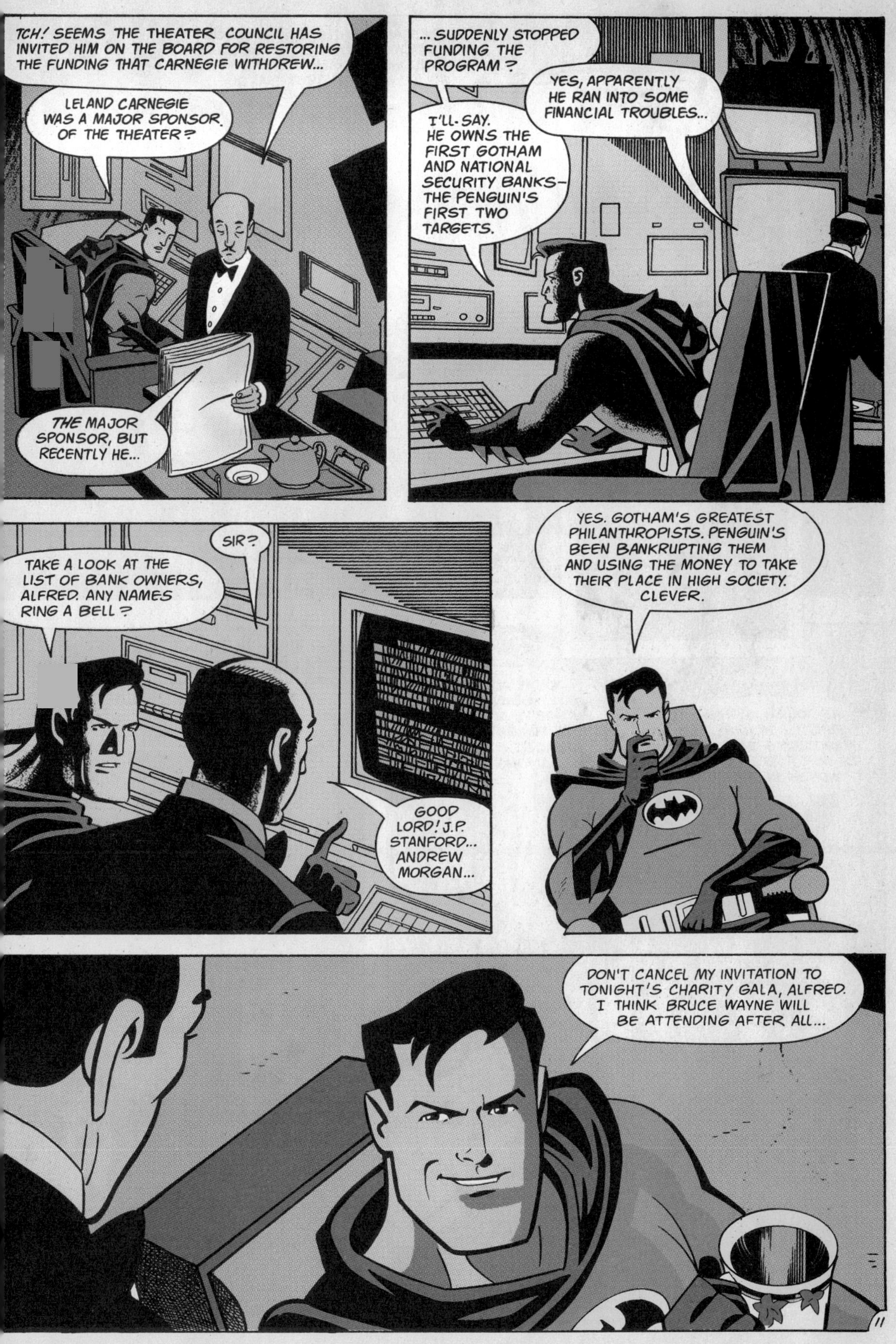
TCH! SEEMS THE THEATER COUNCIL HAS INVITED HIM ON THE BOARD FOR RESTORING THE FUNDING THAT CARNEGIE WITHDREW...
LELAND CARNEGIE WAS A MAJOR SPONSOR OF THE THEATER?
THE MAJOR SPONSOR, BUT RECENTLY HE...
... SUDDENLY STOPPED FUNDING THE PROGRAM?
YES, APPARENTLY HE RAN INTO SOME FINANCIAL TROUBLES...
I'LL SAY. HE OWNS THE FIRST GOTHAM AND NATIONAL SECURITY BANKS— THE PENGUIN'S FIRST TWO TARGETS.
TAKE A LOOK AT THE LIST OF BANK OWNERS, ALFRED. ANY NAMES RING A BELL?
SIR?
GOOD LORD! J.P. STANFORD... ANDREW MORGAN...
YES. GOTHAM'S GREATEST PHILANTHROPISTS. PENGUIN'S BEEN BANKRUPTING THEM AND USING THE MONEY TO TAKE THEIR PLACE IN HIGH SOCIETY. CLEVER.
DON'T CANCEL MY INVITATION TO TONIGHT'S CHARITY GALA, ALFRED. I THINK BRUCE WAYNE WILL BE ATTENDING AFTER ALL...
11

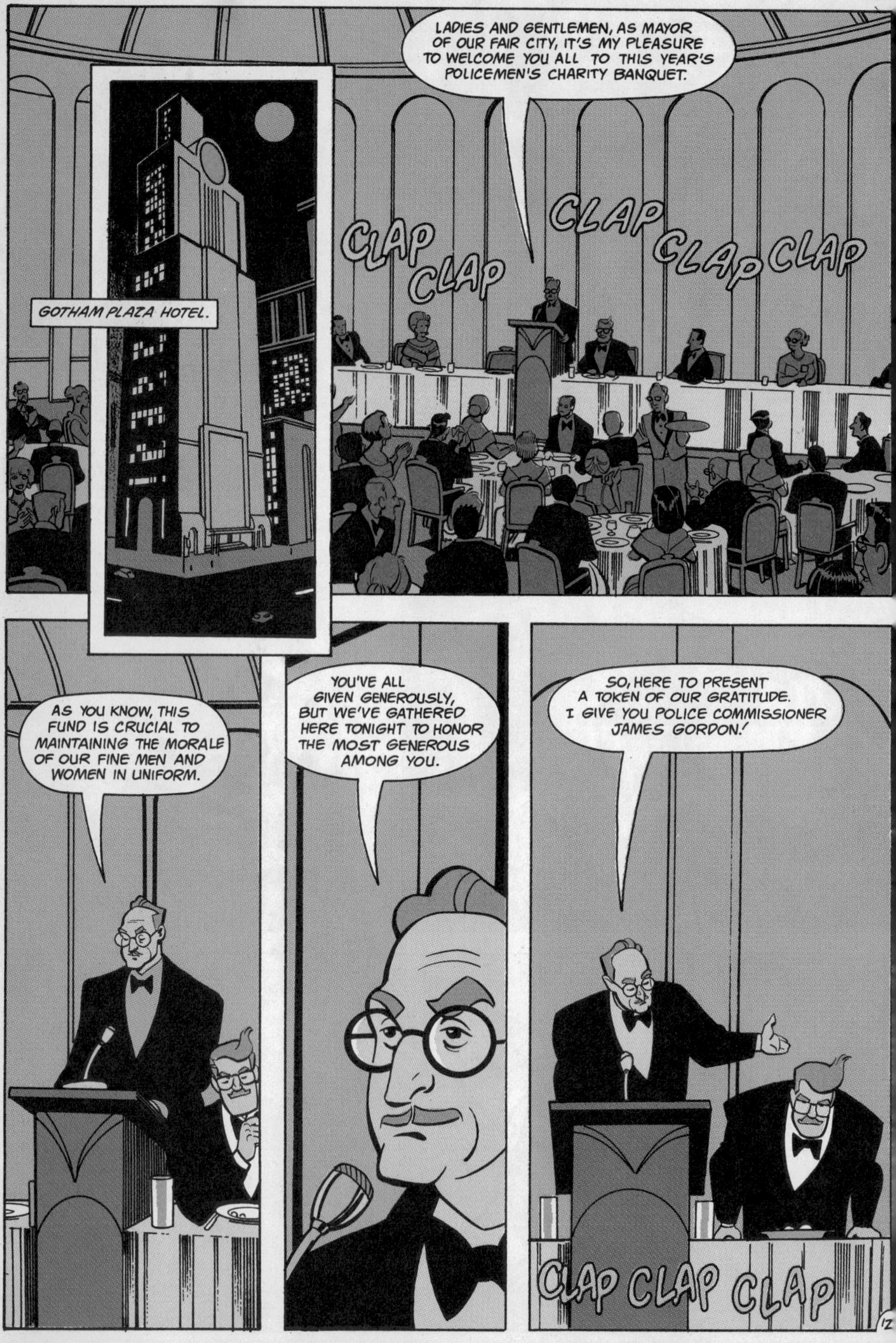

GOTHAM PLAZA HOTEL.
LADIES AND GENTLEMEN, AS MAYOR OF OUR FAIR CITY, IT'S MY PLEASURE TO WELCOME YOU ALL TO THIS YEAR'S POLICEMEN'S CHARITY BANQUET.
CLAP CLAP
CLAP CLAP CLAP
AS YOU KNOW, THIS FUND IS CRUCIAL TO MAINTAINING THE MORALE OF OUR FINE MEN AND WOMEN IN UNIFORM.
YOU'VE ALL GIVEN GENEROUSLY, BUT WE'VE GATHERED HERE TONIGHT TO HONOR THE MOST GENEROUS AMONG YOU.
SO, HERE TO PRESENT A TOKEN OF OUR GRATITUDE. I GIVE YOU POLICE COMMISSIONER JAMES GORDON!
CLAP CLAP CLAP
12

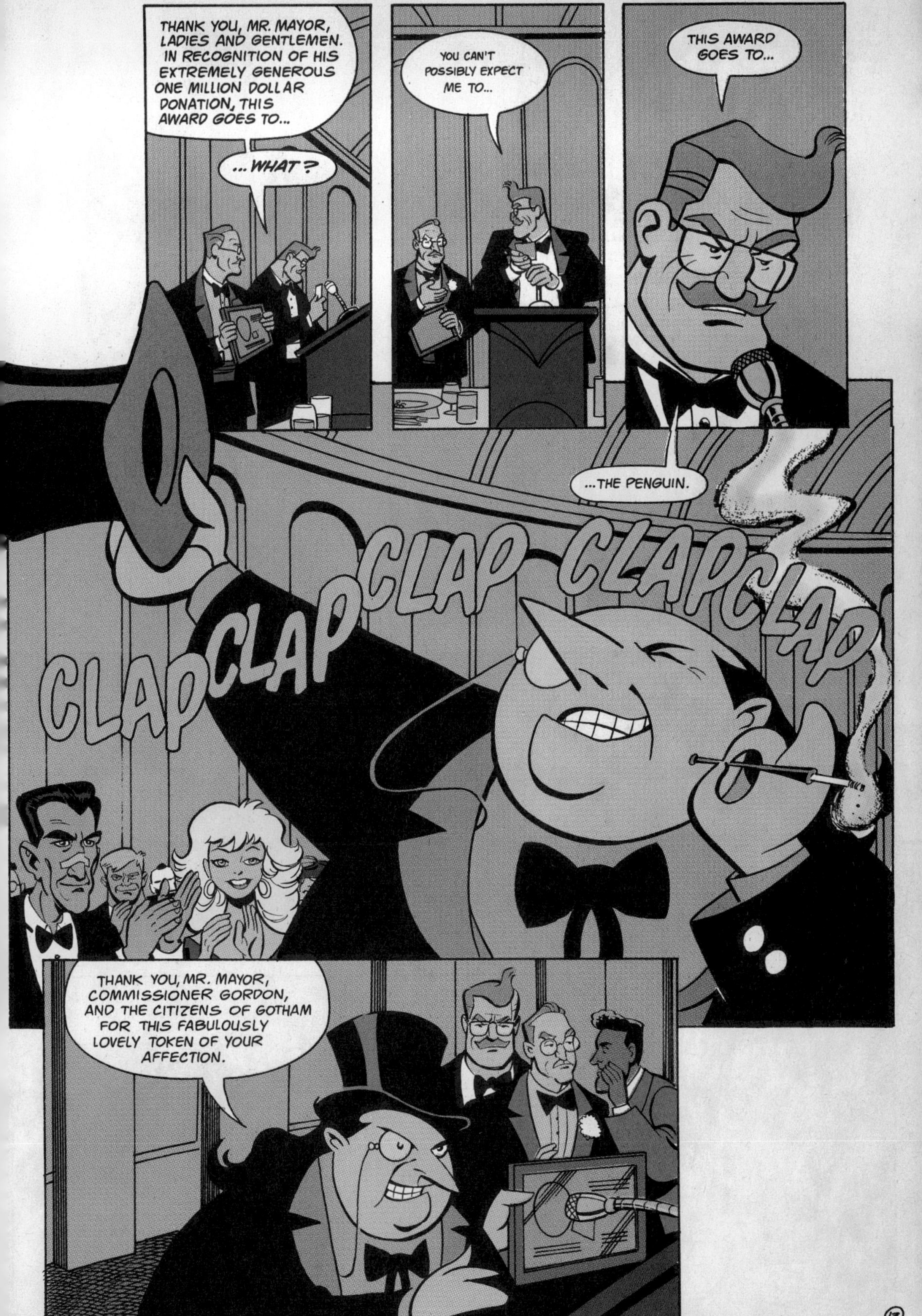
THANK YOU, MR. MAYOR, LADIES AND GENTLEMEN. IN RECOGNITION OF HIS EXTREMELY GENEROUS ONE MILLION DOLLAR DONATION, THIS AWARD GOES TO...
...WHAT?
YOU CAN'T POSSIBLY EXPECT ME TO...
THIS AWARD GOES TO...
...THE PENGUIN.
CLAP CLAP CLAP CLAP CLAP CLAP
THANK YOU, MR. MAYOR, COMMISSIONER GORDON, AND THE CITIZENS OF GOTHAM FOR THIS FABULOUSLY LOVELY TOKEN OF YOUR AFFECTION.
13

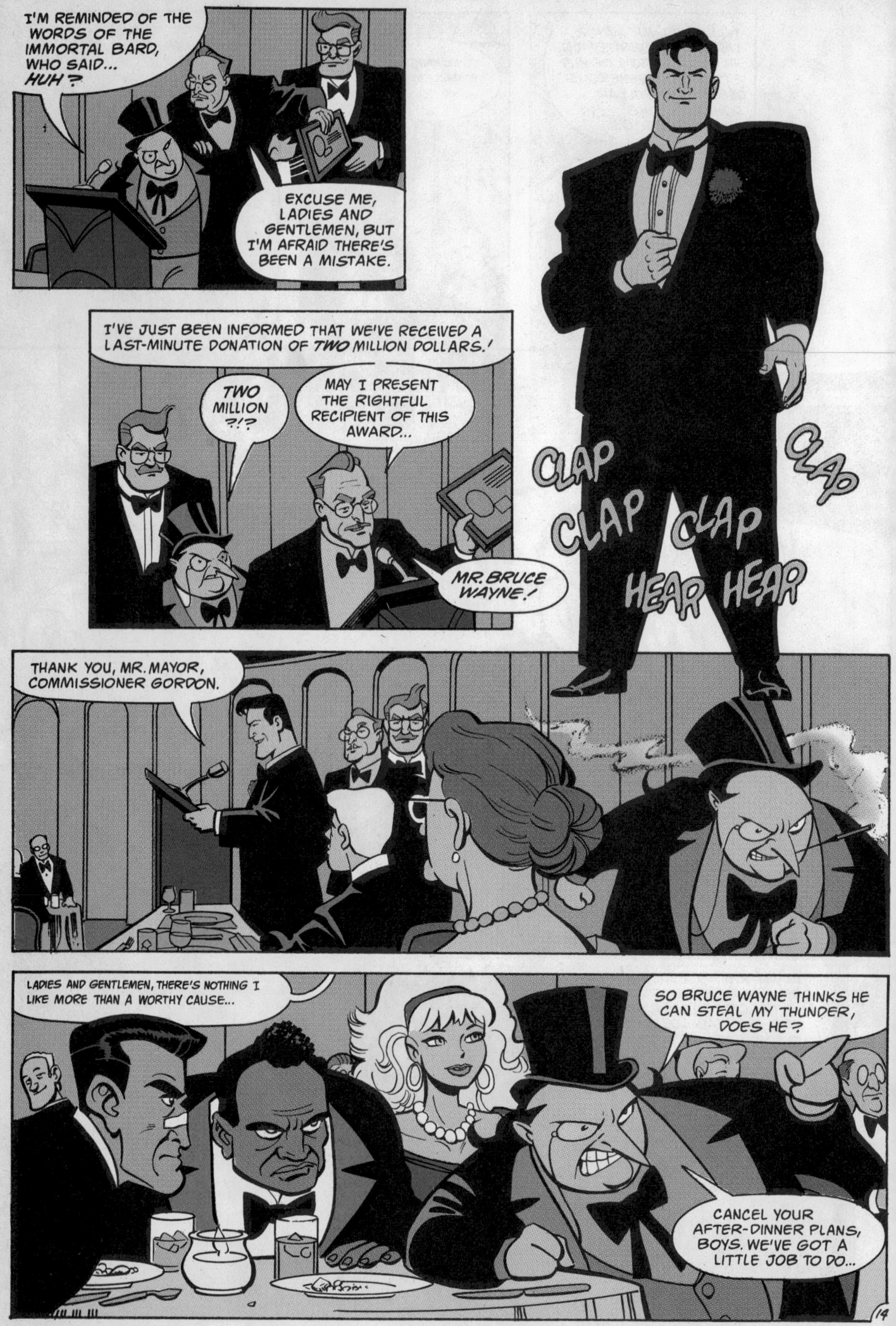
I'M REMINDED OF THE WORDS OF THE IMMORTAL BARD, WHO SAID... HUH?
EXCUSE ME, LADIES AND GENTLEMEN, BUT I'M AFRAID THERE'S BEEN A MISTAKE.
I'VE JUST BEEN INFORMED THAT WE'VE RECEIVED A LAST-MINUTE DONATION OF TWO MILLION DOLLARS!
TWO MILLION ?!?
MAY I PRESENT THE RIGHTFUL RECIPIENT OF THIS AWARD...
MR. BRUCE WAYNE!
CLAP
CLAP
CLAP
CLAP
HEAR HEAR
THANK YOU, MR. MAYOR, COMMISSIONER GORDON.
LADIES AND GENTLEMEN, THERE'S NOTHING I LIKE MORE THAN A WORTHY CAUSE...
SO BRUCE WAYNE THINKS HE CAN STEAL MY THUNDER, DOES HE?
CANCEL YOUR AFTER-DINNER PLANS, BOYS. WE'VE GOT A LITTLE JOB TO DO...
14

16

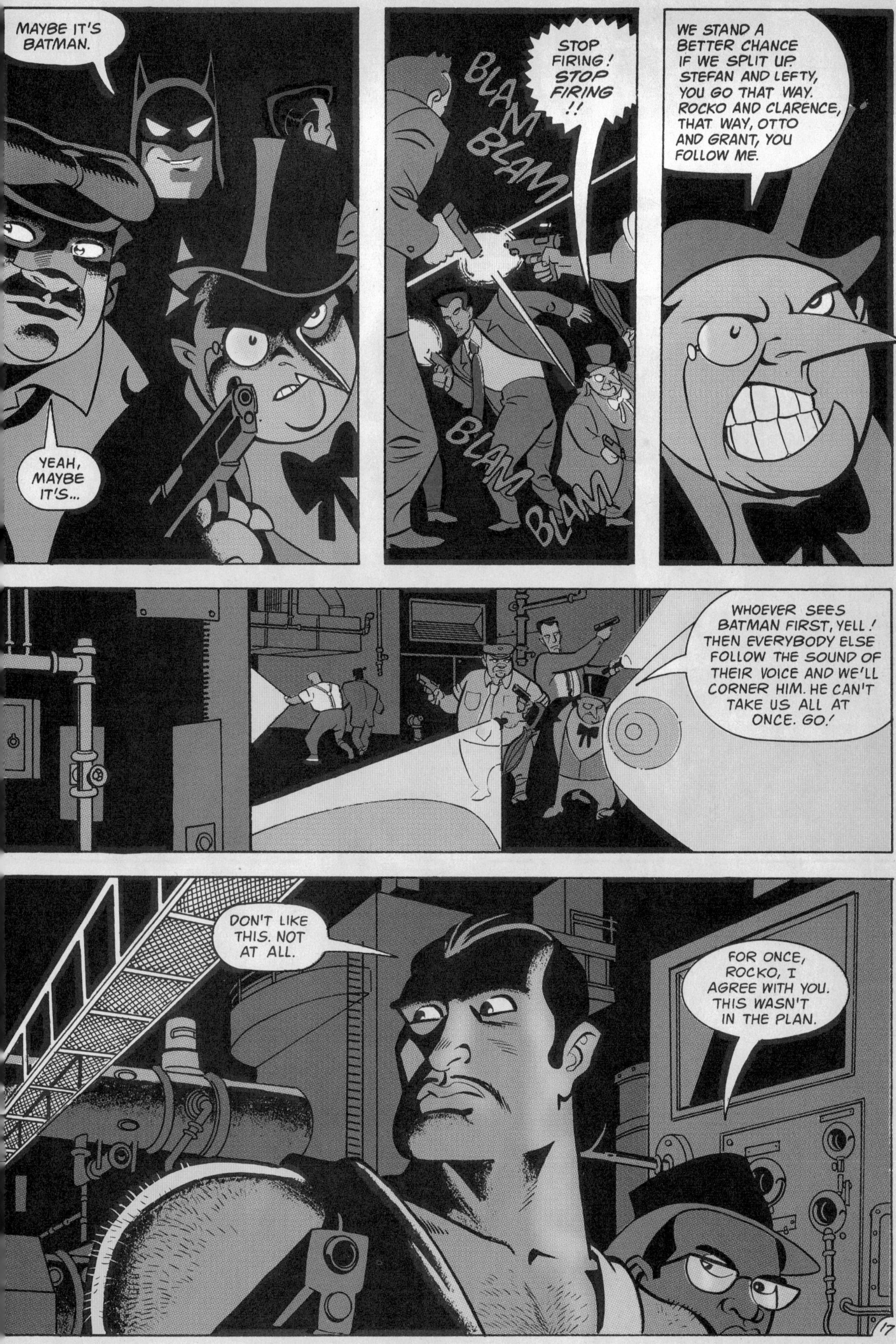
MAYBE IT'S BATMAN.
YEAH, MAYBE IT'S...
BLAM BLAM BLAM
STOP FIRING! STOP FIRING!!
BLAM BLAM
WE STAND A BETTER CHANCE IF WE SPLIT UP. STEFAN AND LEFTY, YOU GO THAT WAY. ROCKO AND CLARENCE, THAT WAY, OTTO AND GRANT, YOU FOLLOW ME.
WHOEVER SEES BATMAN FIRST, YELL! THEN EVERYBODY ELSE FOLLOW THE SOUND OF THEIR VOICE AND WE'LL CORNER HIM. HE CAN'T TAKE US ALL AT ONCE. GO!
DON'T LIKE THIS. NOT AT ALL.
FOR ONCE, ROCKO, I AGREE WITH YOU. THIS WASN'T IN THE PLAN.
17

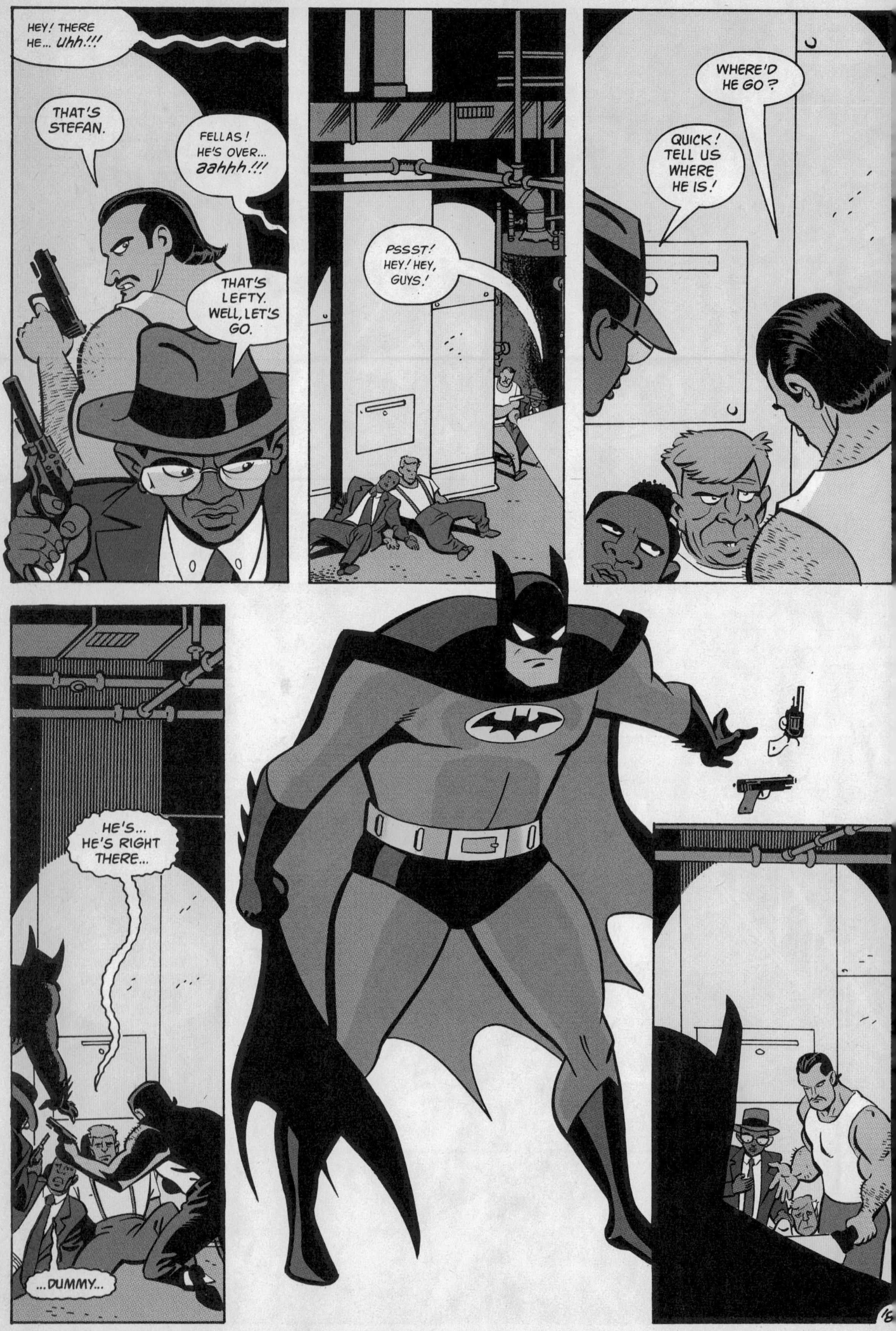
HEY! THERE HE... Uhh!!!
THAT'S STEFAN.
FELLAS! HE'S OVER... aahhh!!!
THAT'S LEFTY. WELL, LET'S GO.
PSSST! HEY! HEY, GUYS!
WHERE'D HE GO?
QUICK! TELL US WHERE HE IS!
HE'S... HE'S RIGHT THERE...
...DUMMY...

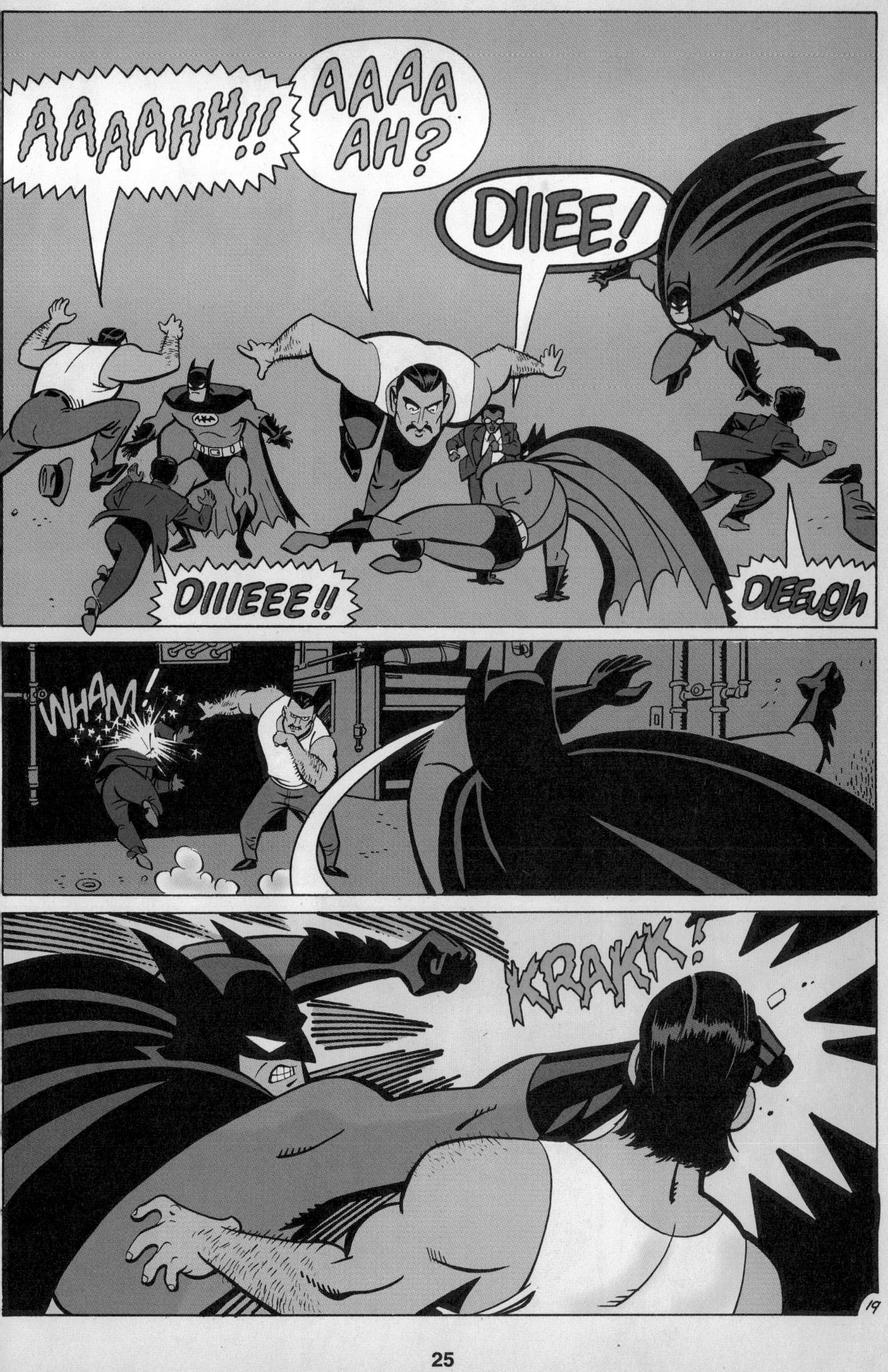
AAAAHH!!
AAAA AH?
DIIEE!
DIIIEEE!!
DIEEugh
WHAM!
KRAKK!
19

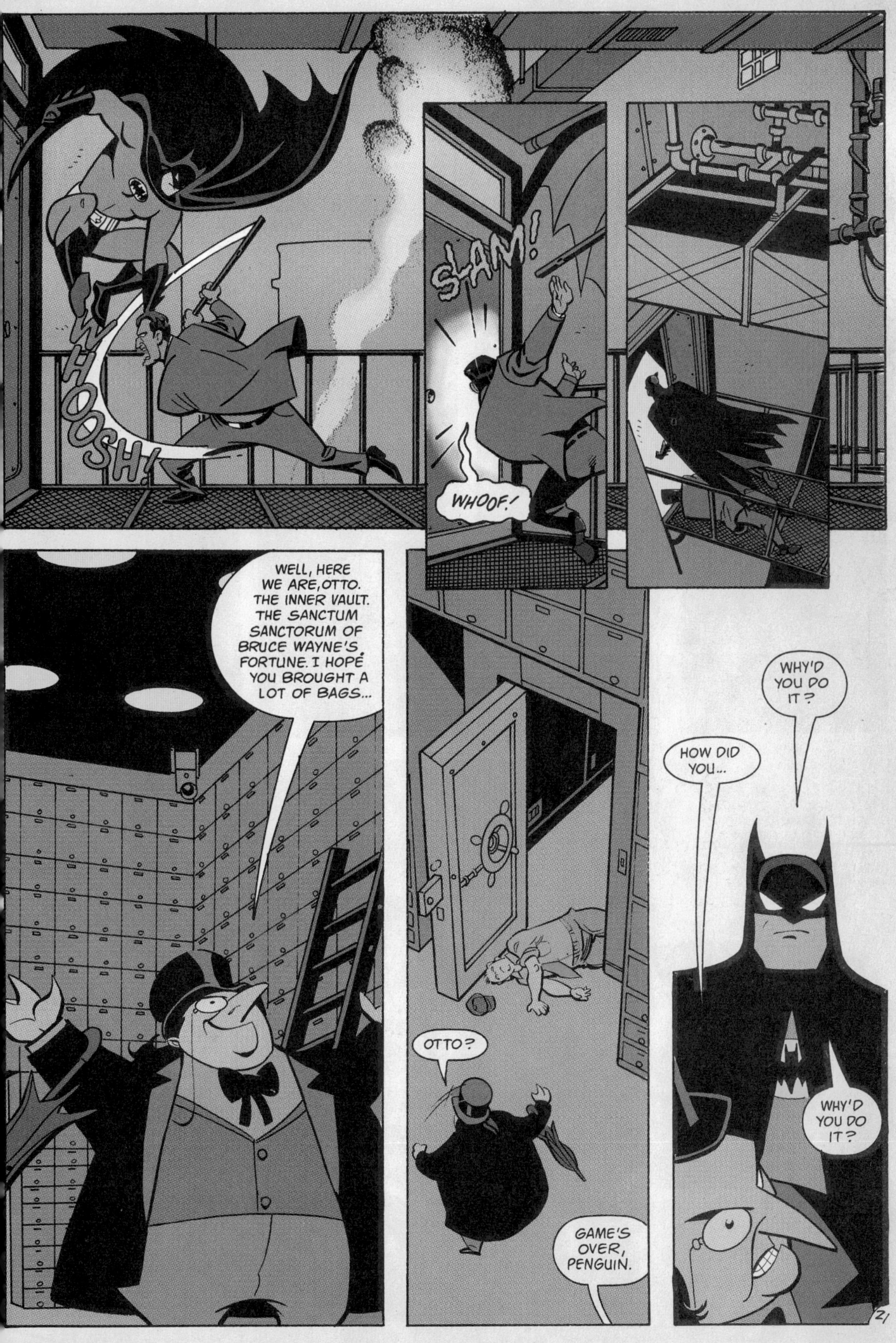
WHOOSH!
SLAM!
WHOOF!
WELL, HERE WE ARE, OTTO. THE INNER VAULT. THE SANCTUM SANCTORUM OF BRUCE WAYNE'S FORTUNE. I HOPE YOU BROUGHT A LOT OF BAGS...
OTTO?
GAME'S OVER, PENGUIN.
WHY'D YOU DO IT?
HOW DID YOU...
WHY'D YOU DO IT?
21

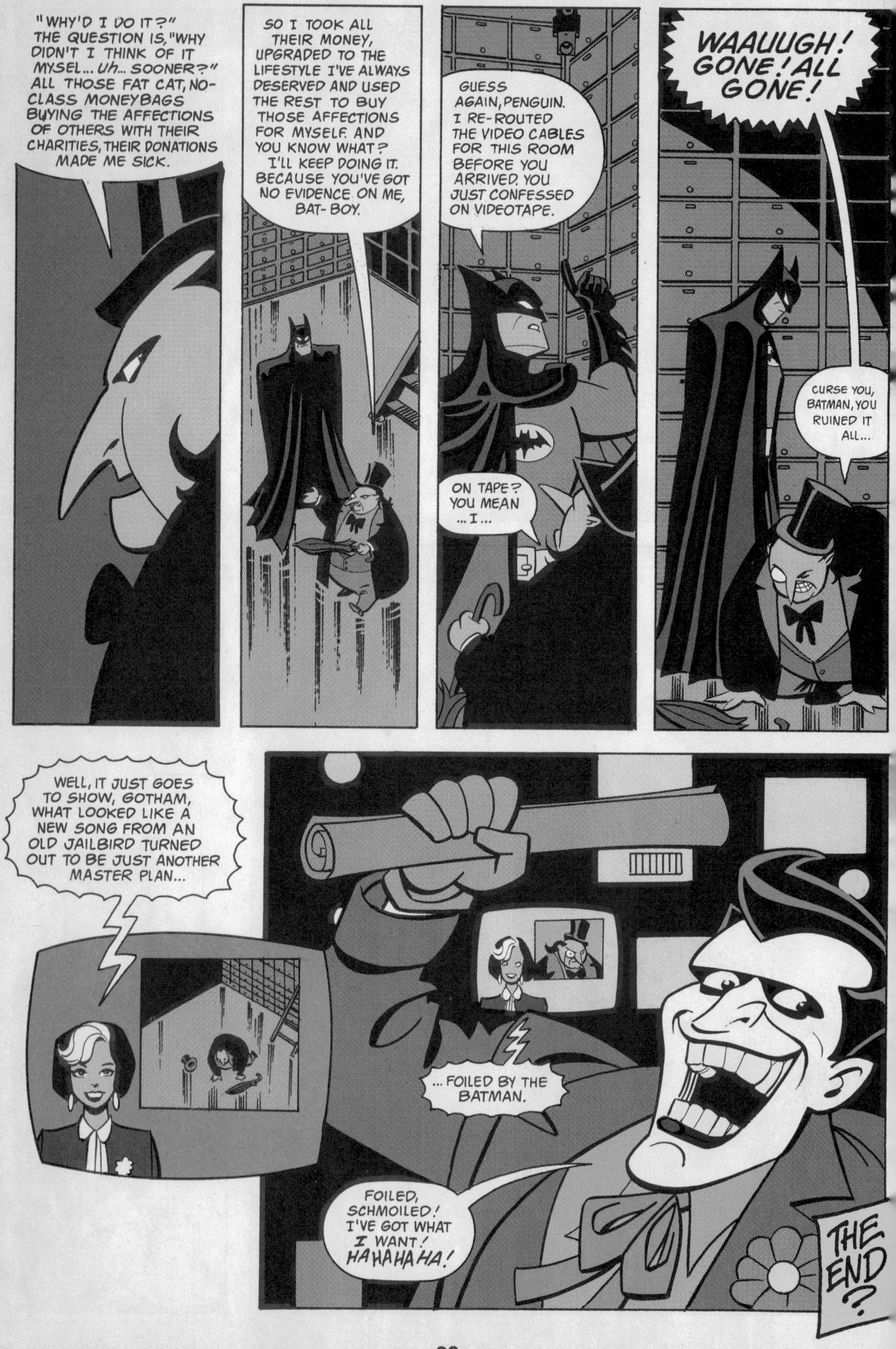
"WHY'D I DO IT?" THE QUESTION IS, "WHY DIDN'T I THINK OF IT MYSEL... *uh*... SOONER?" ALL THOSE FAT CAT, NO-CLASS MONEYBAGS BUYING THE AFFECTIONS OF OTHERS WITH THEIR CHARITIES, THEIR DONATIONS MADE ME SICK.
SO I TOOK ALL THEIR MONEY, UPGRADED TO THE LIFESTYLE I'VE ALWAYS DESERVED AND USED THE REST TO BUY THOSE AFFECTIONS FOR MYSELF. AND YOU KNOW WHAT? I'LL KEEP DOING IT. BECAUSE YOU'VE GOT NO EVIDENCE ON ME, BAT-BOY.
GUESS AGAIN, PENGUIN. I RE-ROUTED THE VIDEO CABLES FOR THIS ROOM BEFORE YOU ARRIVED. YOU JUST CONFESSED ON VIDEOTAPE.
ON TAPE? YOU MEAN ...I...
WAAUUGH! GONE! ALL GONE!
CURSE YOU, BATMAN, YOU RUINED IT ALL...
WELL, IT JUST GOES TO SHOW, GOTHAM, WHAT LOOKED LIKE A NEW SONG FROM AN OLD JAILBIRD TURNED OUT TO BE JUST ANOTHER MASTER PLAN...
...FOILED BY THE BATMAN.
FOILED, SCHMOILED! I'VE GOT WHAT *I* WANT! HAHAHAHA!
THE END?

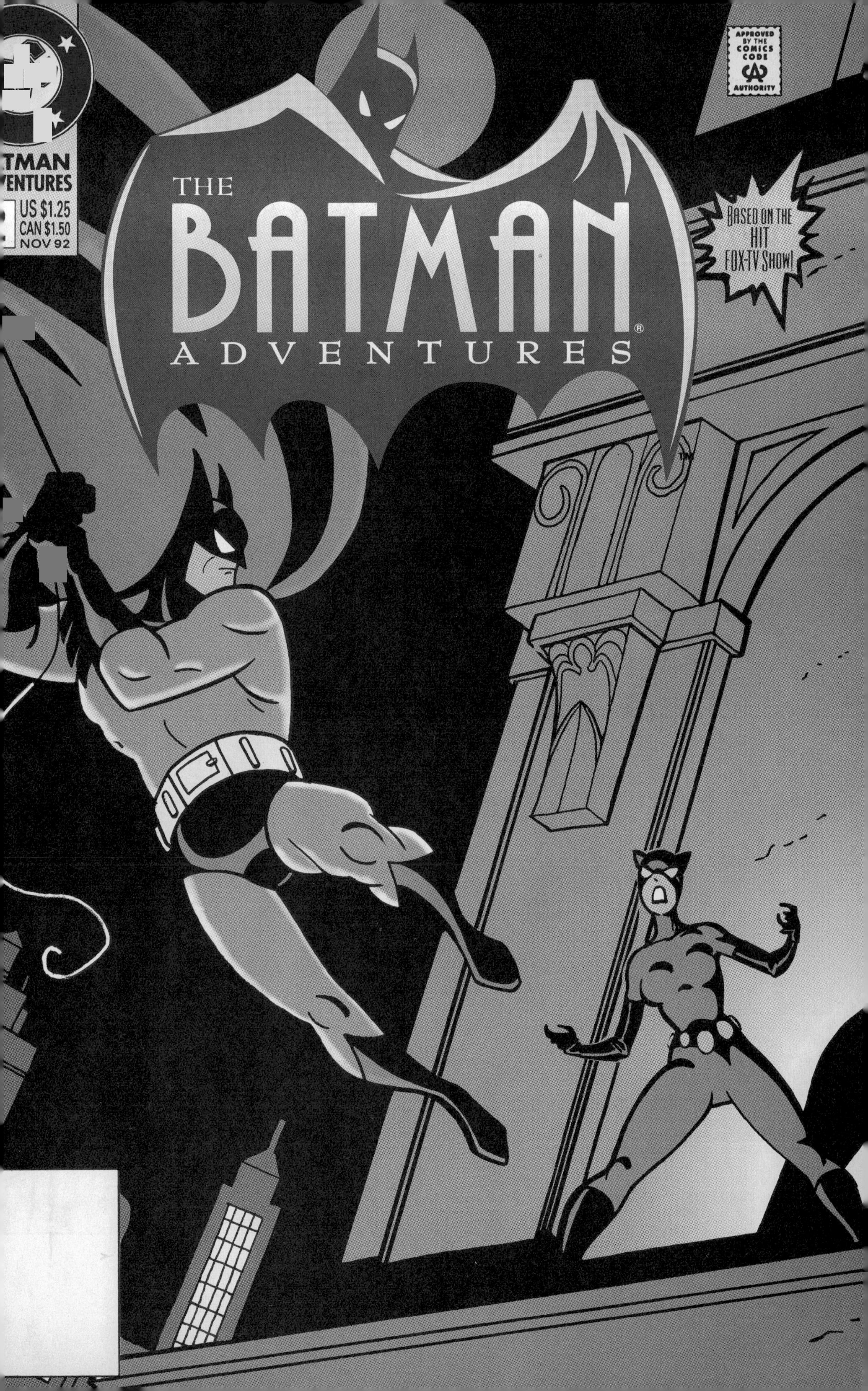
APPROVED BY THE COMICS CODE AUTHORITY
TMAN
ENTURES
US $1.25
CAN $1.50
NOV 92
THE BATMAN ADVENTURES
BASED ON THE HIT FOX-TV SHOW!

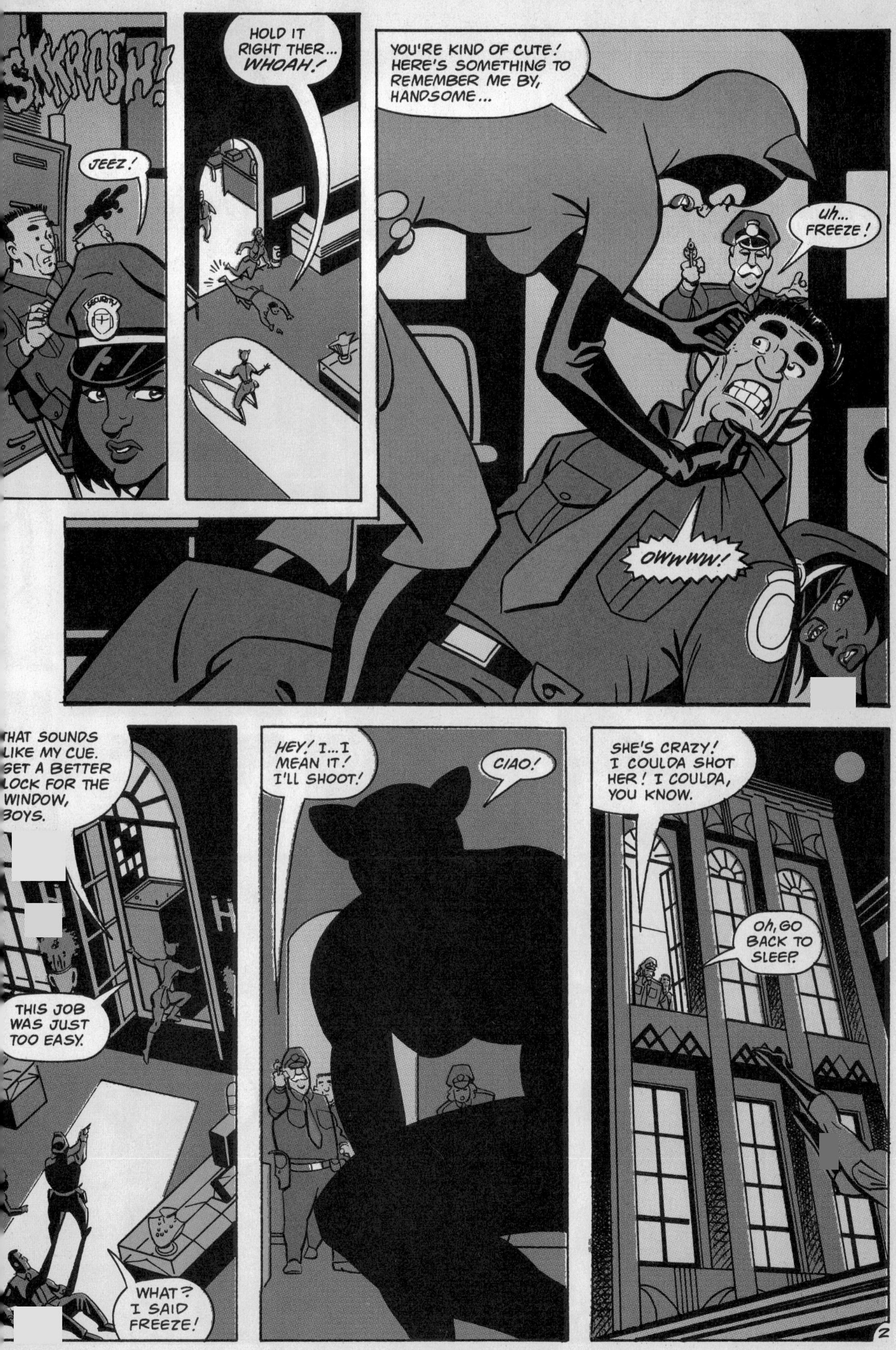
SKKRASH!!
JEEZ!
HOLD IT RIGHT THER... WHOAH!
YOU'RE KIND OF CUTE! HERE'S SOMETHING TO REMEMBER ME BY, HANDSOME...
uh... FREEZE!
OWWWW!
THAT SOUNDS LIKE MY CUE. GET A BETTER LOCK FOR THE WINDOW, BOYS.
THIS JOB WAS JUST TOO EASY.
WHAT? I SAID FREEZE!
HEY! I...I MEAN IT! I'LL SHOOT!
CIAO!
SHE'S CRAZY! I COULDA SHOT HER! I COULDA, YOU KNOW.
Oh, GO BACK TO SLEEP.
2

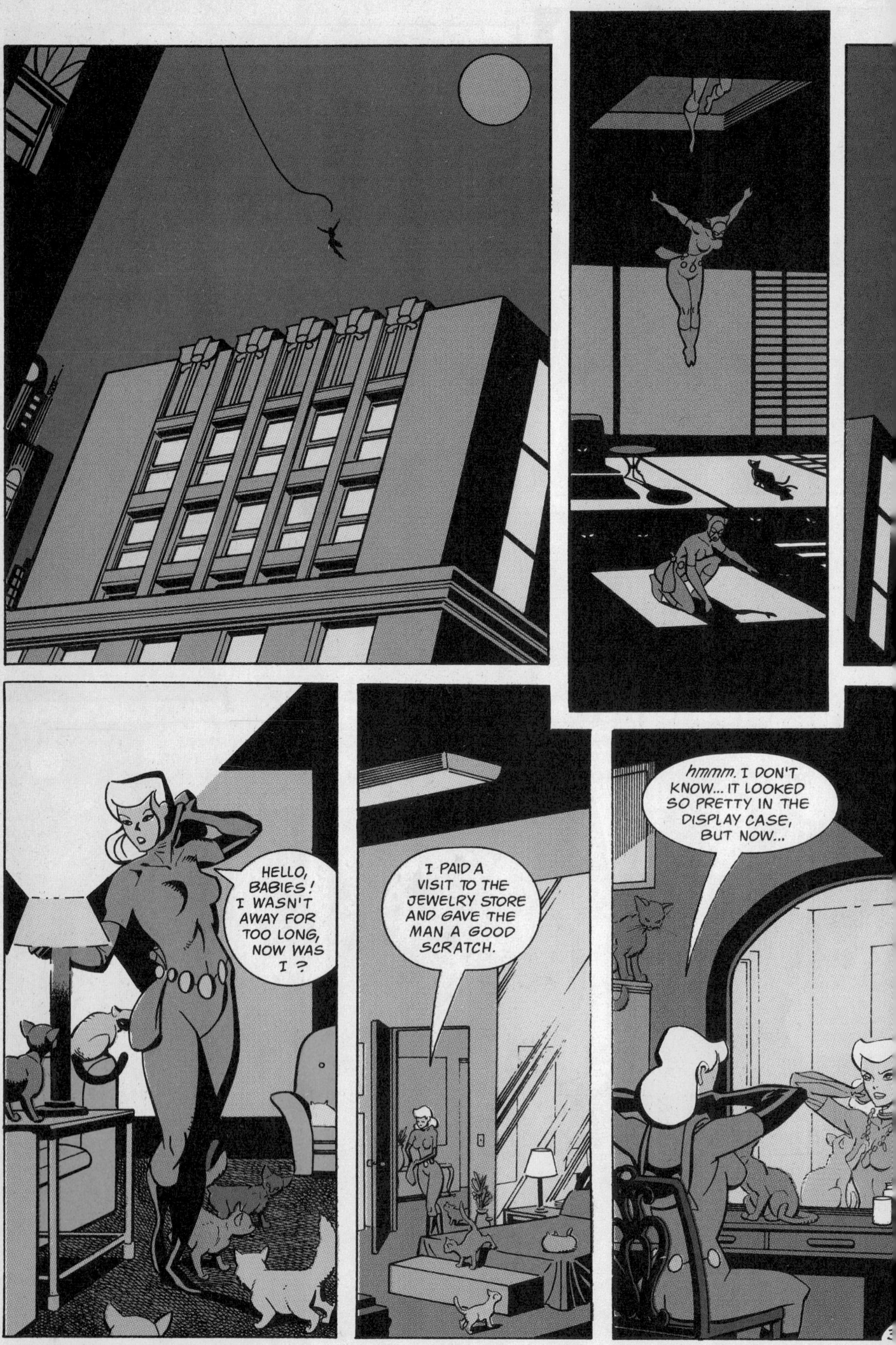
HELLO, BABIES! I WASN'T AWAY FOR TOO LONG, NOW WAS I?
I PAID A VISIT TO THE JEWELRY STORE AND GAVE THE MAN A GOOD SCRATCH.
hmmm. I DON'T KNOW... IT LOOKED SO PRETTY IN THE DISPLAY CASE, BUT NOW...

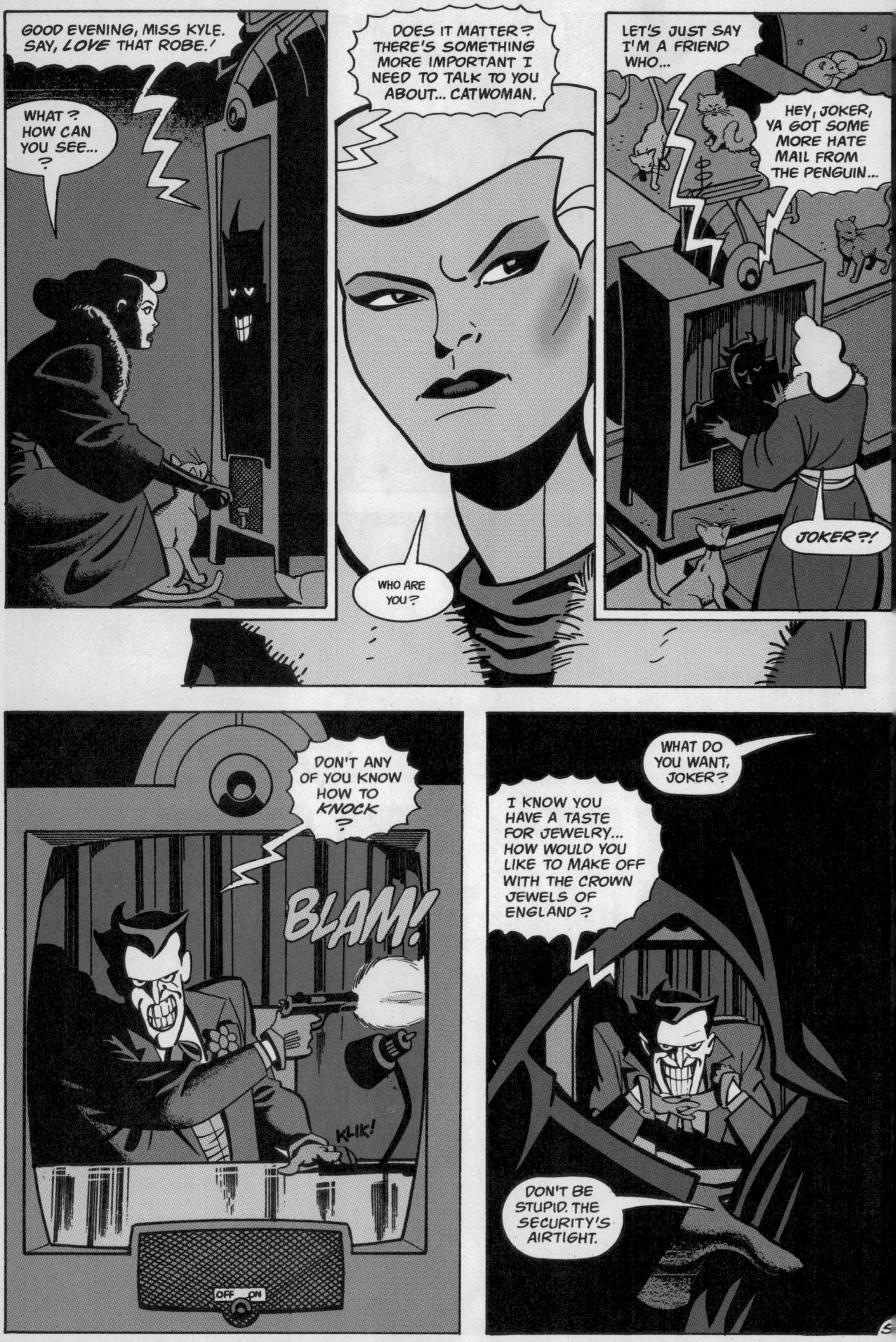
GOOD EVENING, MISS KYLE. SAY, LOVE THAT ROBE.!
WHAT? HOW CAN YOU SEE...?
DOES IT MATTER? THERE'S SOMETHING MORE IMPORTANT I NEED TO TALK TO YOU ABOUT... CATWOMAN.
WHO ARE YOU?
LET'S JUST SAY I'M A FRIEND WHO...
HEY, JOKER, YA GOT SOME MORE HATE MAIL FROM THE PENGUIN...
JOKER?!
DON'T ANY OF YOU KNOW HOW TO KNOCK?
BLAM!
KLIK!
OFF ON
WHAT DO YOU WANT, JOKER?
I KNOW YOU HAVE A TASTE FOR JEWELRY... HOW WOULD YOU LIKE TO MAKE OFF WITH THE CROWN JEWELS OF ENGLAND?
DON'T BE STUPID. THE SECURITY'S AIRTIGHT.
5

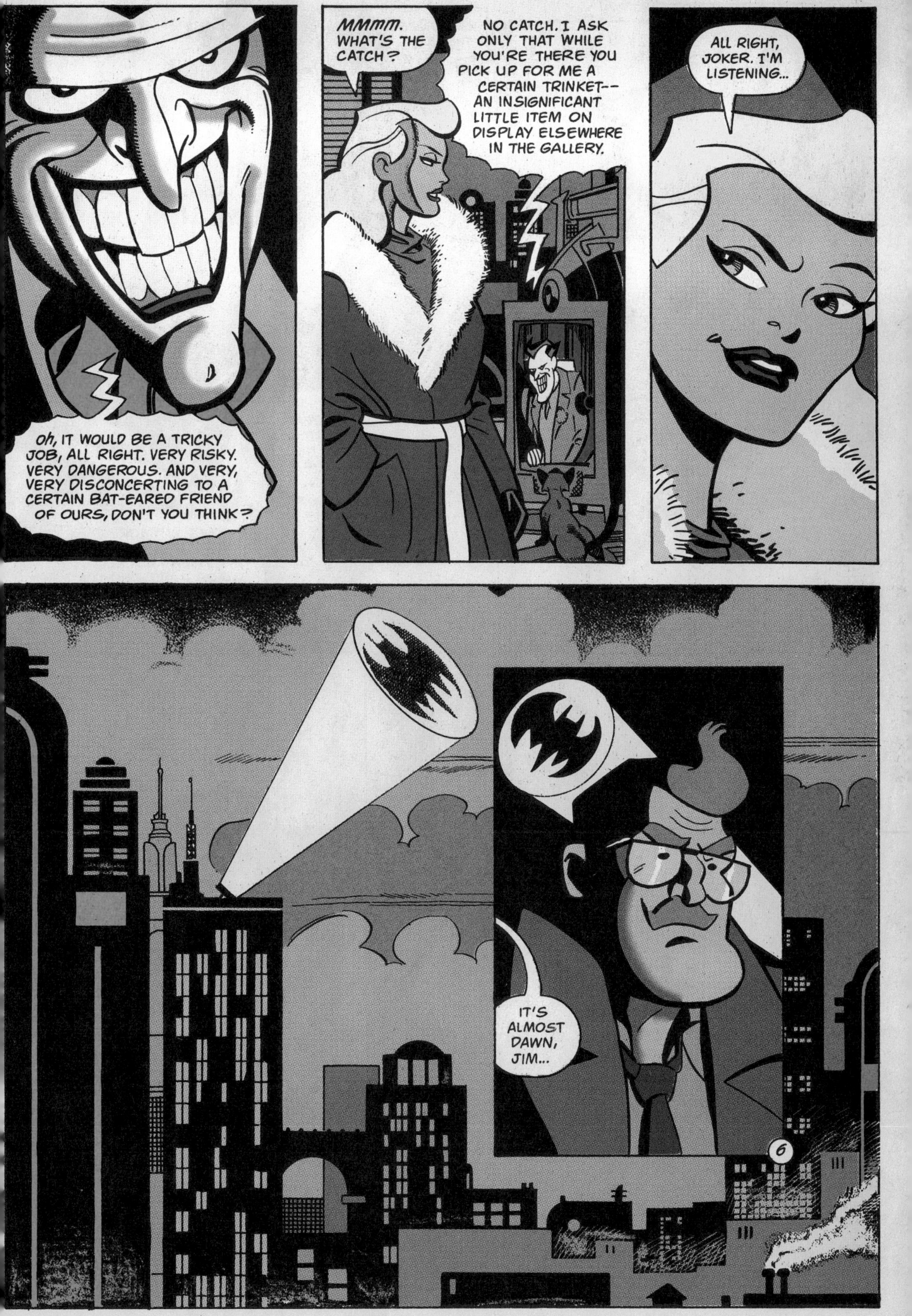
Oh, IT WOULD BE A TRICKY JOB, ALL RIGHT. VERY RISKY. VERY DANGEROUS. AND VERY, VERY DISCONCERTING TO A CERTAIN BAT-EARED FRIEND OF OURS, DON'T YOU THINK?
MMMM. WHAT'S THE CATCH?
NO CATCH. I ASK ONLY THAT WHILE YOU'RE THERE YOU PICK UP FOR ME A CERTAIN TRINKET-- AN INSIGNIFICANT LITTLE ITEM ON DISPLAY ELSEWHERE IN THE GALLERY.
ALL RIGHT, JOKER. I'M LISTENING...
IT'S ALMOST DAWN, JIM...
6

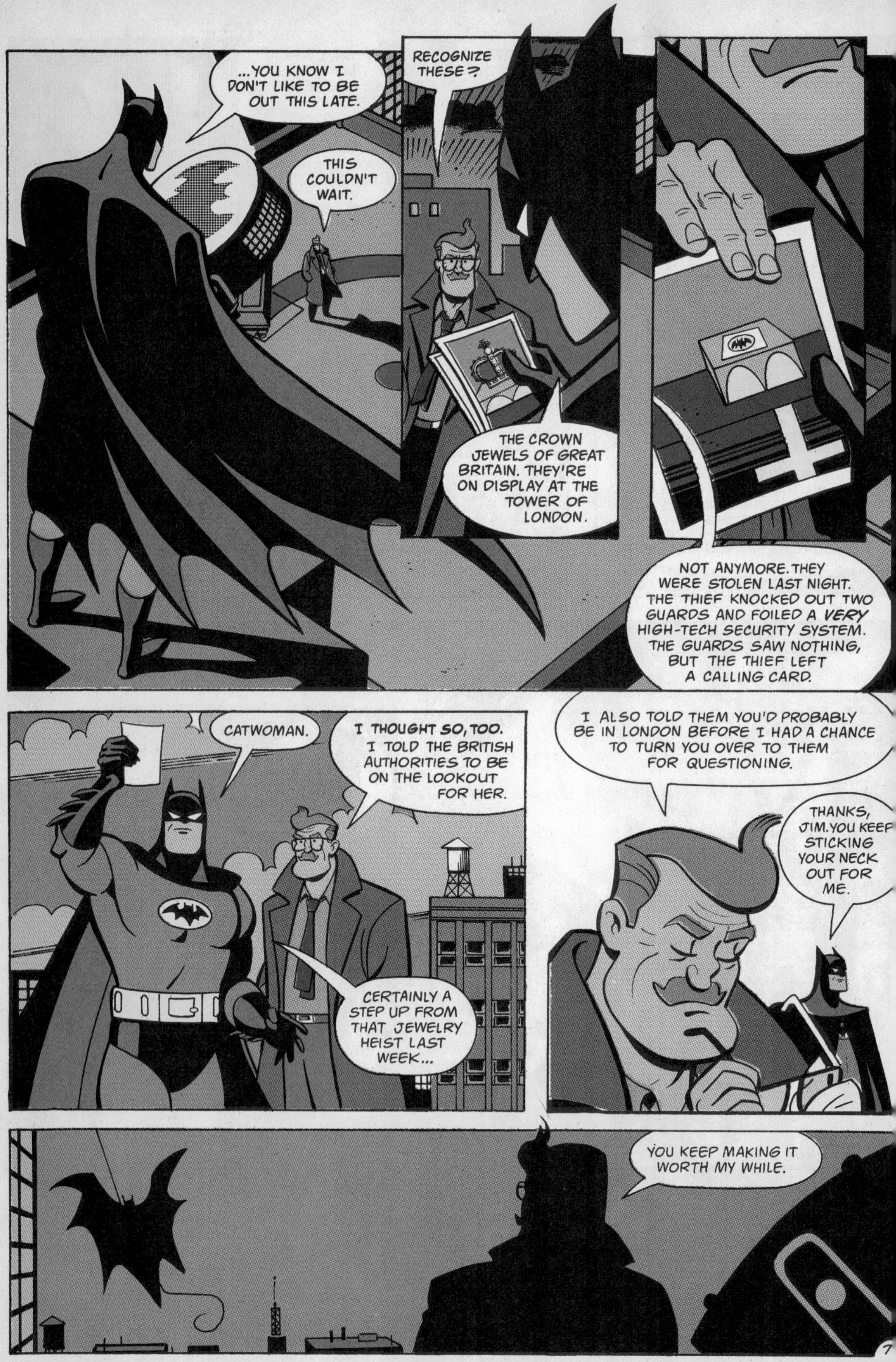
...YOU KNOW I DON'T LIKE TO BE OUT THIS LATE.
THIS COULDN'T WAIT.
RECOGNIZE THESE?
THE CROWN JEWELS OF GREAT BRITAIN. THEY'RE ON DISPLAY AT THE TOWER OF LONDON.
NOT ANYMORE. THEY WERE STOLEN LAST NIGHT. THE THIEF KNOCKED OUT TWO GUARDS AND FOILED A VERY HIGH-TECH SECURITY SYSTEM. THE GUARDS SAW NOTHING, BUT THE THIEF LEFT A CALLING CARD.
CATWOMAN.
I THOUGHT SO, TOO. I TOLD THE BRITISH AUTHORITIES TO BE ON THE LOOKOUT FOR HER.
CERTAINLY A STEP UP FROM THAT JEWELRY HEIST LAST WEEK...
I ALSO TOLD THEM YOU'D PROBABLY BE IN LONDON BEFORE I HAD A CHANCE TO TURN YOU OVER TO THEM FOR QUESTIONING.
THANKS, JIM. YOU KEEP STICKING YOUR NECK OUT FOR ME.
YOU KEEP MAKING IT WORTH MY WHILE.
7

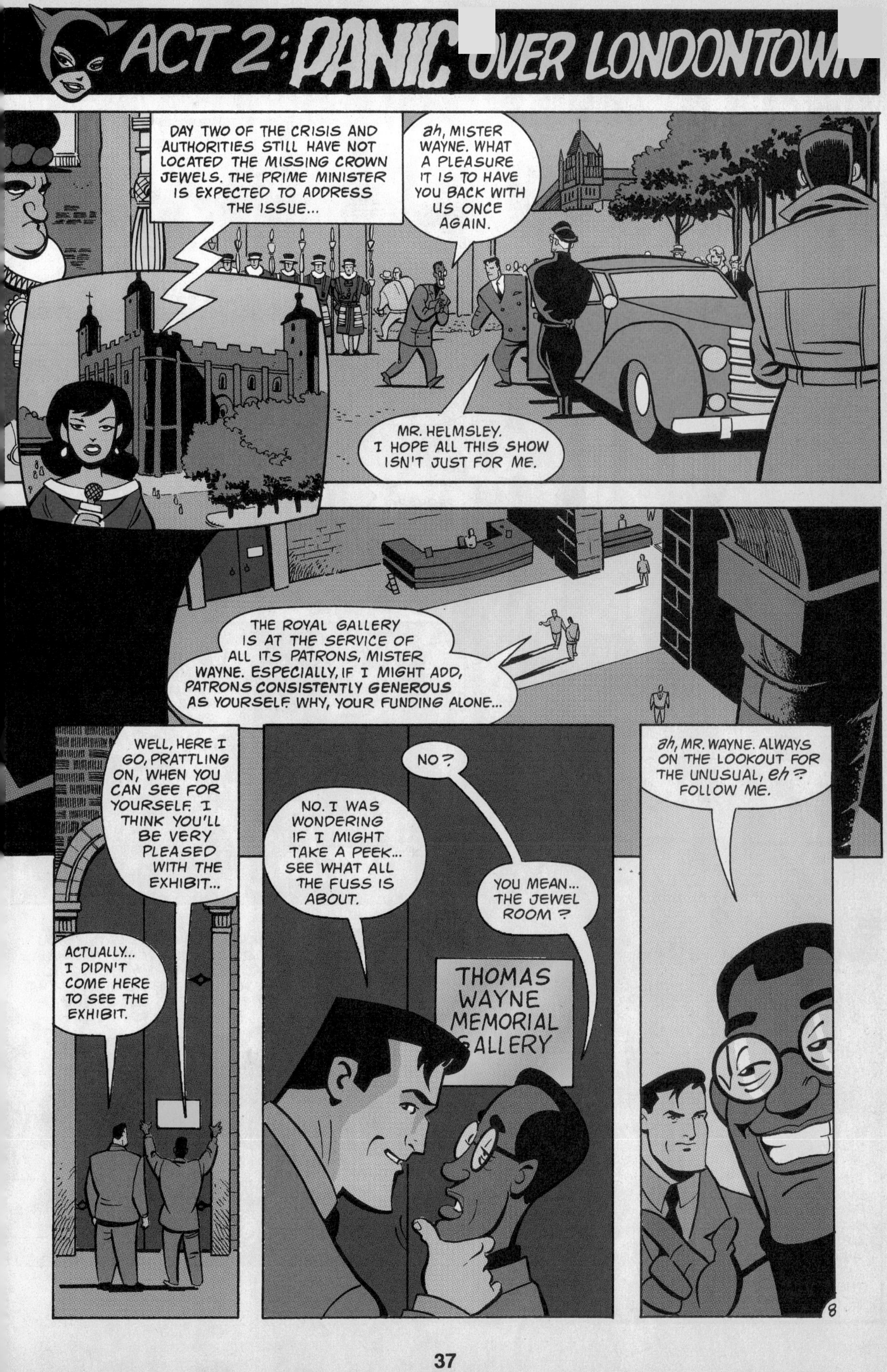
ACT 2: PANIC OVER LONDONTOWN
DAY TWO OF THE CRISIS AND AUTHORITIES STILL HAVE NOT LOCATED THE MISSING CROWN JEWELS. THE PRIME MINISTER IS EXPECTED TO ADDRESS THE ISSUE...
ah, MISTER WAYNE. WHAT A PLEASURE IT IS TO HAVE YOU BACK WITH US ONCE AGAIN.
MR. HELMSLEY. I HOPE ALL THIS SHOW ISN'T JUST FOR ME.
THE ROYAL GALLERY IS AT THE SERVICE OF ALL ITS PATRONS, MISTER WAYNE. ESPECIALLY, IF I MIGHT ADD, PATRONS CONSISTENTLY GENEROUS AS YOURSELF. WHY, YOUR FUNDING ALONE...
WELL, HERE I GO, PRATTLING ON, WHEN YOU CAN SEE FOR YOURSELF. I THINK YOU'LL BE VERY PLEASED WITH THE EXHIBIT...
ACTUALLY... I DIDN'T COME HERE TO SEE THE EXHIBIT.
NO?
NO. I WAS WONDERING IF I MIGHT TAKE A PEEK... SEE WHAT ALL THE FUSS IS ABOUT.
YOU MEAN... THE JEWEL ROOM?
THOMAS WAYNE MEMORIAL GALLERY
ah, MR. WAYNE. ALWAYS ON THE LOOKOUT FOR THE UNUSUAL, eh? FOLLOW ME.
8

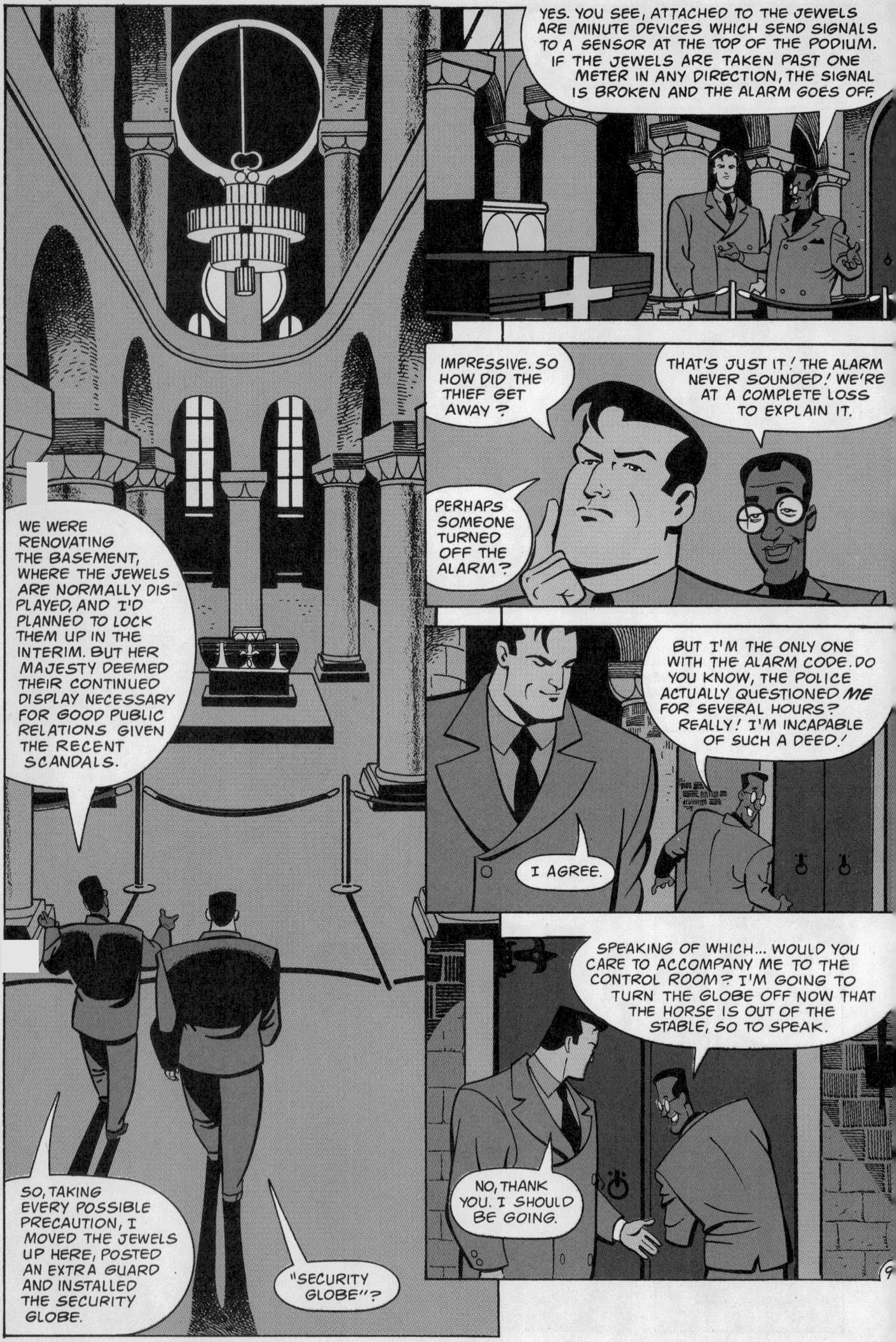
WE WERE RENOVATING THE BASEMENT, WHERE THE JEWELS ARE NORMALLY DISPLAYED, AND I'D PLANNED TO LOCK THEM UP IN THE INTERIM. BUT HER MAJESTY DEEMED THEIR CONTINUED DISPLAY NECESSARY FOR GOOD PUBLIC RELATIONS GIVEN THE RECENT SCANDALS.
SO, TAKING EVERY POSSIBLE PRECAUTION, I MOVED THE JEWELS UP HERE, POSTED AN EXTRA GUARD AND INSTALLED THE SECURITY GLOBE.
"SECURITY GLOBE"?
YES. YOU SEE, ATTACHED TO THE JEWELS ARE MINUTE DEVICES WHICH SEND SIGNALS TO A SENSOR AT THE TOP OF THE PODIUM. IF THE JEWELS ARE TAKEN PAST ONE METER IN ANY DIRECTION, THE SIGNAL IS BROKEN AND THE ALARM GOES OFF.
IMPRESSIVE. SO HOW DID THE THIEF GET AWAY?
THAT'S JUST IT! THE ALARM NEVER SOUNDED! WE'RE AT A COMPLETE LOSS TO EXPLAIN IT.
PERHAPS SOMEONE TURNED OFF THE ALARM?
BUT I'M THE ONLY ONE WITH THE ALARM CODE. DO YOU KNOW, THE POLICE ACTUALLY QUESTIONED ME FOR SEVERAL HOURS? REALLY! I'M INCAPABLE OF SUCH A DEED!
I AGREE.
SPEAKING OF WHICH... WOULD YOU CARE TO ACCOMPANY ME TO THE CONTROL ROOM? I'M GOING TO TURN THE GLOBE OFF NOW THAT THE HORSE IS OUT OF THE STABLE, SO TO SPEAK.
NO, THANK YOU. I SHOULD BE GOING.

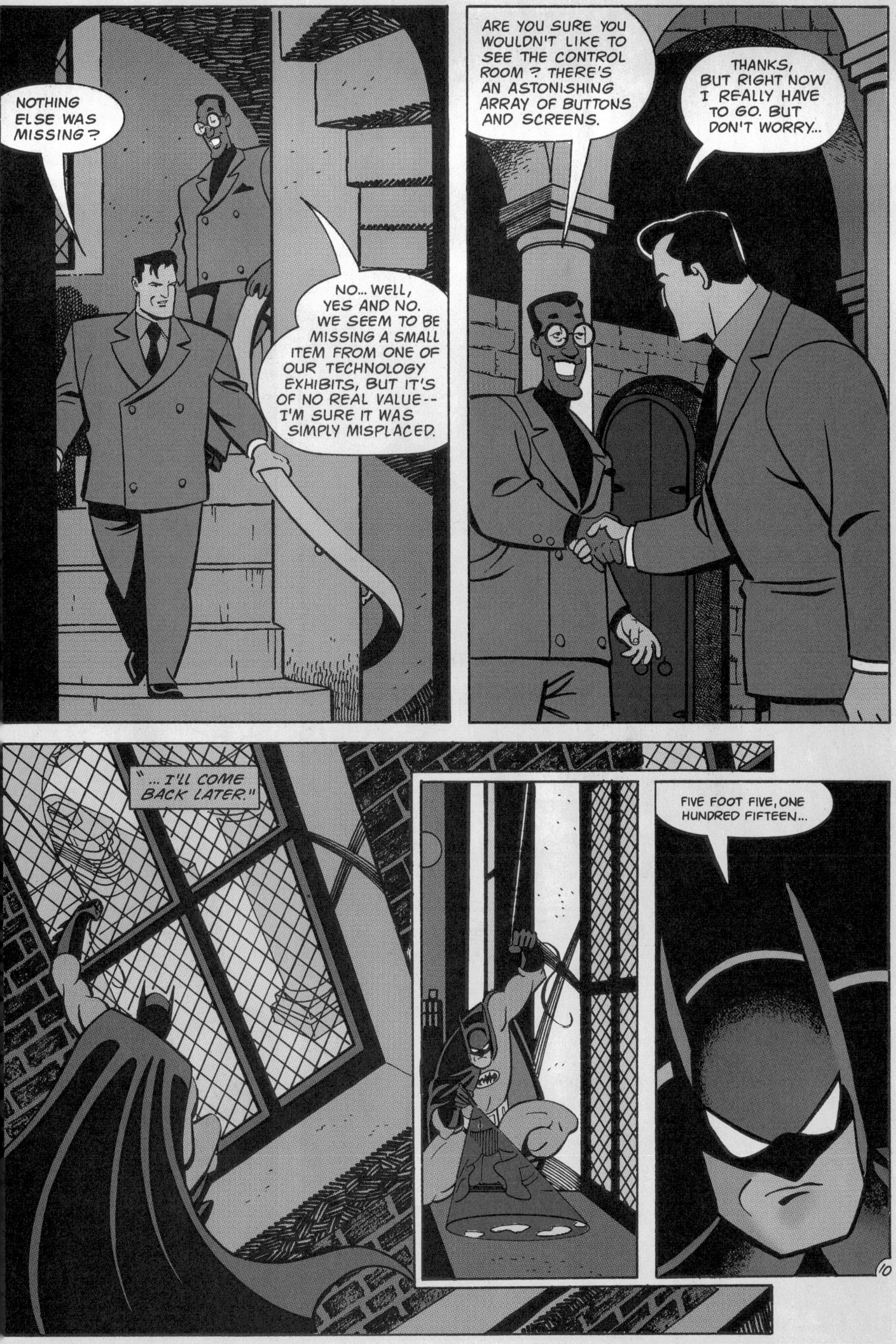
NOTHING ELSE WAS MISSING?
NO... WELL, YES AND NO. WE SEEM TO BE MISSING A SMALL ITEM FROM ONE OF OUR TECHNOLOGY EXHIBITS, BUT IT'S OF NO REAL VALUE-- I'M SURE IT WAS SIMPLY MISPLACED.
ARE YOU SURE YOU WOULDN'T LIKE TO SEE THE CONTROL ROOM? THERE'S AN ASTONISHING ARRAY OF BUTTONS AND SCREENS.
THANKS, BUT RIGHT NOW I REALLY HAVE TO GO. BUT DON'T WORRY...
"...I'LL COME BACK LATER."
FIVE FOOT FIVE, ONE HUNDRED FIFTEEN...
10

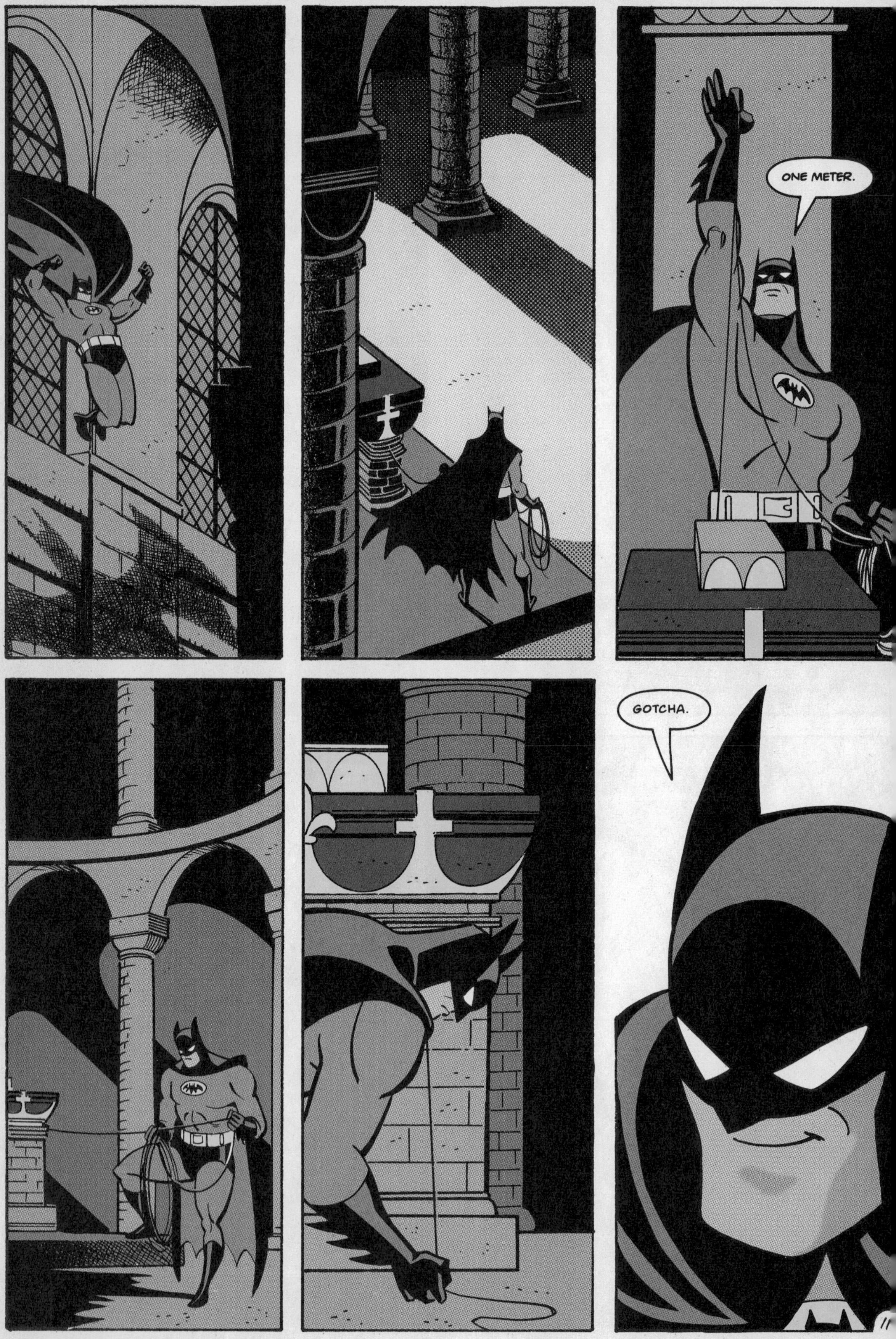
ONE METER.
GOTCHA.

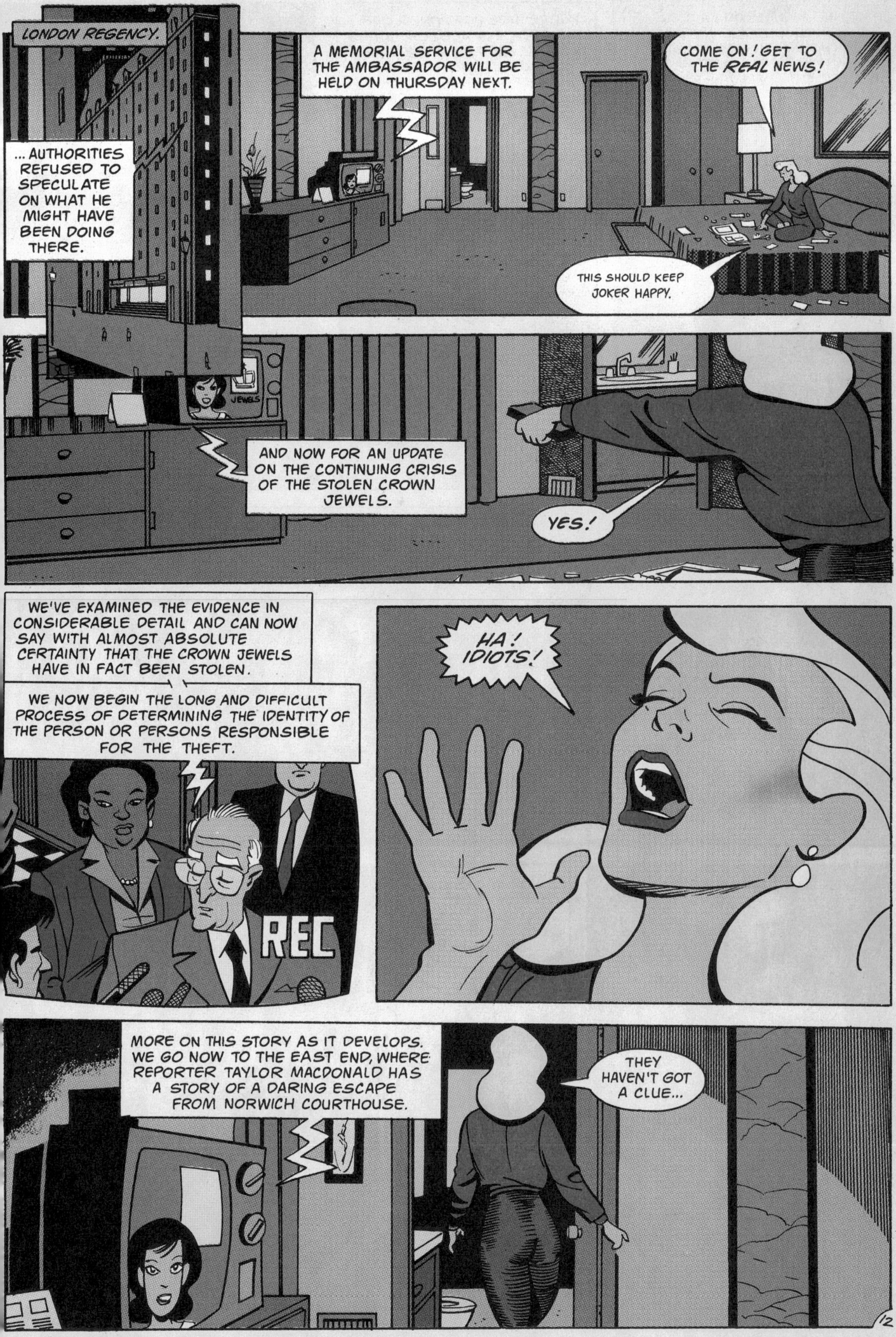
LONDON REGENCY.
...AUTHORITIES REFUSED TO SPECULATE ON WHAT HE MIGHT HAVE BEEN DOING THERE.
A MEMORIAL SERVICE FOR THE AMBASSADOR WILL BE HELD ON THURSDAY NEXT.
COME ON! GET TO THE REAL NEWS!
THIS SHOULD KEEP JOKER HAPPY.
JEWELS
AND NOW FOR AN UPDATE ON THE CONTINUING CRISIS OF THE STOLEN CROWN JEWELS.
YES!
WE'VE EXAMINED THE EVIDENCE IN CONSIDERABLE DETAIL AND CAN NOW SAY WITH ALMOST ABSOLUTE CERTAINTY THAT THE CROWN JEWELS HAVE IN FACT BEEN STOLEN.
WE NOW BEGIN THE LONG AND DIFFICULT PROCESS OF DETERMINING THE IDENTITY OF THE PERSON OR PERSONS RESPONSIBLE FOR THE THEFT.
REC
HA! IDIOTS!
MORE ON THIS STORY AS IT DEVELOPS. WE GO NOW TO THE EAST END, WHERE REPORTER TAYLOR MACDONALD HAS A STORY OF A DARING ESCAPE FROM NORWICH COURTHOUSE.
THEY HAVEN'T GOT A CLUE...
12

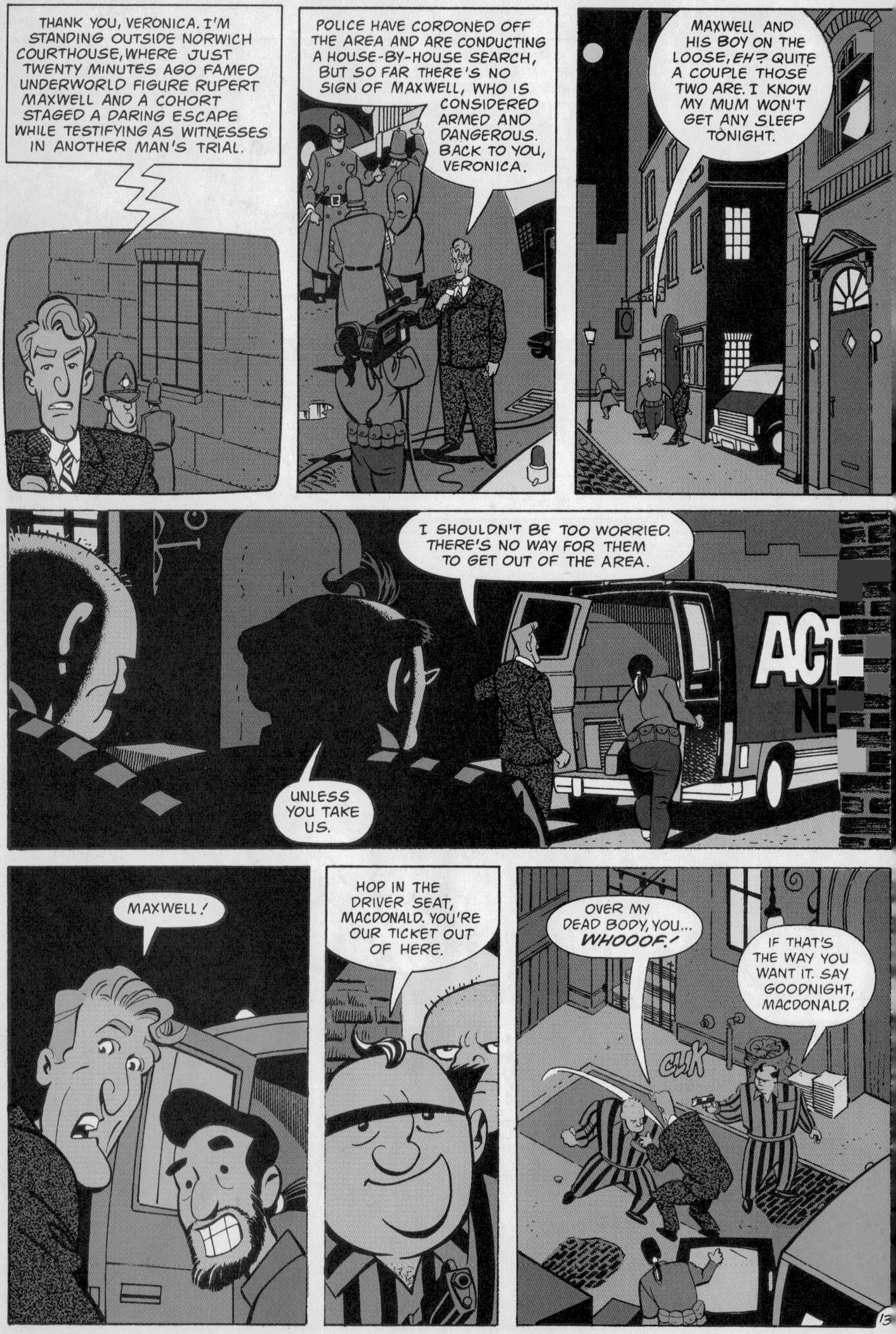
THANK YOU, VERONICA. I'M STANDING OUTSIDE NORWICH COURTHOUSE, WHERE JUST TWENTY MINUTES AGO FAMED UNDERWORLD FIGURE RUPERT MAXWELL AND A COHORT STAGED A DARING ESCAPE WHILE TESTIFYING AS WITNESSES IN ANOTHER MAN'S TRIAL.
POLICE HAVE CORDONED OFF THE AREA AND ARE CONDUCTING A HOUSE-BY-HOUSE SEARCH, BUT SO FAR THERE'S NO SIGN OF MAXWELL, WHO IS CONSIDERED ARMED AND DANGEROUS. BACK TO YOU, VERONICA.
MAXWELL AND HIS BOY ON THE LOOSE, EH? QUITE A COUPLE THOSE TWO ARE. I KNOW MY MUM WON'T GET ANY SLEEP TONIGHT.
I SHOULDN'T BE TOO WORRIED. THERE'S NO WAY FOR THEM TO GET OUT OF THE AREA.
UNLESS YOU TAKE US.
MAXWELL!
HOP IN THE DRIVER SEAT, MACDONALD. YOU'RE OUR TICKET OUT OF HERE.
OVER MY DEAD BODY, YOU... WHOOOF!
IF THAT'S THE WAY YOU WANT IT. SAY GOODNIGHT, MACDONALD.
CLIK

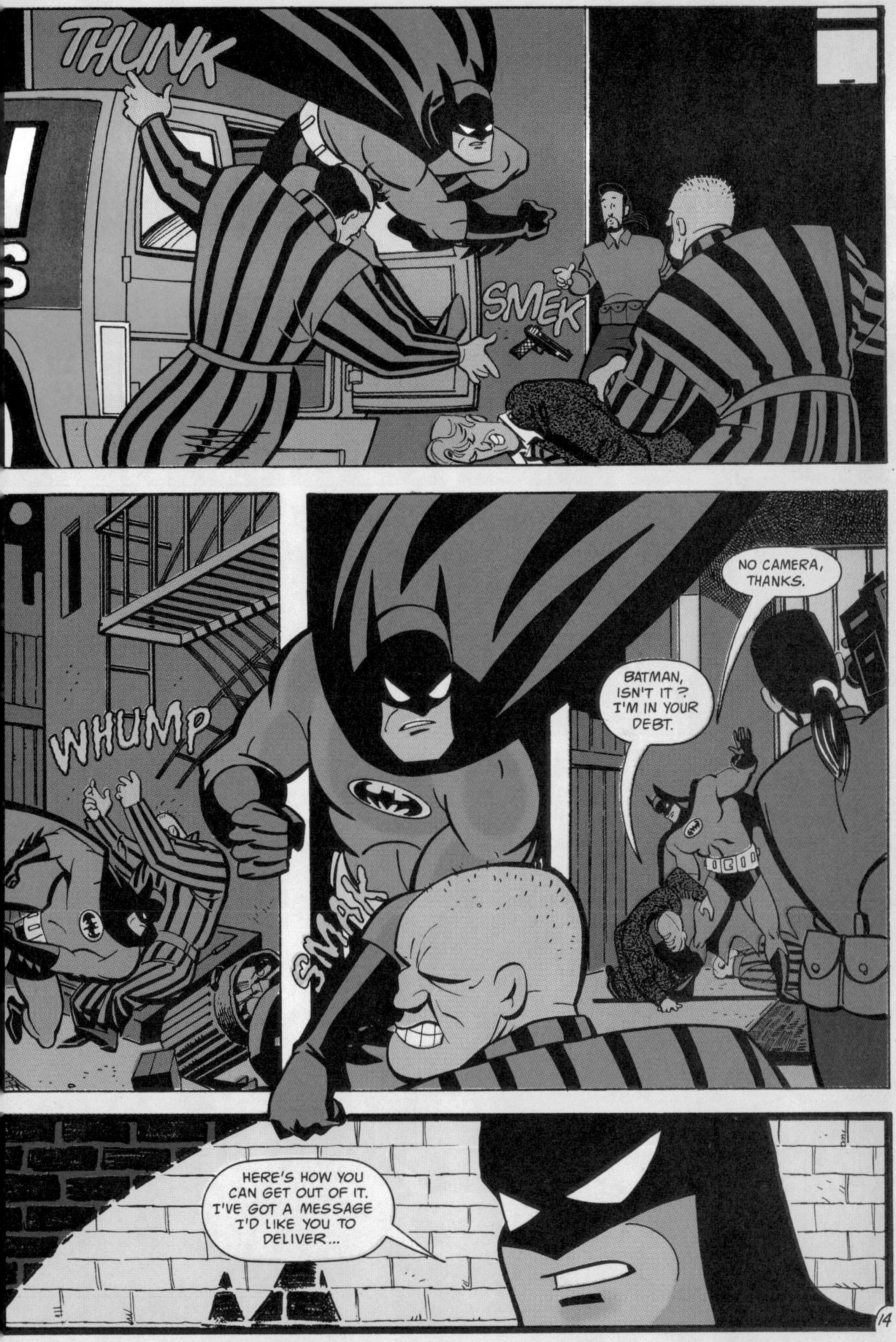
THUNK
SMEK
WHUMP
SMAK
NO CAMERA, THANKS.
BATMAN, ISN'T IT? I'M IN YOUR DEBT.
HERE'S HOW YOU CAN GET OUT OF IT. I'VE GOT A MESSAGE I'D LIKE YOU TO DELIVER...
14

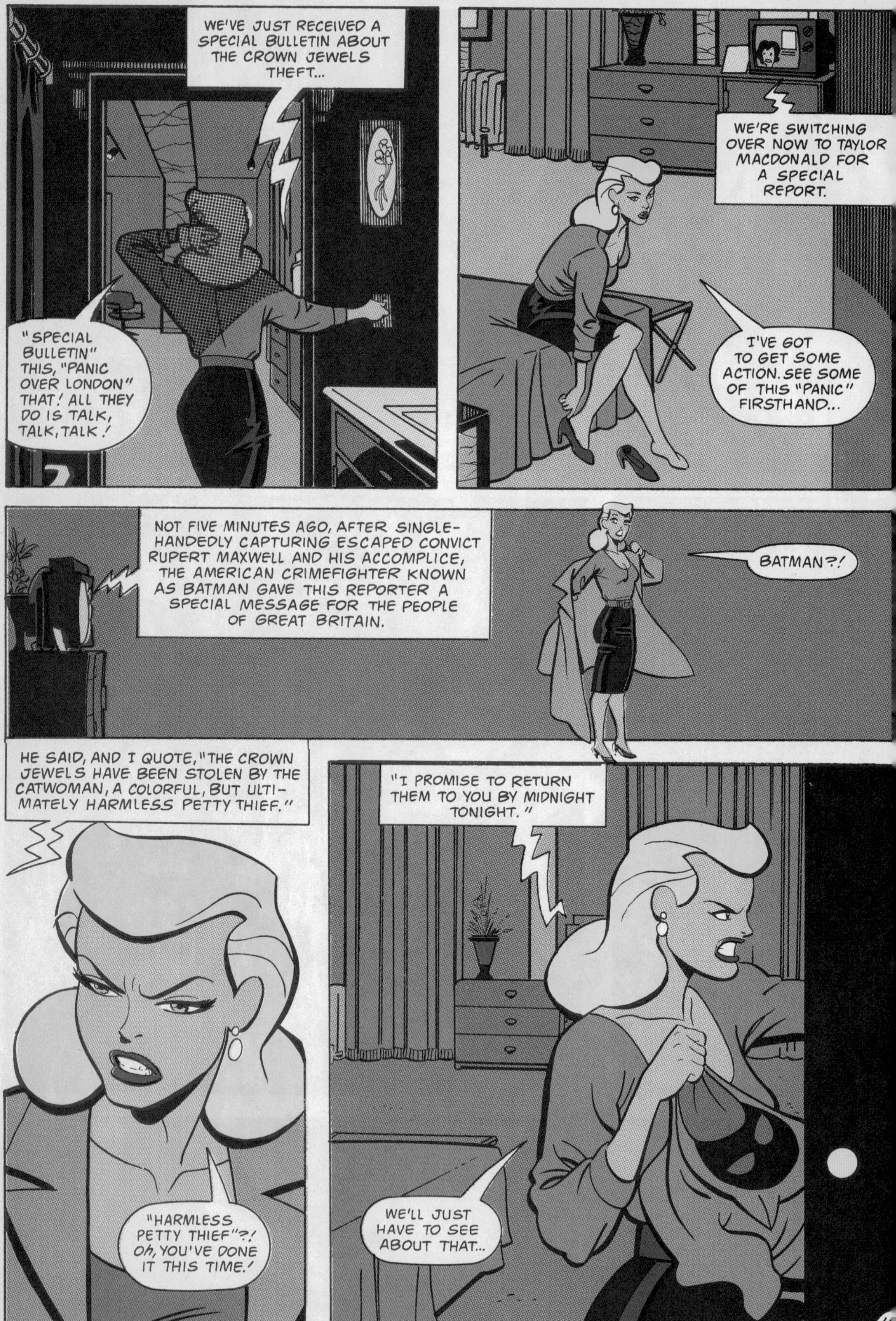
WE'VE JUST RECEIVED A SPECIAL BULLETIN ABOUT THE CROWN JEWELS THEFT...
"SPECIAL BULLETIN" THIS, "PANIC OVER LONDON" THAT! ALL THEY DO IS TALK, TALK, TALK!
WE'RE SWITCHING OVER NOW TO TAYLOR MACDONALD FOR A SPECIAL REPORT.
I'VE GOT TO GET SOME ACTION. SEE SOME OF THIS "PANIC" FIRSTHAND...
NOT FIVE MINUTES AGO, AFTER SINGLE-HANDEDLY CAPTURING ESCAPED CONVICT RUPERT MAXWELL AND HIS ACCOMPLICE, THE AMERICAN CRIMEFIGHTER KNOWN AS BATMAN GAVE THIS REPORTER A SPECIAL MESSAGE FOR THE PEOPLE OF GREAT BRITAIN.
BATMAN?!
HE SAID, AND I QUOTE, "THE CROWN JEWELS HAVE BEEN STOLEN BY THE CATWOMAN, A COLORFUL, BUT ULTIMATELY HARMLESS PETTY THIEF."
"HARMLESS PETTY THIEF"?! Oh, YOU'VE DONE IT THIS TIME!
"I PROMISE TO RETURN THEM TO YOU BY MIDNIGHT TONIGHT."
WE'LL JUST HAVE TO SEE ABOUT THAT...

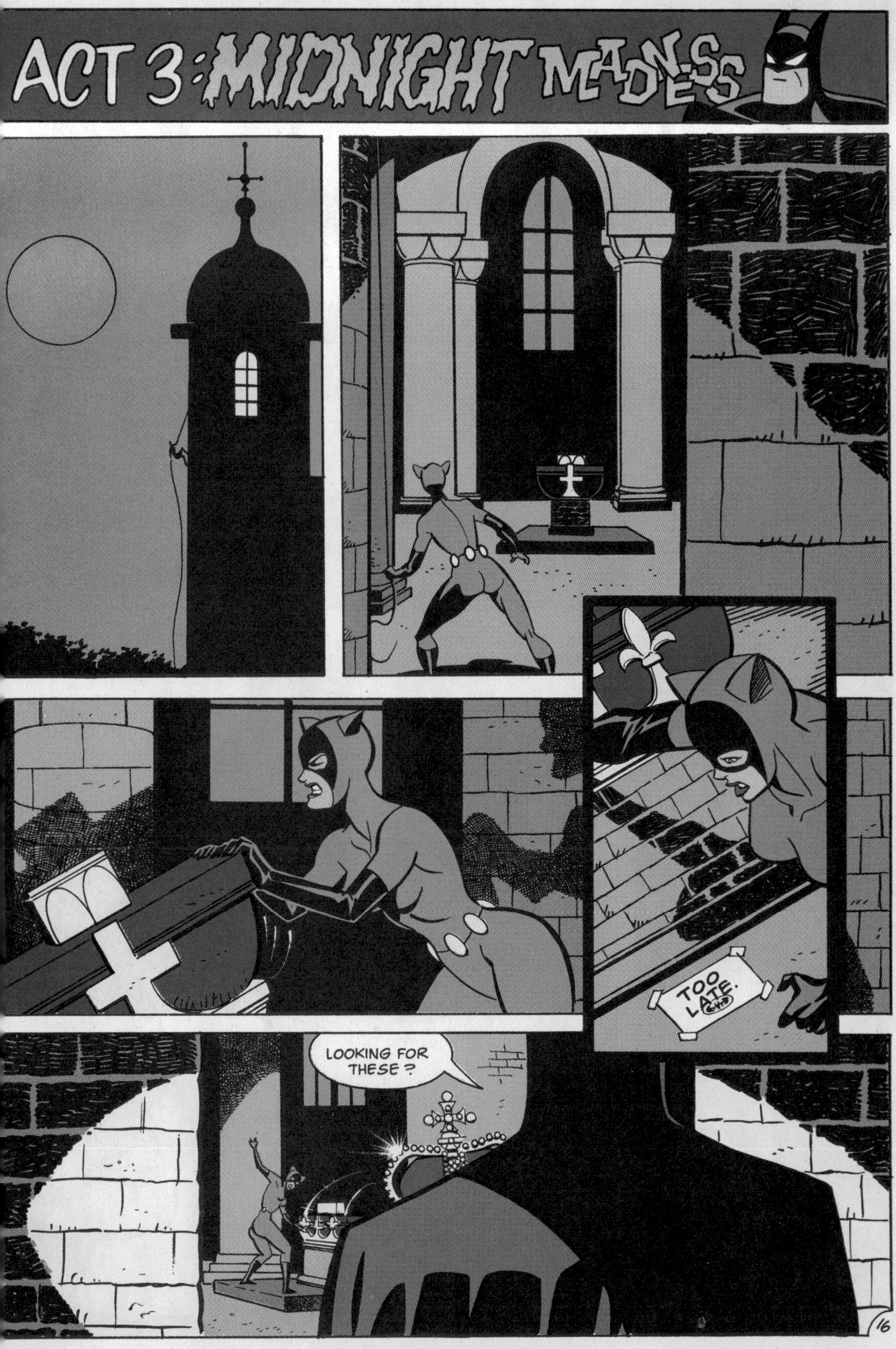
ACT 3: MIDNIGHT MADNESS
TOO LATE.
LOOKING FOR THESE?
16

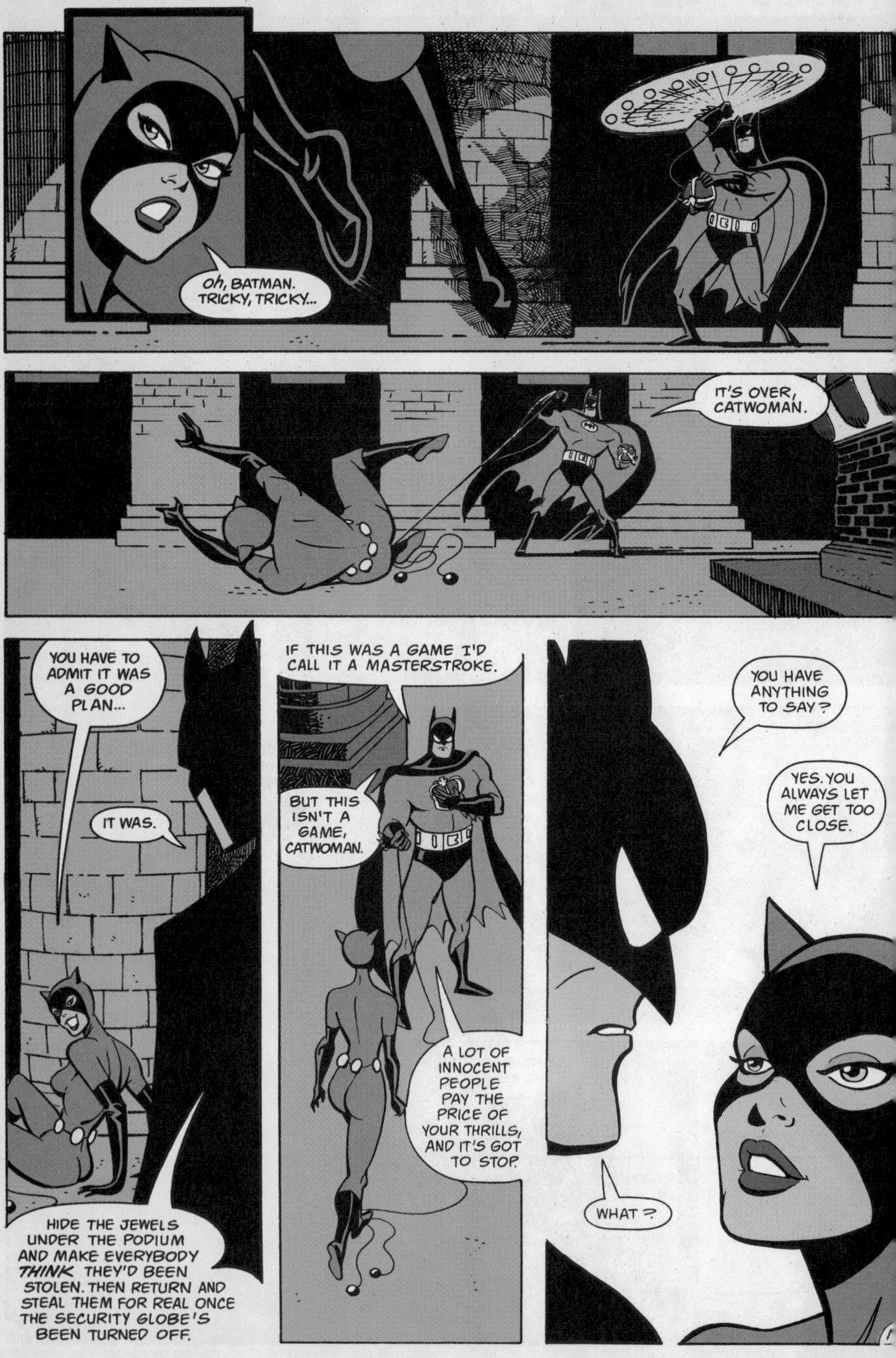
Oh, BATMAN. TRICKY, TRICKY...
IT'S OVER, CATWOMAN.
YOU HAVE TO ADMIT IT WAS A GOOD PLAN...
IT WAS.
HIDE THE JEWELS UNDER THE PODIUM AND MAKE EVERYBODY THINK THEY'D BEEN STOLEN. THEN RETURN AND STEAL THEM FOR REAL ONCE THE SECURITY GLOBE'S BEEN TURNED OFF.
IF THIS WAS A GAME I'D CALL IT A MASTERSTROKE.
BUT THIS ISN'T A GAME, CATWOMAN.
A LOT OF INNOCENT PEOPLE PAY THE PRICE OF YOUR THRILLS, AND IT'S GOT TO STOP.
YOU HAVE ANYTHING TO SAY?
YES. YOU ALWAYS LET ME GET TOO CLOSE.
WHAT?

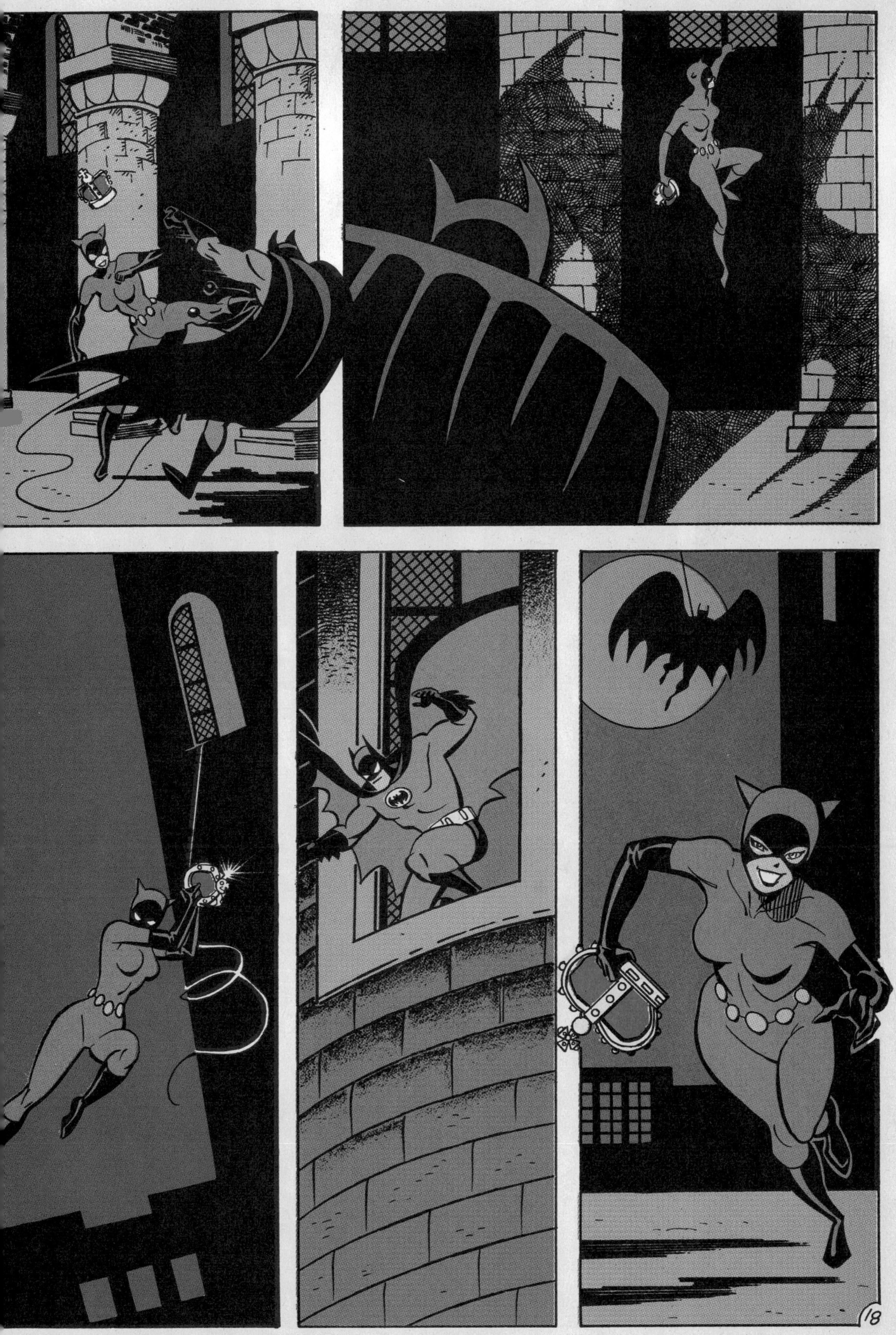
18

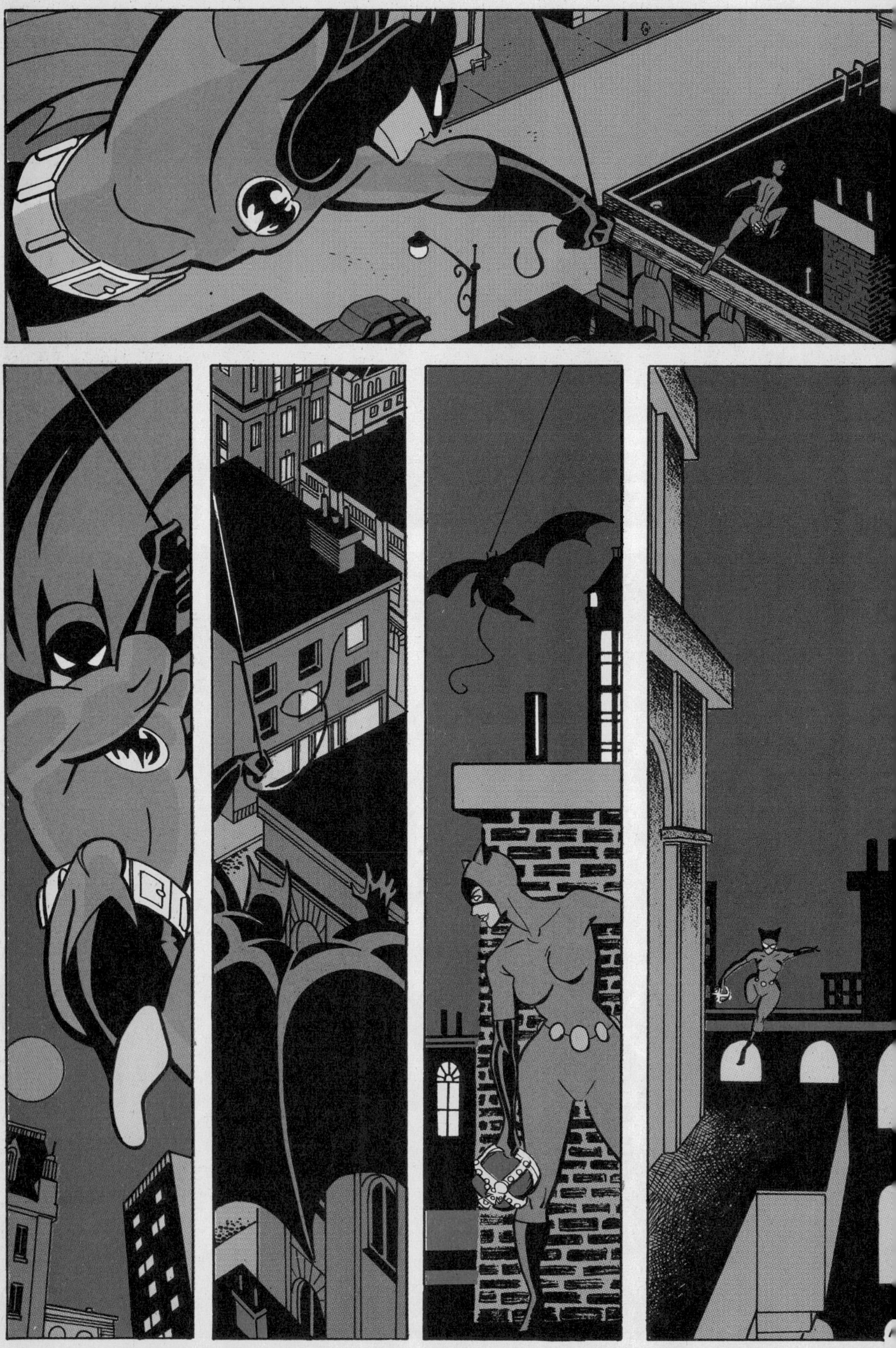

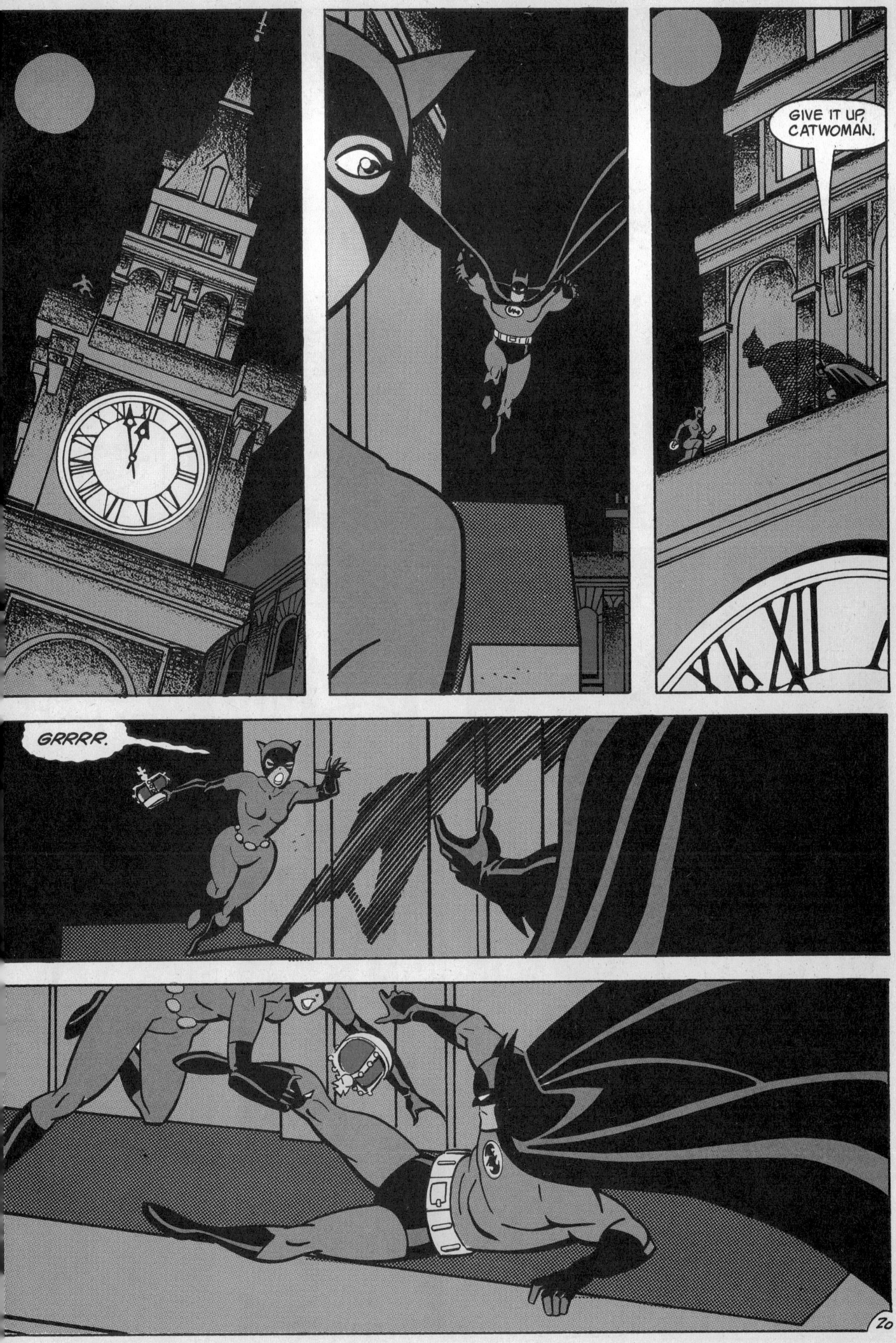
GIVE IT UP, CATWOMAN.
GRRRR.
20

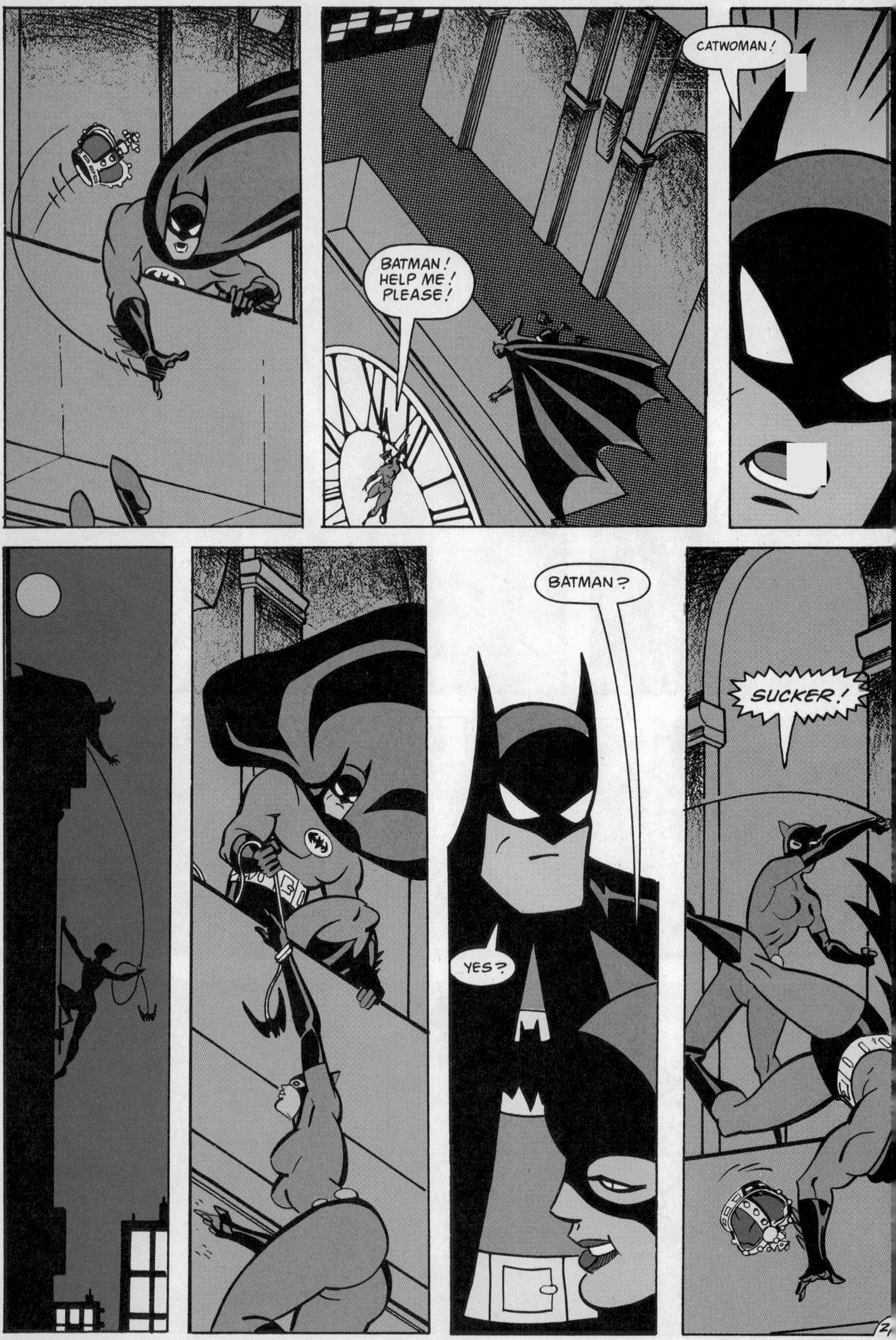
BATMAN! HELP ME! PLEASE!
CATWOMAN!
BATMAN?
YES?
SUCKER!

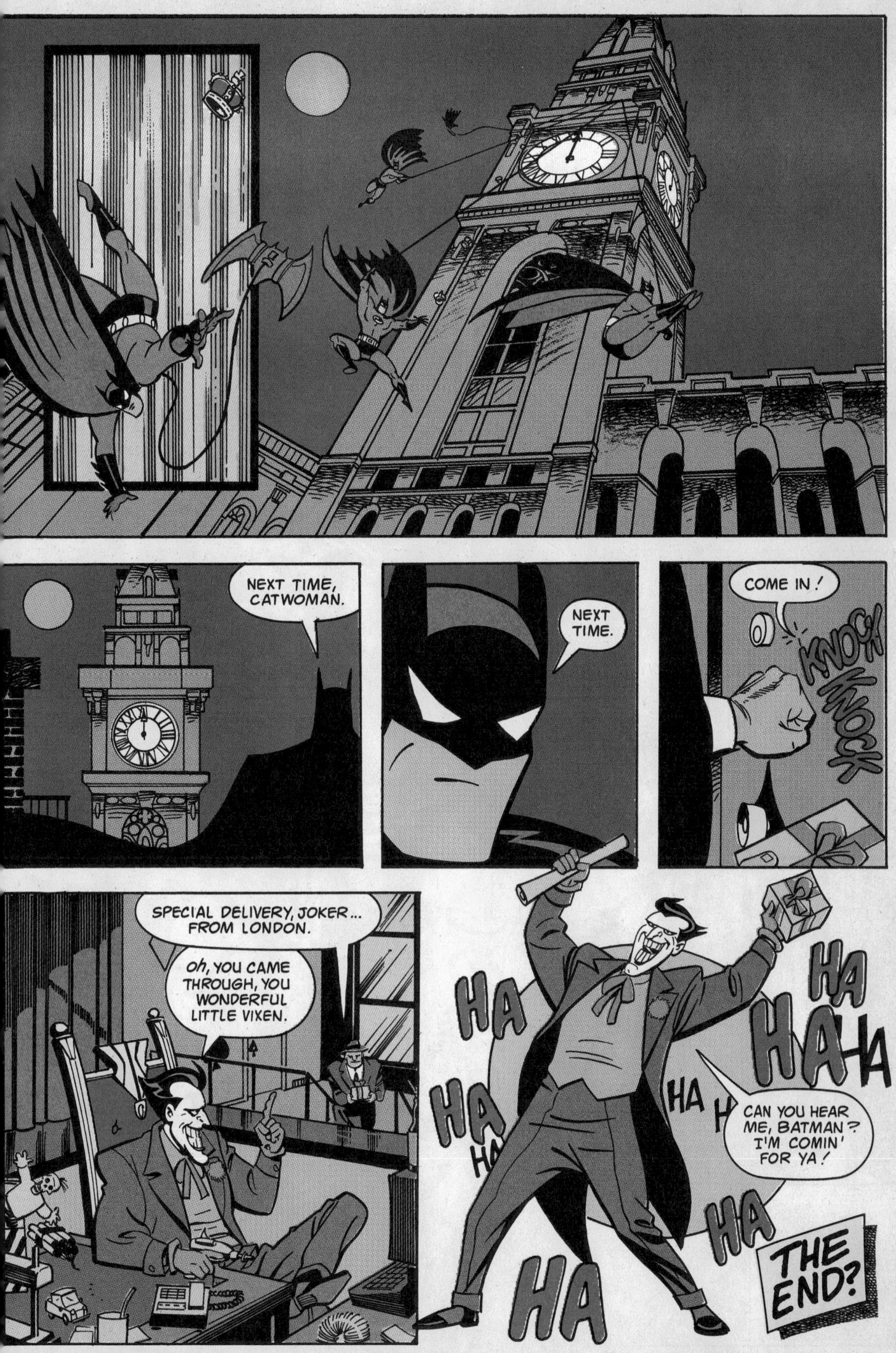
NEXT TIME, CATWOMAN.
NEXT TIME.
COME IN!
KNOCK KNOCK
SPECIAL DELIVERY, JOKER... FROM LONDON.
Oh, YOU CAME THROUGH, YOU WONDERFUL LITTLE VIXEN.
HA HA HA HA HA HA HA HA HA HA HA
CAN YOU HEAR ME, BATMAN? I'M COMIN' FOR YA!
THE END?

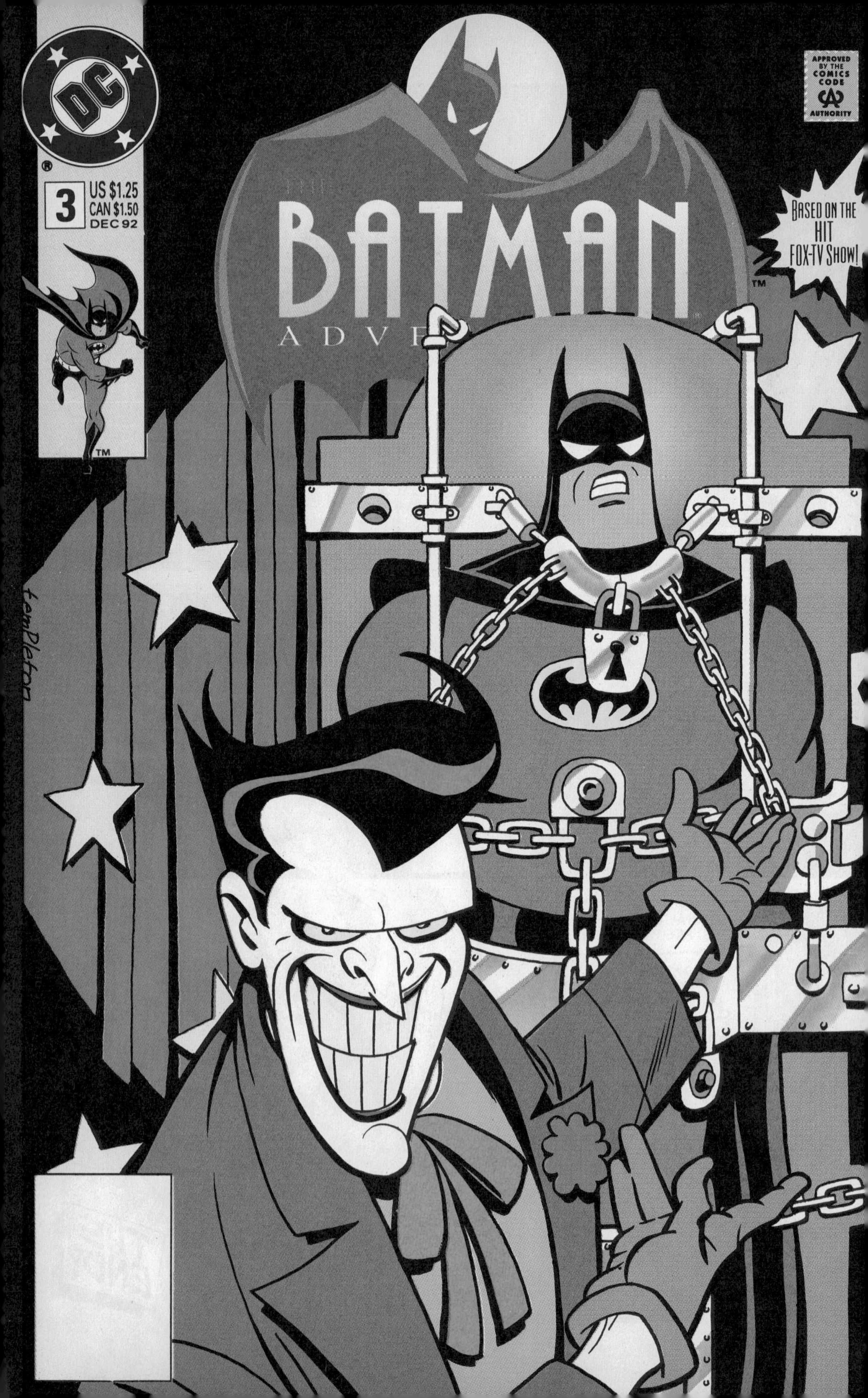
DC
3
US $1.25
CAN $1.50
DEC 92
APPROVED BY THE COMICS CODE AUTHORITY
BATMAN
ADVE
BASED ON THE HIT FOX-TV SHOW!
TM
templeton

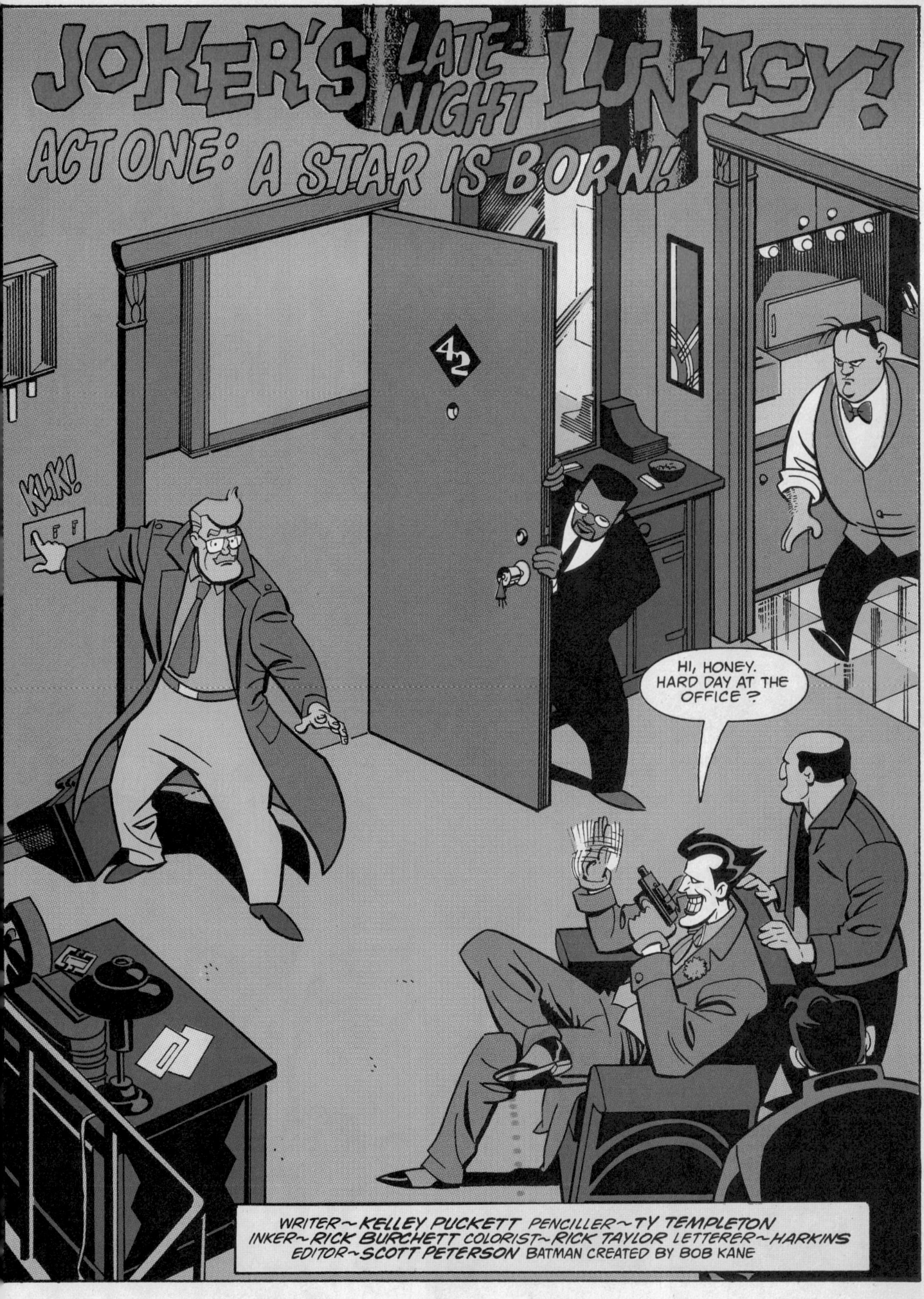
JOKER'S LATE-NIGHT LUNACY!
ACT ONE: A STAR IS BORN!
KLIK!
42
HI, HONEY. HARD DAY AT THE OFFICE?
WRITER~KELLEY PUCKETT PENCILLER~TY TEMPLETON
INKER~RICK BURCHETT COLORIST~RICK TAYLOR LETTERER~HARKINS
EDITOR~SCOTT PETERSON BATMAN CREATED BY BOB KANE

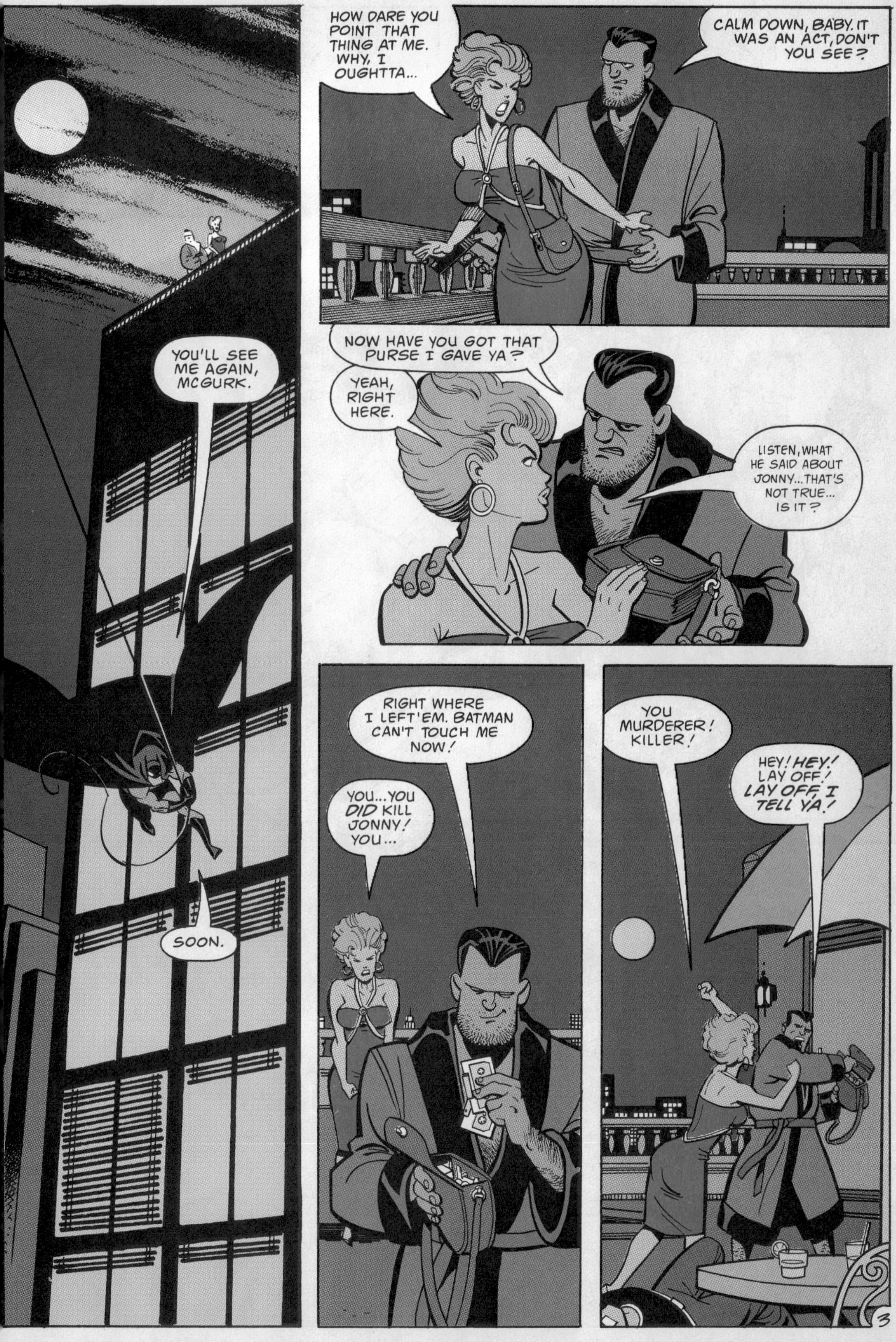
YOU'LL SEE ME AGAIN, MCGURK.
SOON.
HOW DARE YOU POINT THAT THING AT ME. WHY, I OUGHTTA...
CALM DOWN, BABY. IT WAS AN ACT, DON'T YOU SEE?
NOW HAVE YOU GOT THAT PURSE I GAVE YA?
YEAH, RIGHT HERE.
LISTEN, WHAT HE SAID ABOUT JONNY...THAT'S NOT TRUE... IS IT?
RIGHT WHERE I LEFT 'EM. BATMAN CAN'T TOUCH ME NOW!
YOU...YOU DID KILL JONNY! YOU...
YOU MURDERER! KILLER!
HEY! HEY! LAY OFF! LAY OFF, I TELL YA!
3

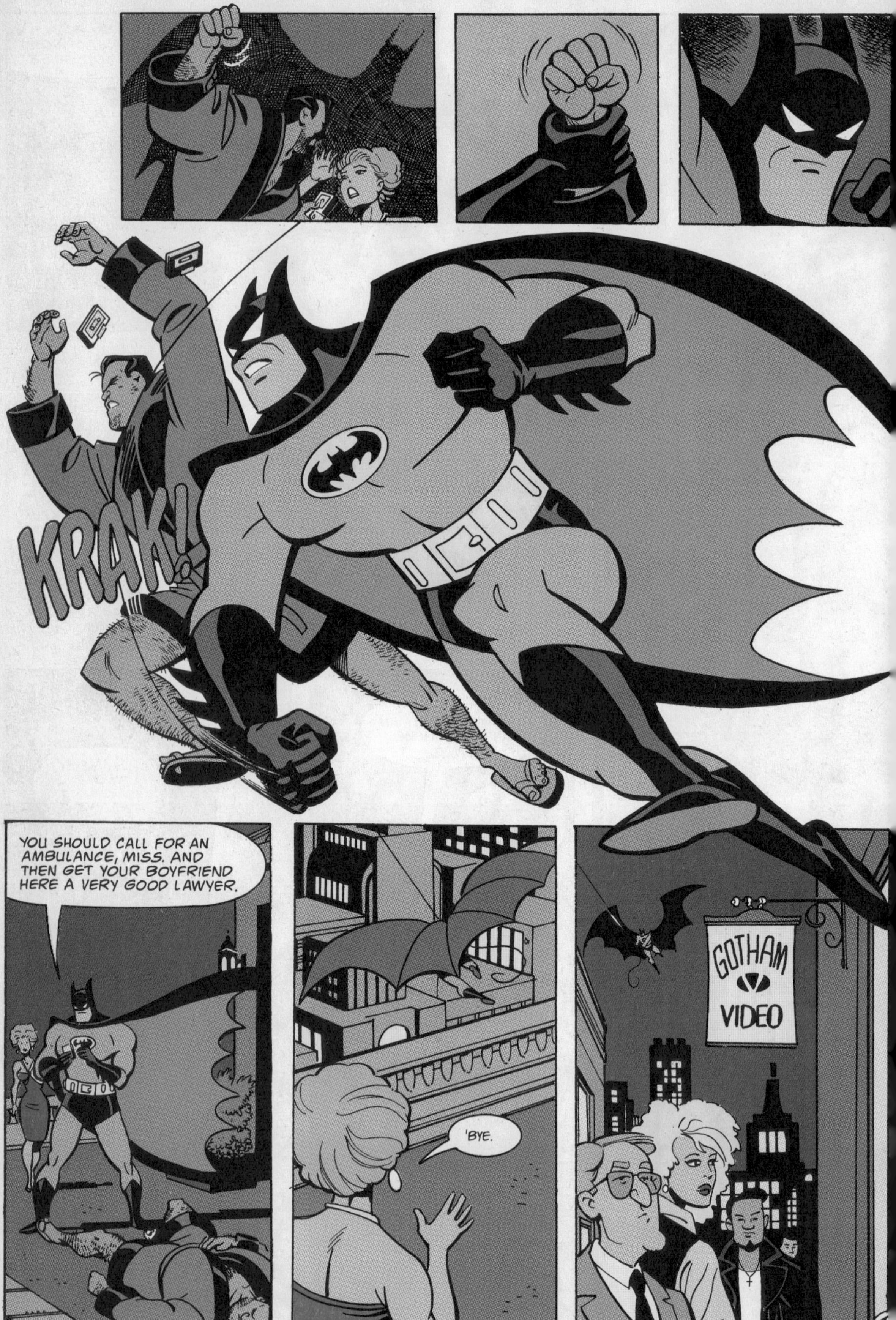
KRAK!
YOU SHOULD CALL FOR AN AMBULANCE, MISS. AND THEN GET YOUR BOYFRIEND HERE A VERY GOOD LAWYER.
'BYE.
GOTHAM VIDEO

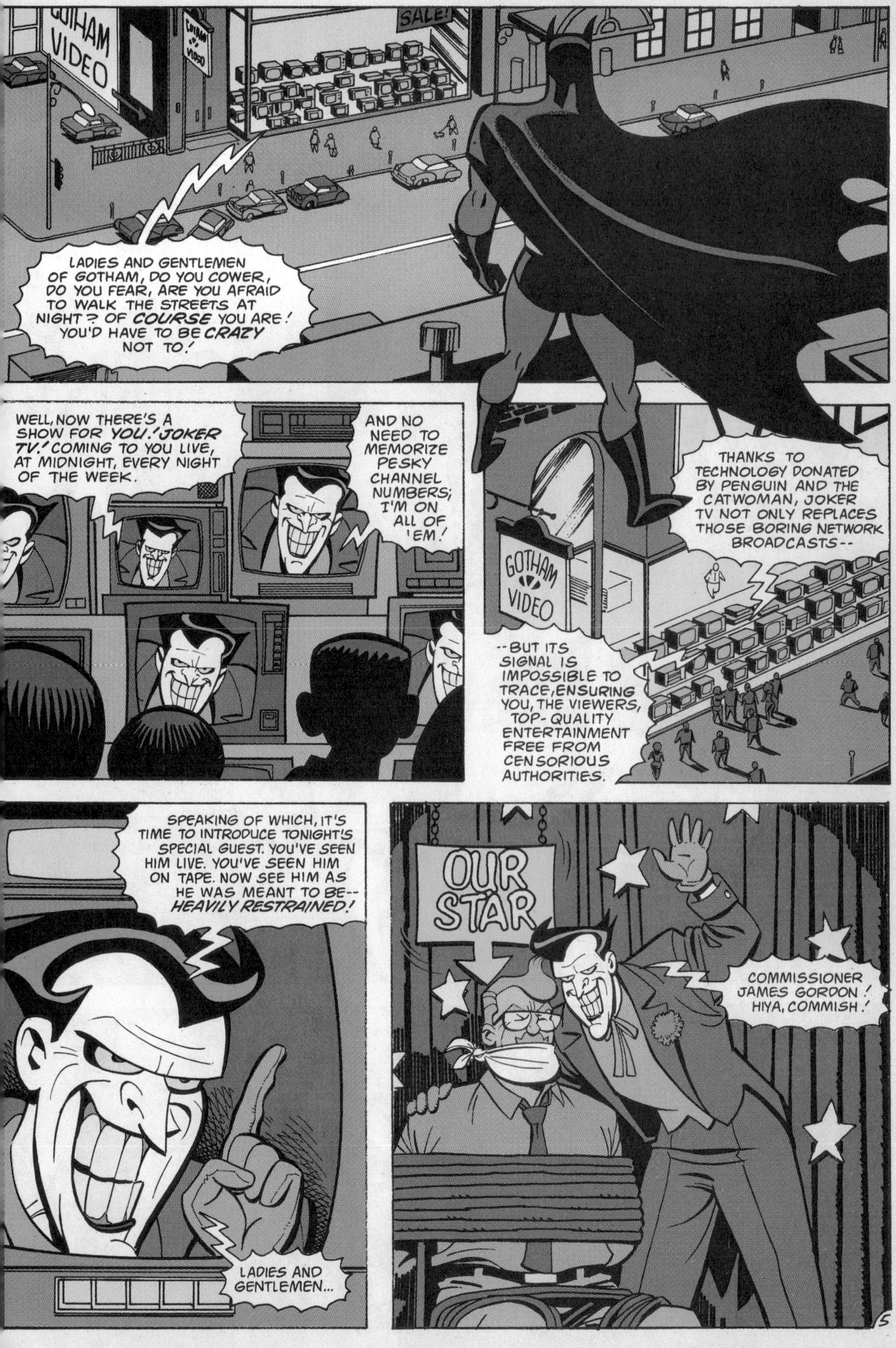
GOTHAM VIDEO
SALE!
LADIES AND GENTLEMEN OF GOTHAM, DO YOU COWER, DO YOU FEAR, ARE YOU AFRAID TO WALK THE STREETS AT NIGHT? OF COURSE YOU ARE! YOU'D HAVE TO BE CRAZY NOT TO!
WELL, NOW THERE'S A SHOW FOR YOU! JOKER TV! COMING TO YOU LIVE, AT MIDNIGHT, EVERY NIGHT OF THE WEEK.
AND NO NEED TO MEMORIZE PESKY CHANNEL NUMBERS; I'M ON ALL OF 'EM!
THANKS TO TECHNOLOGY DONATED BY PENGUIN AND THE CATWOMAN, JOKER TV NOT ONLY REPLACES THOSE BORING NETWORK BROADCASTS--
GOTHAM VIDEO
--BUT ITS SIGNAL IS IMPOSSIBLE TO TRACE, ENSURING YOU, THE VIEWERS, TOP-QUALITY ENTERTAINMENT FREE FROM CENSORIOUS AUTHORITIES.
SPEAKING OF WHICH, IT'S TIME TO INTRODUCE TONIGHT'S SPECIAL GUEST. YOU'VE SEEN HIM LIVE. YOU'VE SEEN HIM ON TAPE. NOW SEE HIM AS HE WAS MEANT TO BE-- HEAVILY RESTRAINED!
LADIES AND GENTLEMEN...
OUR STAR
COMMISSIONER JAMES GORDON! HIYA, COMMISH!
5

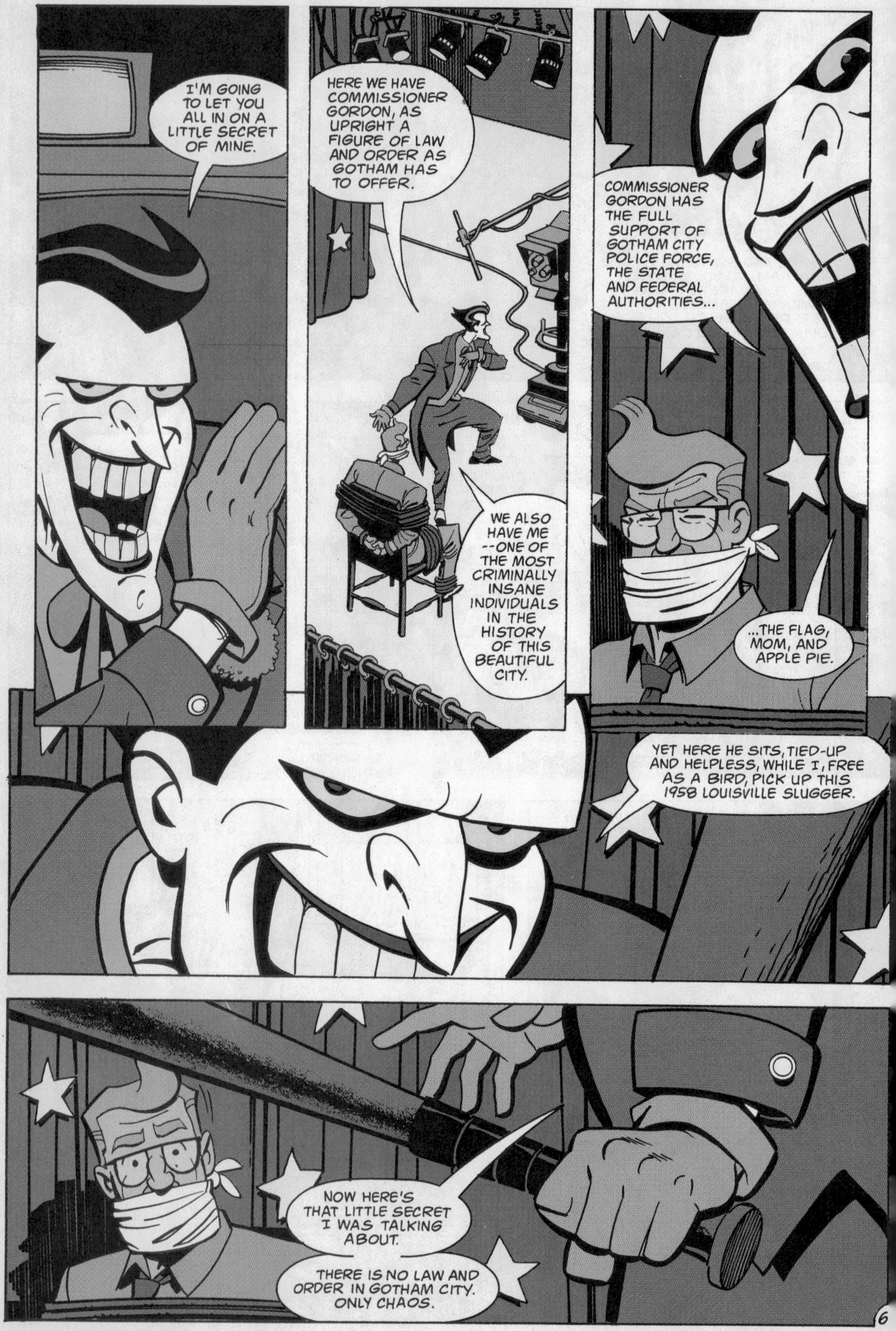
I'M GOING TO LET YOU ALL IN ON A LITTLE SECRET OF MINE.
HERE WE HAVE COMMISSIONER GORDON, AS UPRIGHT A FIGURE OF LAW AND ORDER AS GOTHAM HAS TO OFFER.
WE ALSO HAVE ME --ONE OF THE MOST CRIMINALLY INSANE INDIVIDUALS IN THE HISTORY OF THIS BEAUTIFUL CITY.
COMMISSIONER GORDON HAS THE FULL SUPPORT OF GOTHAM CITY POLICE FORCE, THE STATE AND FEDERAL AUTHORITIES...
...THE FLAG, MOM, AND APPLE PIE.
YET HERE HE SITS, TIED-UP AND HELPLESS, WHILE I, FREE AS A BIRD, PICK UP THIS 1958 LOUISVILLE SLUGGER.
NOW HERE'S THAT LITTLE SECRET I WAS TALKING ABOUT.
THERE IS NO LAW AND ORDER IN GOTHAM CITY. ONLY CHAOS.
6

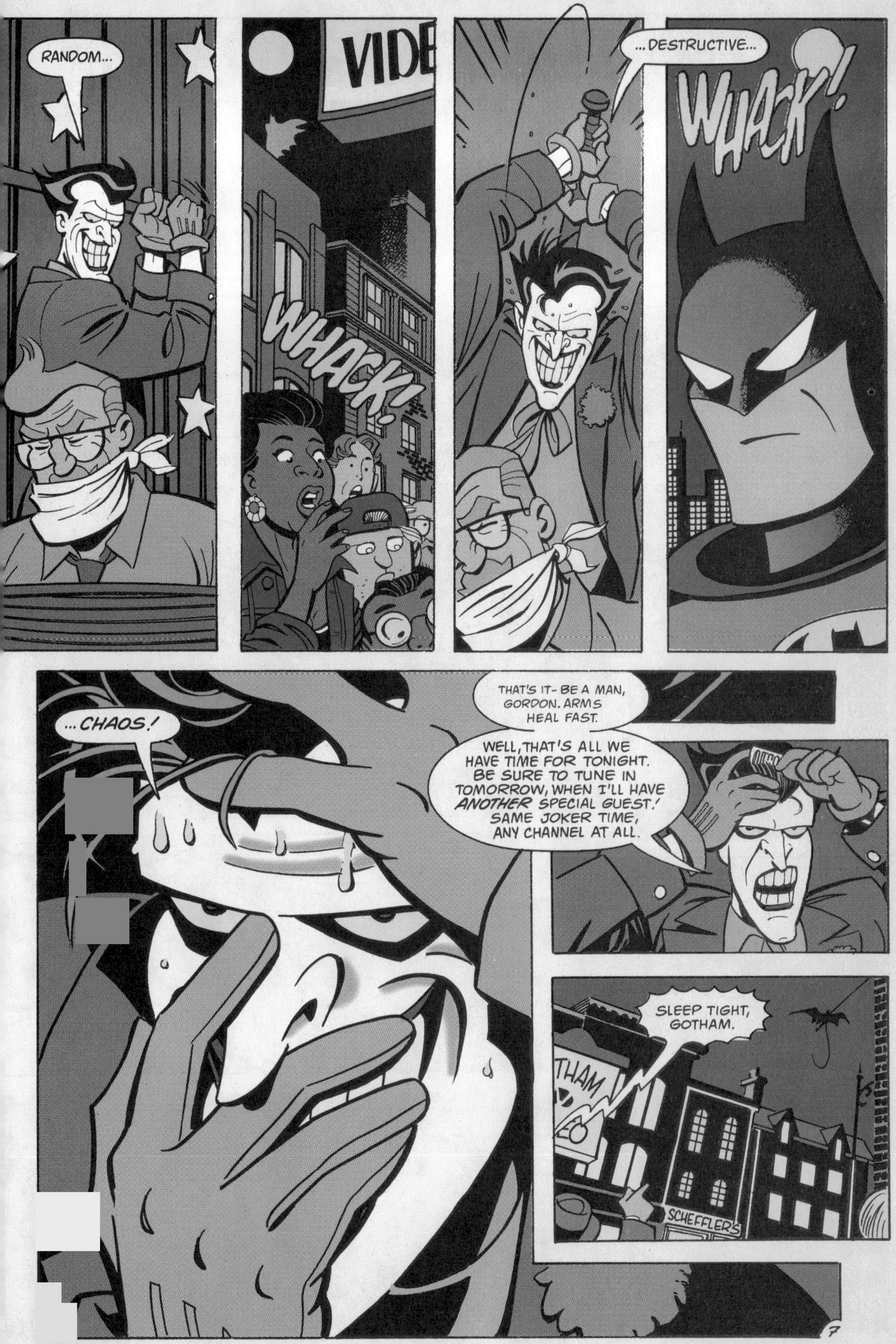
RANDOM...
VIDE
WHACK!
...DESTRUCTIVE...
WHACK!
...CHAOS!
THAT'S IT- BE A MAN, GORDON. ARMS HEAL FAST.
WELL, THAT'S ALL WE HAVE TIME FOR TONIGHT. BE SURE TO TUNE IN TOMORROW, WHEN I'LL HAVE ANOTHER SPECIAL GUEST! SAME JOKER TIME, ANY CHANNEL AT ALL.
SLEEP TIGHT, GOTHAM.
THAM
SCHEFFLER'S
7

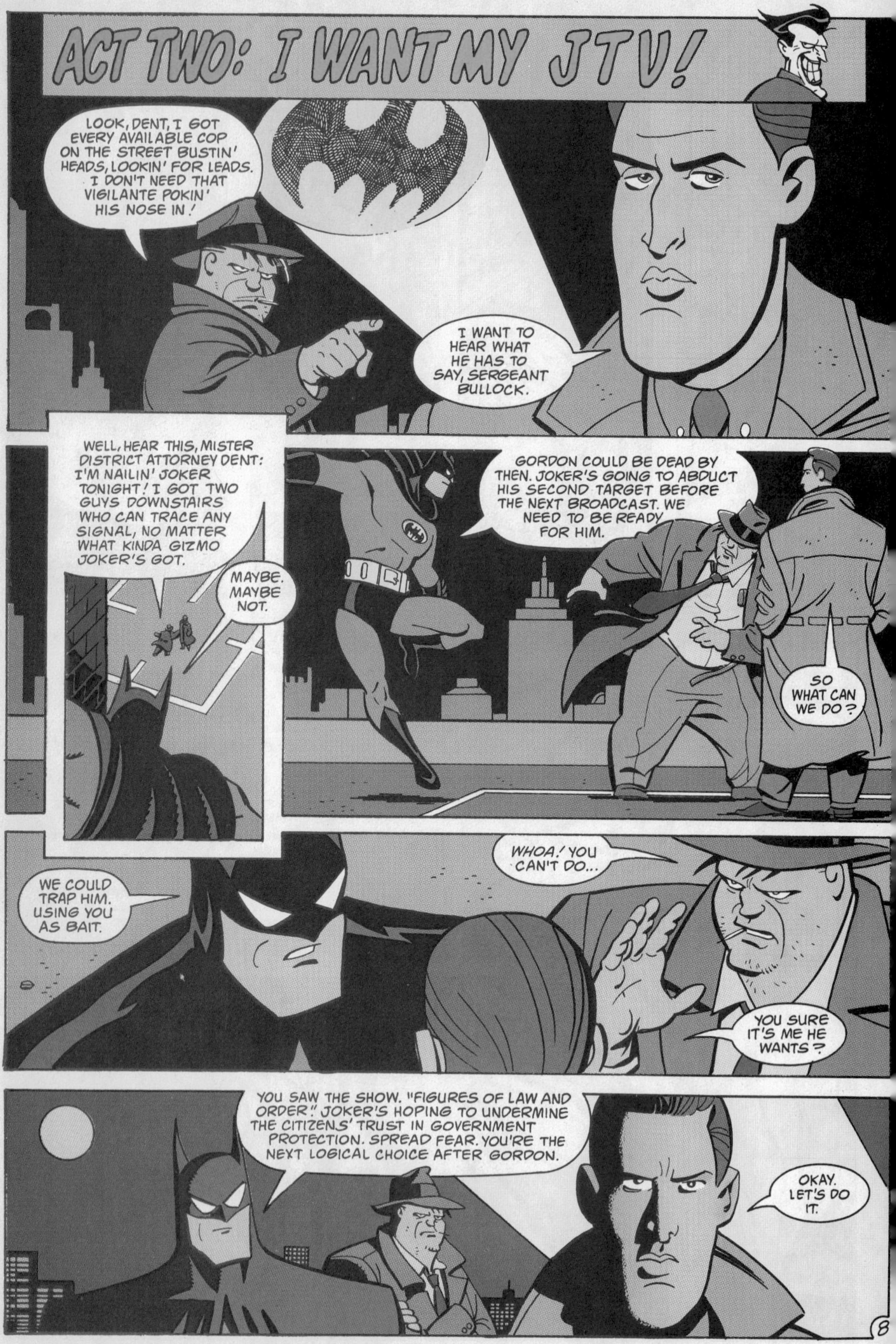
ACT TWO: I WANT MY JTV!
LOOK, DENT, I GOT EVERY AVAILABLE COP ON THE STREET BUSTIN' HEADS, LOOKIN' FOR LEADS. I DON'T NEED THAT VIGILANTE POKIN' HIS NOSE IN!
I WANT TO HEAR WHAT HE HAS TO SAY, SERGEANT BULLOCK.
WELL, HEAR THIS, MISTER DISTRICT ATTORNEY DENT: I'M NAILIN' JOKER TONIGHT! I GOT TWO GUYS DOWNSTAIRS WHO CAN TRACE ANY SIGNAL, NO MATTER WHAT KINDA GIZMO JOKER'S GOT.
MAYBE. MAYBE NOT.
GORDON COULD BE DEAD BY THEN. JOKER'S GOING TO ABDUCT HIS SECOND TARGET BEFORE THE NEXT BROADCAST. WE NEED TO BE READY FOR HIM.
SO WHAT CAN WE DO?
WE COULD TRAP HIM. USING YOU AS BAIT.
WHOA! YOU CAN'T DO...
YOU SURE IT'S ME HE WANTS?
YOU SAW THE SHOW. "FIGURES OF LAW AND ORDER." JOKER'S HOPING TO UNDERMINE THE CITIZENS' TRUST IN GOVERNMENT PROTECTION. SPREAD FEAR. YOU'RE THE NEXT LOGICAL CHOICE AFTER GORDON.
OKAY. LET'S DO IT.
8

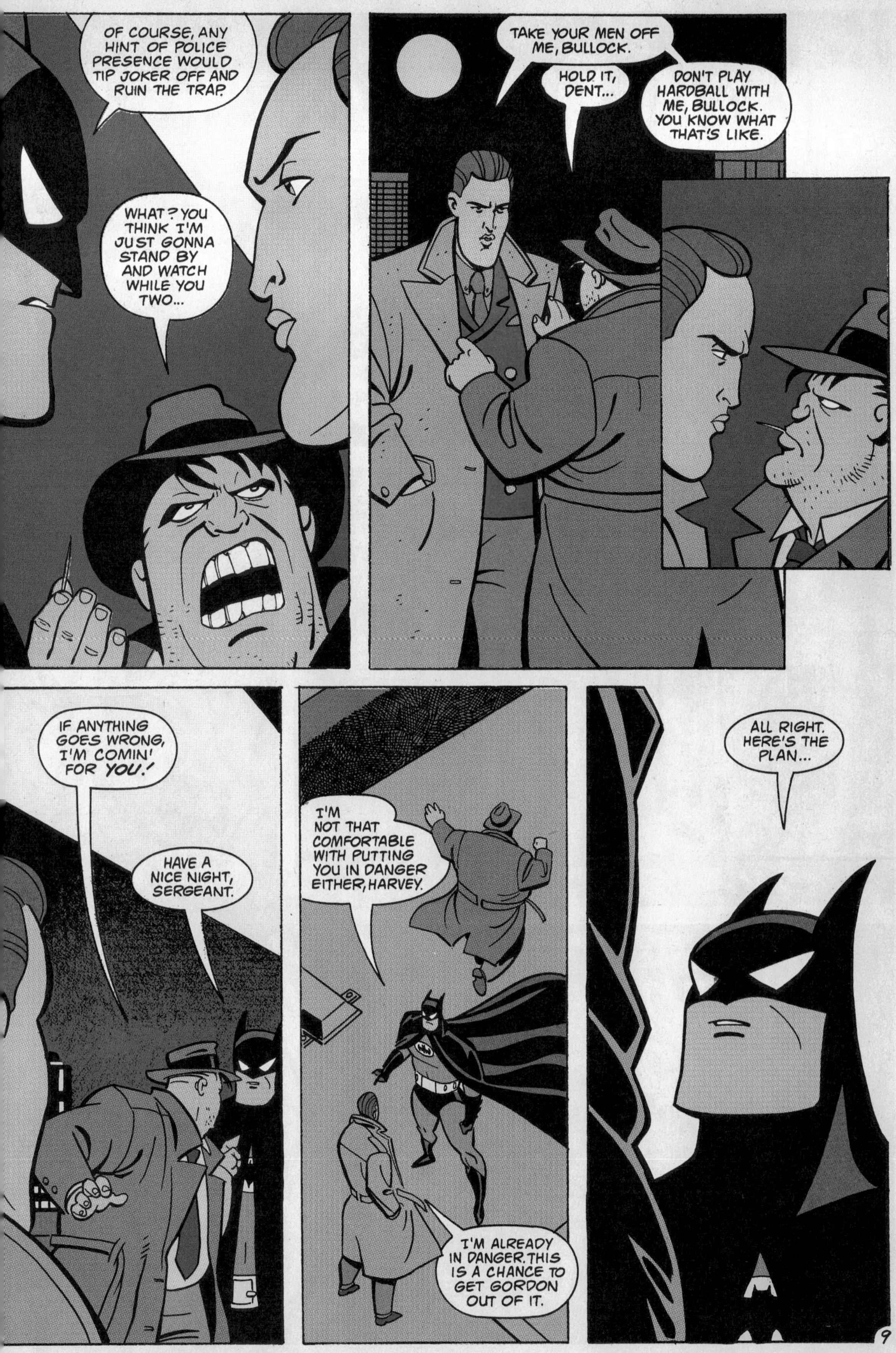
OF COURSE, ANY HINT OF POLICE PRESENCE WOULD TIP JOKER OFF AND RUIN THE TRAP.
WHAT? YOU THINK I'M JUST GONNA STAND BY AND WATCH WHILE YOU TWO...
TAKE YOUR MEN OFF ME, BULLOCK.
HOLD IT, DENT...
DON'T PLAY HARDBALL WITH ME, BULLOCK. YOU KNOW WHAT THAT'S LIKE.
IF ANYTHING GOES WRONG, I'M COMIN' FOR YOU!
HAVE A NICE NIGHT, SERGEANT.
I'M NOT THAT COMFORTABLE WITH PUTTING YOU IN DANGER EITHER, HARVEY.
I'M ALREADY IN DANGER. THIS IS A CHANCE TO GET GORDON OUT OF IT.
ALL RIGHT. HERE'S THE PLAN...
9

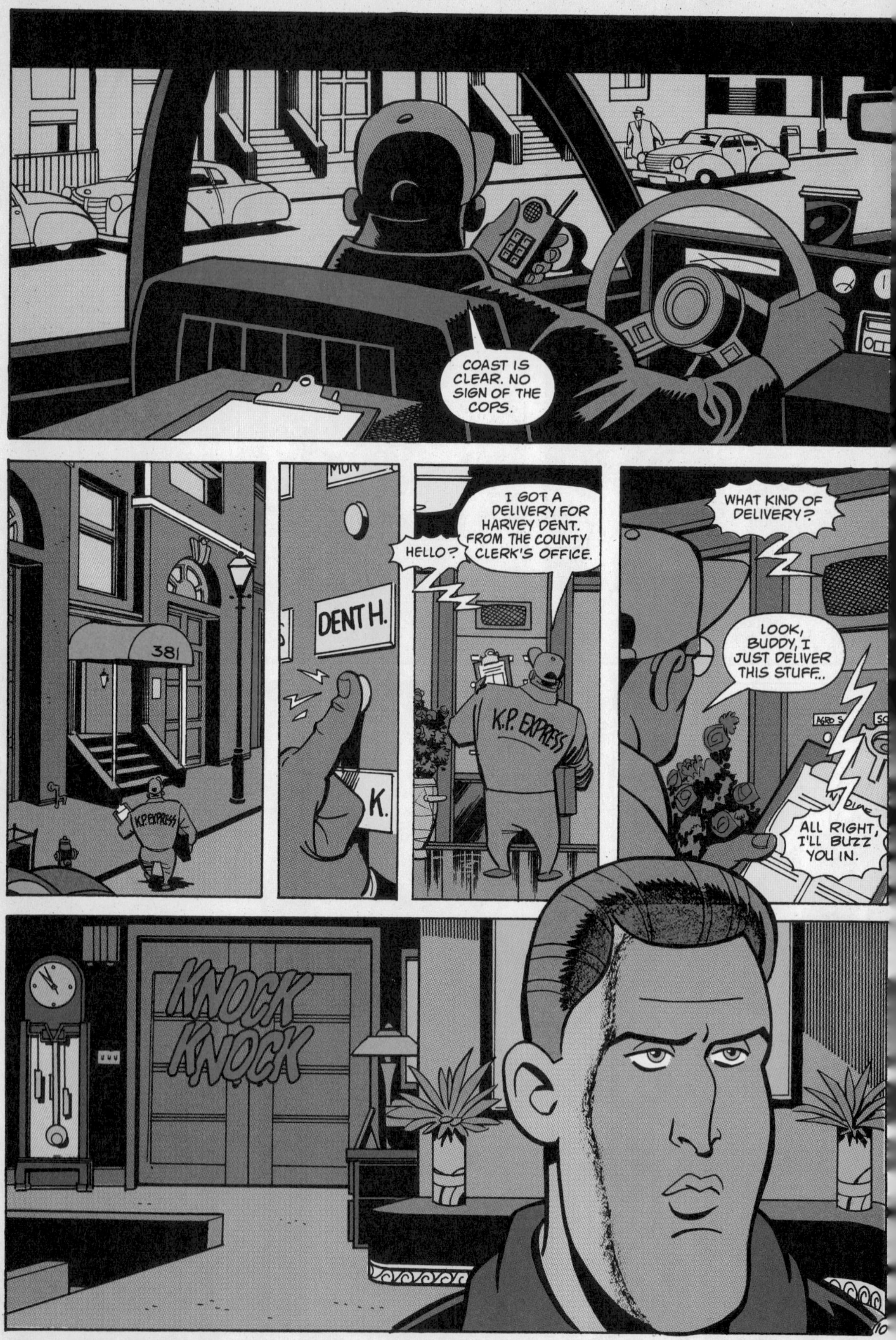

COAST IS CLEAR. NO SIGN OF THE COPS.
DENT H.
K.
HELLO?
I GOT A DELIVERY FOR HARVEY DENT. FROM THE COUNTY CLERK'S OFFICE.
K.P. EXPRESS
WHAT KIND OF DELIVERY?
LOOK, BUDDY, I JUST DELIVER THIS STUFF...
ALL RIGHT, I'LL BUZZ YOU IN.
KNOCK KNOCK

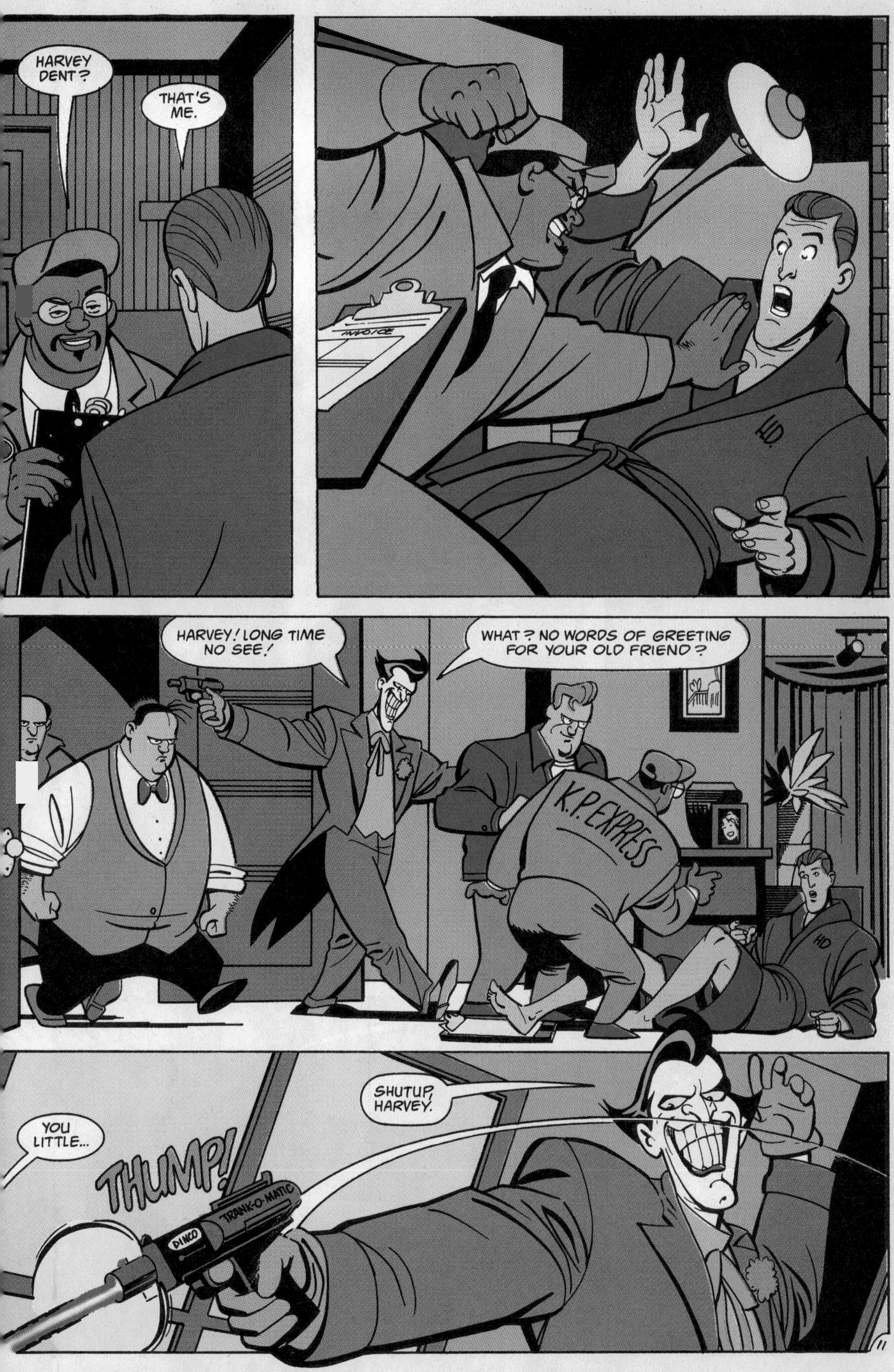
HARVEY DENT?
THAT'S ME.
INVOICE
HD
HARVEY! LONG TIME NO SEE!
WHAT? NO WORDS OF GREETING FOR YOUR OLD FRIEND?
K.P. EXPRESS
HD
SHUTUP, HARVEY.
YOU LITTLE...
THUMP!
TRANK-O-MATIC
DINCO

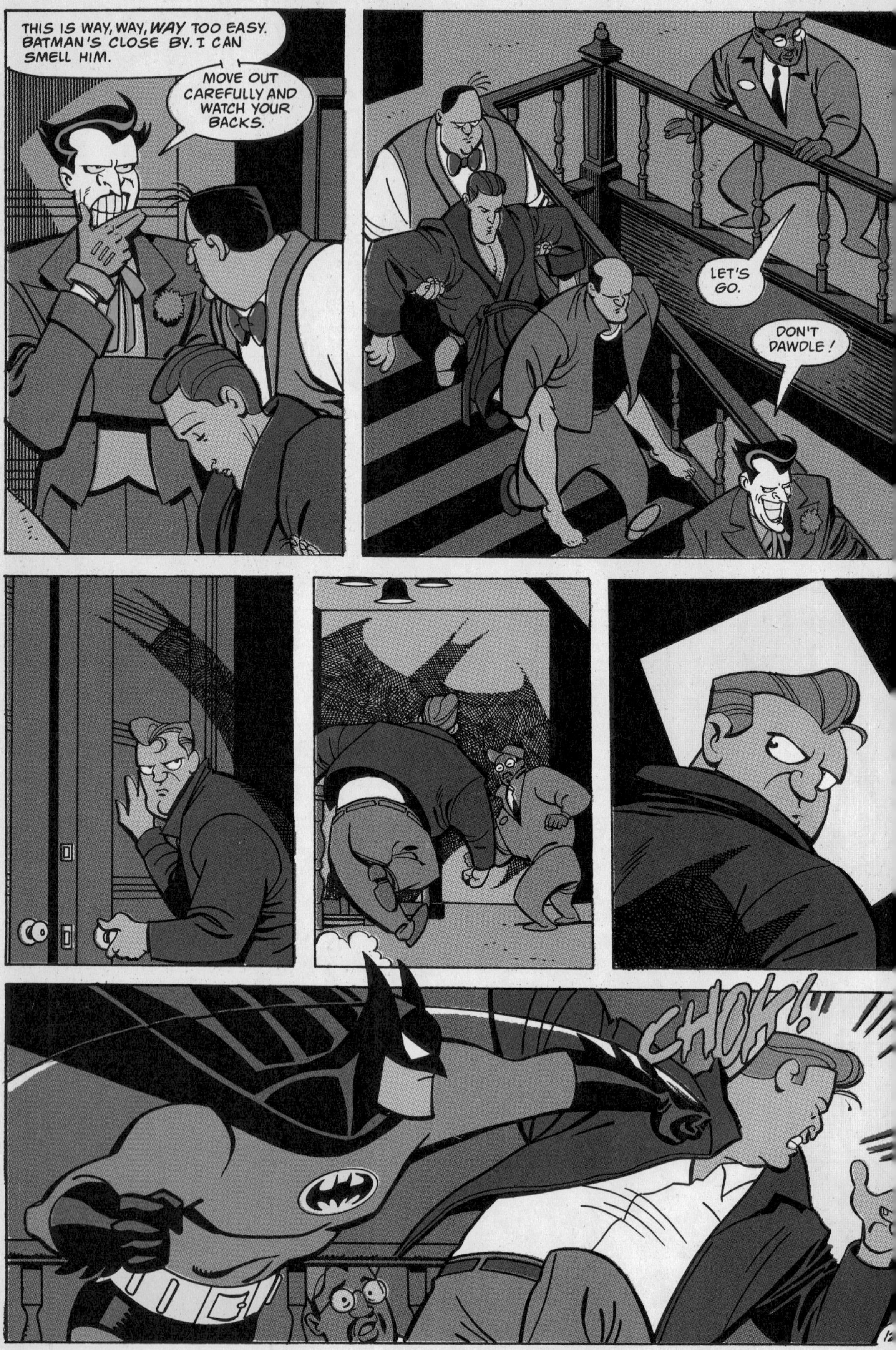
THIS IS WAY, WAY, WAY TOO EASY. BATMAN'S CLOSE BY. I CAN SMELL HIM.
MOVE OUT CAREFULLY AND WATCH YOUR BACKS.
LET'S GO.
DON'T DAWDLE!
CHOK!

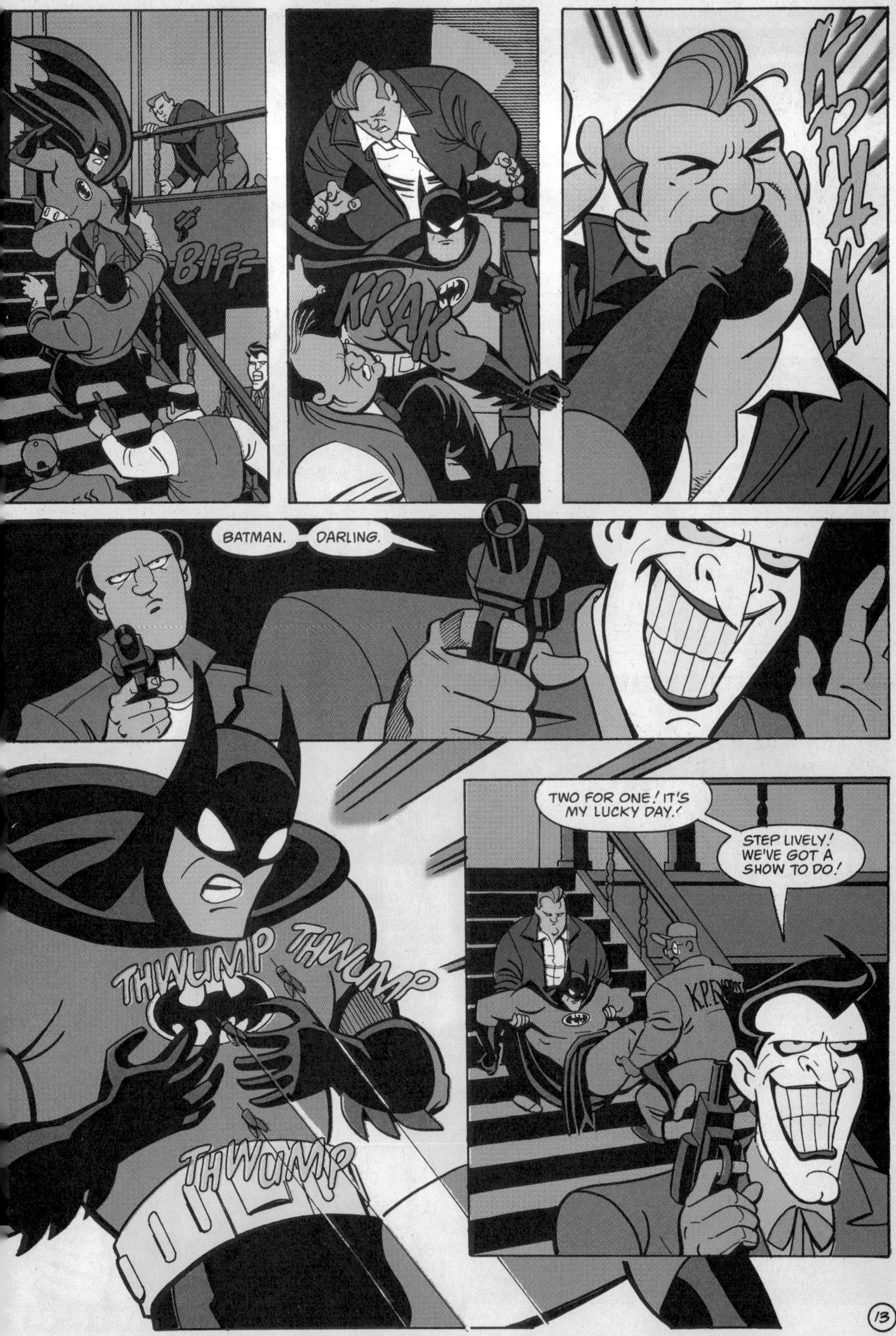
BIFF
KRAK
KRAK
BATMAN.
DARLING.
THWUMP THWUMP
THWUMP
TWO FOR ONE! IT'S MY LUCKY DAY!
STEP LIVELY! WE'VE GOT A SHOW TO DO!
13

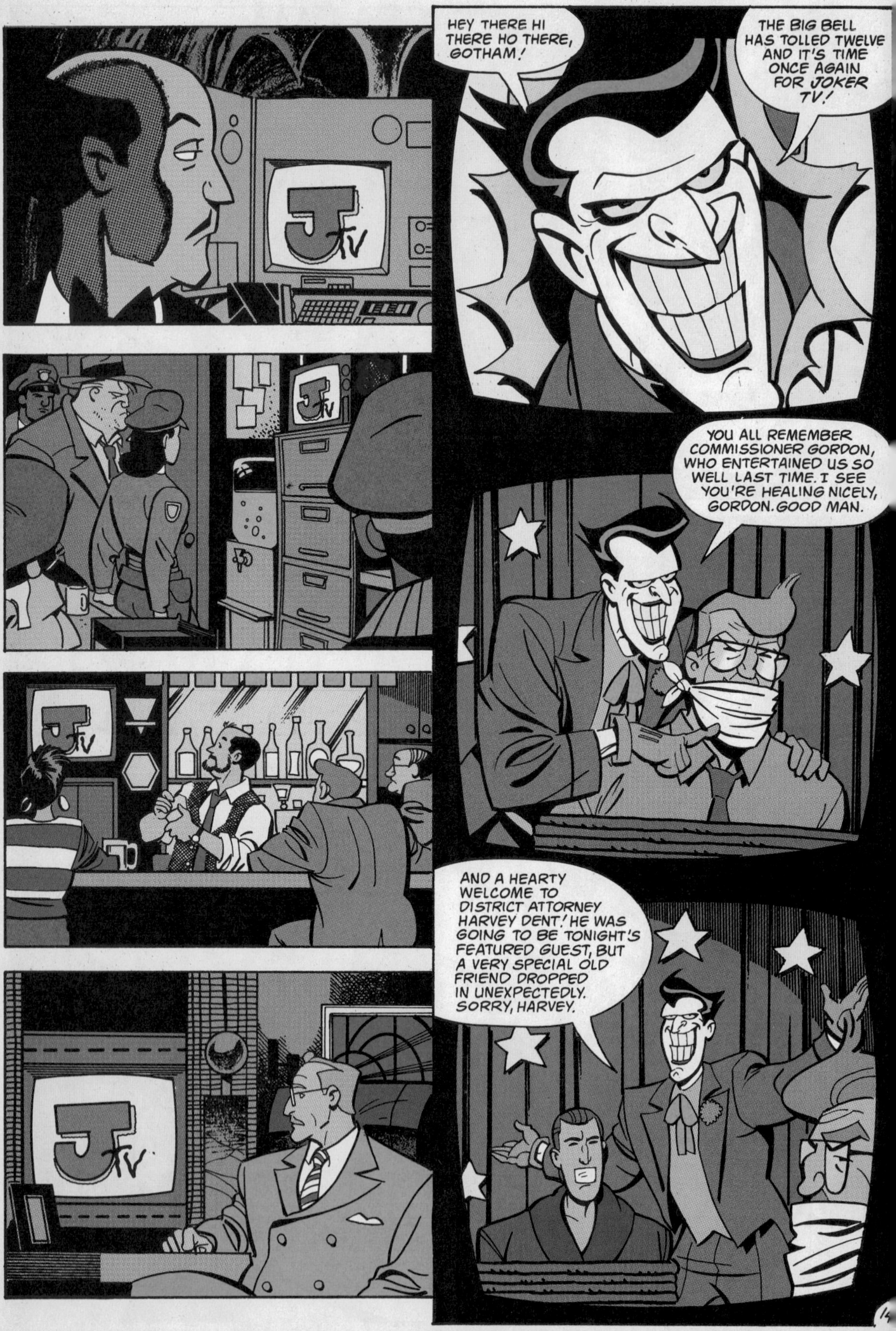
HEY THERE HI THERE HO THERE, GOTHAM!
THE BIG BELL HAS TOLLED TWELVE AND IT'S TIME ONCE AGAIN FOR JOKER TV!
YOU ALL REMEMBER COMMISSIONER GORDON, WHO ENTERTAINED US SO WELL LAST TIME. I SEE YOU'RE HEALING NICELY, GORDON. GOOD MAN.
AND A HEARTY WELCOME TO DISTRICT ATTORNEY HARVEY DENT! HE WAS GOING TO BE TONIGHT'S FEATURED GUEST, BUT A VERY SPECIAL OLD FRIEND DROPPED IN UNEXPECTEDLY. SORRY, HARVEY.

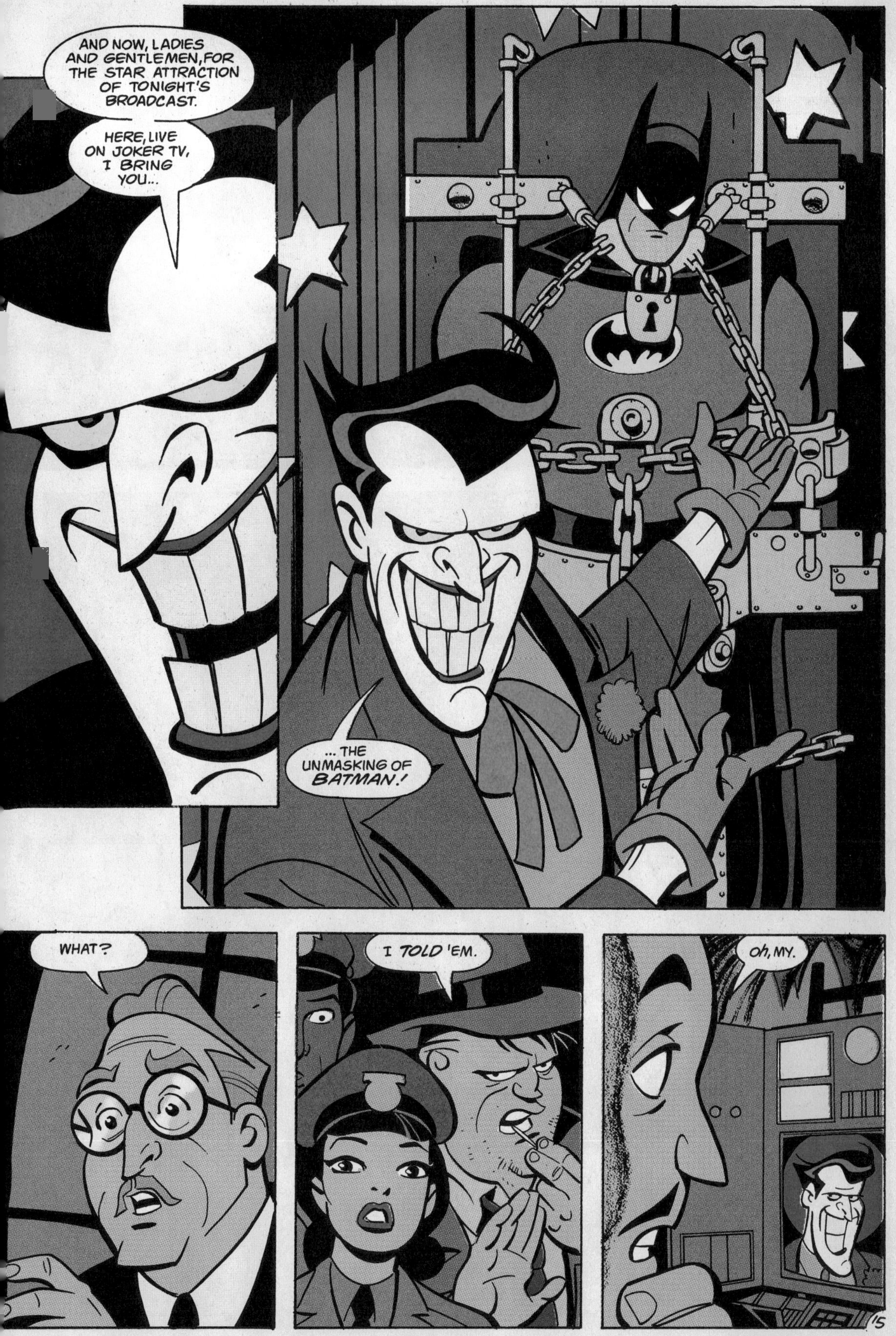

AND NOW, LADIES AND GENTLEMEN, FOR THE STAR ATTRACTION OF TONIGHT'S BROADCAST.
HERE, LIVE ON JOKER TV, I BRING YOU...
... THE UNMASKING OF BATMAN!
WHAT?
I TOLD 'EM.
Oh, MY.
15

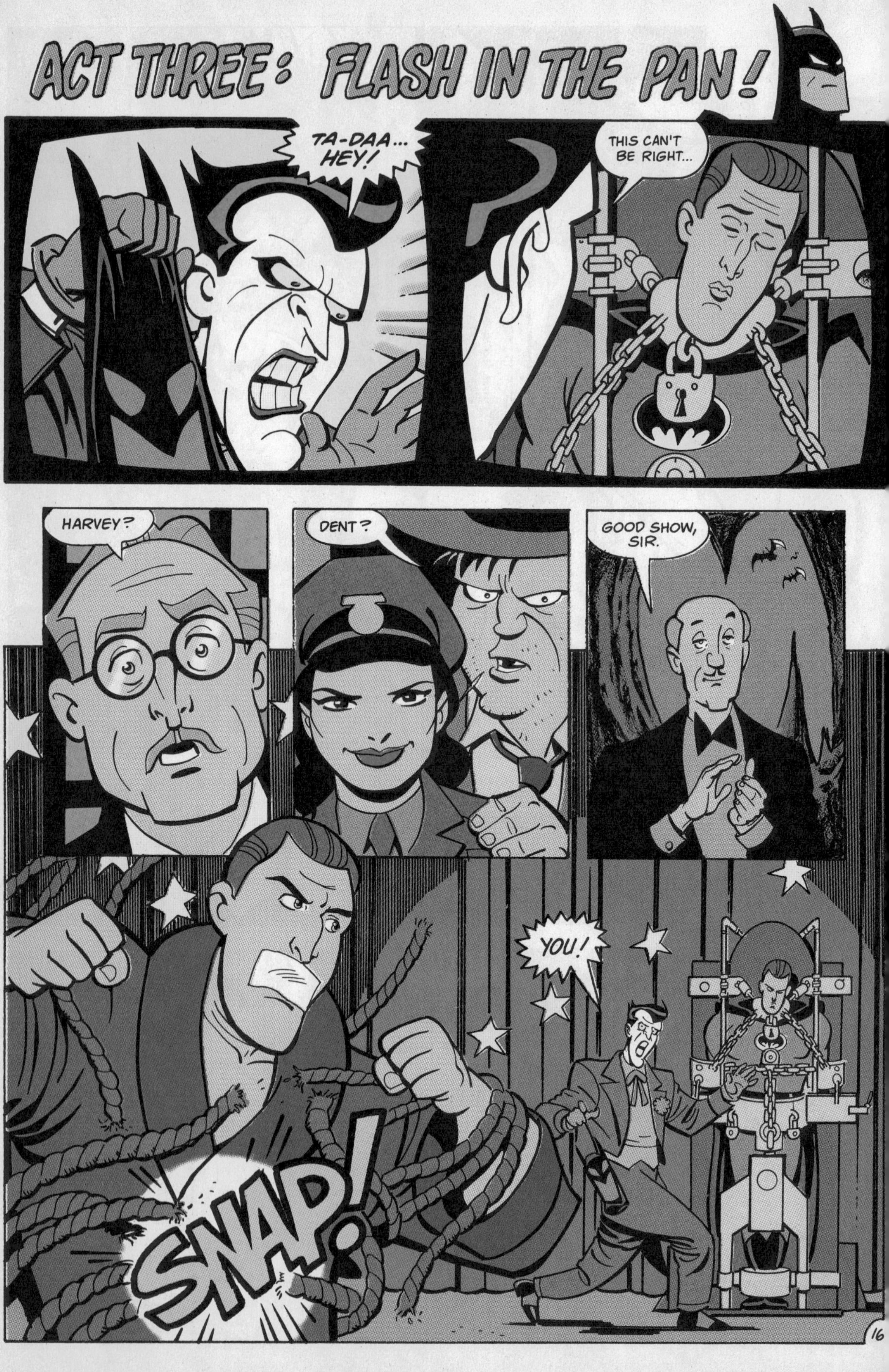
ACT THREE: FLASH IN THE PAN!
TA-DAA... HEY!
THIS CAN'T BE RIGHT...
HARVEY?
DENT?
GOOD SHOW, SIR.
YOU!
SNAP!
16

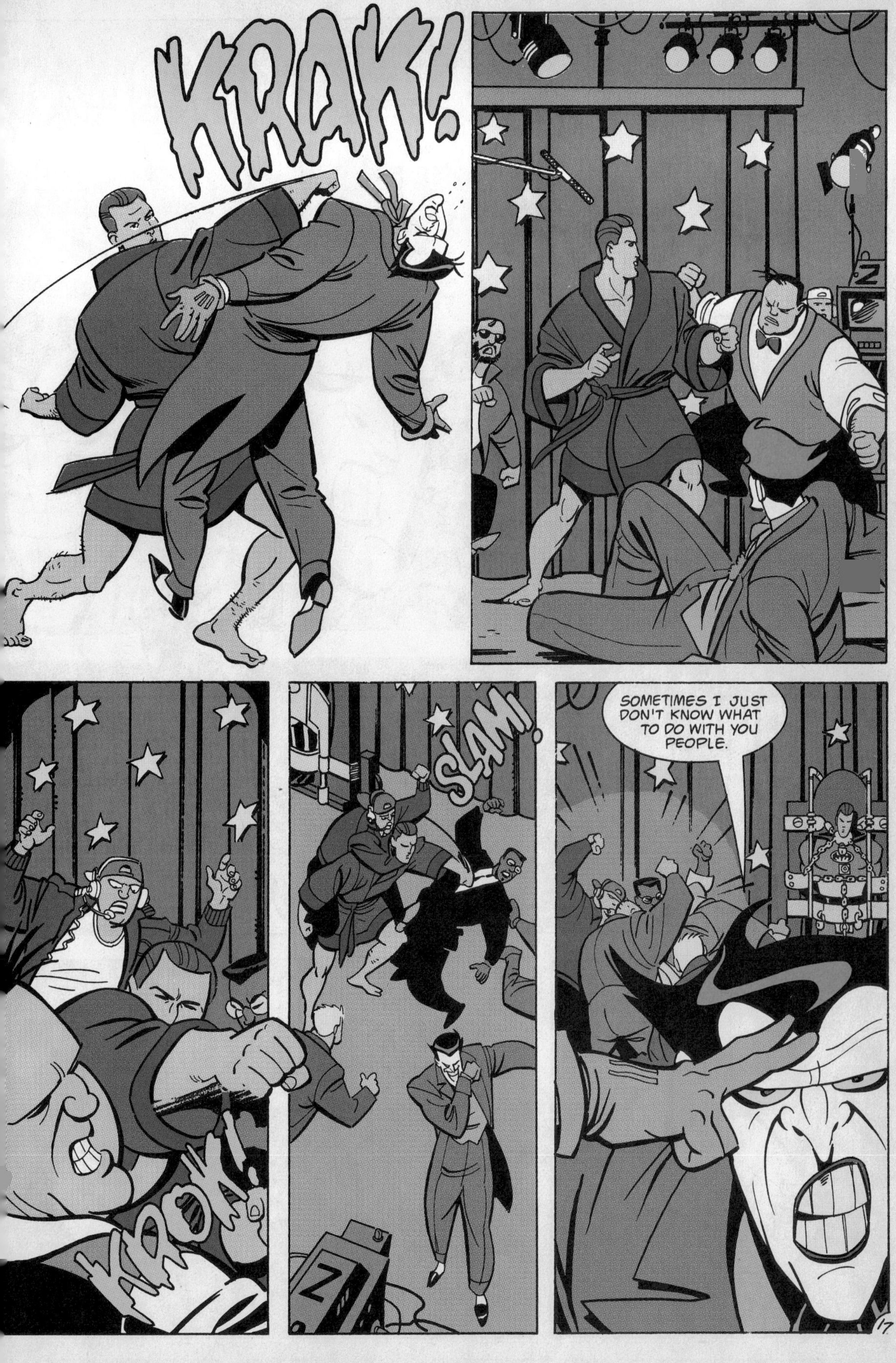
KRAK!
SLAM!
SOMETIMES I JUST DON'T KNOW WHAT TO DO WITH YOU PEOPLE.

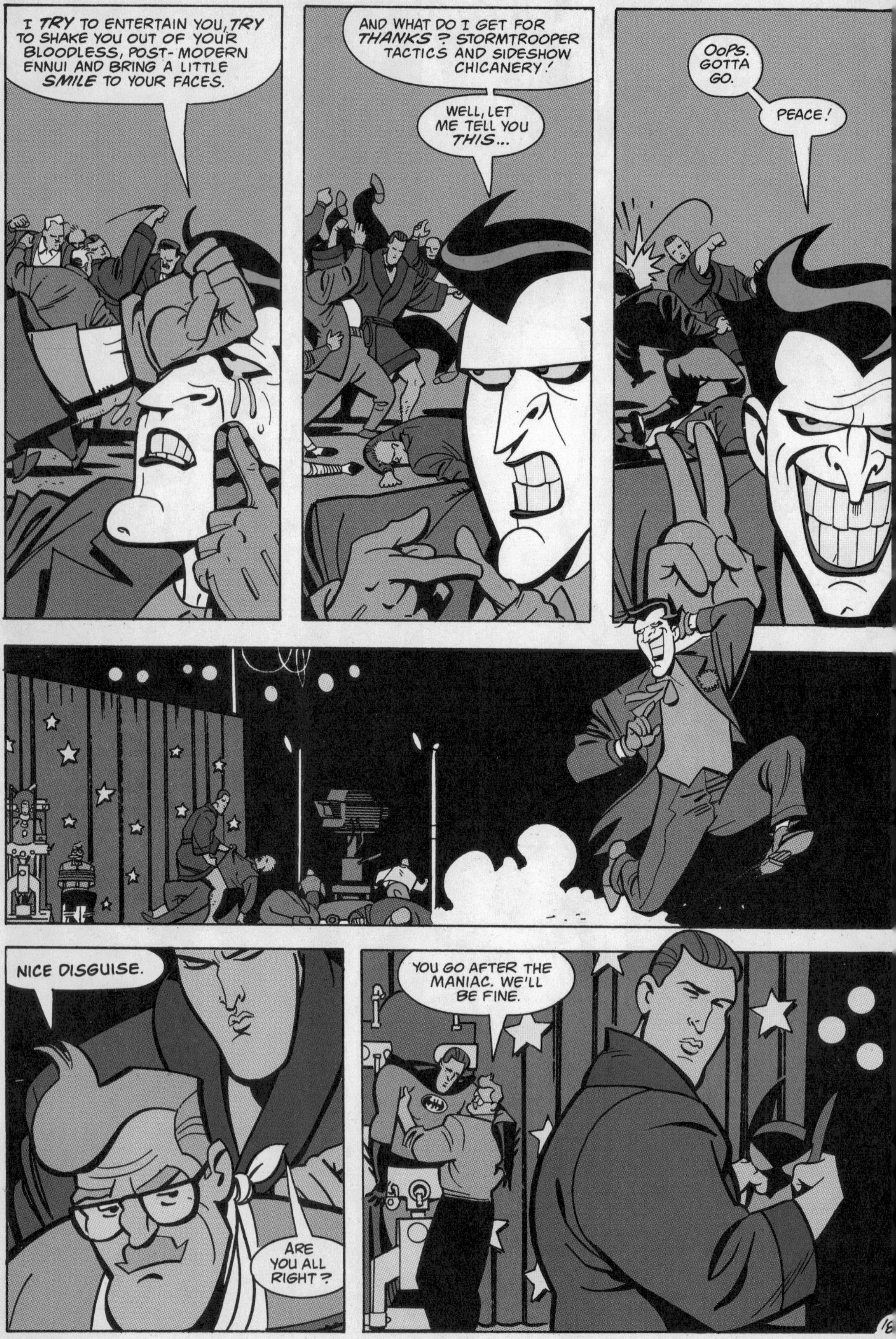
I TRY TO ENTERTAIN YOU, TRY TO SHAKE YOU OUT OF YOUR BLOODLESS, POST-MODERN ENNUI AND BRING A LITTLE SMILE TO YOUR FACES.
AND WHAT DO I GET FOR THANKS? STORMTROOPER TACTICS AND SIDESHOW CHICANERY!
WELL, LET ME TELL YOU THIS...
OOPS. GOTTA GO.
PEACE!
NICE DISGUISE.
ARE YOU ALL RIGHT?
YOU GO AFTER THE MANIAC. WE'LL BE FINE.

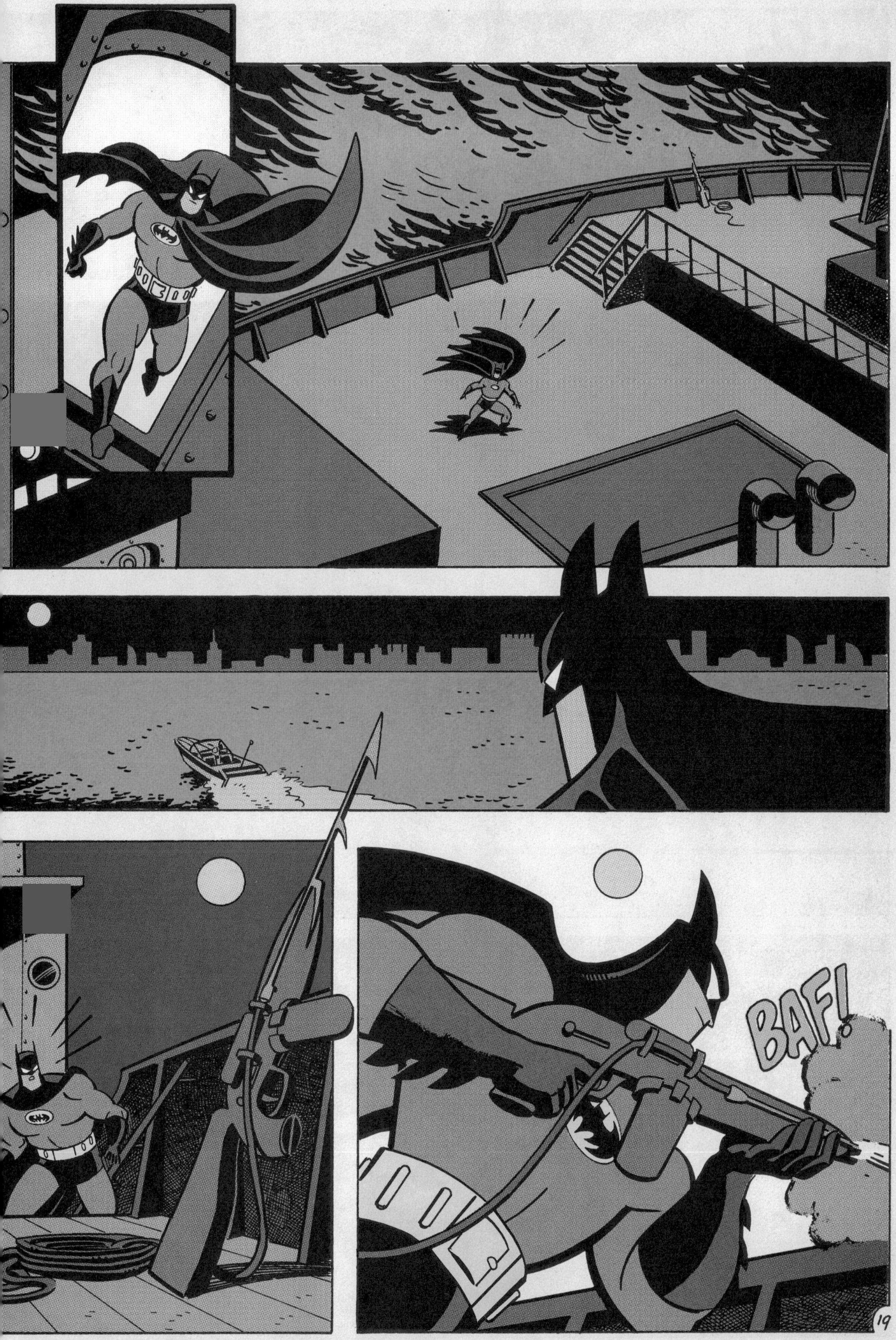
BAF!
19

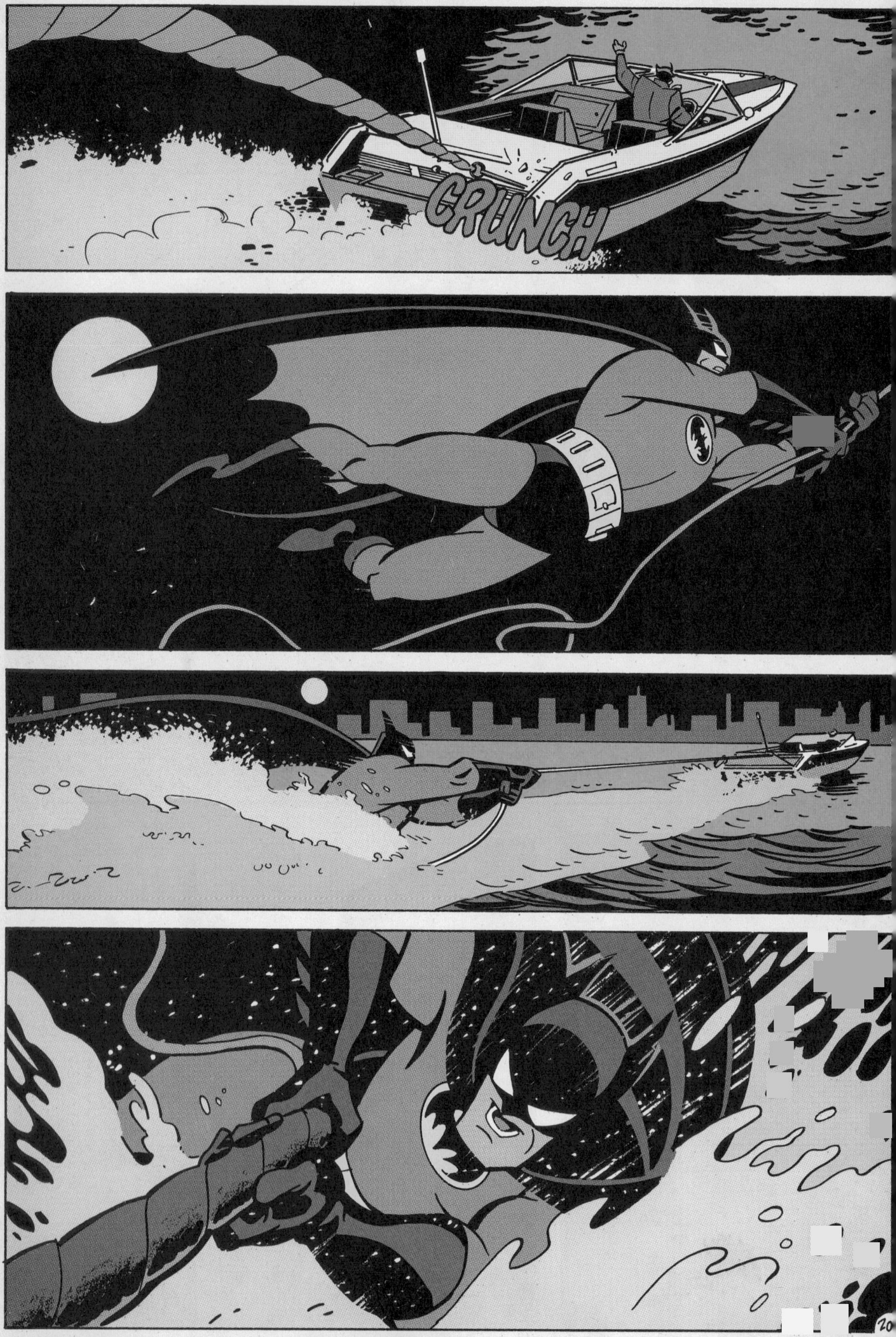
CRUNCH

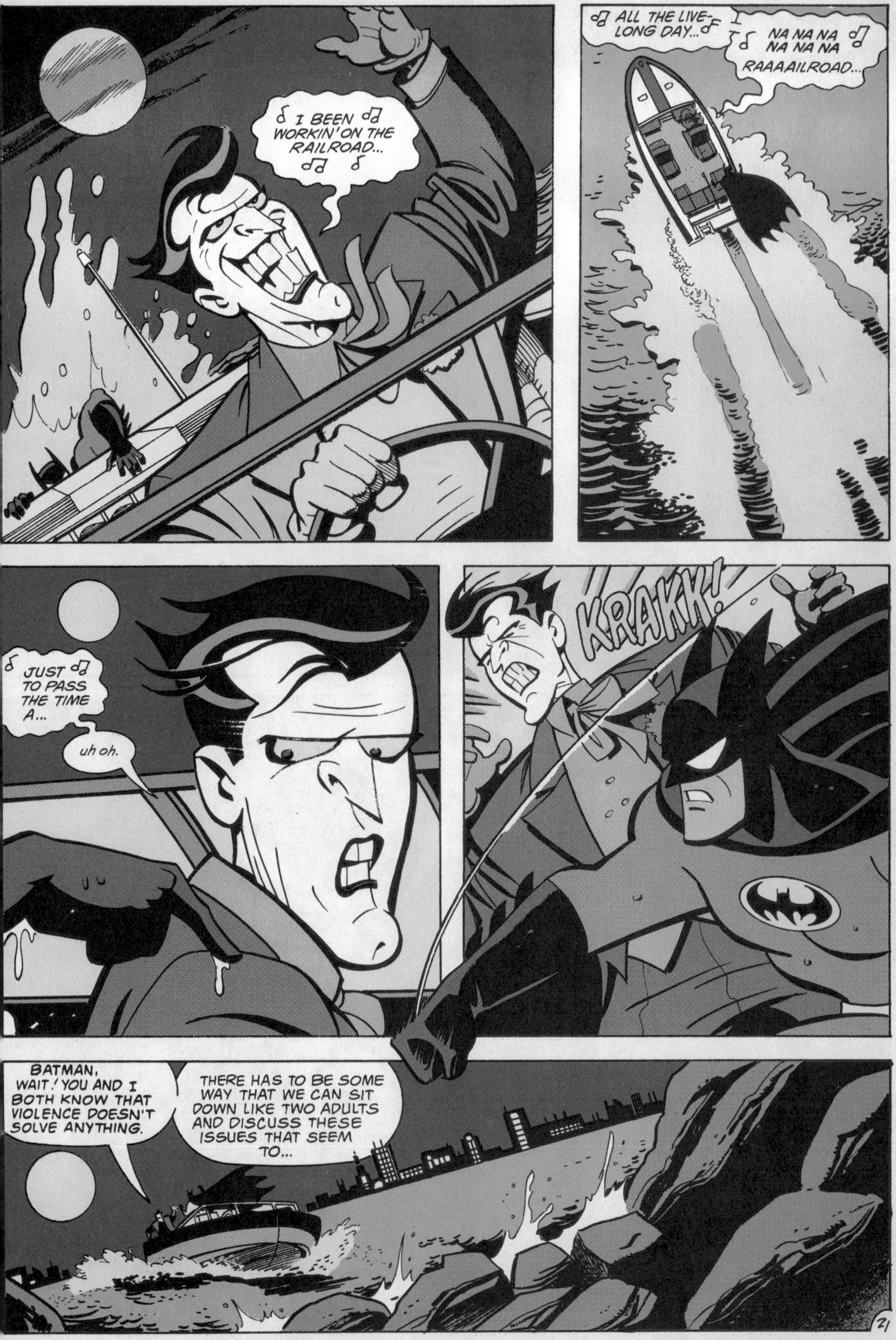
I BEEN WORKIN' ON THE RAILROAD...
ALL THE LIVE-LONG DAY...
NA NA NA NA NA NA RAAAAILROAD...
JUST TO PASS THE TIME A...
uh oh.
KRAKK!
BATMAN, WAIT! YOU AND I BOTH KNOW THAT VIOLENCE DOESN'T SOLVE ANYTHING.
THERE HAS TO BE SOME WAY THAT WE CAN SIT DOWN LIKE TWO ADULTS AND DISCUSS THESE ISSUES THAT SEEM TO...
21

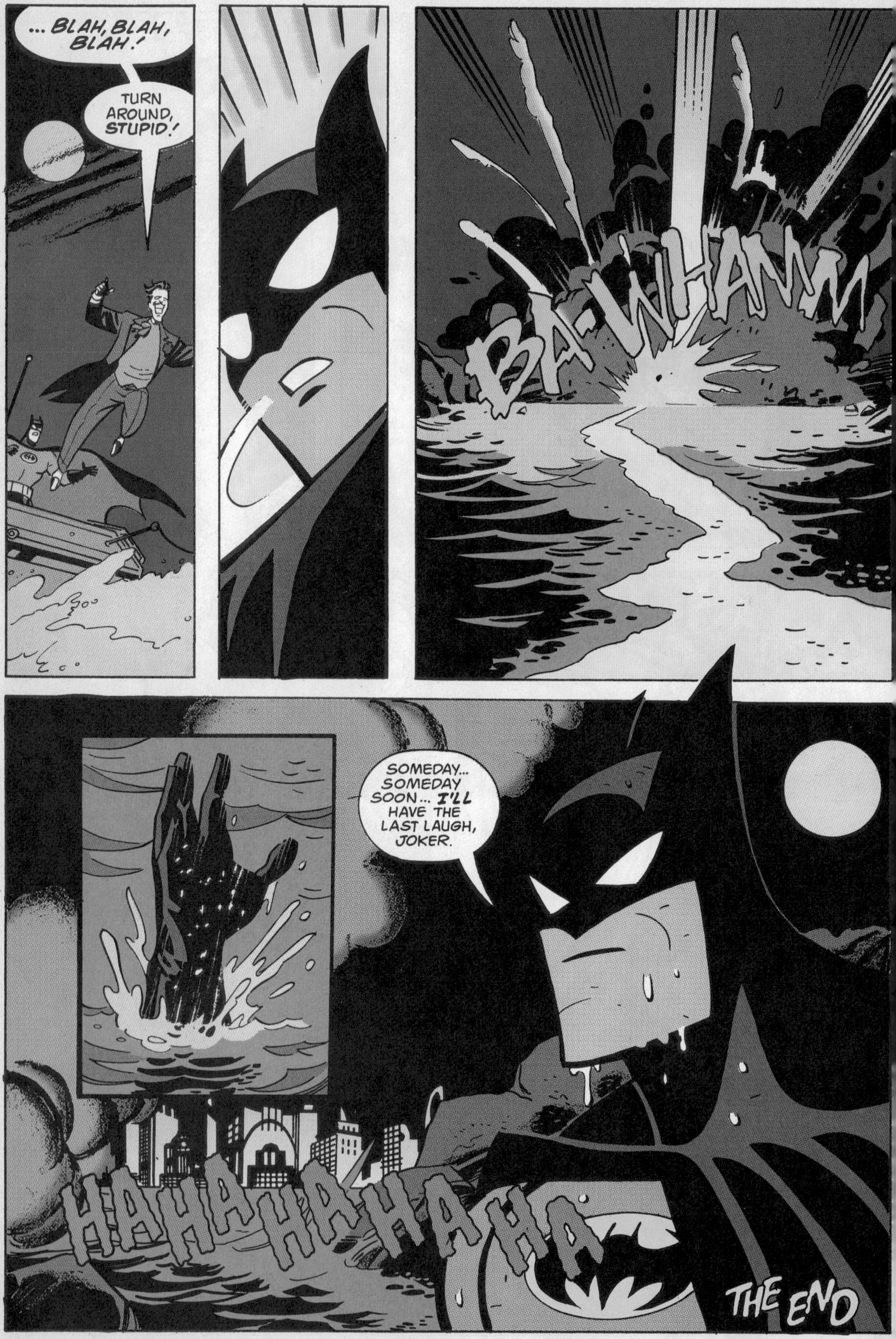

... BLAH, BLAH, BLAH!
TURN AROUND, STUPID!
BA-WHAMM
SOMEDAY... SOMEDAY SOON... I'LL HAVE THE LAST LAUGH, JOKER.
HAHAHAHAHAHA
THE END

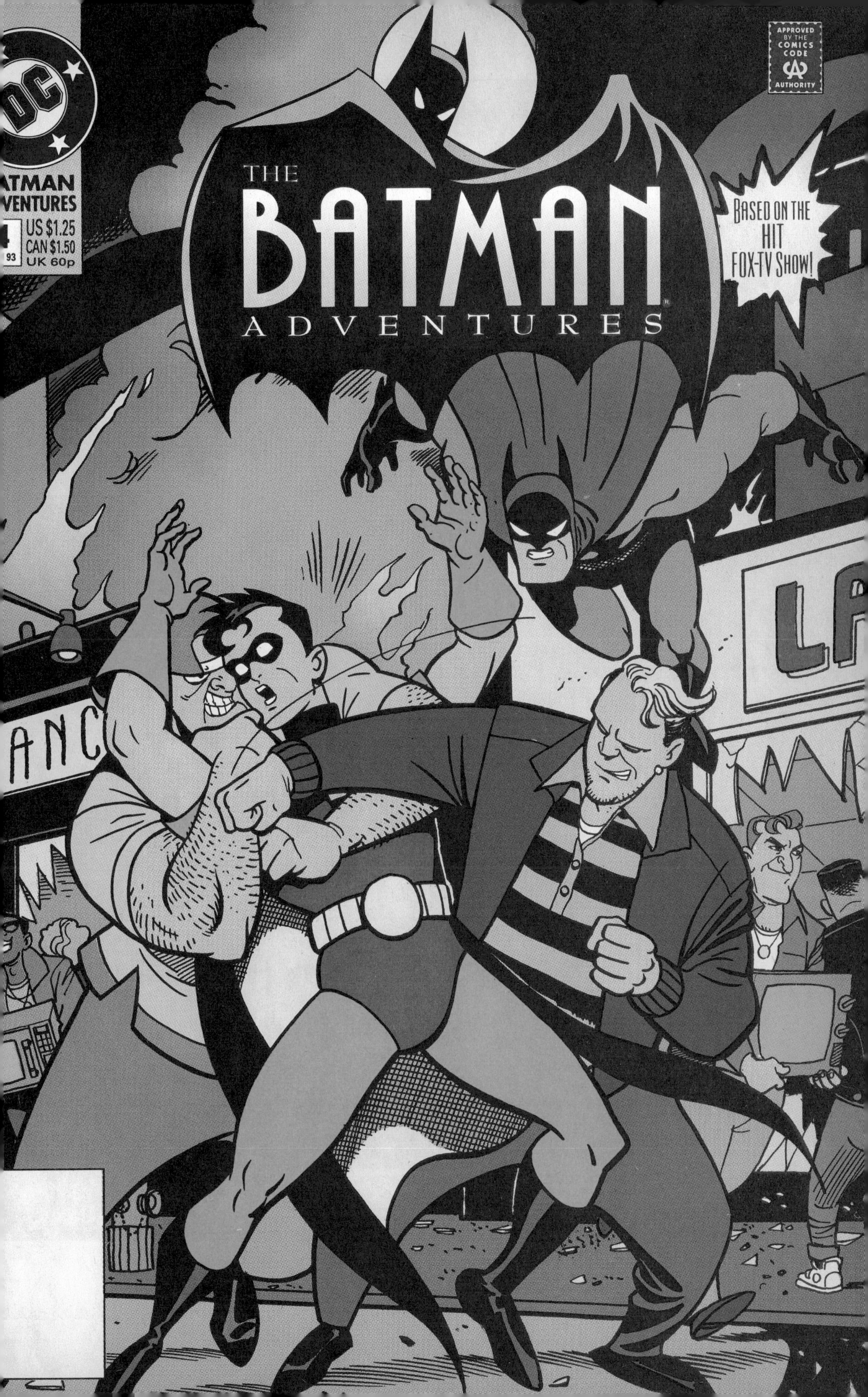
DC
BATMAN ADVENTURES
4
US $1.25
CAN $1.50
UK 60p
93
APPROVED BY THE COMICS CODE AUTHORITY
THE BATMAN ADVENTURES
BASED ON THE HIT FOX-TV SHOW!

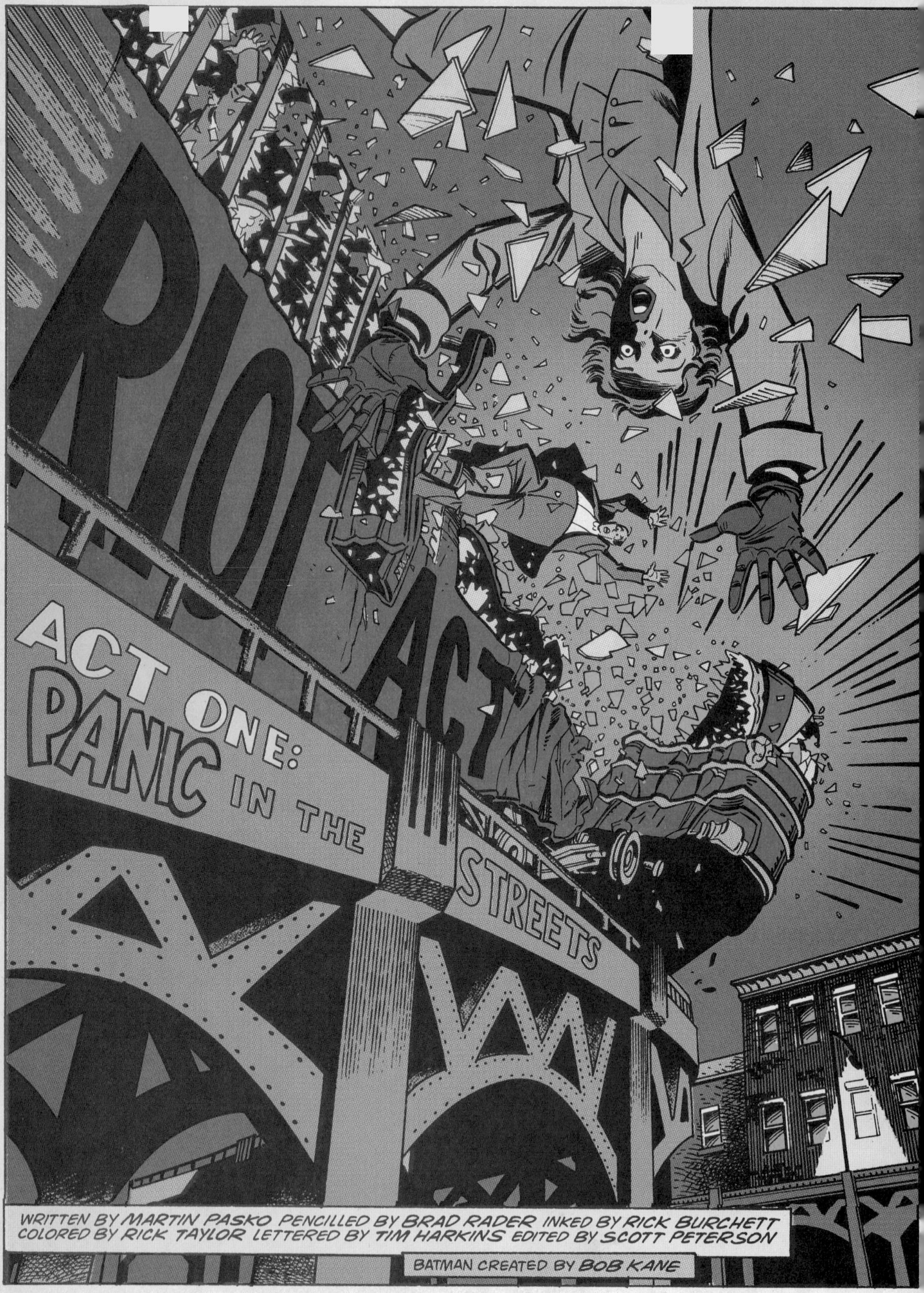
RIOT ACT
ACT ONE: PANIC IN THE STREETS
WRITTEN BY MARTIN PASKO PENCILLED BY BRAD RADER INKED BY RICK BURCHETT
COLORED BY RICK TAYLOR LETTERED BY TIM HARKINS EDITED BY SCOTT PETERSON
BATMAN CREATED BY BOB KANE

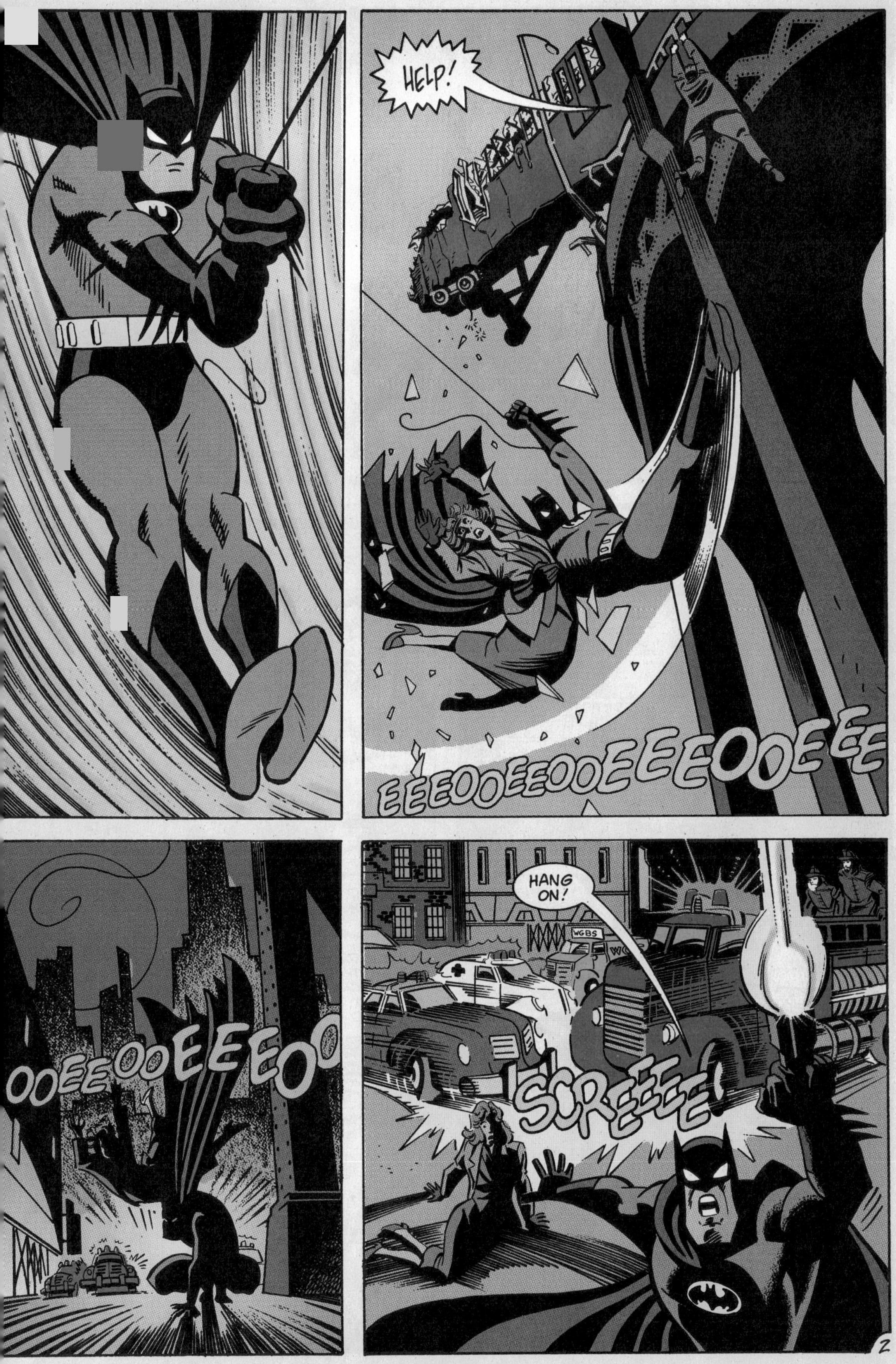

HELP!
EEEOOEEEOOEEEOOEEE
OOEEOOEEEOO
HANG ON!
SCREEEE
2

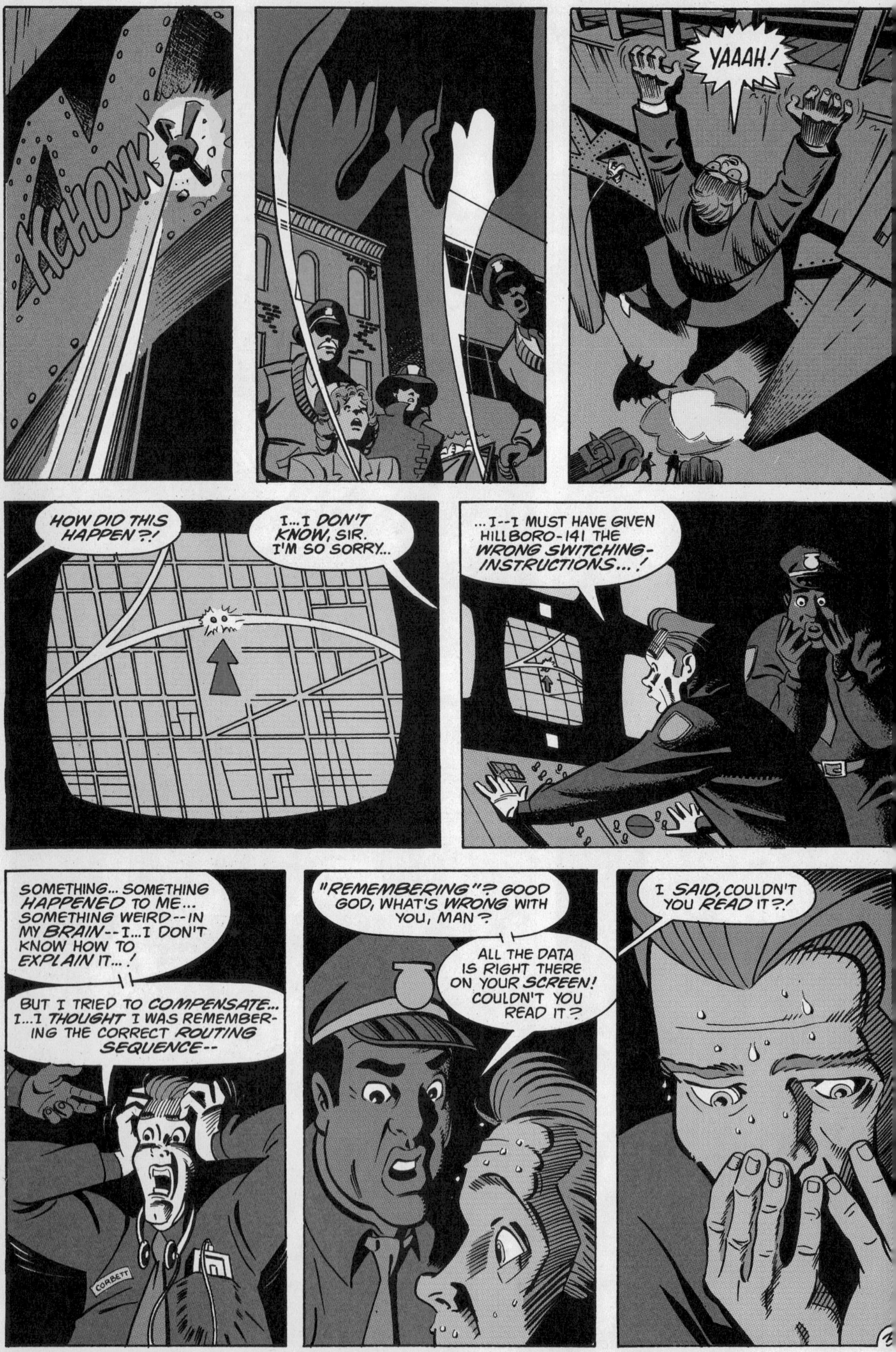
KCHONK
YAAAH!
HOW DID THIS HAPPEN?!
I...I DON'T KNOW, SIR. I'M SO SORRY...
...I--I MUST HAVE GIVEN HILLBORO-141 THE WRONG SWITCHING-INSTRUCTIONS...!
SOMETHING... SOMETHING HAPPENED TO ME... SOMETHING WEIRD--IN MY BRAIN--I...I DON'T KNOW HOW TO EXPLAIN IT...!
BUT I TRIED TO COMPENSATE... I...I THOUGHT I WAS REMEMBERING THE CORRECT ROUTING SEQUENCE--
CORBETT
"REMEMBERING"? GOOD GOD, WHAT'S WRONG WITH YOU, MAN?
ALL THE DATA IS RIGHT THERE ON YOUR SCREEN! COULDN'T YOU READ IT?
I SAID, COULDN'T YOU READ IT?!

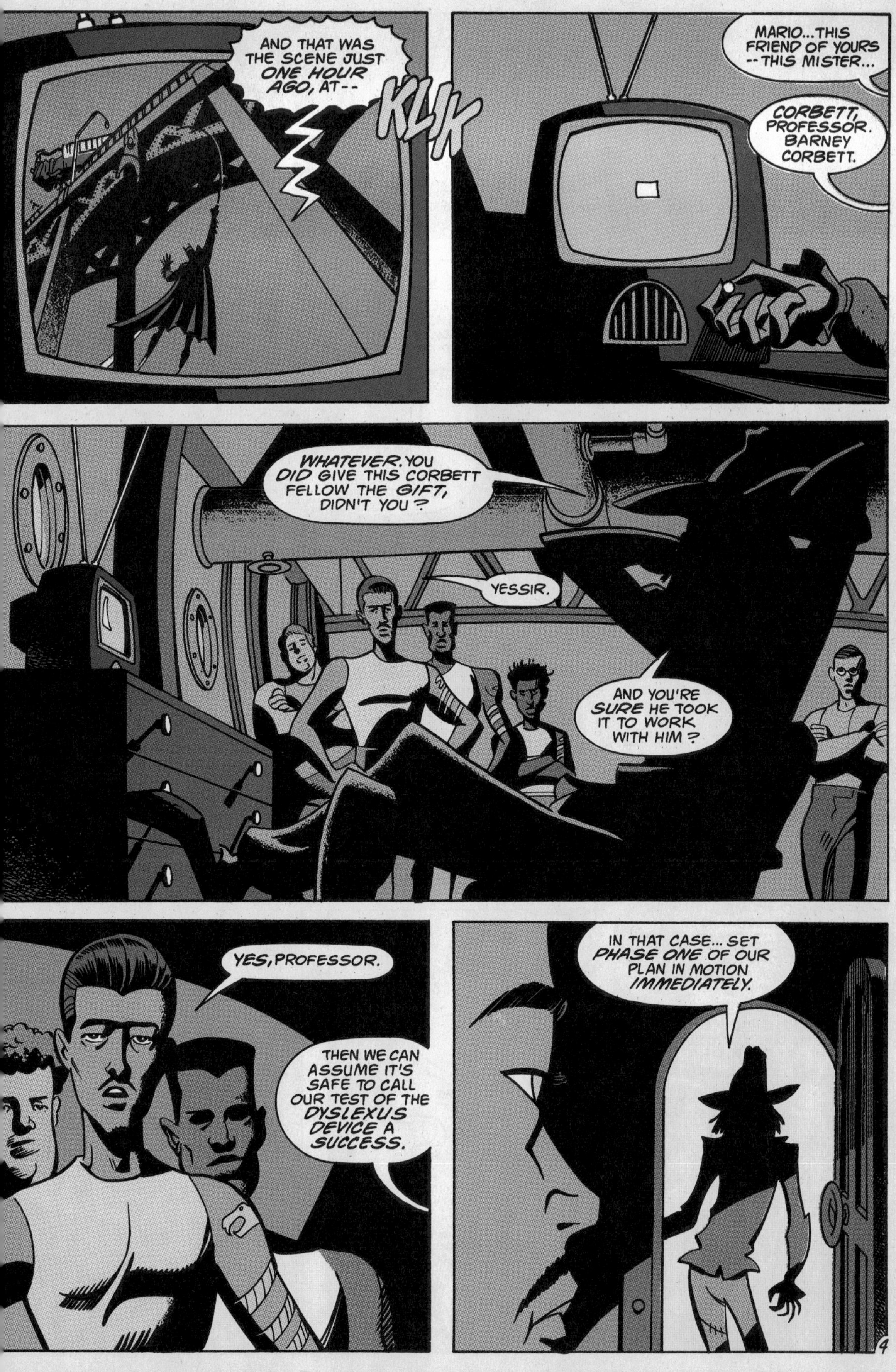
AND THAT WAS THE SCENE JUST ONE HOUR AGO, AT--
KLIK
MARIO...THIS FRIEND OF YOURS --THIS MISTER...
CORBETT, PROFESSOR. BARNEY CORBETT.
WHATEVER. YOU DID GIVE THIS CORBETT FELLOW THE GIFT, DIDN'T YOU?
YESSIR.
AND YOU'RE SURE HE TOOK IT TO WORK WITH HIM?
YES, PROFESSOR.
THEN WE CAN ASSUME IT'S SAFE TO CALL OUR TEST OF THE DYSLEXUS DEVICE A SUCCESS.
IN THAT CASE... SET PHASE ONE OF OUR PLAN IN MOTION IMMEDIATELY.
4

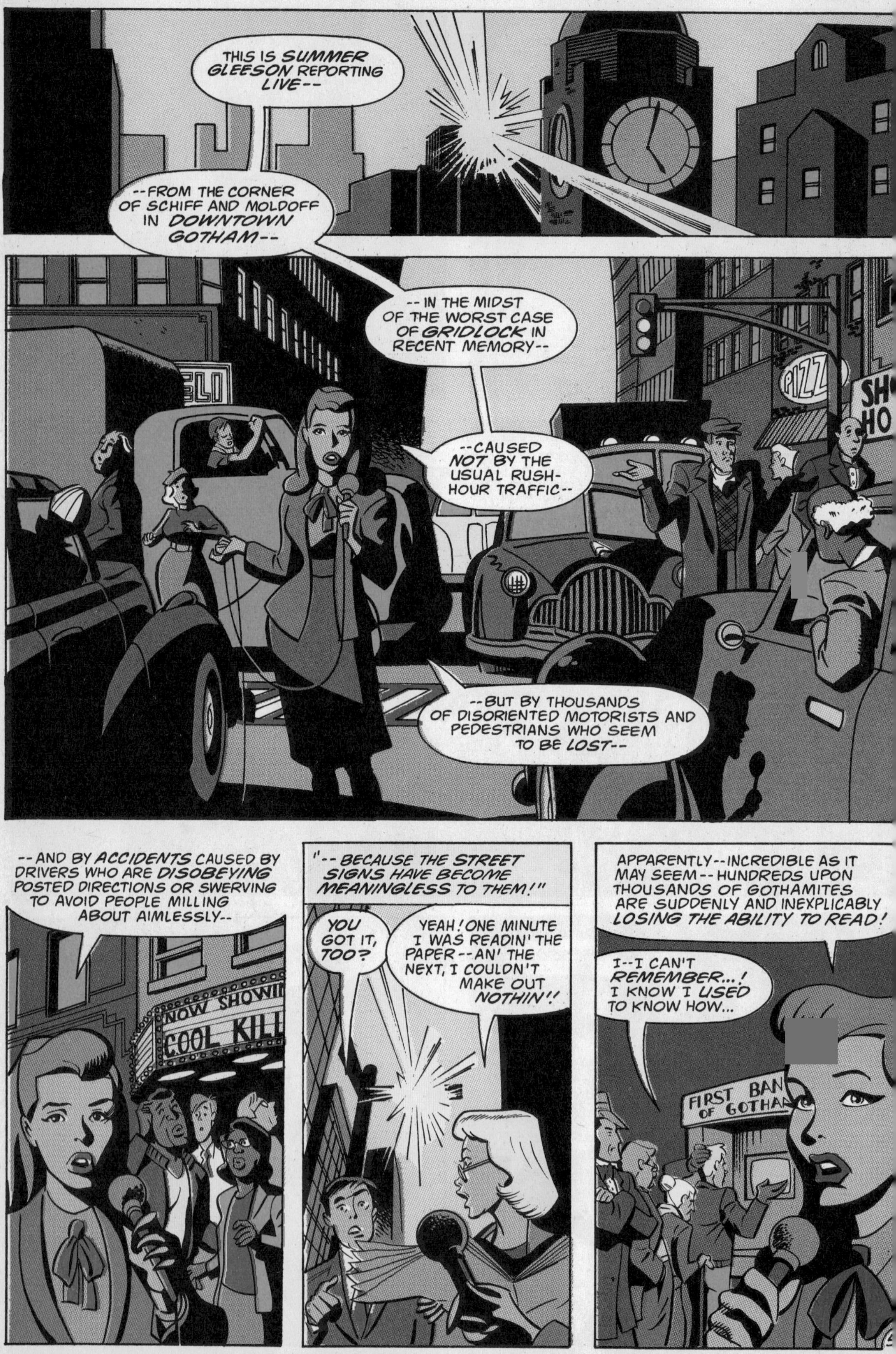
THIS IS SUMMER GLEESON REPORTING LIVE--
--FROM THE CORNER OF SCHIFF AND MOLDOFF IN DOWNTOWN GOTHAM--
--IN THE MIDST OF THE WORST CASE OF GRIDLOCK IN RECENT MEMORY--
--CAUSED NOT BY THE USUAL RUSH-HOUR TRAFFIC--
--BUT BY THOUSANDS OF DISORIENTED MOTORISTS AND PEDESTRIANS WHO SEEM TO BE LOST--
PIZZ
--AND BY ACCIDENTS CAUSED BY DRIVERS WHO ARE DISOBEYING POSTED DIRECTIONS OR SWERVING TO AVOID PEOPLE MILLING ABOUT AIMLESSLY--
NOW SHOWIN
COOL KILL
"--BECAUSE THE STREET SIGNS HAVE BECOME MEANINGLESS TO THEM!"
YOU GOT IT, TOO?
YEAH! ONE MINUTE I WAS READIN' THE PAPER--AN' THE NEXT, I COULDN'T MAKE OUT NOTHIN'!
APPARENTLY--INCREDIBLE AS IT MAY SEEM--HUNDREDS UPON THOUSANDS OF GOTHAMITES ARE SUDDENLY AND INEXPLICABLY LOSING THE ABILITY TO READ!
I--I CAN'T REMEMBER...! I KNOW I USED TO KNOW HOW...
FIRST BAN OF GOTHA

...BUT I *CAN'T* ANY-MORE! IT'S LIKE A PART OF MY BRAIN *BURNED OUT* OR SUMPIN'...!

FIRST OF GOTH

BUSINESS ALL OVER THE CITY, AS WELL AS *PUBLIC TRANSPORTATION* AND MANY *OTHER* MUNICIPAL SERVICES HAVE BEEN THROWN INTO DISARRAY--

-- AND SOME MAY BE FORCED TO *SHUT DOWN* ALTOGETHER UNTIL THE CAUSE OF THIS *BIZARRE* PHENOMENON IS DISCOVERED AND ITS EFFECTS *REVERSED.*

NOW BACK TO DIRK BRICKER IN THE *WGBS* NEWSROOM. DIRK...?

THANK YOU, SUMMER. WE'LL CONTINUE WITH OUR ONGOING COVERAGE OF THE STRANGE *CRISIS* GRIPPING GOTHAM IN JUST A MOMENT.

BUT RIGHT NOW, THESE OTHER HEADLINES AT THE TOP OF THE NEWS: MAYOR HILL HAS...

CHANNEL NEWS 1

...CALLED A PRESS CONFERENCE...

CALLED A PRESS CONFERENC TO ANNOUNCE THE FORMATION OF A COALITION THAT WILL

...TO... TO...

...TO...

PLEASE STAND BY

MY WORD...!

6

ATTENTION, GOTHAMITES!-- THIS IS THE ARCHITECT OF YOUR CITY'S *NEW ORDER*, BREAKING IN ON REGULAR TV- AND RADIO TRANSMISSIONS FOR A BRIEF ANNOUNCEMENT.

PLEASE STAND BY

NOT THAT THERE WILL *BE* REGULAR TRANSMISSIONS FOR MUCH LONGER.

YOU SEE, THE TECHNICIANS CAN'T KNOW WHAT *TAPES* TO BROADCAST, OR WHICH *BUTTONS* TO *PUSH*, IF THEY *CAN'T READ THE LABELS* ON THEM!

NOW, AS YOU FACE THE VIRTUAL *END* OF LIFE AS YOU *KNOW* IT... I WANT TO TELL YOU *WHO* YOU HAVE TO THANK FOR THAT: *YOURSELVES!*

AFTER ALL, YOU LOW-BROWED LITTLE VERMIN, *YOU* ELECTED YOUR CRETINOUS *MAYOR HILL* AND A *CITY COUNCIL* FULL OF *MORONS*--

--*NONE* OF WHOM HAS MADE A *PRIORITY* OF *EDUCATING* YOUR YOUTH!

AND *YOU* REFUSED TO PAY MORE *TAXES* TO IMPROVE YOUR *SCHOOL SYSTEM.* IN SO DOING, YOU HAVE *ENRAGED* ME.

HOW AND *WHY* IS UNIMPORTANT-- SUFFICE IT TO SAY I NOW PURSUE MY *JUSTICE...*

--AND AT THE SAME TIME GIVE YOU A TASTE OF WHAT THE *FUTURE* HOLDS -- IF YOU CONTINUE DOWN THE PATH OF THE *YAHOO.*

I CAN PROMISE GOTHAM'S RULING CLASS THAT ITS *WORST NIGHTMARES* WILL COME *TRUE*--

--UNLESS IT AGREES TO PAY THE *RANSOM* I'VE DEMANDED--

KNOK KNOK

BEGGING YOUR PARDON, MASTER BRUCE, I SHOULDN'T WISH TO *DISTURB* YOU...

ALFRED, I FEEL AS IF EVERY MUSCLE IN MY BODY HAS BEEN PULLED THROUGH A *PAPER-SHREDDER.*

I SHOULDN'T WONDER...

...YOU HAD QUITE A BUSY NIGHT EVEN *BEFORE* YOU SAVED THOSE TRAIN PASSENGERS.

"BUSY"? YOU COULD SAY THAT.

DO YOU HAVE ANY IDEA WHAT IT FEELS LIKE TO GO UP AGAINST A GUY WHO CAN TURN HIS *HANDS* INTO *ANVILS* BEFORE HE *PUNCHES* YOU?

AH, YES... *CLAYFACE.* NASTY BUSINESS, THAT.

HOWEVER --

THEN AT LEAST LET ME *TRY* TO GET A FEW HOURS' SLEEP, WILL YOU?

VERY GOOD, SIR. MIGHT I SUGGEST YOU TURN ON THE TELLY WITH THE SLEEPTIMER ON? IT MIGHT *RELAX* YOU.

KLIK

ALFRED! ALFRED, YOU'RE --

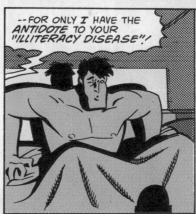

-- FOR ONLY *I* HAVE THE *ANTIDOTE* TO YOUR *"ILLITERACY DISEASE"!*

-- *MUCH* TOO GOOD AT FOLLOWING THE ORDERS I GIVE YOU.

8

83

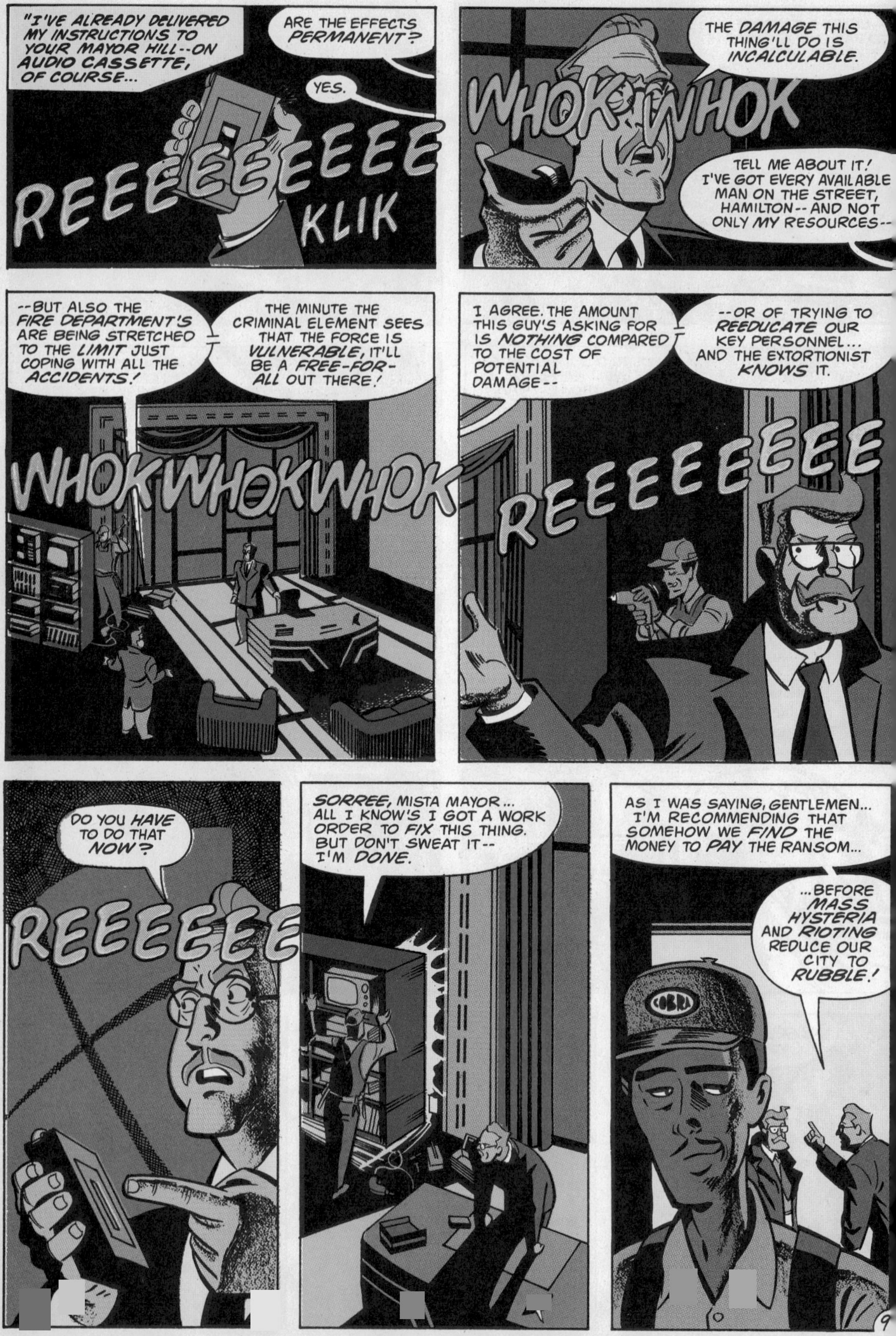
"I'VE ALREADY DELIVERED MY INSTRUCTIONS TO YOUR MAYOR HILL--ON AUDIO CASSETTE, OF COURSE...
ARE THE EFFECTS PERMANENT?
YES.
REEEEEEEEEE
KLIK
THE DAMAGE THIS THING'LL DO IS INCALCULABLE.
WHOK WHOK
TELL ME ABOUT IT! I'VE GOT EVERY AVAILABLE MAN ON THE STREET, HAMILTON--AND NOT ONLY MY RESOURCES--
--BUT ALSO THE FIRE DEPARTMENT'S ARE BEING STRETCHED TO THE LIMIT JUST COPING WITH ALL THE ACCIDENTS!
THE MINUTE THE CRIMINAL ELEMENT SEES THAT THE FORCE IS VULNERABLE, IT'LL BE A FREE-FOR-ALL OUT THERE!
WHOKWHOKWHOK
I AGREE. THE AMOUNT THIS GUY'S ASKING FOR IS NOTHING COMPARED TO THE COST OF POTENTIAL DAMAGE--
--OR OF TRYING TO REEDUCATE OUR KEY PERSONNEL... AND THE EXTORTIONIST KNOWS IT.
REEEEEEEEE
DO YOU HAVE TO DO THAT NOW?
REEEEEEE
SORREE, MISTA MAYOR... ALL I KNOW'S I GOT A WORK ORDER TO FIX THIS THING. BUT DON'T SWEAT IT-- I'M DONE.
AS I WAS SAYING, GENTLEMEN... I'M RECOMMENDING THAT SOMEHOW WE FIND THE MONEY TO PAY THE RANSOM...
...BEFORE MASS HYSTERIA AND RIOTING REDUCE OUR CITY TO RUBBLE!
COBRA
9

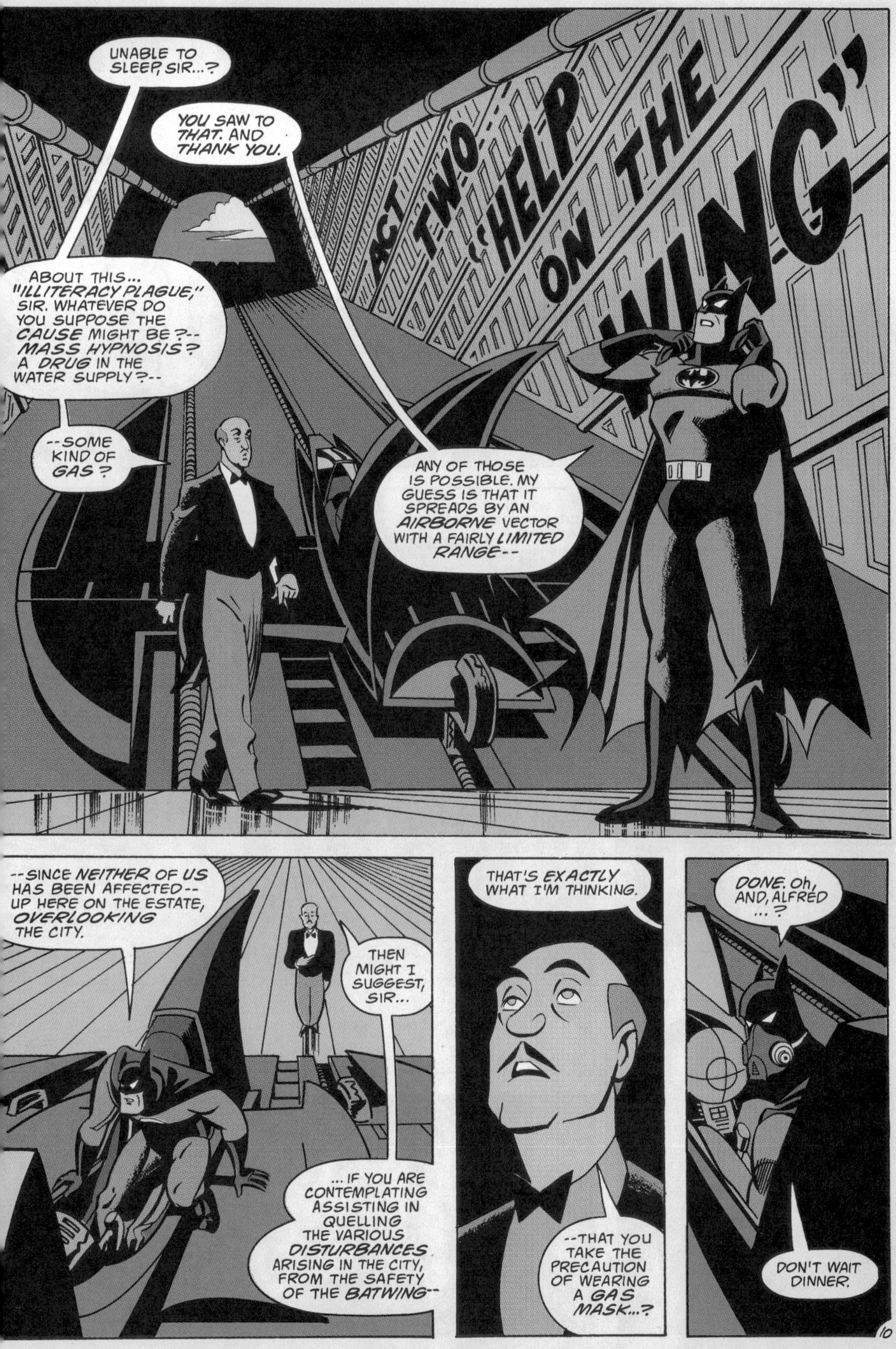
UNABLE TO SLEEP, SIR...?
YOU SAW TO THAT. AND THANK YOU.
ACT TWO "HELP ON THE WING"
ABOUT THIS... "ILLITERACY PLAGUE," SIR. WHATEVER DO YOU SUPPOSE THE CAUSE MIGHT BE?-- MASS HYPNOSIS? A DRUG IN THE WATER SUPPLY?--
--SOME KIND OF GAS?
ANY OF THOSE IS POSSIBLE. MY GUESS IS THAT IT SPREADS BY AN AIRBORNE VECTOR WITH A FAIRLY LIMITED RANGE--
--SINCE NEITHER OF US HAS BEEN AFFECTED-- UP HERE ON THE ESTATE, OVERLOOKING THE CITY.
THEN MIGHT I SUGGEST, SIR...
...IF YOU ARE CONTEMPLATING ASSISTING IN QUELLING THE VARIOUS DISTURBANCES ARISING IN THE CITY, FROM THE SAFETY OF THE BATWING--
THAT'S EXACTLY WHAT I'M THINKING.
--THAT YOU TAKE THE PRECAUTION OF WEARING A GAS MASK...?
DONE. Oh, AND, ALFRED ...?
DON'T WAIT DINNER.
10

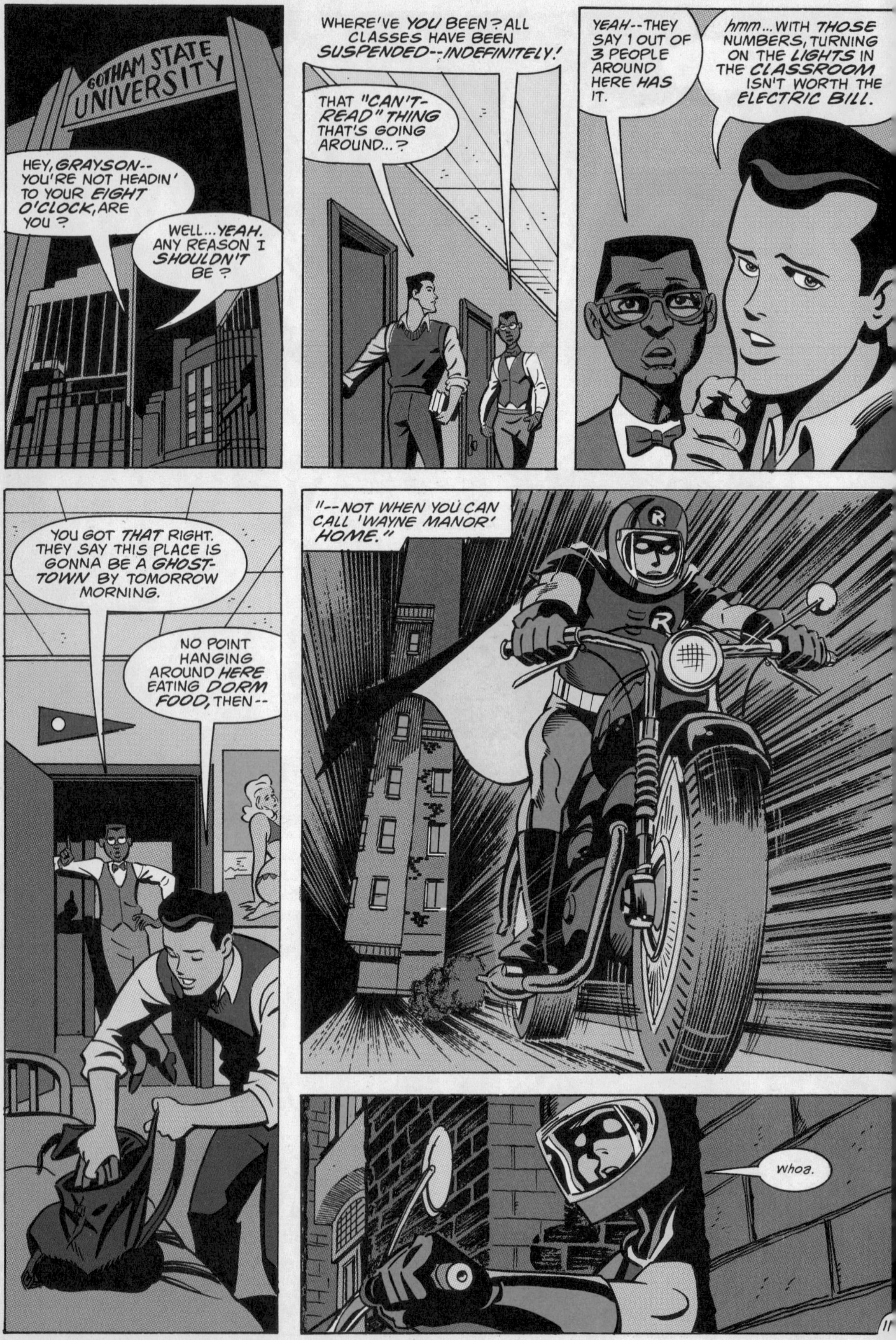
GOTHAM STATE UNIVERSITY
HEY, GRAYSON-- YOU'RE NOT HEADIN' TO YOUR EIGHT O'CLOCK, ARE YOU?
WELL...YEAH. ANY REASON I SHOULDN'T BE?
WHERE'VE YOU BEEN? ALL CLASSES HAVE BEEN SUSPENDED--INDEFINITELY!
THAT "CAN'T-READ" THING THAT'S GOING AROUND...?
YEAH--THEY SAY 1 OUT OF 3 PEOPLE AROUND HERE HAS IT.
hmm...WITH THOSE NUMBERS, TURNING ON THE LIGHTS IN THE CLASSROOM ISN'T WORTH THE ELECTRIC BILL.
YOU GOT THAT RIGHT. THEY SAY THIS PLACE IS GONNA BE A GHOST-TOWN BY TOMORROW MORNING.
NO POINT HANGING AROUND HERE EATING DORM FOOD, THEN--
"--NOT WHEN YOU CAN CALL 'WAYNE MANOR' HOME."
Whoa.
11

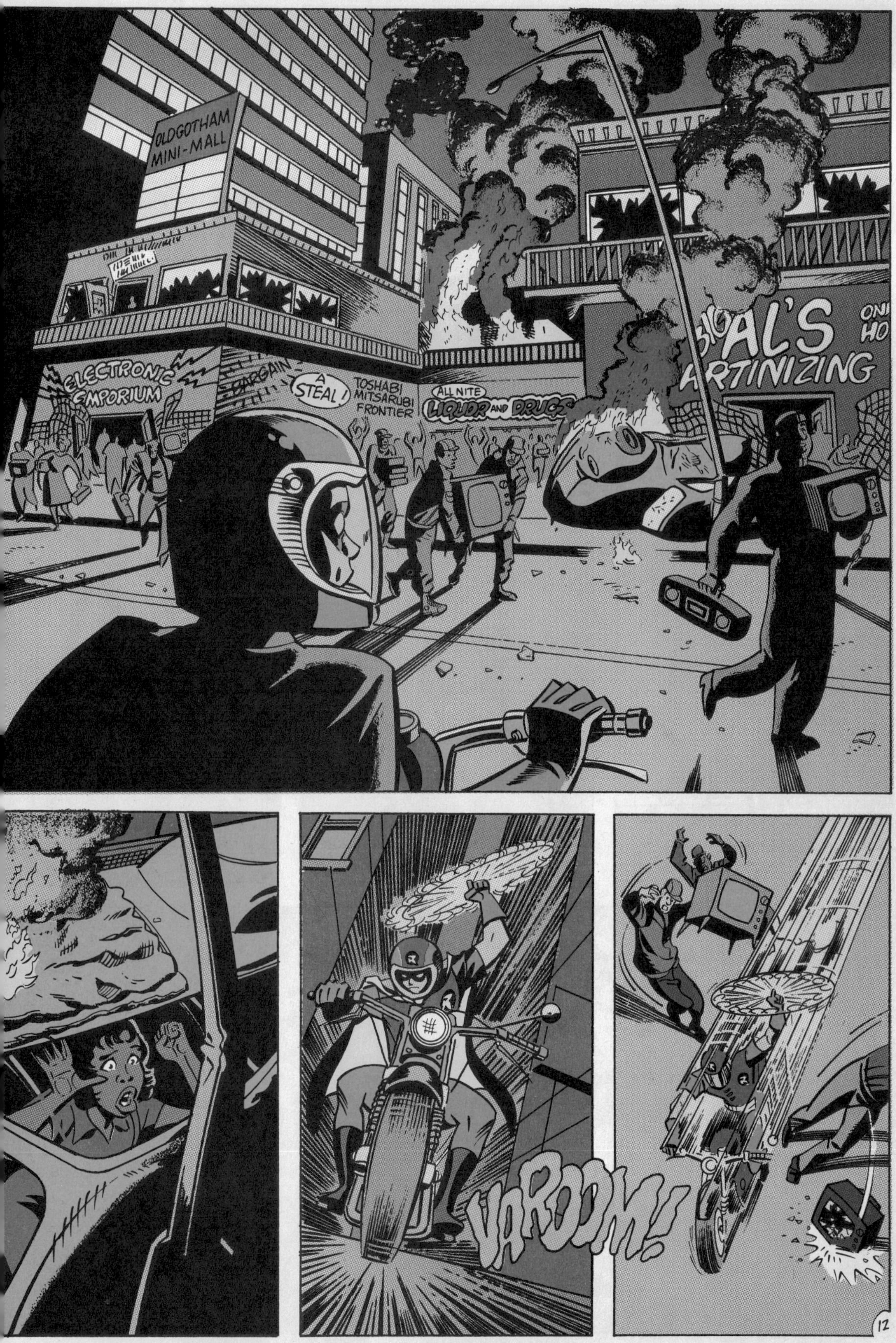
OLDGOTHAM MINI-MALL
ELECTRONIC EMPORIUM
BARGAIN
A STEAL!
TOSHABI MITSARUBI FRONTIER
ALL NITE LIQUOR AND DRUGS
AL'S
VAROOM!!
12

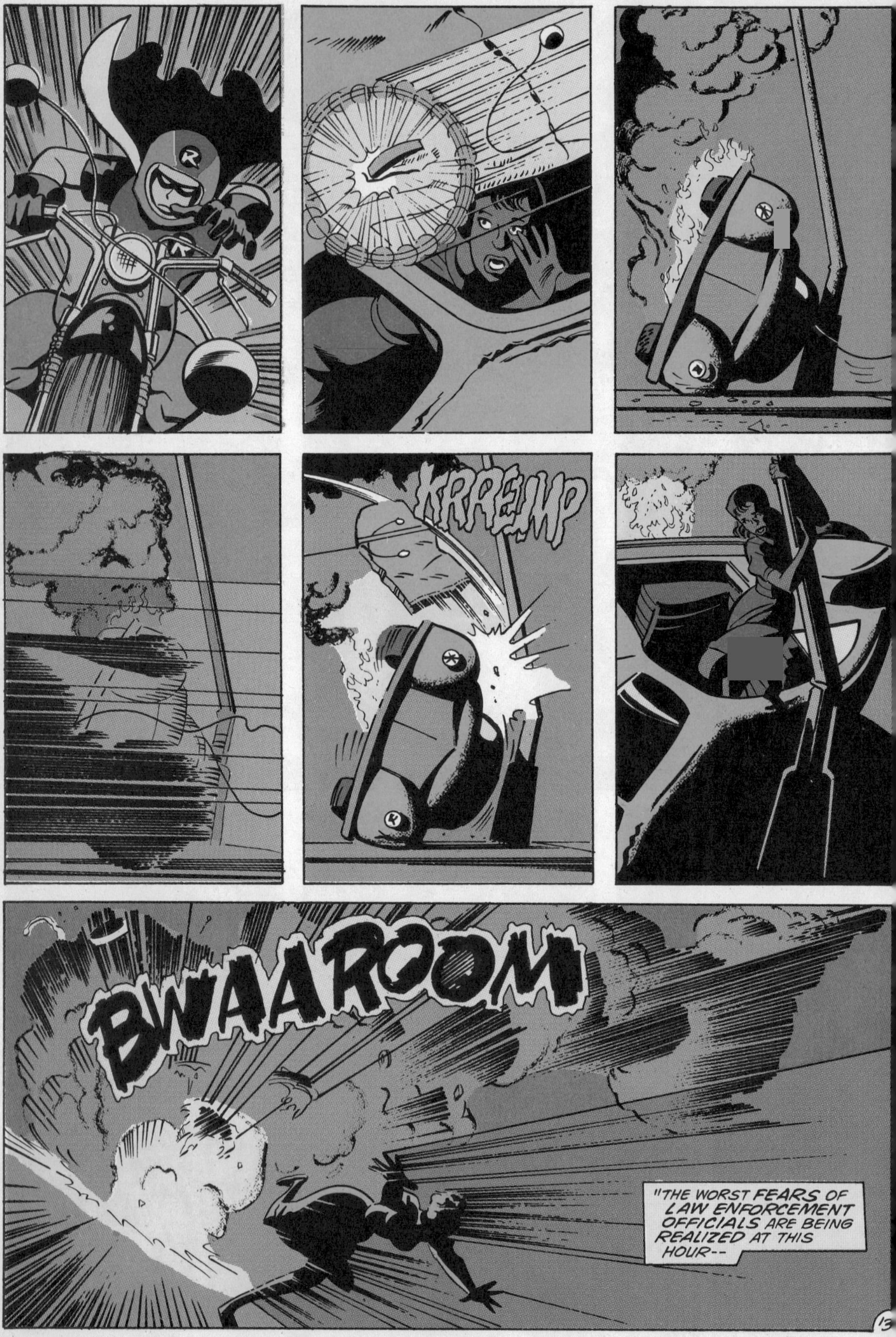
KRREMP
BWAAROOM
"THE WORST FEARS OF LAW ENFORCEMENT OFFICIALS ARE BEING REALIZED AT THIS HOUR--
13

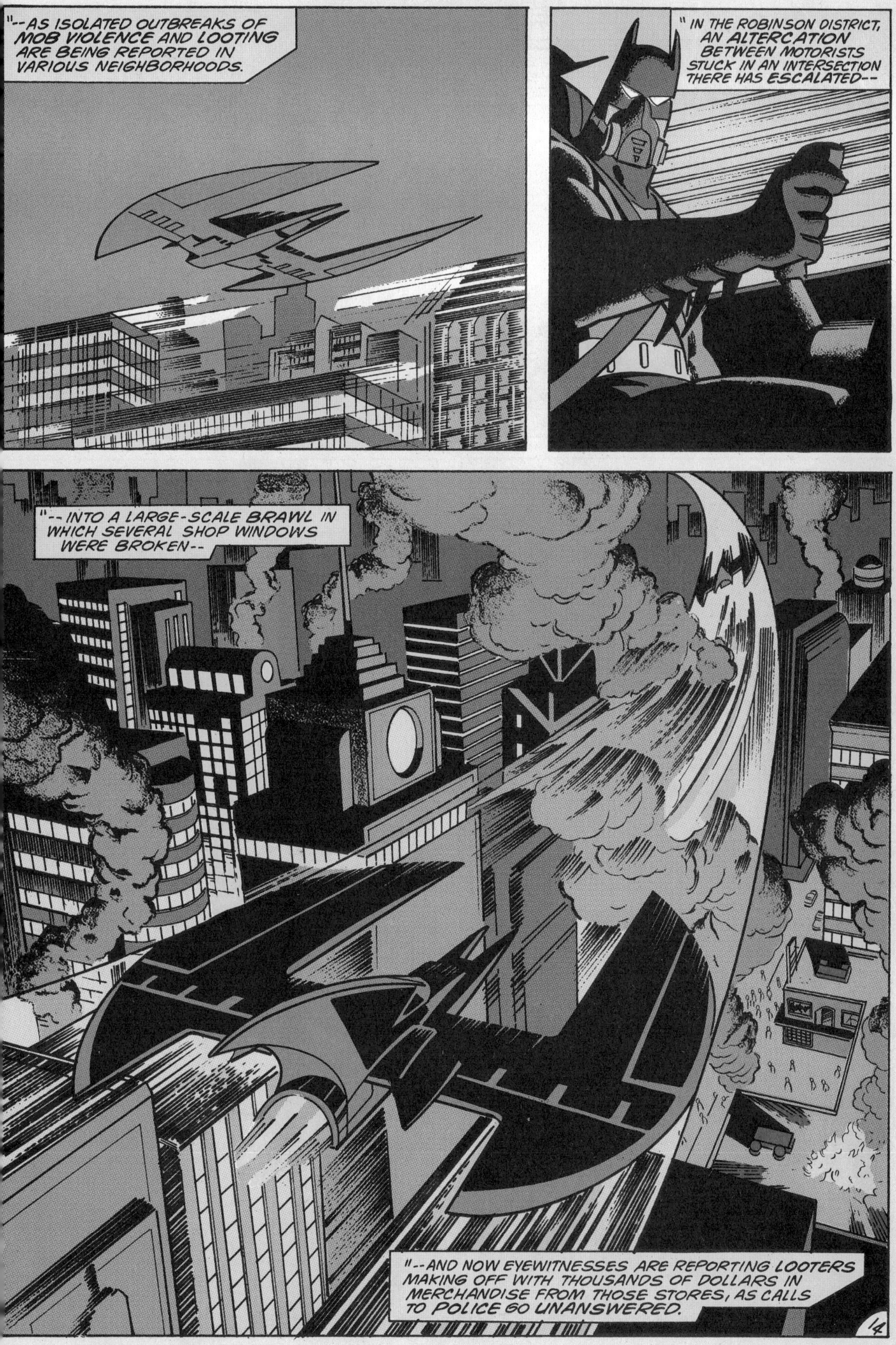
"--AS ISOLATED OUTBREAKS OF MOB VIOLENCE AND LOOTING ARE BEING REPORTED IN VARIOUS NEIGHBORHOODS.
"IN THE ROBINSON DISTRICT, AN ALTERCATION BETWEEN MOTORISTS STUCK IN AN INTERSECTION THERE HAS ESCALATED--
"--INTO A LARGE-SCALE BRAWL IN WHICH SEVERAL SHOP WINDOWS WERE BROKEN--
"--AND NOW EYEWITNESSES ARE REPORTING LOOTERS MAKING OFF WITH THOUSANDS OF DOLLARS IN MERCHANDISE FROM THOSE STORES, AS CALLS TO POLICE GO UNANSWERED.
14

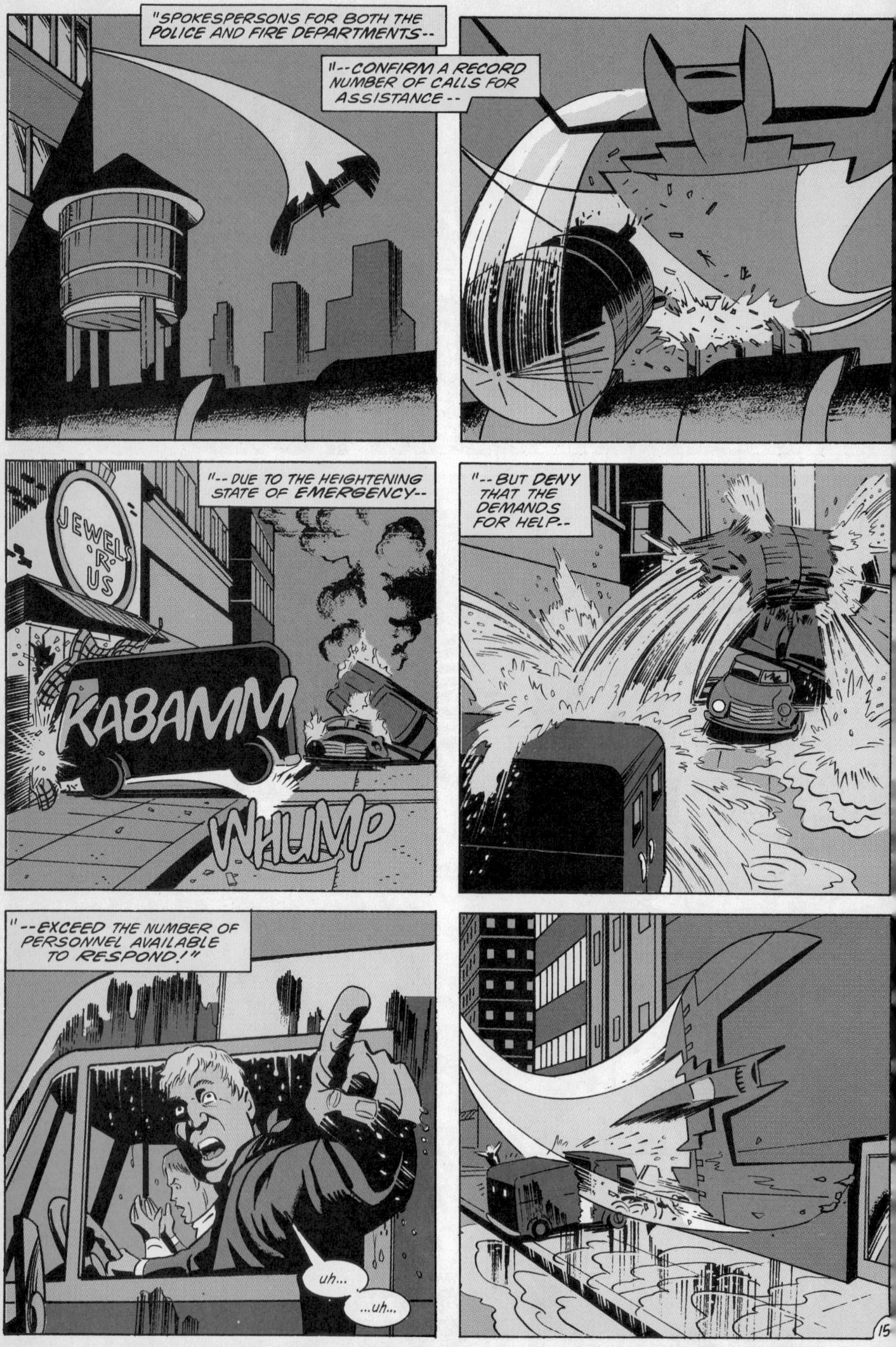
"SPOKESPERSONS FOR BOTH THE POLICE AND FIRE DEPARTMENTS--
"--CONFIRM A RECORD NUMBER OF CALLS FOR ASSISTANCE--
"--DUE TO THE HEIGHTENING STATE OF EMERGENCY--
JEWELS 'R' US
KABAMM
WHUMP
"--BUT DENY THAT THE DEMANDS FOR HELP--
"--EXCEED THE NUMBER OF PERSONNEL AVAILABLE TO RESPOND!"
uh...
...uh...
15

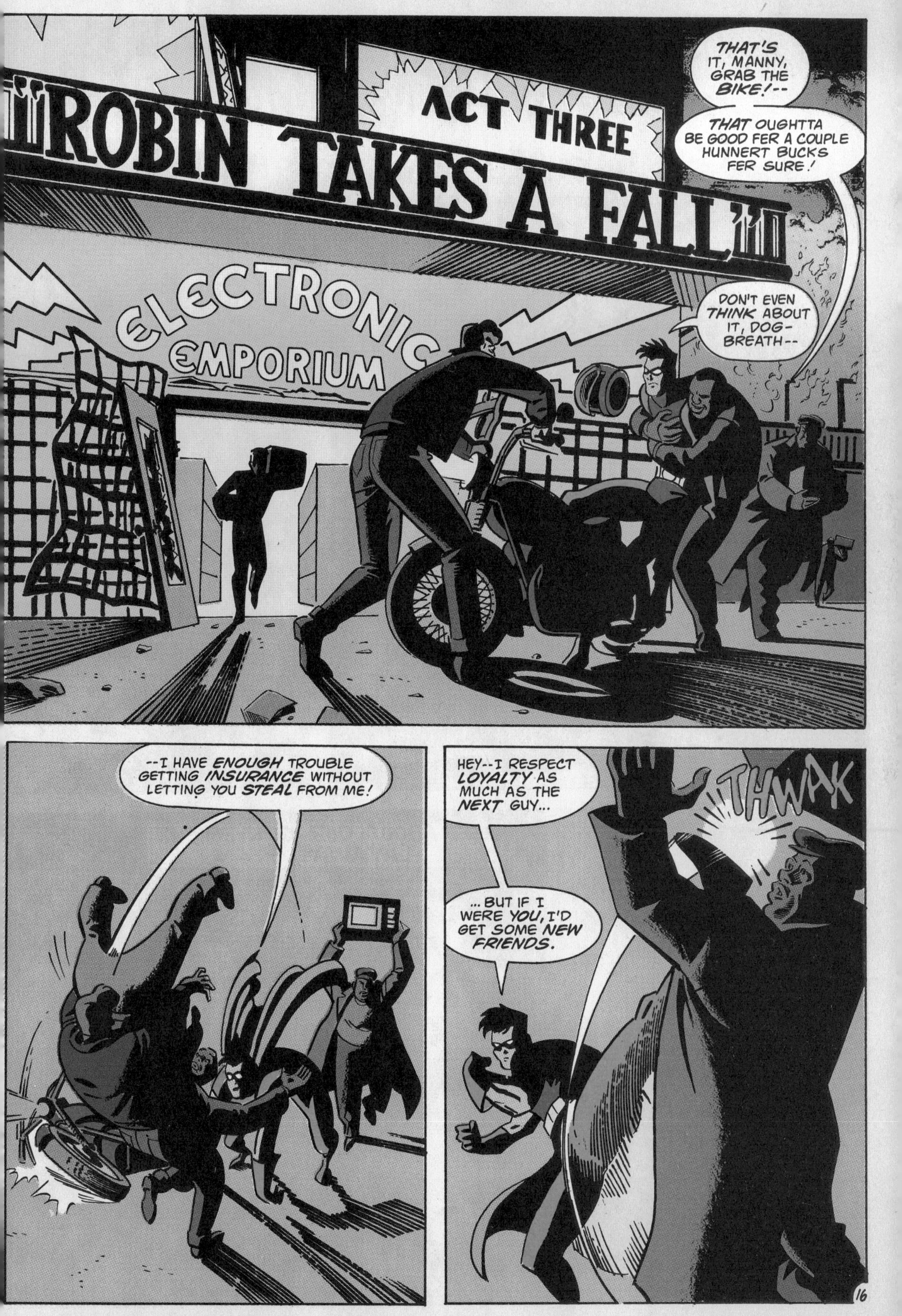
"ROBIN TAKES A FALL"
ACT THREE
ELECTRONIC EMPORIUM
THAT'S IT, MANNY, GRAB THE BIKE!--
THAT OUGHTTA BE GOOD FER A COUPLE HUNNERT BUCKS FER SURE!
DON'T EVEN THINK ABOUT IT, DOG-BREATH--
--I HAVE ENOUGH TROUBLE GETTING INSURANCE WITHOUT LETTING YOU STEAL FROM ME!
HEY--I RESPECT LOYALTY AS MUCH AS THE NEXT GUY...
THWAK
... BUT IF I WERE YOU, I'D GET SOME NEW FRIENDS.
16

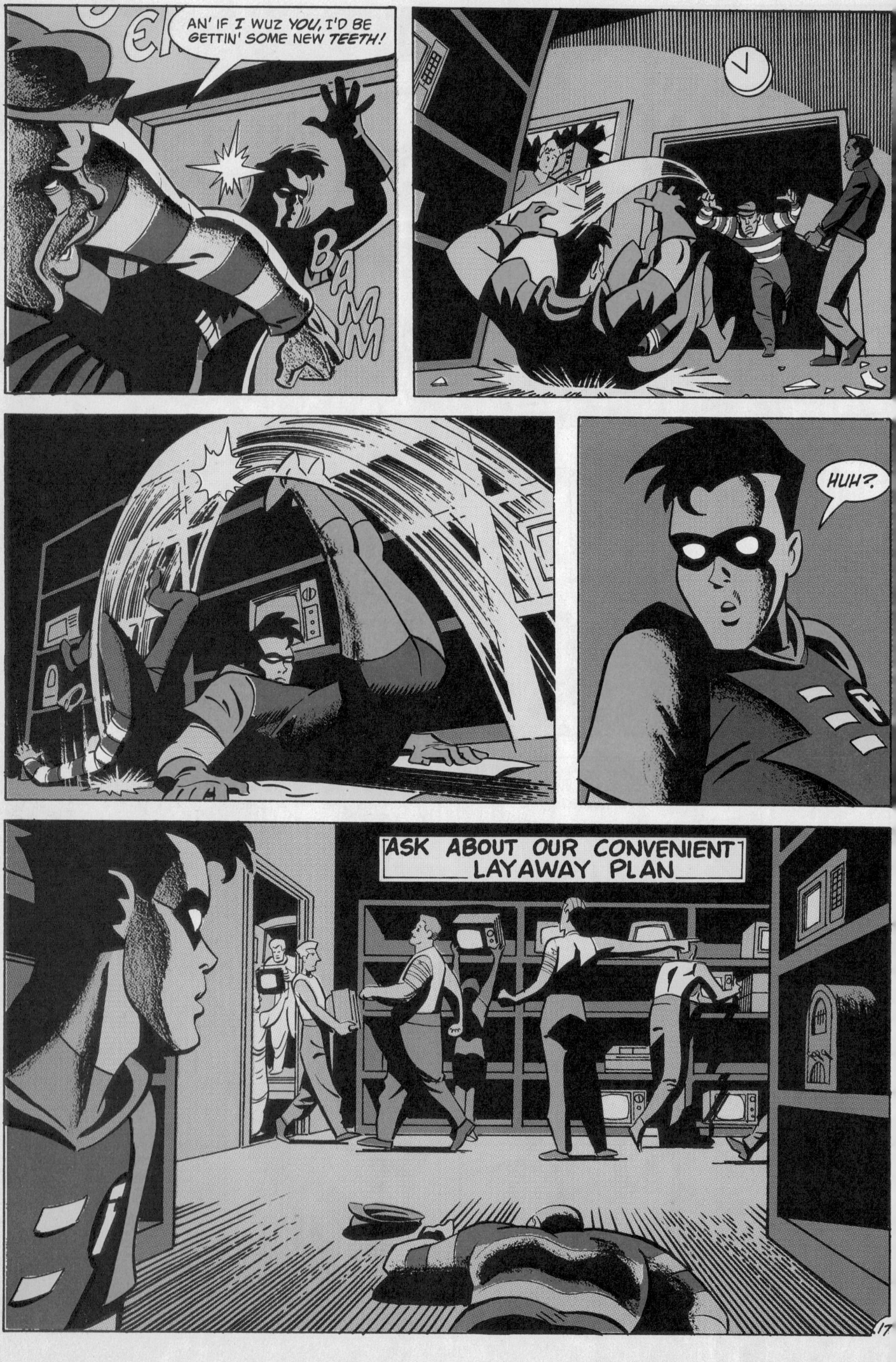
AN' IF I WUZ YOU, I'D BE GETTIN' SOME NEW TEETH!
BAMM
HUH?
ASK ABOUT OUR CONVENIENT LAYAWAY PLAN
17

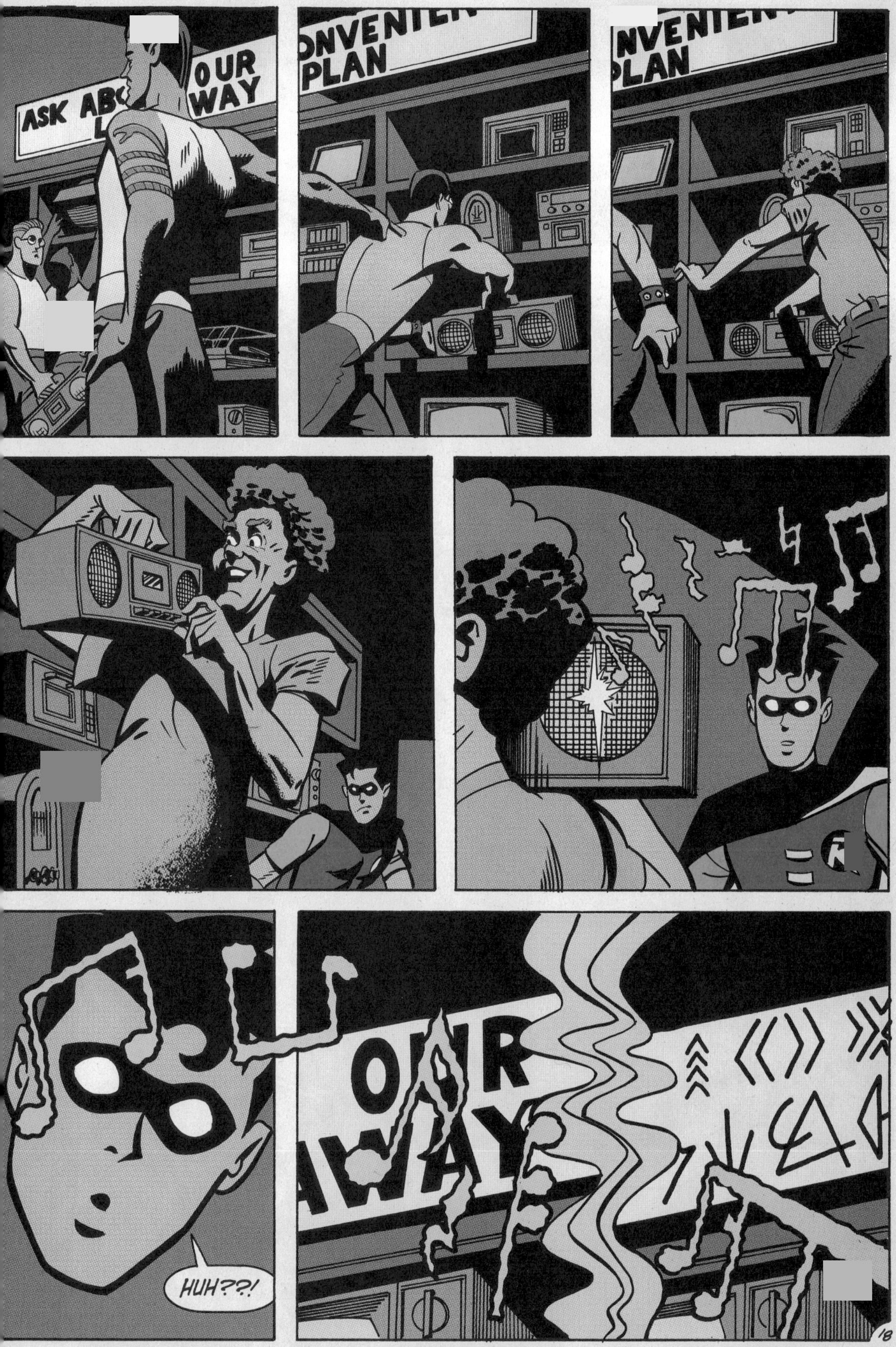
ASK ABO
OUR
WAY
ONVENTEN
PLAN
NVENTEN
PLAN
HUH??!
18

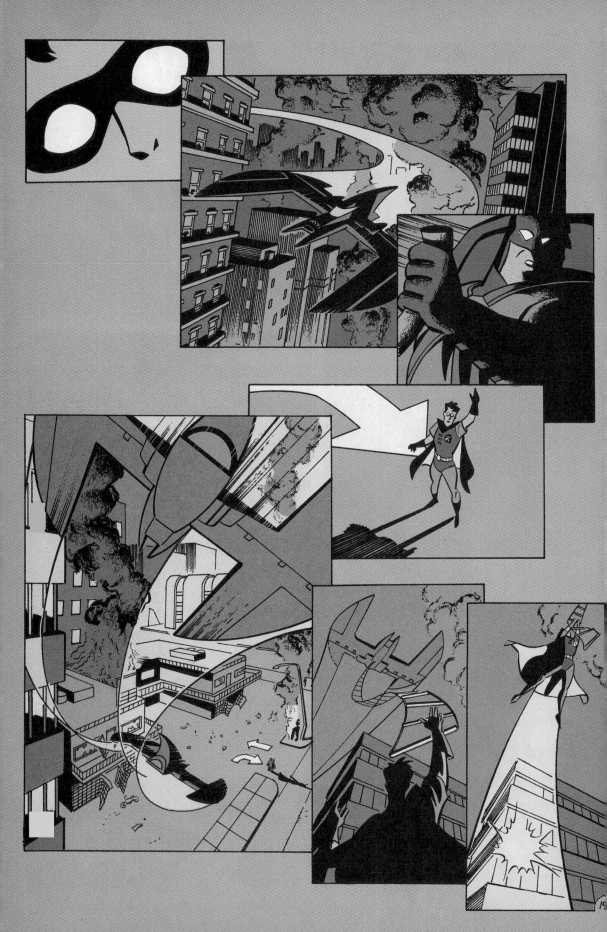

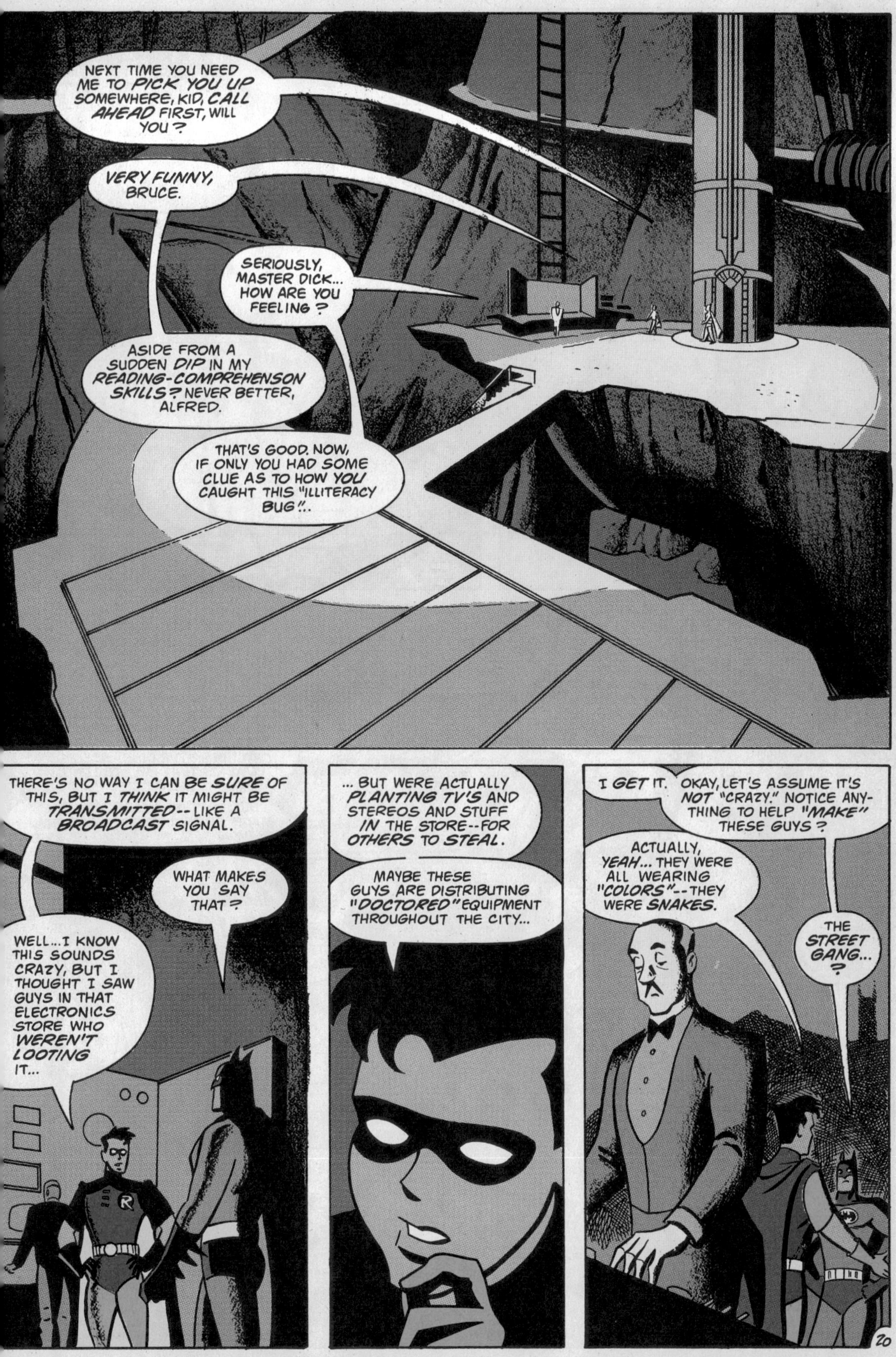
NEXT TIME YOU NEED ME TO PICK YOU UP SOMEWHERE, KID, CALL AHEAD FIRST, WILL YOU?
VERY FUNNY, BRUCE.
SERIOUSLY, MASTER DICK... HOW ARE YOU FEELING?
ASIDE FROM A SUDDEN DIP IN MY READING-COMPREHENSON SKILLS? NEVER BETTER, ALFRED.
THAT'S GOOD. NOW, IF ONLY YOU HAD SOME CLUE AS TO HOW YOU CAUGHT THIS "ILLITERACY BUG"..
THERE'S NO WAY I CAN BE SURE OF THIS, BUT I THINK IT MIGHT BE TRANSMITTED--LIKE A BROADCAST SIGNAL.
WHAT MAKES YOU SAY THAT?
WELL...I KNOW THIS SOUNDS CRAZY, BUT I THOUGHT I SAW GUYS IN THAT ELECTRONICS STORE WHO WEREN'T LOOTING IT...
... BUT WERE ACTUALLY PLANTING TV'S AND STEREOS AND STUFF IN THE STORE--FOR OTHERS TO STEAL.
MAYBE THESE GUYS ARE DISTRIBUTING "DOCTORED" EQUIPMENT THROUGHOUT THE CITY...
I GET IT.
OKAY, LET'S ASSUME IT'S NOT "CRAZY." NOTICE ANYTHING TO HELP "MAKE" THESE GUYS?
ACTUALLY, YEAH... THEY WERE ALL WEARING "COLORS"--THEY WERE SNAKES.
THE STREET GANG...?
20

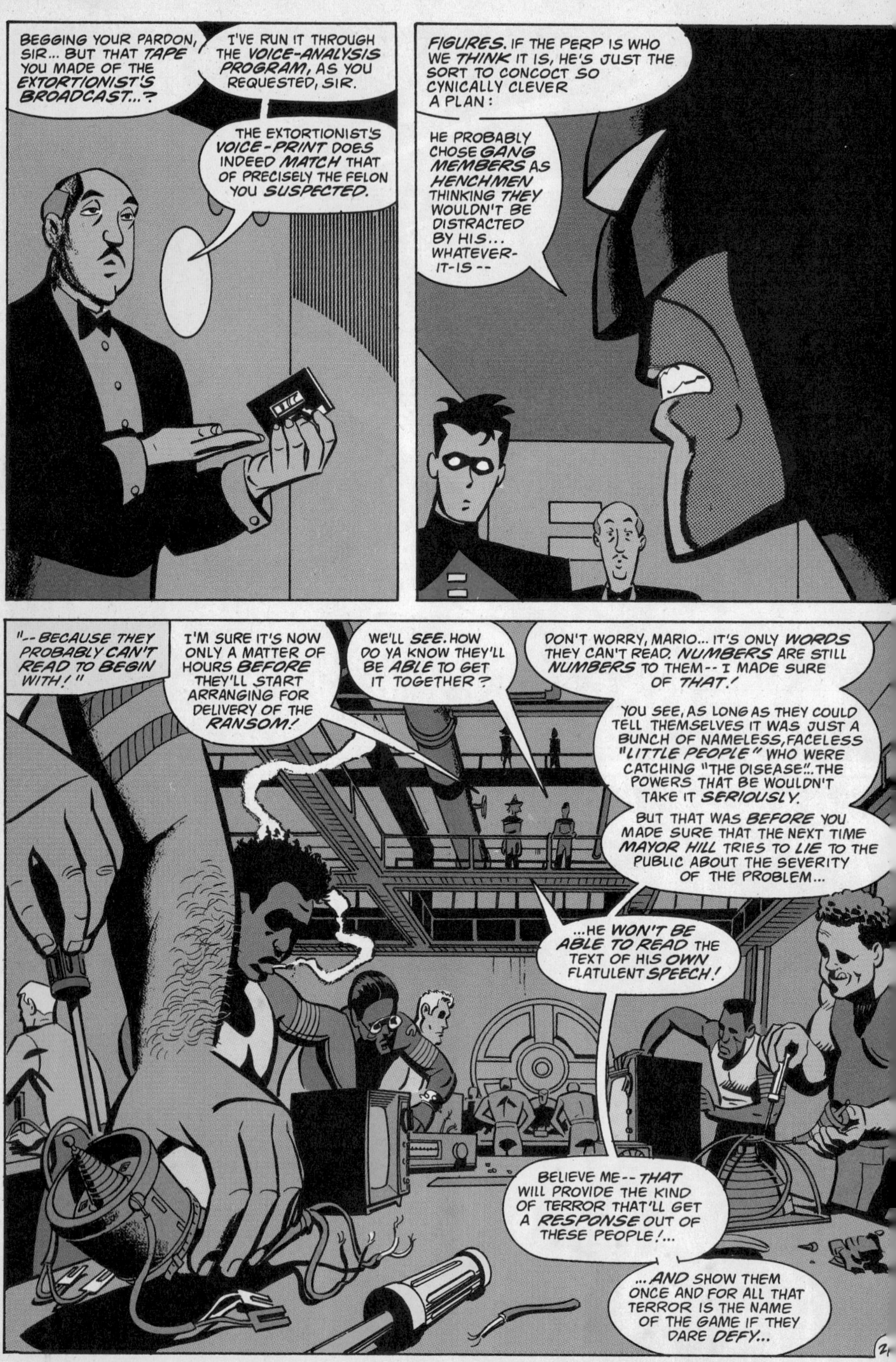
BEGGING YOUR PARDON, SIR... BUT THAT TAPE YOU MADE OF THE EXTORTIONIST'S BROADCAST...?
I'VE RUN IT THROUGH THE VOICE-ANALYSIS PROGRAM, AS YOU REQUESTED, SIR.
THE EXTORTIONIST'S VOICE-PRINT DOES INDEED MATCH THAT OF PRECISELY THE FELON YOU SUSPECTED.
FIGURES. IF THE PERP IS WHO WE THINK IT IS, HE'S JUST THE SORT TO CONCOCT SO CYNICALLY CLEVER A PLAN:
HE PROBABLY CHOSE GANG MEMBERS AS HENCHMEN THINKING THEY WOULDN'T BE DISTRACTED BY HIS... WHATEVER-IT-IS --
"-- BECAUSE THEY PROBABLY CAN'T READ TO BEGIN WITH!"
I'M SURE IT'S NOW ONLY A MATTER OF HOURS BEFORE THEY'LL START ARRANGING FOR DELIVERY OF THE RANSOM!
WE'LL SEE. HOW DO YA KNOW THEY'LL BE ABLE TO GET IT TOGETHER?
DON'T WORRY, MARIO... IT'S ONLY WORDS THEY CAN'T READ. NUMBERS ARE STILL NUMBERS TO THEM -- I MADE SURE OF THAT!
YOU SEE, AS LONG AS THEY COULD TELL THEMSELVES IT WAS JUST A BUNCH OF NAMELESS, FACELESS "LITTLE PEOPLE" WHO WERE CATCHING "THE DISEASE"... THE POWERS THAT BE WOULDN'T TAKE IT SERIOUSLY.
BUT THAT WAS BEFORE YOU MADE SURE THAT THE NEXT TIME MAYOR HILL TRIES TO LIE TO THE PUBLIC ABOUT THE SEVERITY OF THE PROBLEM...
...HE WON'T BE ABLE TO READ THE TEXT OF HIS OWN FLATULENT SPEECH!
BELIEVE ME -- THAT WILL PROVIDE THE KIND OF TERROR THAT'LL GET A RESPONSE OUT OF THESE PEOPLE!...
...AND SHOW THEM ONCE AND FOR ALL THAT TERROR IS THE NAME OF THE GAME IF THEY DARE DEFY...

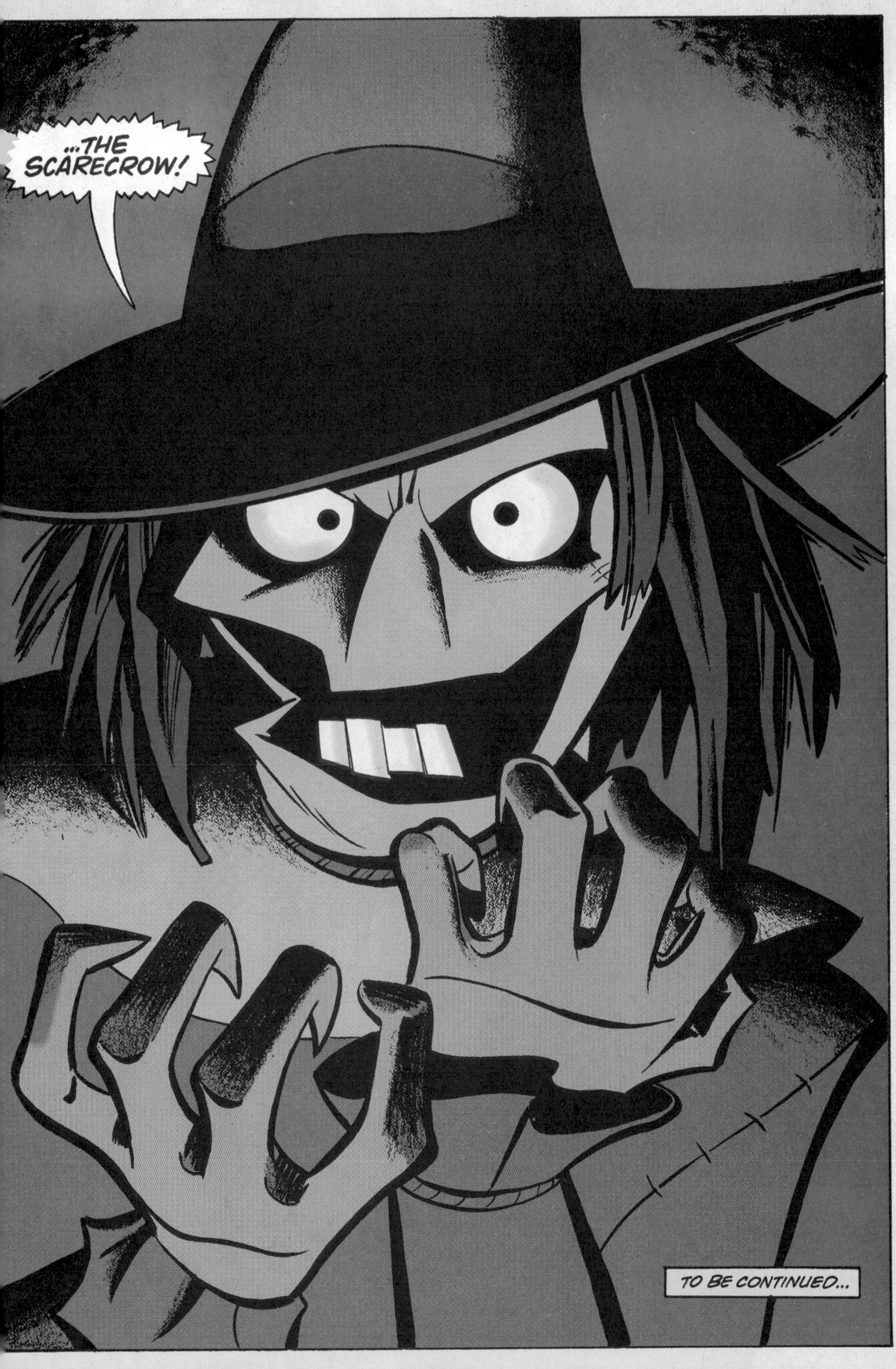
...THE SCARECROW!
TO BE CONTINUED...

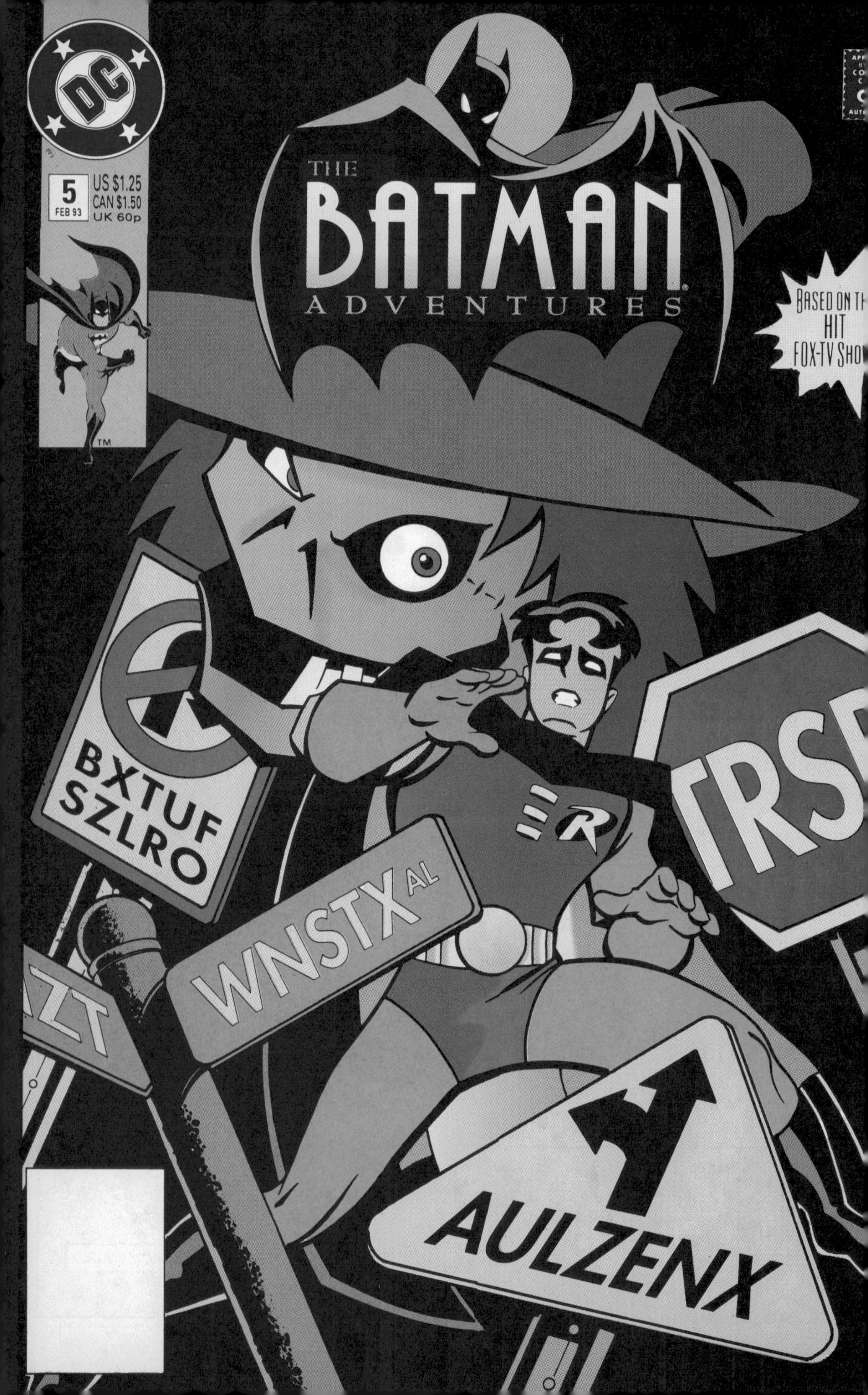
DC
5
FEB 93
US $1.25
CAN $1.50
UK 60p
THE BATMAN ADVENTURES
BXTUF SZLRO
WNSTX AL
AULZENX

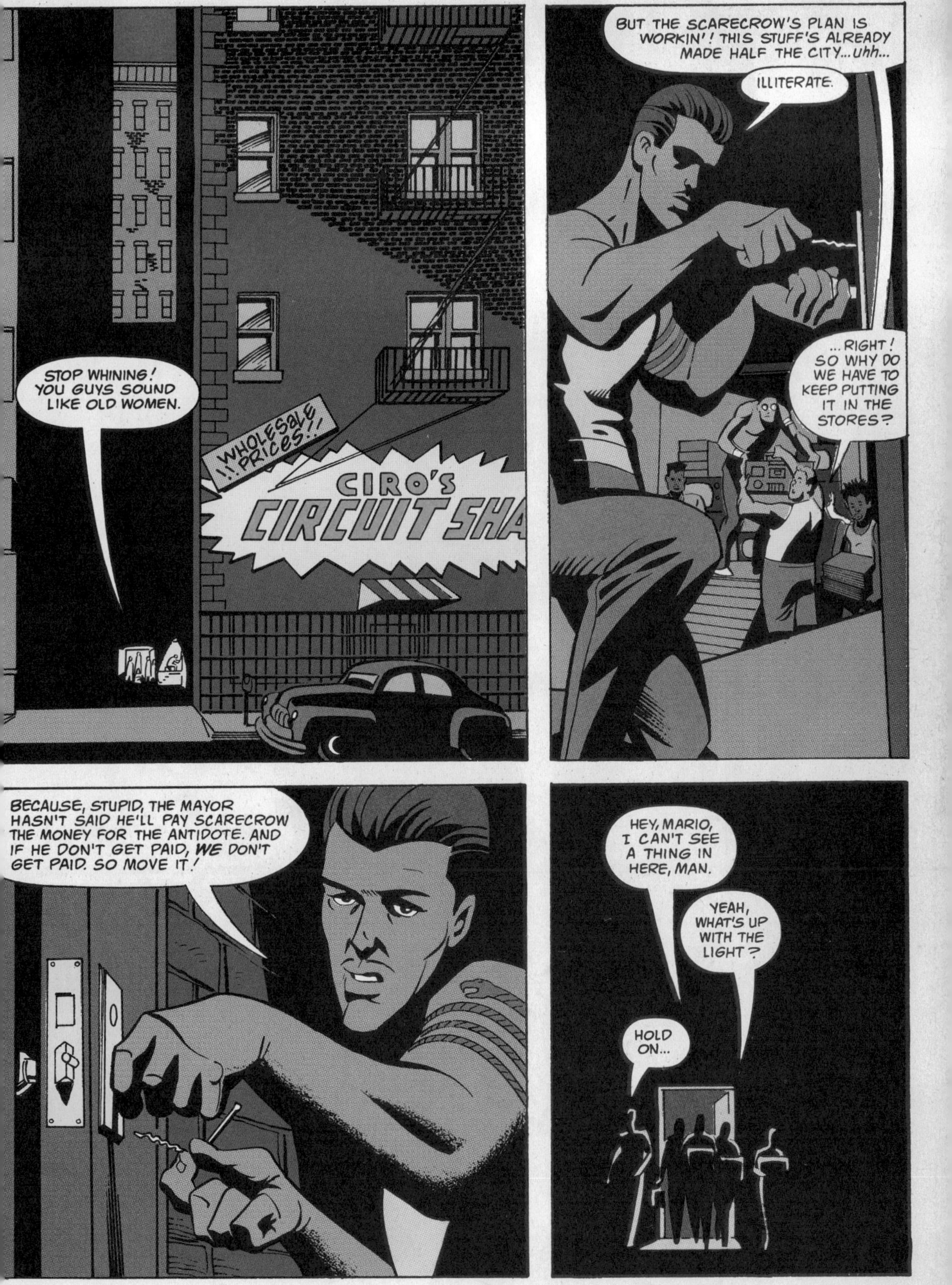
STOP WHINING! YOU GUYS SOUND LIKE OLD WOMEN.
!! WHOLESALE PRICES !!
CIRO'S
CIRCUIT SHA
BUT THE SCARECROW'S PLAN IS WORKIN'! THIS STUFF'S ALREADY MADE HALF THE CITY... *uhh...*
ILLITERATE.
...RIGHT! SO WHY DO WE HAVE TO KEEP PUTTING IT IN THE STORES?
BECAUSE, STUPID, THE MAYOR HASN'T SAID HE'LL PAY SCARECROW THE MONEY FOR THE ANTIDOTE. AND IF HE DON'T GET PAID, *WE* DON'T GET PAID. SO MOVE IT!
HEY, MARIO, I CAN'T SEE A THING IN HERE, MAN.
YEAH, WHAT'S UP WITH THE LIGHT?
HOLD ON...

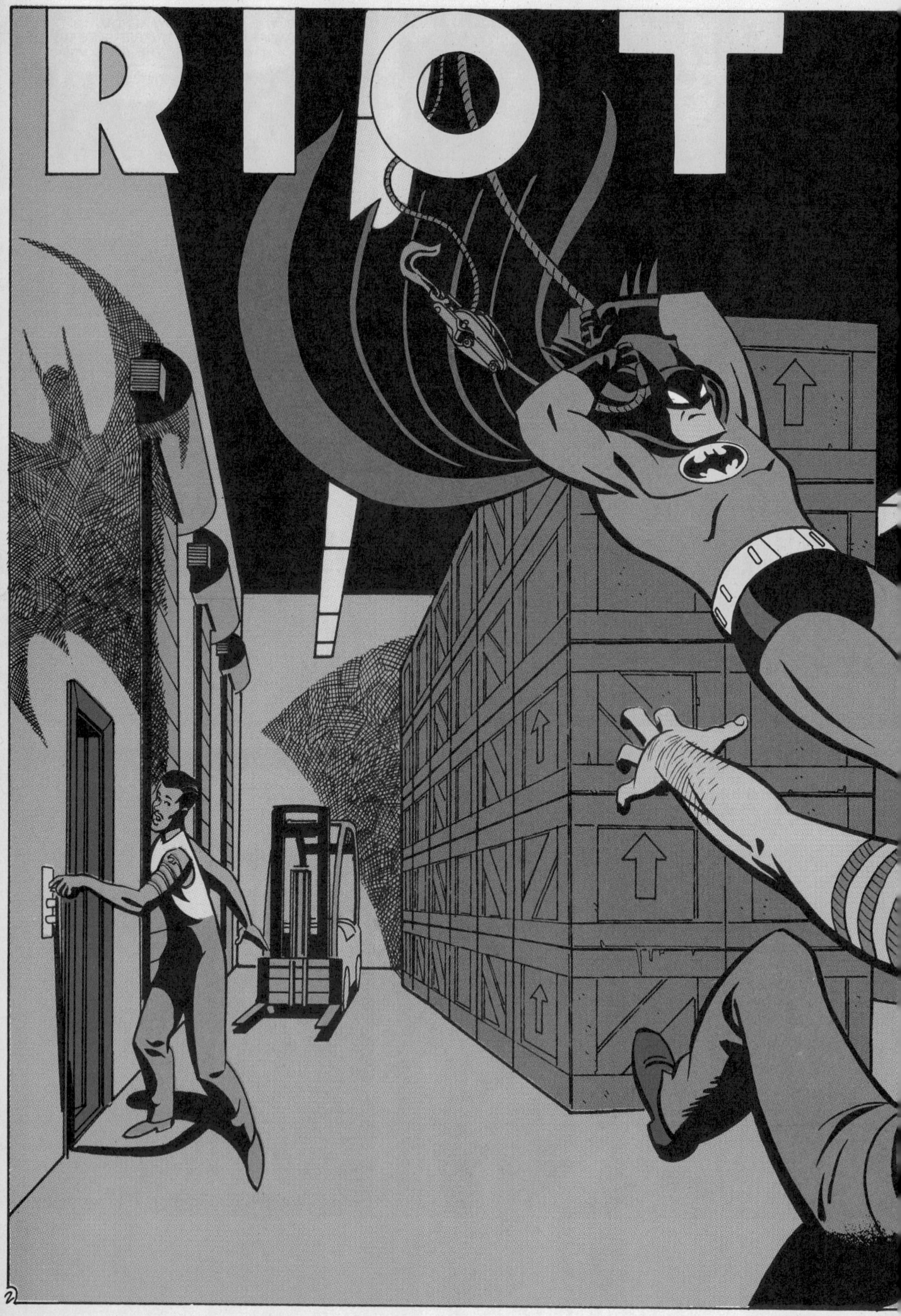
RIOT

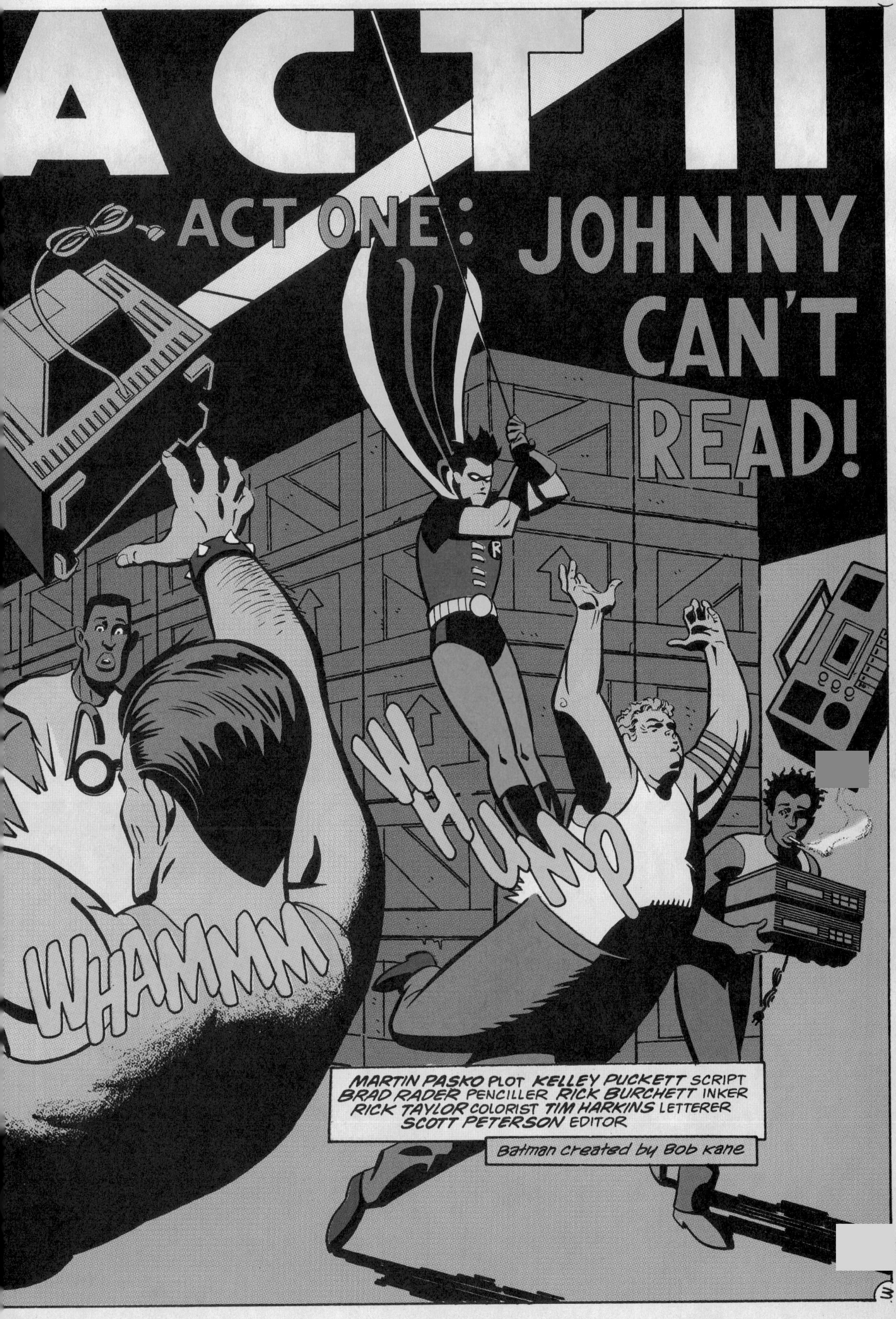

ACT II
ACT ONE: JOHNNY CAN'T READ!
WHUMP
WHAMMM
MARTIN PASKO PLOT KELLEY PUCKETT SCRIPT
BRAD RADER PENCILLER RICK BURCHETT INKER
RICK TAYLOR COLORIST TIM HARKINS LETTERER
SCOTT PETERSON EDITOR
Batman created by Bob Kane

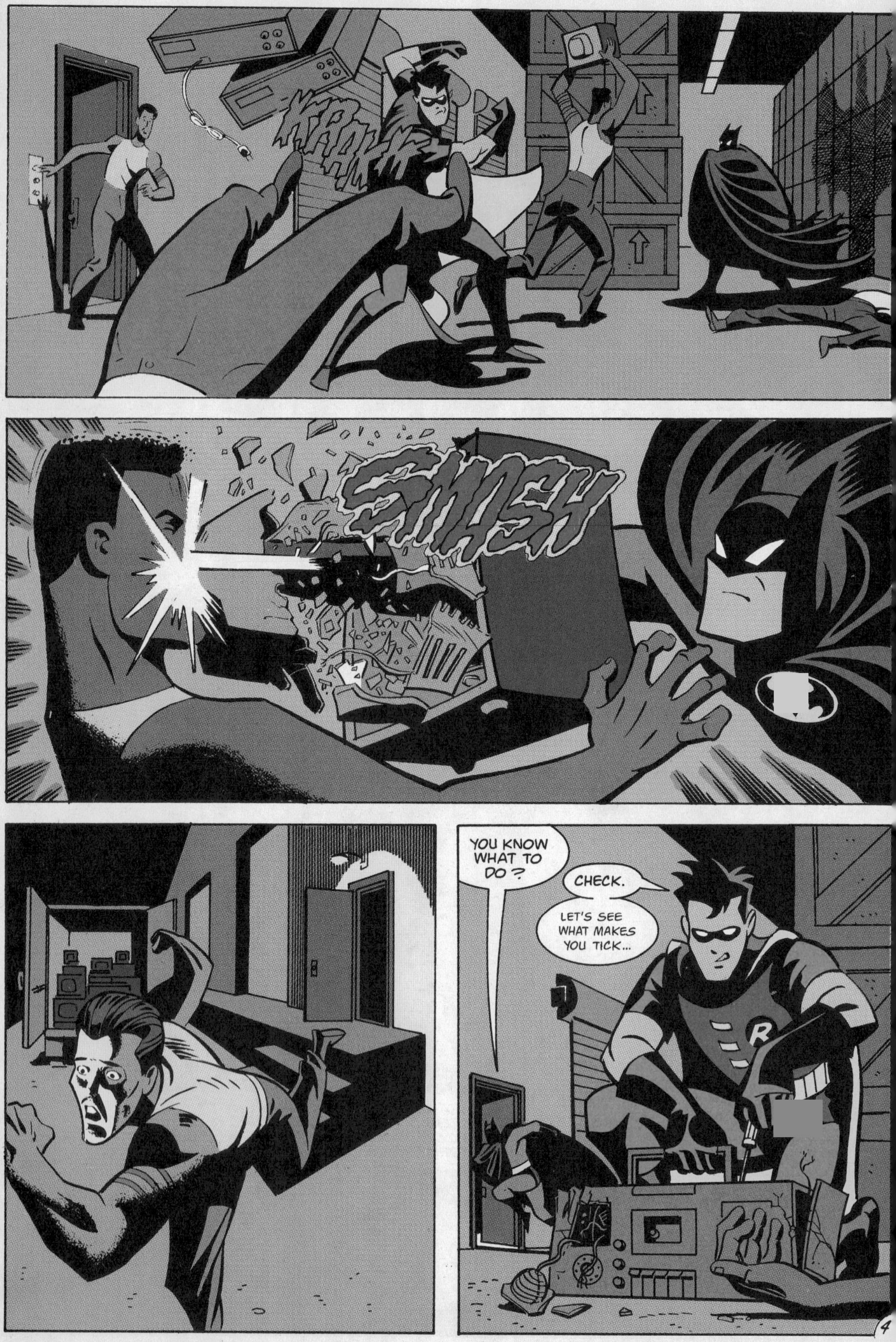
SMASH
YOU KNOW WHAT TO DO?
CHECK.
LET'S SEE WHAT MAKES YOU TICK...

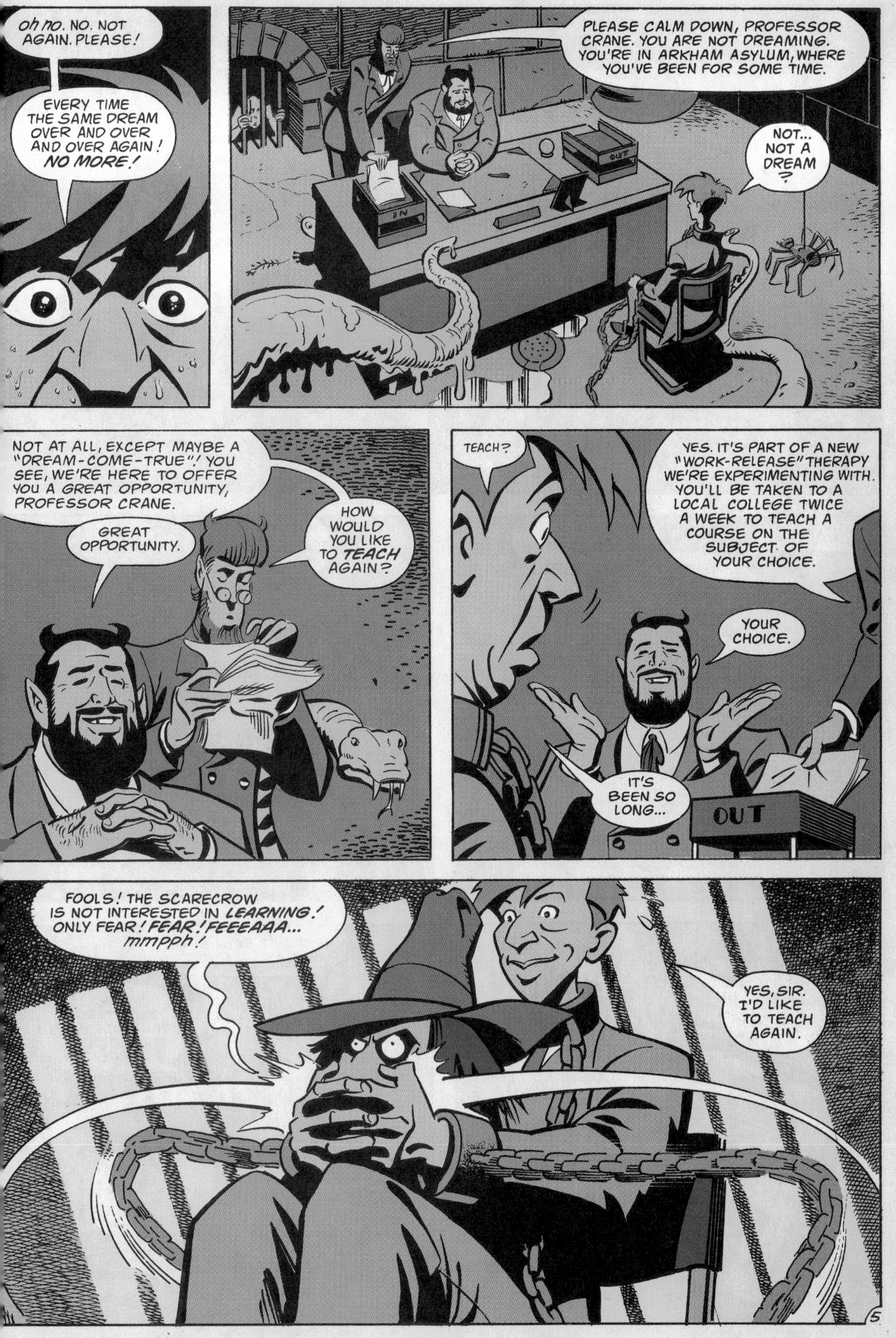
oh no. NO. NOT AGAIN. PLEASE!
EVERY TIME THE SAME DREAM OVER AND OVER AND OVER AGAIN! NO MORE!
PLEASE CALM DOWN, PROFESSOR CRANE. YOU ARE NOT DREAMING. YOU'RE IN ARKHAM ASYLUM, WHERE YOU'VE BEEN FOR SOME TIME.
NOT... NOT A DREAM?
OUT
IN
NOT AT ALL, EXCEPT MAYBE A "DREAM-COME-TRUE"! YOU SEE, WE'RE HERE TO OFFER YOU A GREAT OPPORTUNITY, PROFESSOR CRANE.
GREAT OPPORTUNITY.
HOW WOULD YOU LIKE TO TEACH AGAIN?
TEACH?
YES. IT'S PART OF A NEW "WORK-RELEASE" THERAPY WE'RE EXPERIMENTING WITH. YOU'LL BE TAKEN TO A LOCAL COLLEGE TWICE A WEEK TO TEACH A COURSE ON THE SUBJECT OF YOUR CHOICE.
YOUR CHOICE.
IT'S BEEN SO LONG...
OUT
FOOLS! THE SCARECROW IS NOT INTERESTED IN LEARNING! ONLY FEAR! FEAR! FEEEAAA... mmpph!
YES, SIR. I'D LIKE TO TEACH AGAIN.
5

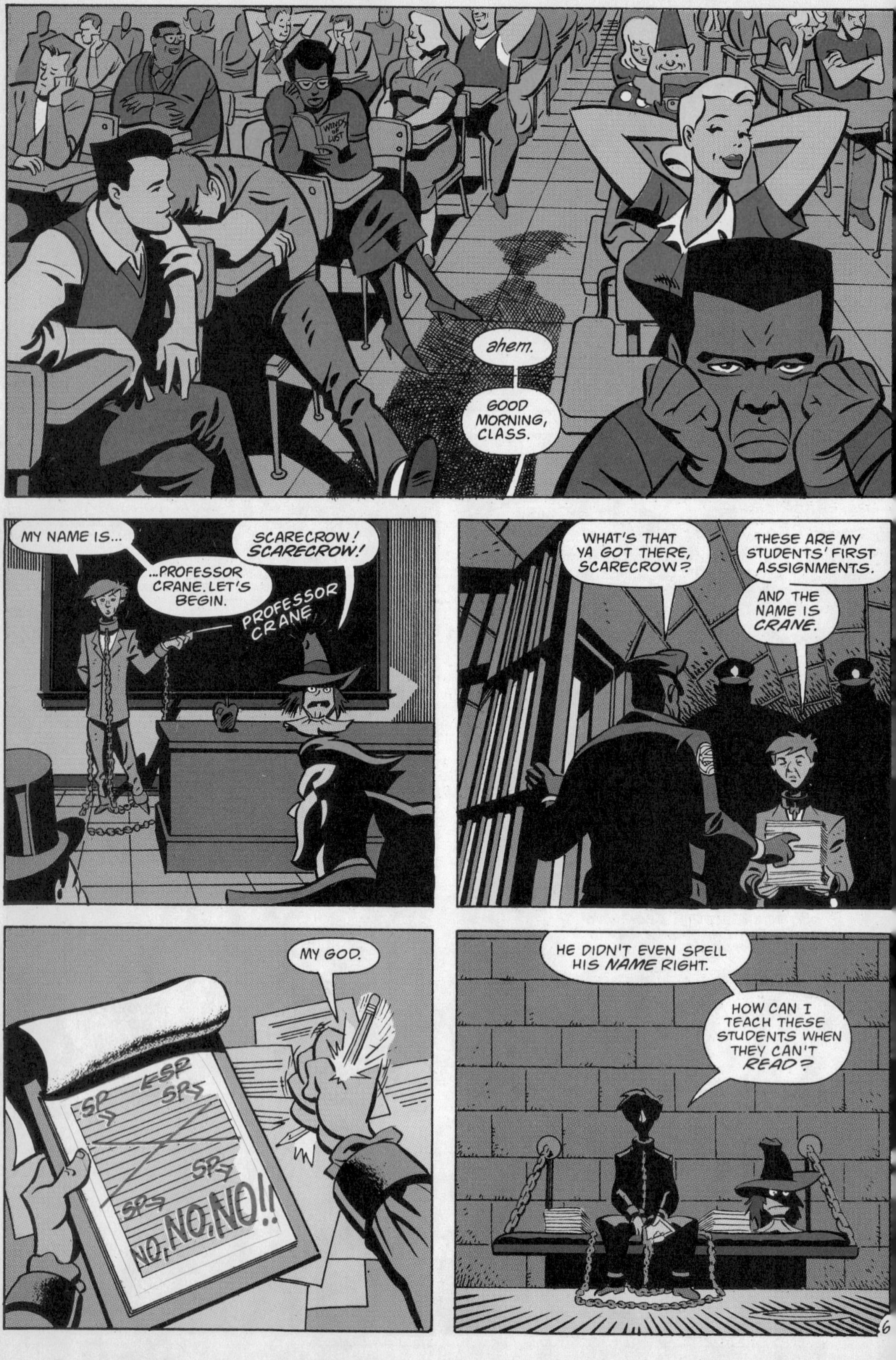
WINDS OF LUST
ahem.
GOOD MORNING, CLASS.
MY NAME IS...
...PROFESSOR CRANE. LET'S BEGIN.
SCARECROW! SCARECROW!
PROFESSOR CRANE
WHAT'S THAT YA GOT THERE, SCARECROW?
THESE ARE MY STUDENTS' FIRST ASSIGNMENTS.
AND THE NAME IS CRANE.
MY GOD.
SP
ESP
SPS
SPS
SPS
NO, NO, NO!!
HE DIDN'T EVEN SPELL HIS NAME RIGHT.
HOW CAN I TEACH THESE STUDENTS WHEN THEY CAN'T READ?
6

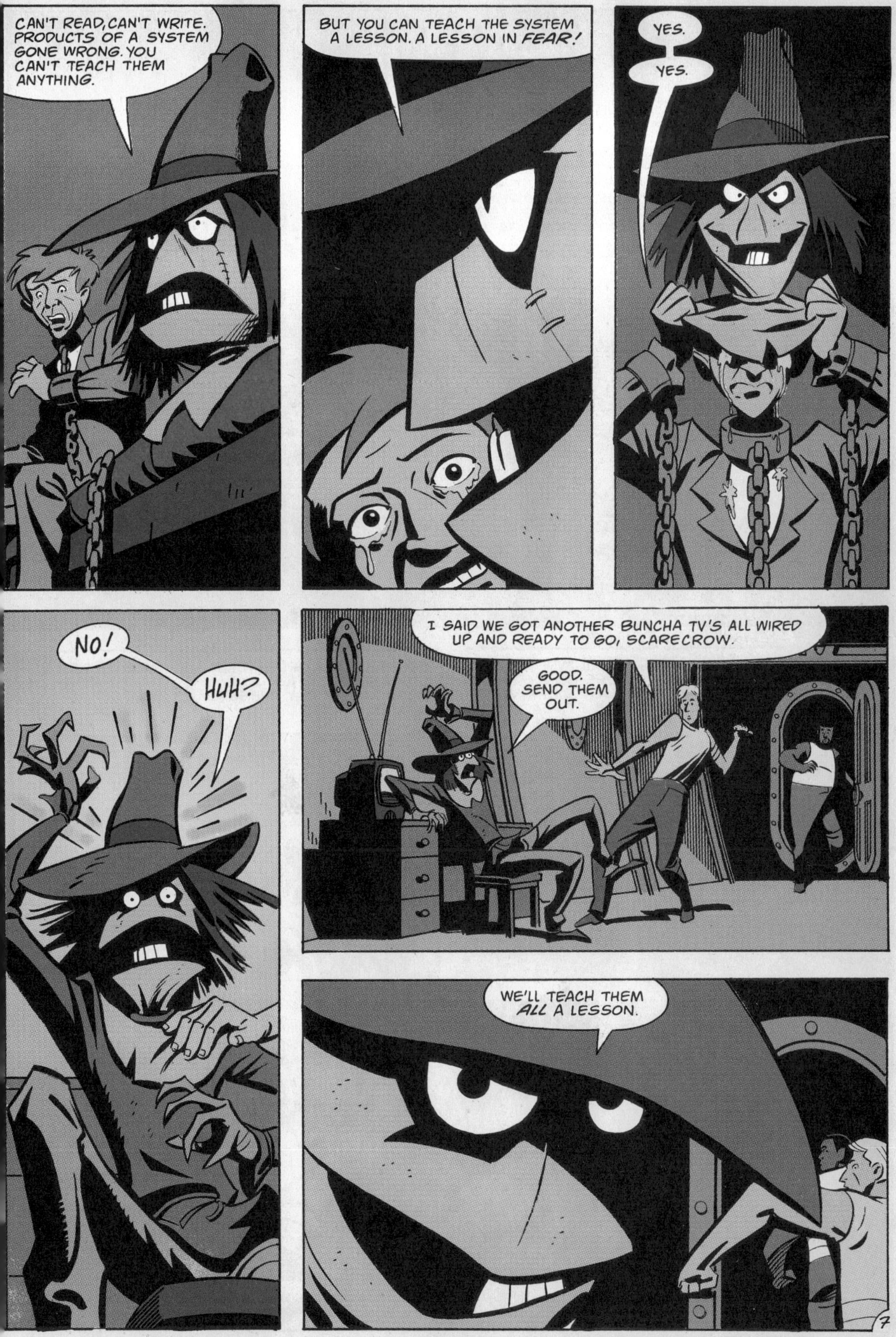
CAN'T READ, CAN'T WRITE. PRODUCTS OF A SYSTEM GONE WRONG. YOU CAN'T TEACH THEM ANYTHING.
BUT YOU CAN TEACH THE SYSTEM A LESSON. A LESSON IN FEAR!
YES.
YES.
NO!
HUH?
I SAID WE GOT ANOTHER BUNCHA TV'S ALL WIRED UP AND READY TO GO, SCARECROW.
GOOD. SEND THEM OUT.
WE'LL TEACH THEM ALL A LESSON.
7

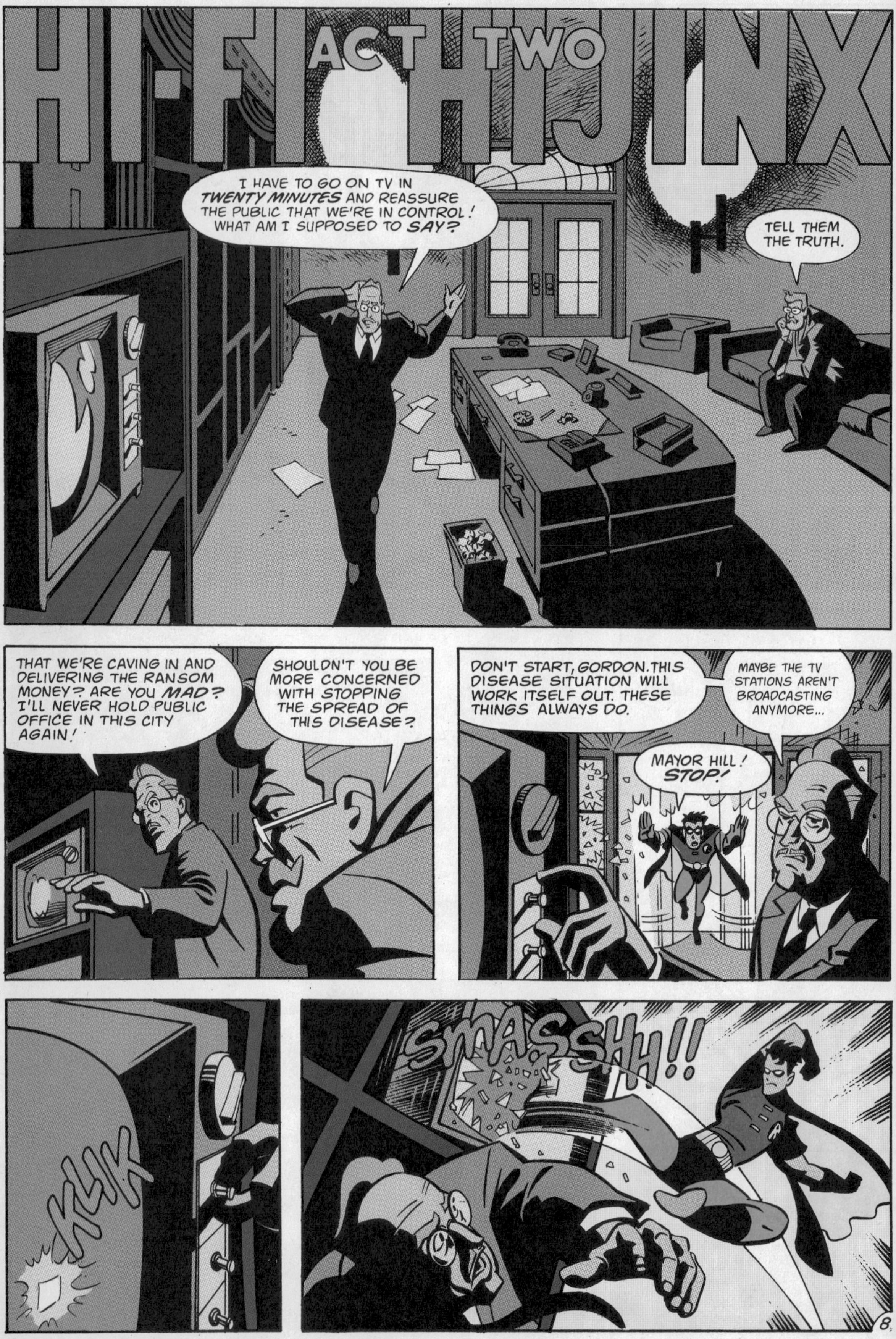
HI-FI HIJINX
ACT TWO
I HAVE TO GO ON TV IN TWENTY MINUTES AND REASSURE THE PUBLIC THAT WE'RE IN CONTROL! WHAT AM I SUPPOSED TO SAY?
TELL THEM THE TRUTH.
THAT WE'RE CAVING IN AND DELIVERING THE RANSOM MONEY? ARE YOU MAD? I'LL NEVER HOLD PUBLIC OFFICE IN THIS CITY AGAIN!
SHOULDN'T YOU BE MORE CONCERNED WITH STOPPING THE SPREAD OF THIS DISEASE?
DON'T START, GORDON. THIS DISEASE SITUATION WILL WORK ITSELF OUT. THESE THINGS ALWAYS DO.
MAYBE THE TV STATIONS AREN'T BROADCASTING ANYMORE...
MAYOR HILL! STOP!
KLIK
SMASSHH!!
8

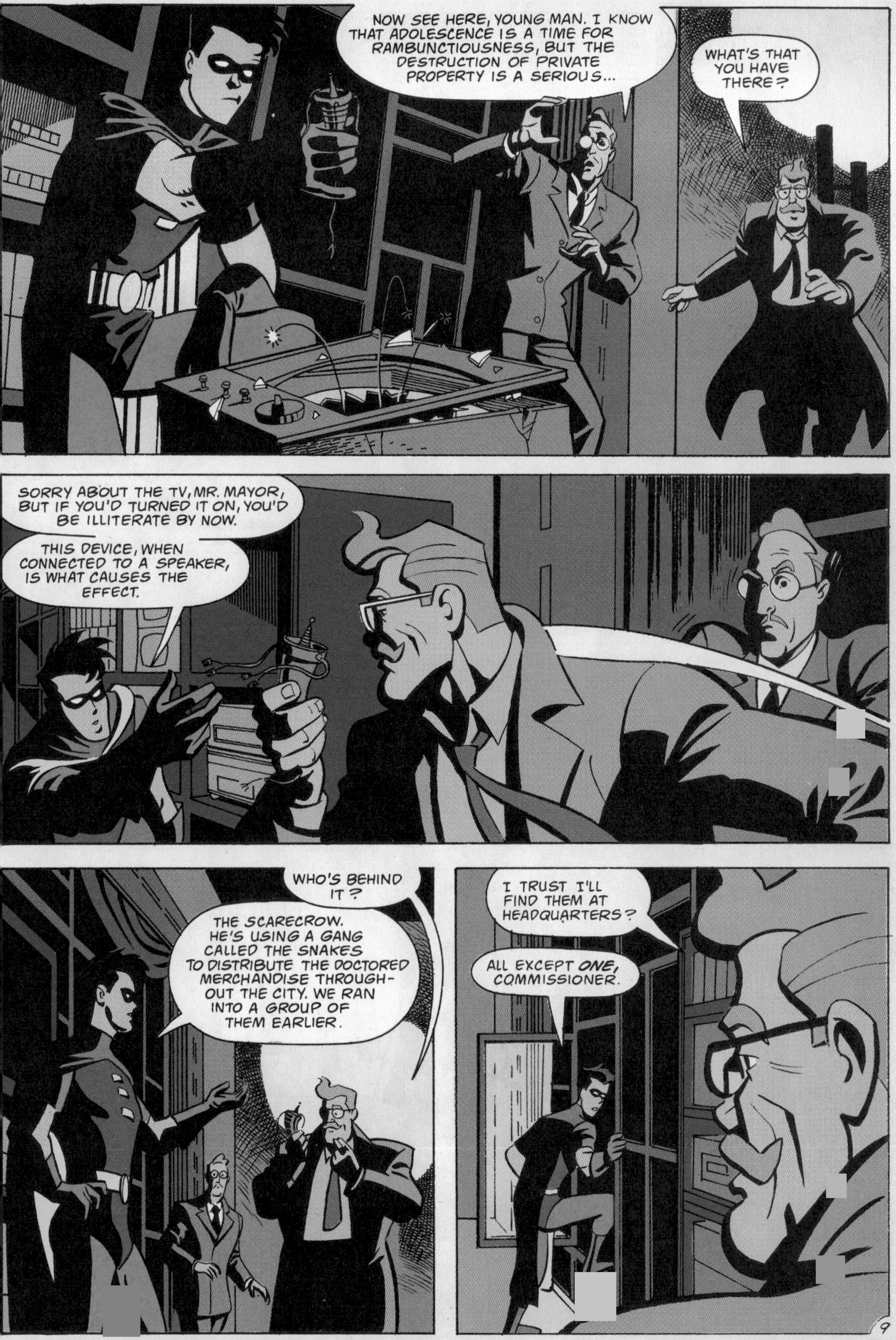
NOW SEE HERE, YOUNG MAN. I KNOW THAT ADOLESCENCE IS A TIME FOR RAMBUNCTIOUSNESS, BUT THE DESTRUCTION OF PRIVATE PROPERTY IS A SERIOUS...
WHAT'S THAT YOU HAVE THERE?
SORRY ABOUT THE TV, MR. MAYOR, BUT IF YOU'D TURNED IT ON, YOU'D BE ILLITERATE BY NOW.
THIS DEVICE, WHEN CONNECTED TO A SPEAKER, IS WHAT CAUSES THE EFFECT.
WHO'S BEHIND IT?
THE SCARECROW. HE'S USING A GANG CALLED THE SNAKES TO DISTRIBUTE THE DOCTORED MERCHANDISE THROUGH-OUT THE CITY. WE RAN INTO A GROUP OF THEM EARLIER.
I TRUST I'LL FIND THEM AT HEADQUARTERS?
ALL EXCEPT *ONE*, COMMISSIONER.
9

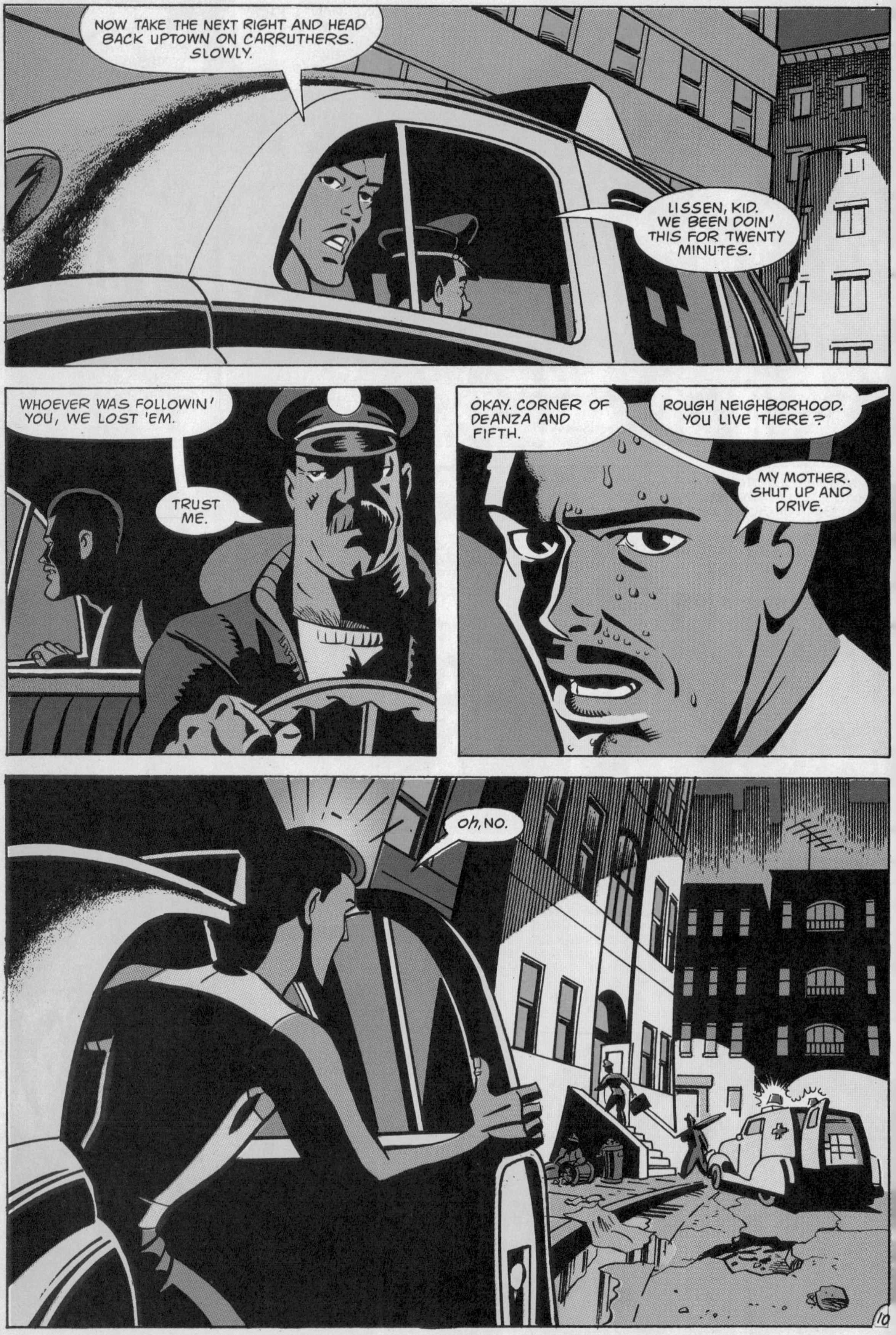
NOW TAKE THE NEXT RIGHT AND HEAD BACK UPTOWN ON CARRUTHERS. SLOWLY.
LISSEN, KID. WE BEEN DOIN' THIS FOR TWENTY MINUTES.
WHOEVER WAS FOLLOWIN' YOU, WE LOST 'EM.
TRUST ME.
OKAY. CORNER OF DEANZA AND FIFTH.
ROUGH NEIGHBORHOOD. YOU LIVE THERE?
MY MOTHER. SHUT UP AND DRIVE.
oh, NO.
10

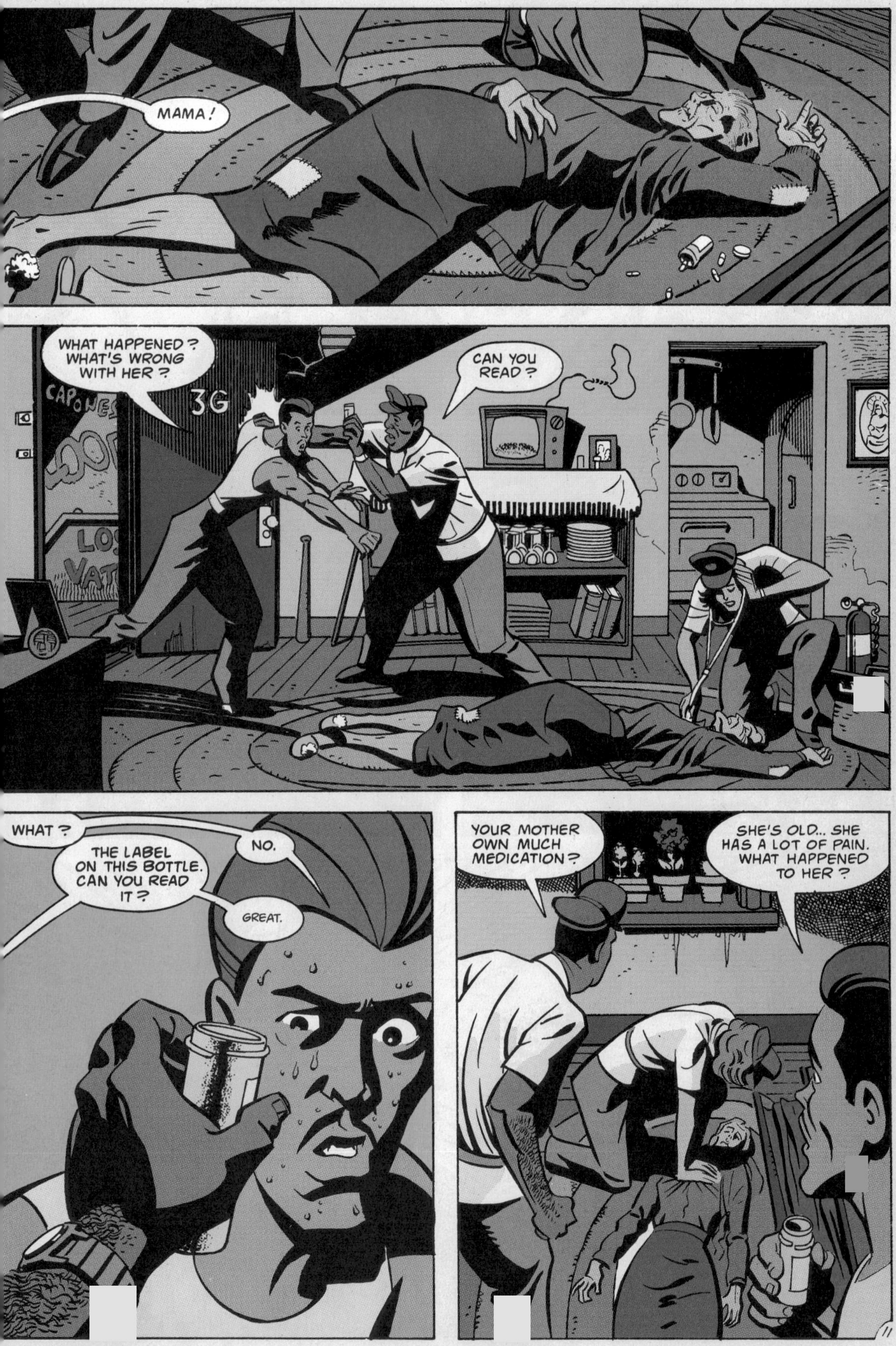
MAMA!
WHAT HAPPENED? WHAT'S WRONG WITH HER?
CAPONES
LOS VATOS
3G
CAN YOU READ?
WHAT?
NO.
THE LABEL ON THIS BOTTLE. CAN YOU READ IT?
GREAT.
YOUR MOTHER OWN MUCH MEDICATION?
SHE'S OLD... SHE HAS A LOT OF PAIN. WHAT HAPPENED TO HER?

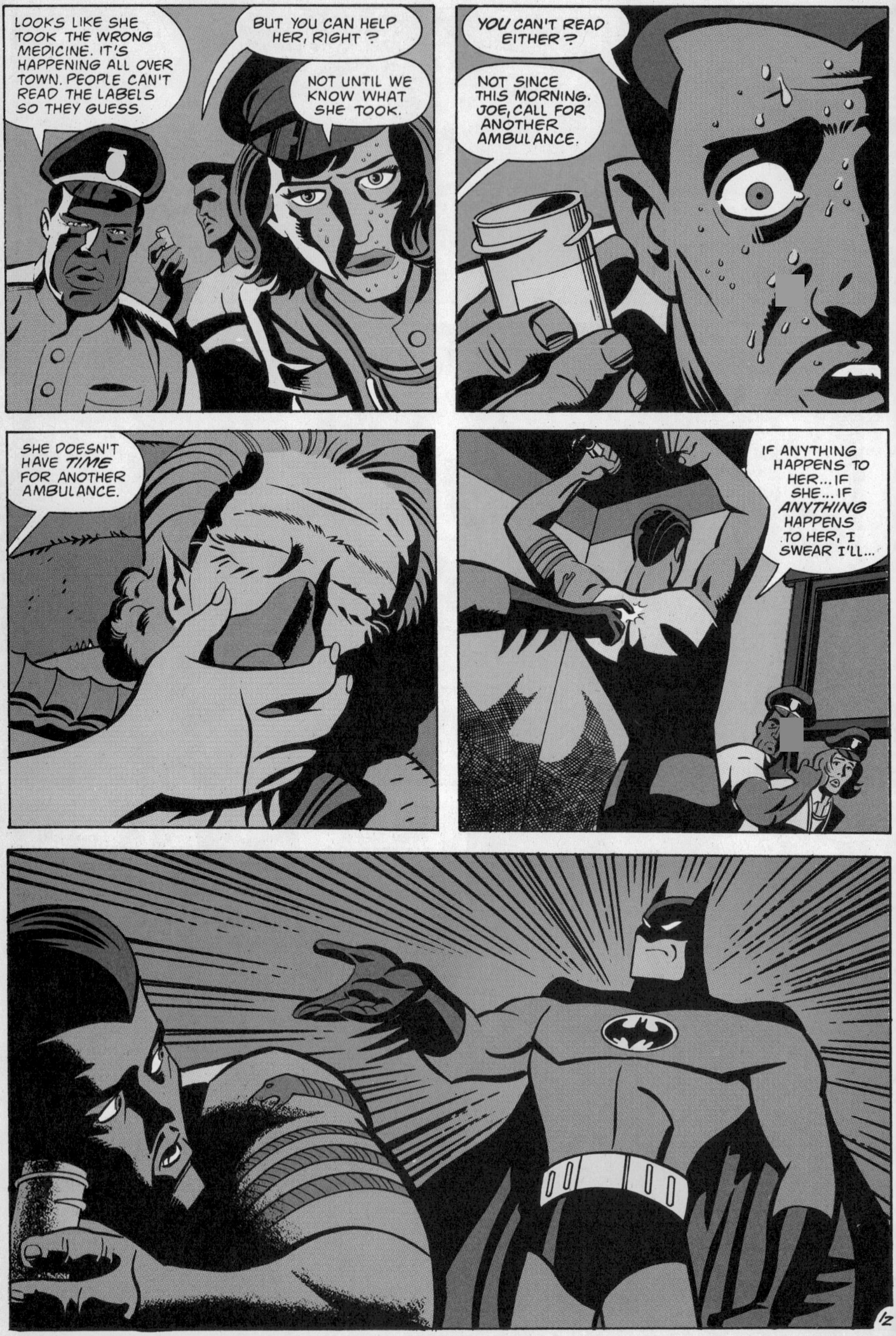
LOOKS LIKE SHE TOOK THE WRONG MEDICINE. IT'S HAPPENING ALL OVER TOWN. PEOPLE CAN'T READ THE LABELS SO THEY GUESS.
BUT YOU CAN HELP HER, RIGHT?
NOT UNTIL WE KNOW WHAT SHE TOOK.
YOU CAN'T READ EITHER?
NOT SINCE THIS MORNING. JOE, CALL FOR ANOTHER AMBULANCE.
SHE DOESN'T HAVE TIME FOR ANOTHER AMBULANCE.
IF ANYTHING HAPPENS TO HER... IF SHE... IF ANYTHING HAPPENS TO HER, I SWEAR I'LL...
12

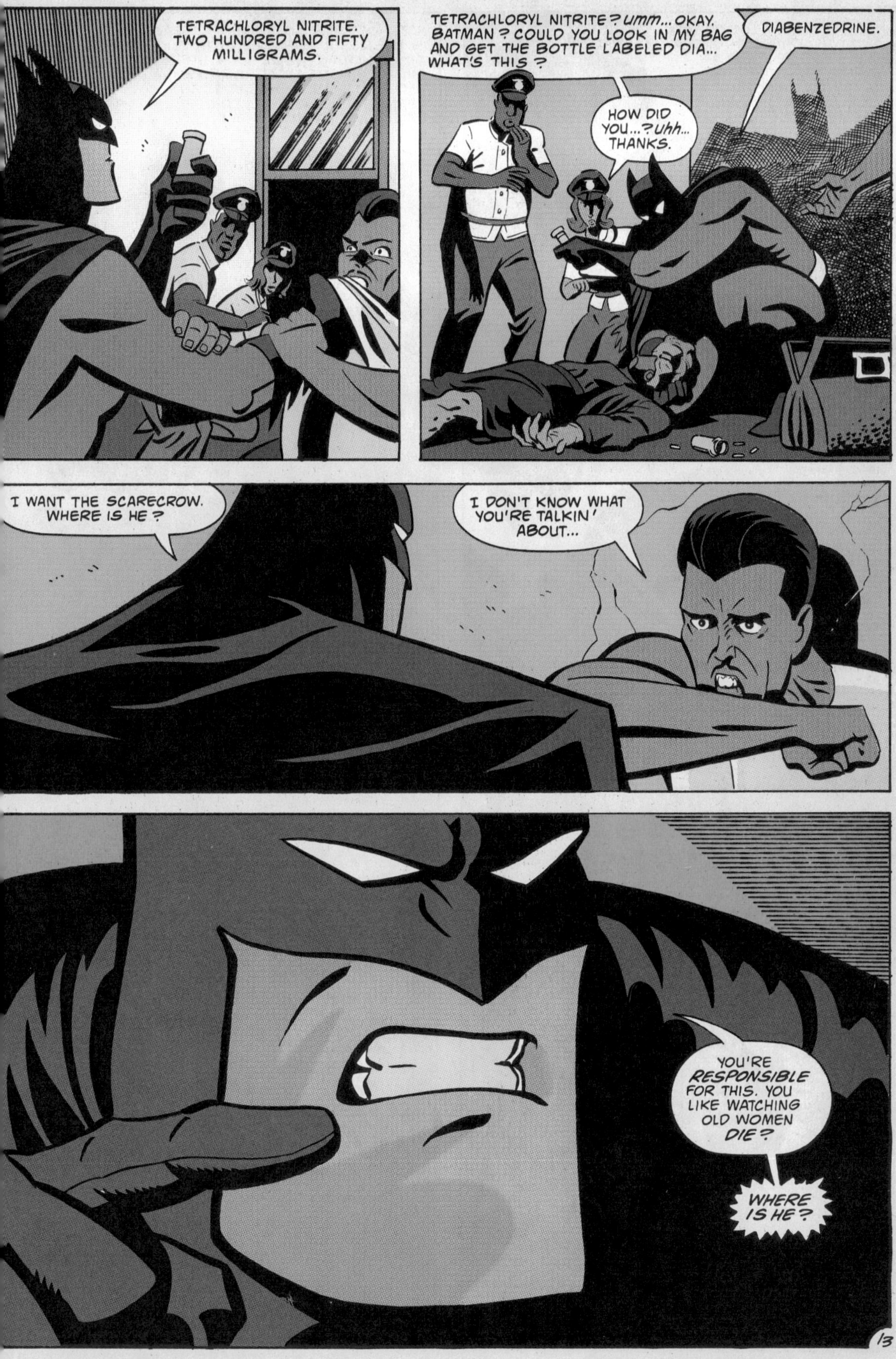

TETRACHLORYL NITRITE. TWO HUNDRED AND FIFTY MILLIGRAMS.
TETRACHLORYL NITRITE? umm... OKAY. BATMAN? COULD YOU LOOK IN MY BAG AND GET THE BOTTLE LABELED DIA... WHAT'S THIS?
DIABENZEDRINE.
HOW DID YOU...? uhh... THANKS.
I WANT THE SCARECROW. WHERE IS HE?
I DON'T KNOW WHAT YOU'RE TALKIN' ABOUT...
YOU'RE RESPONSIBLE FOR THIS. YOU LIKE WATCHING OLD WOMEN DIE?
WHERE IS HE?
13

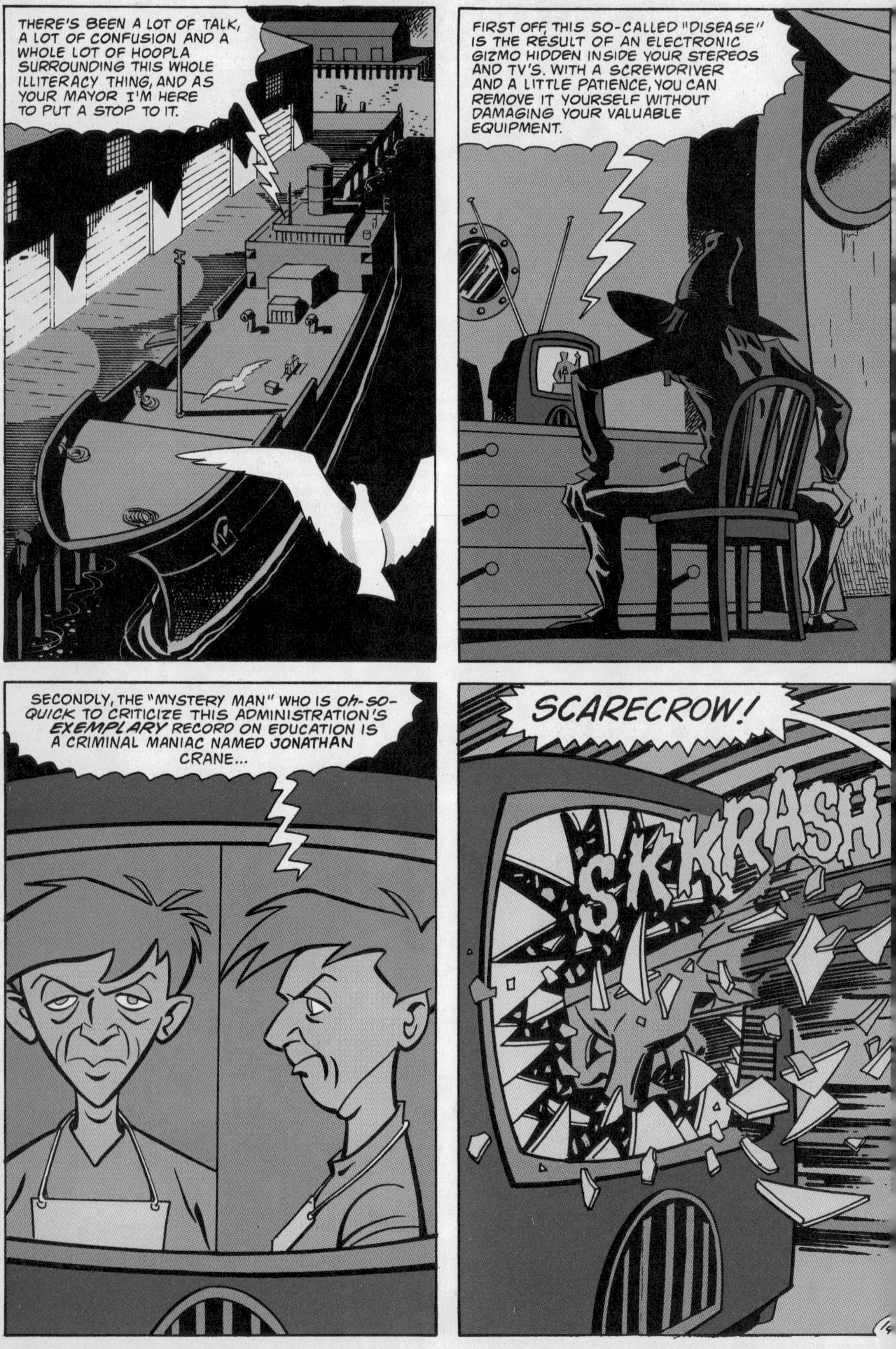
THERE'S BEEN A LOT OF TALK, A LOT OF CONFUSION AND A WHOLE LOT OF HOOPLA SURROUNDING THIS WHOLE ILLITERACY THING, AND AS YOUR MAYOR I'M HERE TO PUT A STOP TO IT.
FIRST OFF, THIS SO-CALLED "DISEASE" IS THE RESULT OF AN ELECTRONIC GIZMO HIDDEN INSIDE YOUR STEREOS AND TV'S. WITH A SCREWDRIVER AND A LITTLE PATIENCE, YOU CAN REMOVE IT YOURSELF WITHOUT DAMAGING YOUR VALUABLE EQUIPMENT.
SECONDLY, THE "MYSTERY MAN" WHO IS *oh-SO-QUICK* TO CRITICIZE THIS ADMINISTRATION'S *EXEMPLARY* RECORD ON EDUCATION IS A CRIMINAL MANIAC NAMED JONATHAN CRANE...
SCARECROW!
SKKRASH

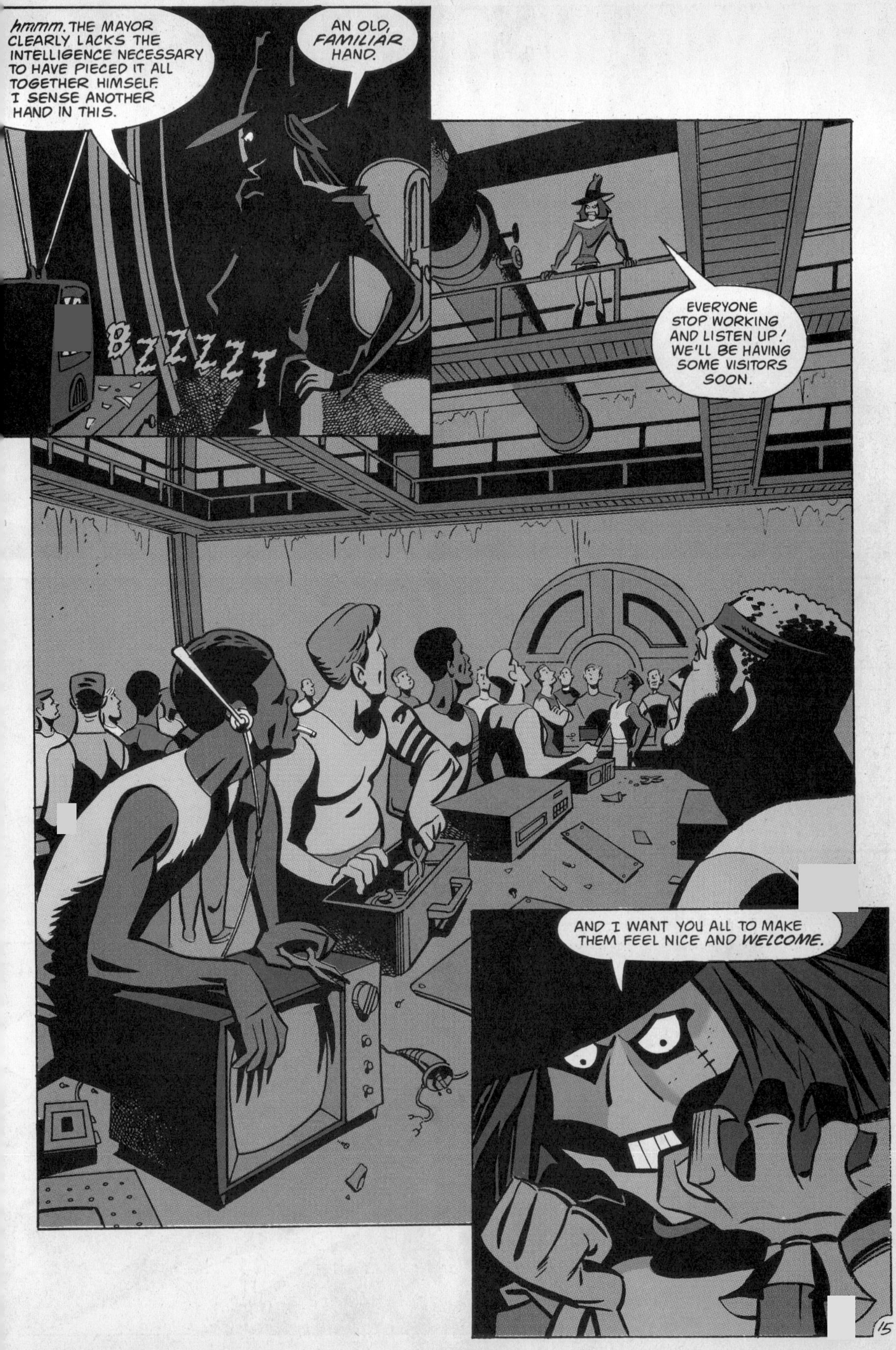

hmmm. THE MAYOR CLEARLY LACKS THE INTELLIGENCE NECESSARY TO HAVE PIECED IT ALL TOGETHER HIMSELF. I SENSE ANOTHER HAND IN THIS.
AN OLD, FAMILIAR HAND.
BZZZZZT
EVERYONE STOP WORKING AND LISTEN UP! WE'LL BE HAVING SOME VISITORS SOON.
AND I WANT YOU ALL TO MAKE THEM FEEL NICE AND WELCOME.
15

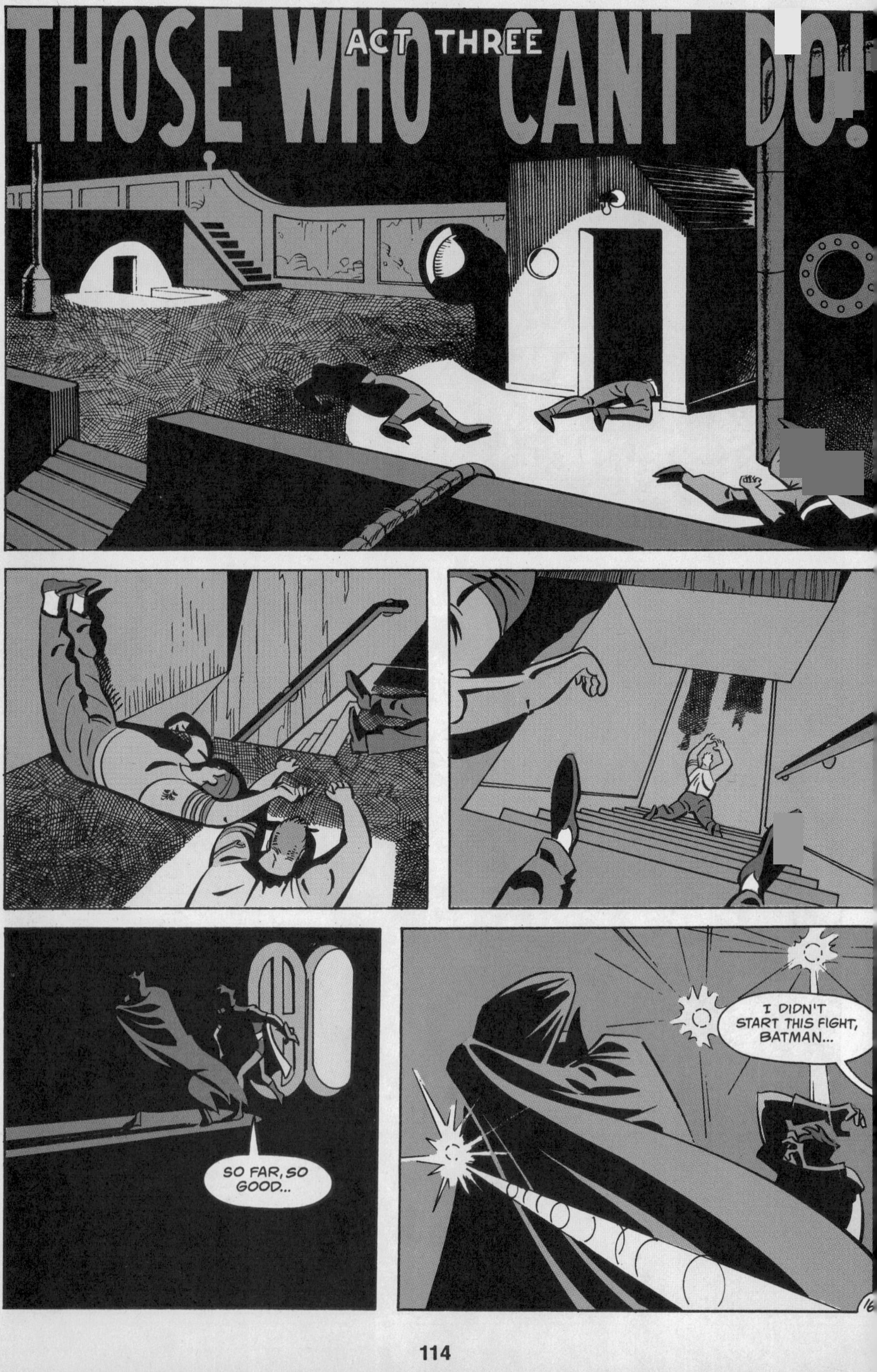
ACT THREE
THOSE WHO CANT DO!
SO FAR, SO GOOD...
I DIDN'T START THIS FIGHT, BATMAN...

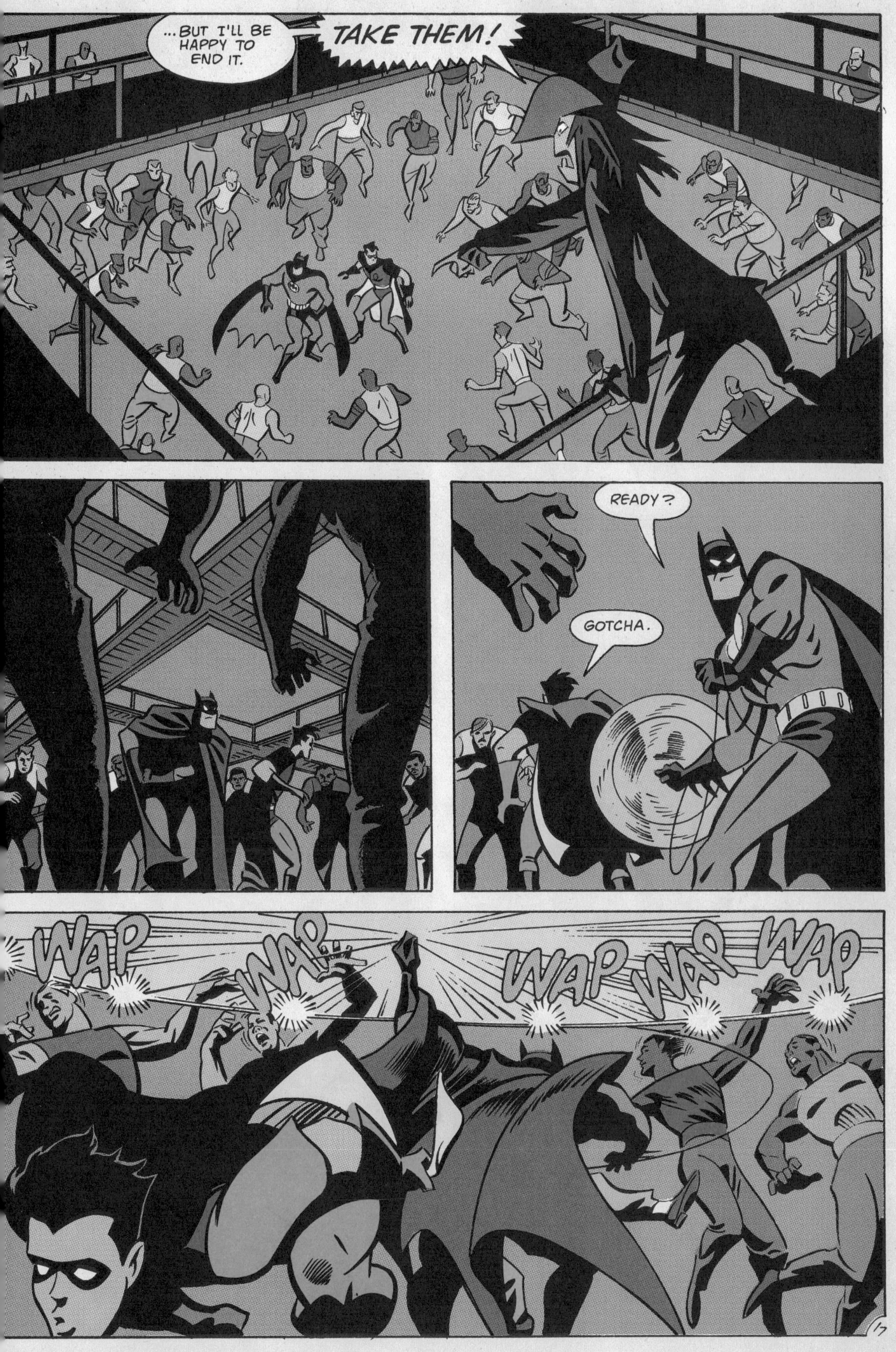
...BUT I'LL BE HAPPY TO END IT.
TAKE THEM!
READY?
GOTCHA.
WAP
WAP
WAP
WAP
WAP
17

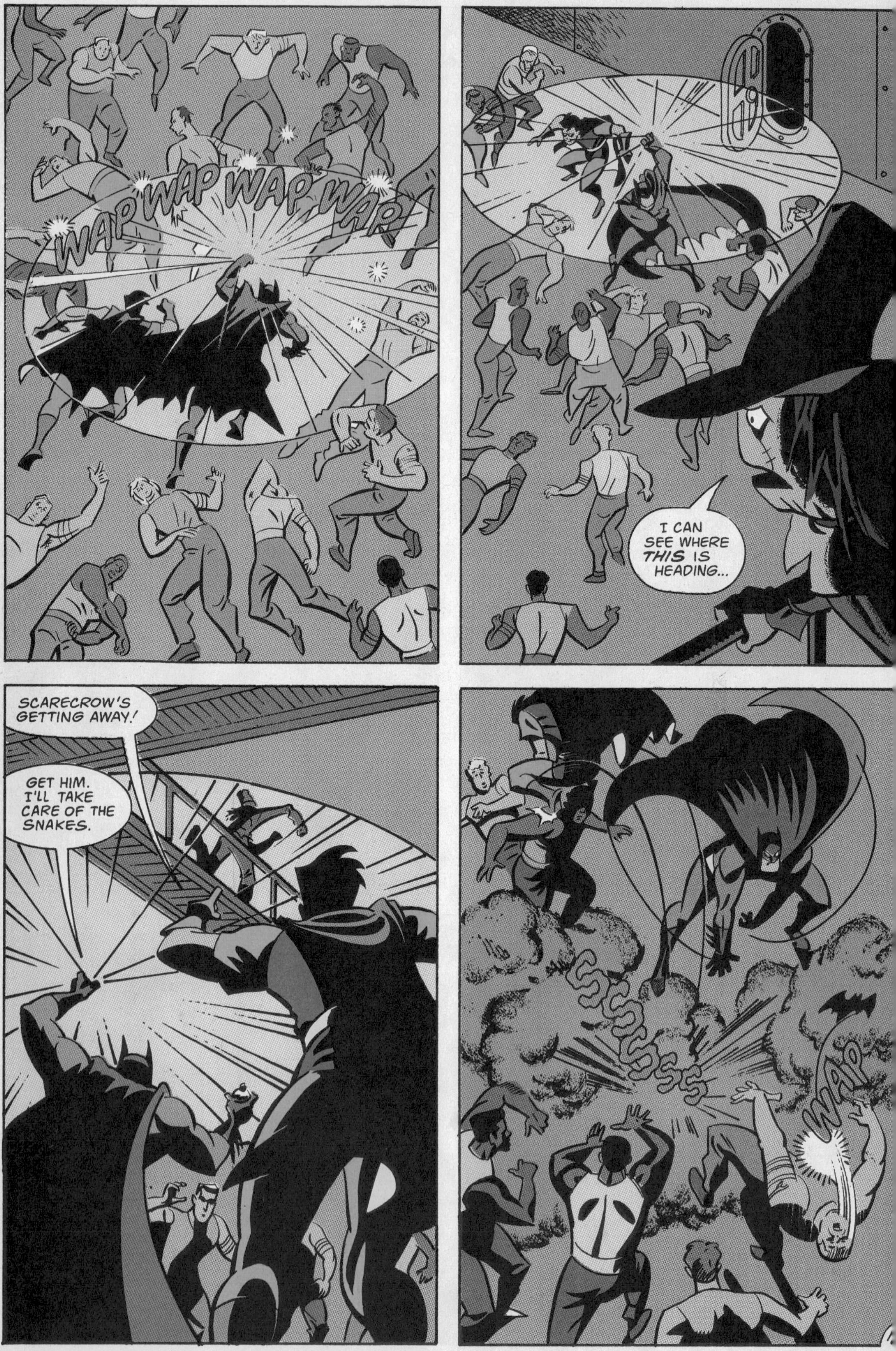
WAP WAP WAP WAP
I CAN SEE WHERE THIS IS HEADING...
SCARECROW'S GETTING AWAY!
GET HIM. I'LL TAKE CARE OF THE SNAKES.
WAP

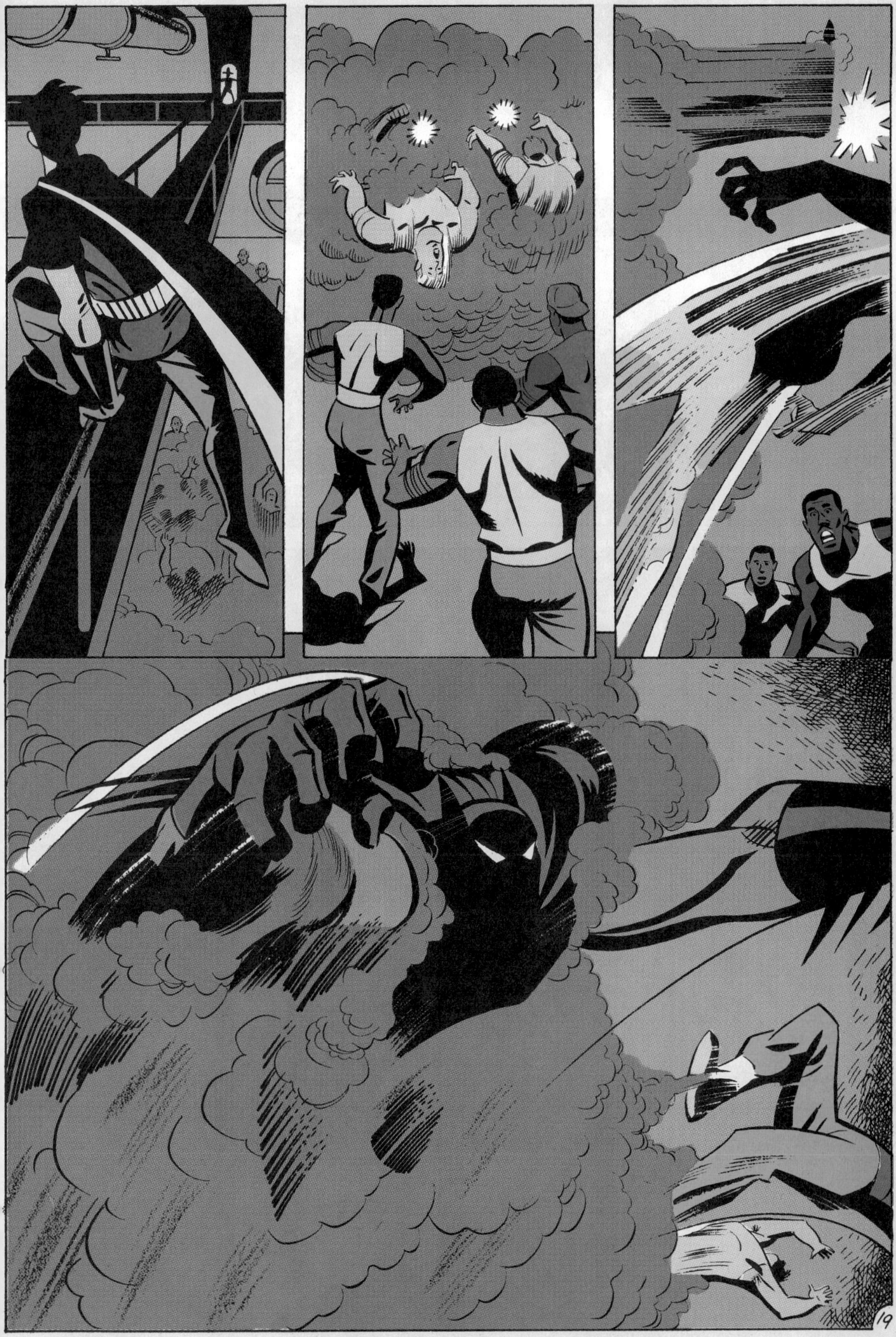
19

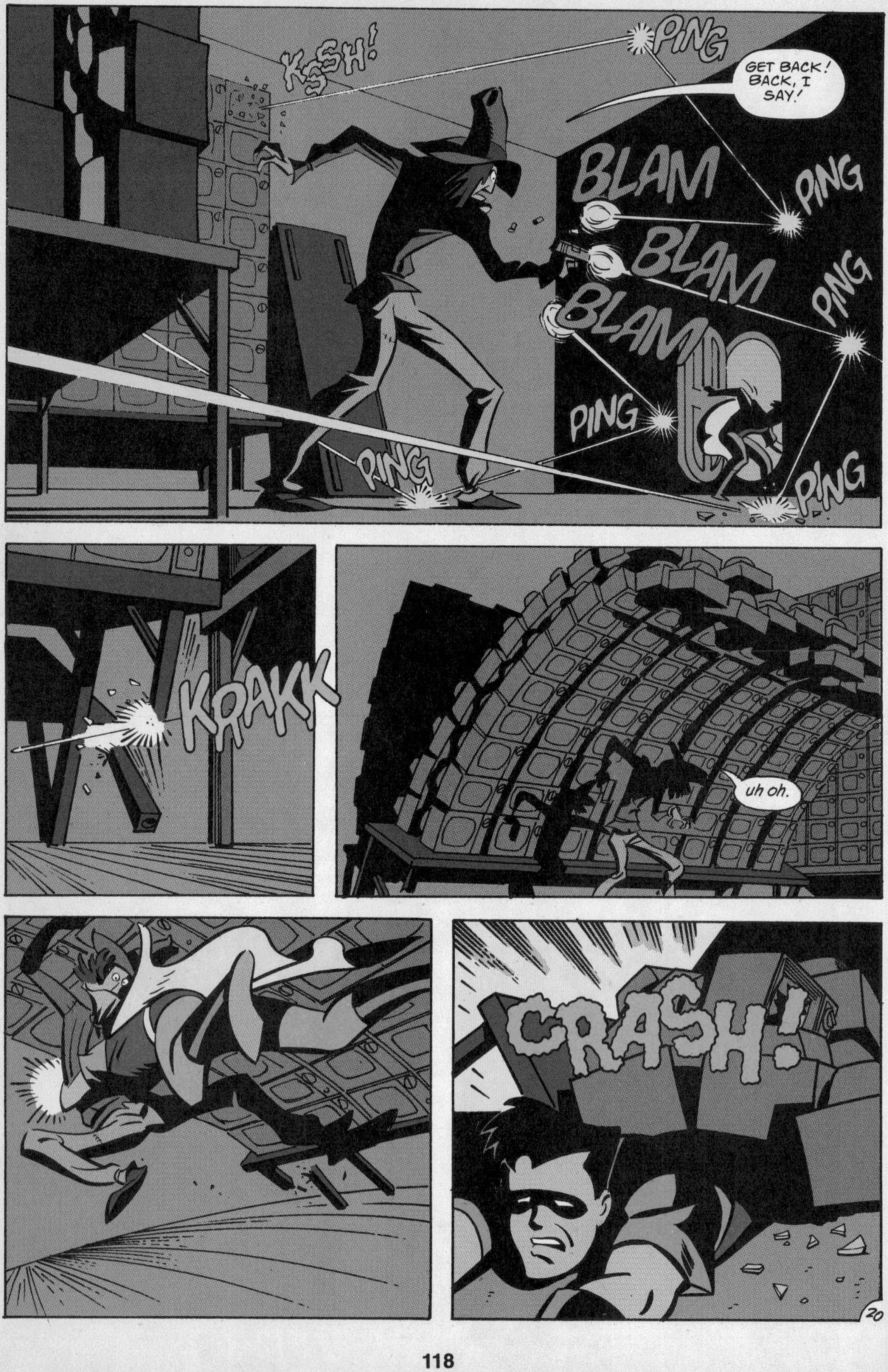
KSSH!
PING
GET BACK! BACK, I SAY!
BLAM
PING
BLAM
PING
BLAM
PING
PING
PING
KRAKK
uh oh.
CRASH!
20

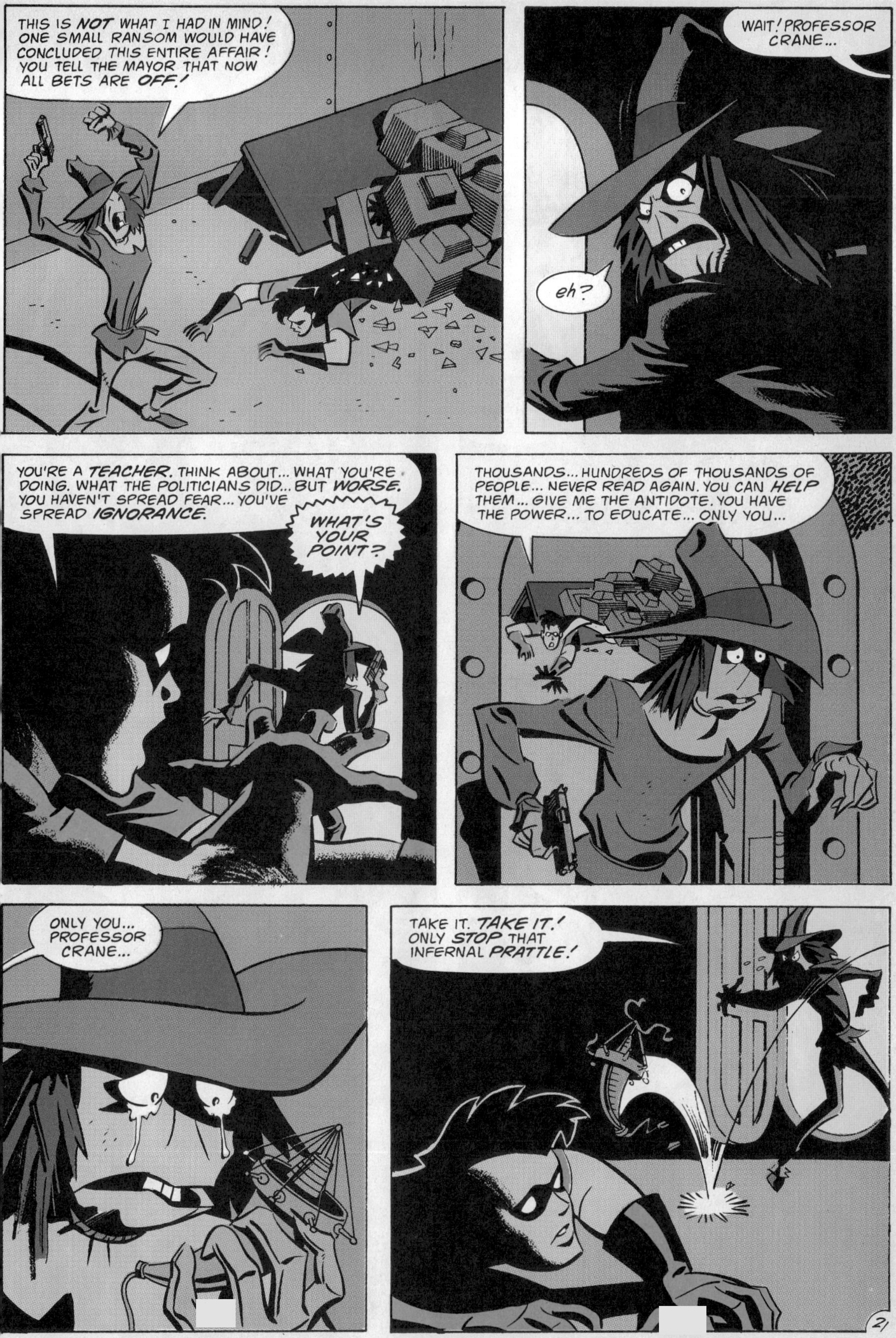
THIS IS NOT WHAT I HAD IN MIND! ONE SMALL RANSOM WOULD HAVE CONCLUDED THIS ENTIRE AFFAIR! YOU TELL THE MAYOR THAT NOW ALL BETS ARE OFF!
WAIT! PROFESSOR CRANE...
eh?
YOU'RE A TEACHER. THINK ABOUT... WHAT YOU'RE DOING. WHAT THE POLITICIANS DID... BUT WORSE. YOU HAVEN'T SPREAD FEAR... YOU'VE SPREAD IGNORANCE.
WHAT'S YOUR POINT?
THOUSANDS... HUNDREDS OF THOUSANDS OF PEOPLE... NEVER READ AGAIN. YOU CAN HELP THEM... GIVE ME THE ANTIDOTE. YOU HAVE THE POWER... TO EDUCATE... ONLY YOU...
ONLY YOU... PROFESSOR CRANE...
TAKE IT. TAKE IT! ONLY STOP THAT INFERNAL PRATTLE!
21

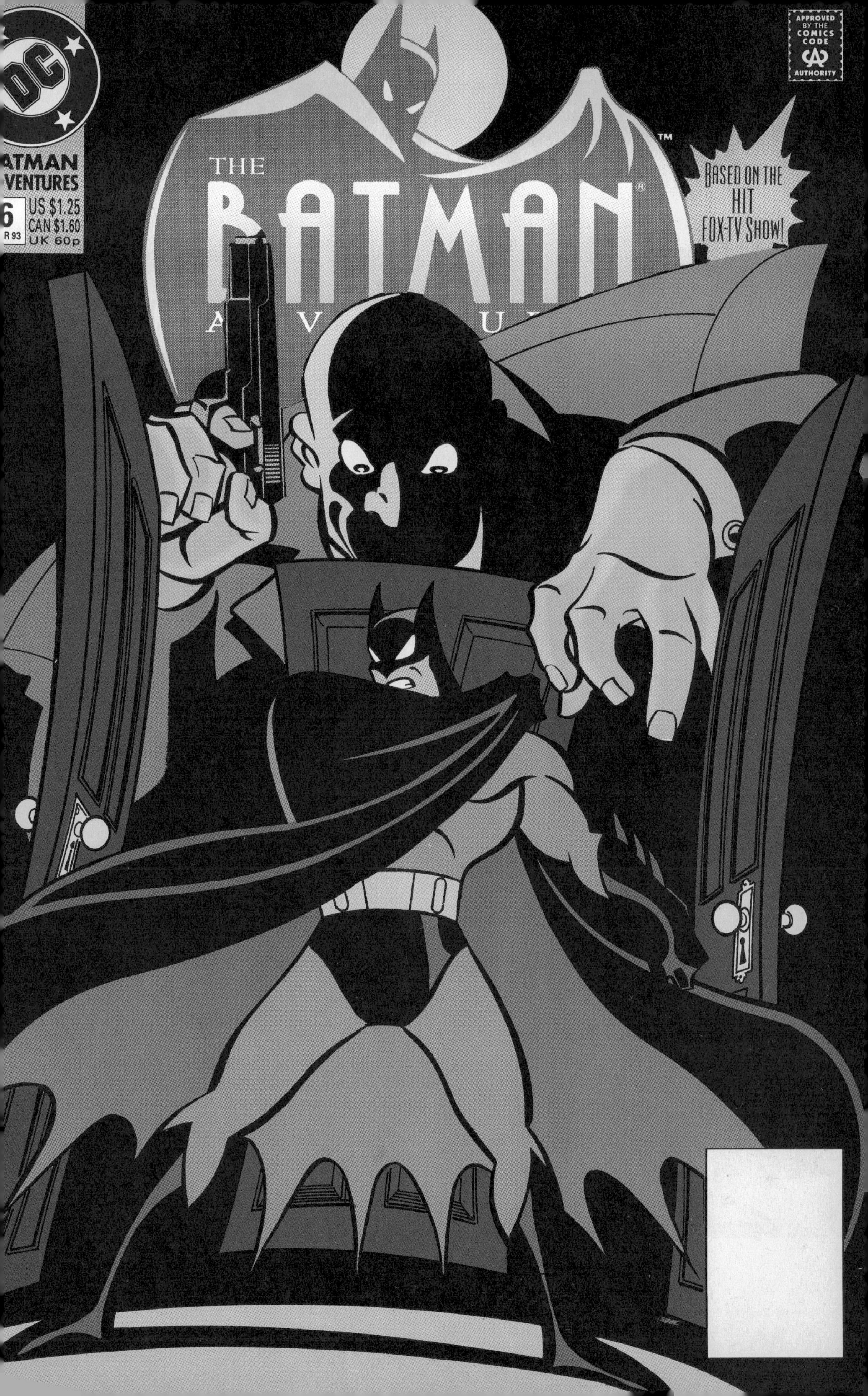

DC
BATMAN ADVENTURES
6
US $1.25
CAN $1.60
UK 60p
THE BATMAN ADVENTURES
BASED ON THE HIT FOX-TV SHOW!
APPROVED BY THE COMICS CODE AUTHORITY

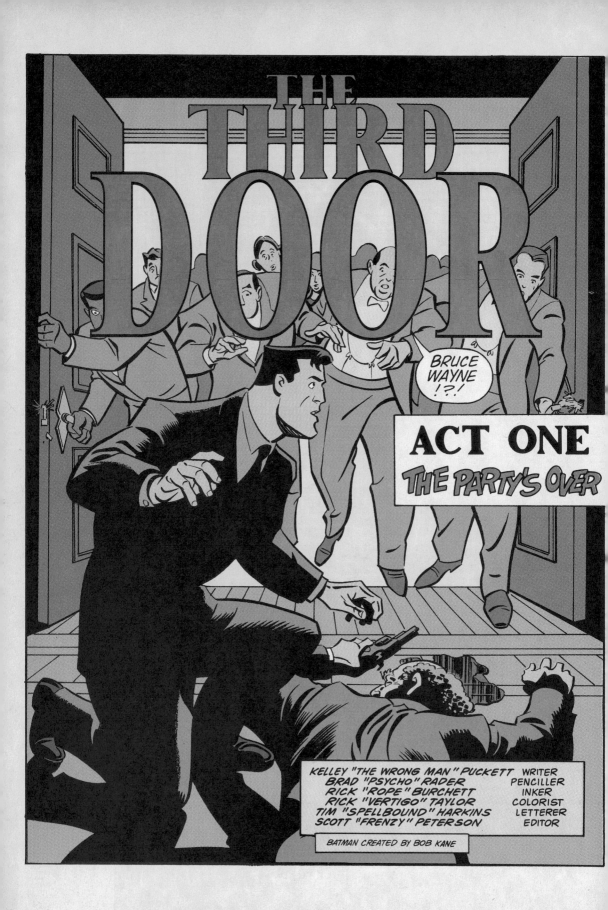

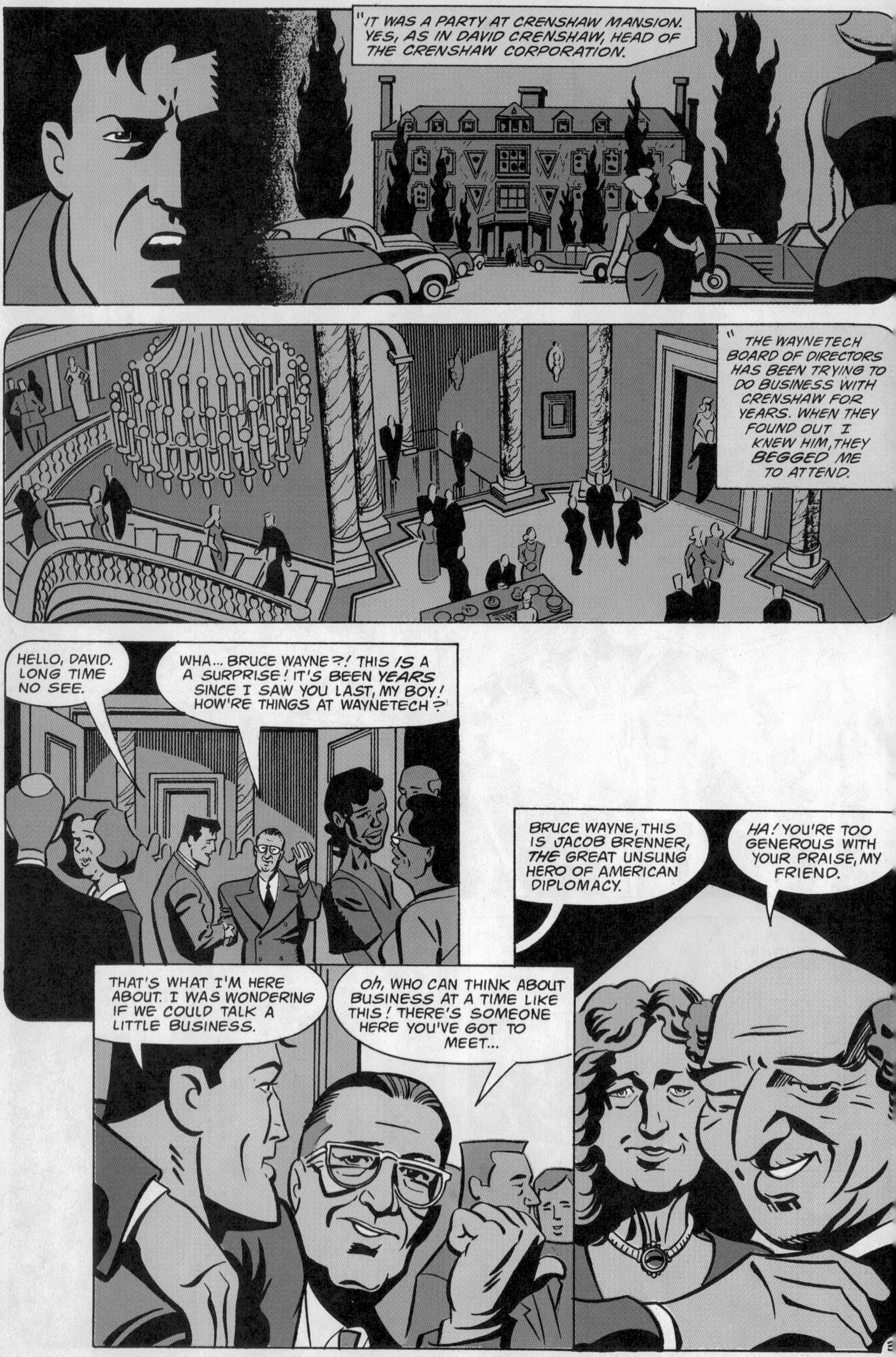
"IT WAS A PARTY AT CRENSHAW MANSION. YES, AS IN DAVID CRENSHAW, HEAD OF THE CRENSHAW CORPORATION.
"THE WAYNETECH BOARD OF DIRECTORS HAS BEEN TRYING TO DO BUSINESS WITH CRENSHAW FOR YEARS. WHEN THEY FOUND OUT I KNEW HIM, THEY BEGGED ME TO ATTEND.
HELLO, DAVID. LONG TIME NO SEE.
WHA... BRUCE WAYNE?! THIS IS A SURPRISE! IT'S BEEN YEARS SINCE I SAW YOU LAST, MY BOY! HOW'RE THINGS AT WAYNETECH?
THAT'S WHAT I'M HERE ABOUT. I WAS WONDERING IF WE COULD TALK A LITTLE BUSINESS.
OH, WHO CAN THINK ABOUT BUSINESS AT A TIME LIKE THIS! THERE'S SOMEONE HERE YOU'VE GOT TO MEET...
BRUCE WAYNE, THIS IS JACOB BRENNER, THE GREAT UNSUNG HERO OF AMERICAN DIPLOMACY.
HA! YOU'RE TOO GENEROUS WITH YOUR PRAISE, MY FRIEND.

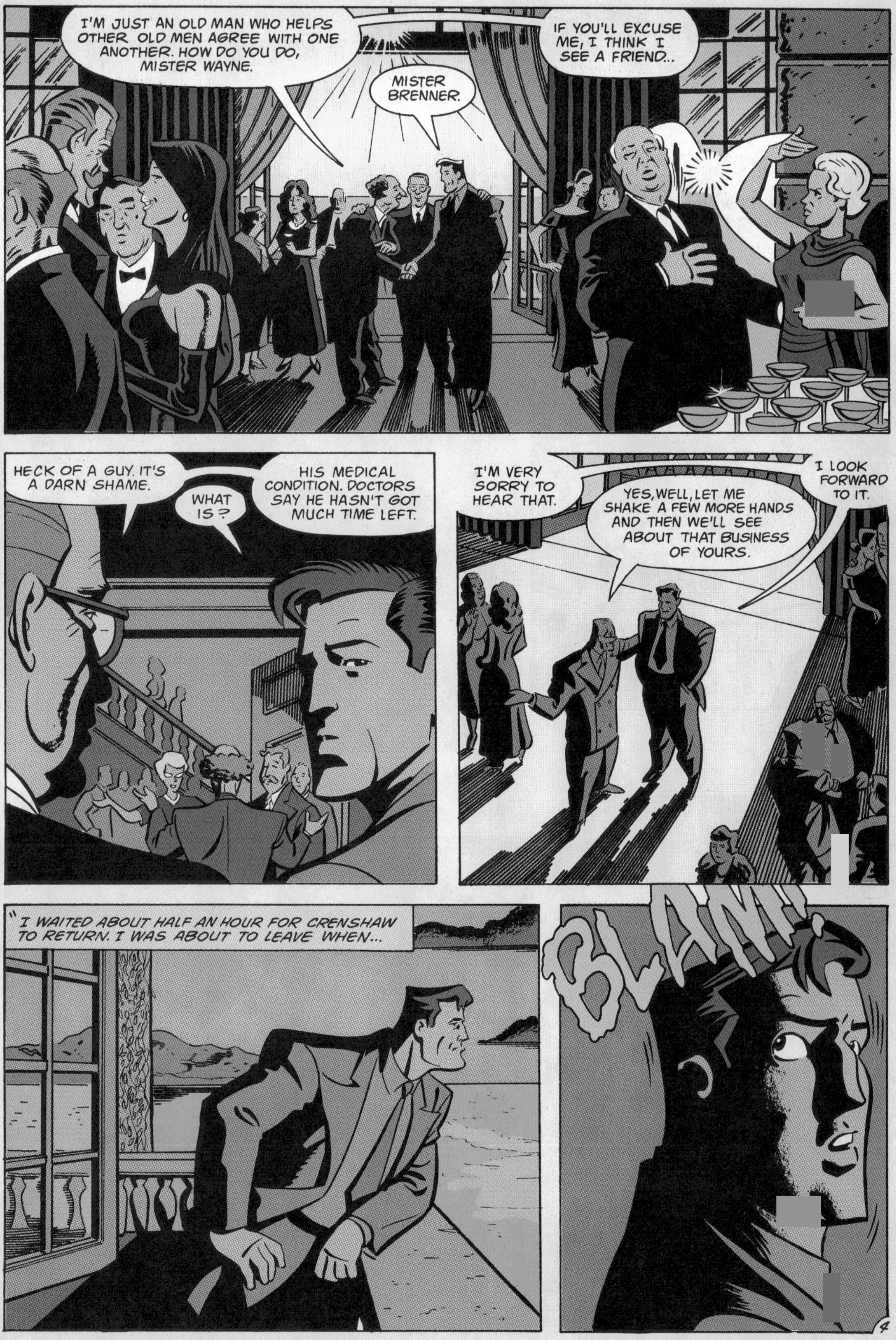
I'M JUST AN OLD MAN WHO HELPS OTHER OLD MEN AGREE WITH ONE ANOTHER. HOW DO YOU DO, MISTER WAYNE.
MISTER BRENNER.
IF YOU'LL EXCUSE ME, I THINK I SEE A FRIEND...
HECK OF A GUY. IT'S A DARN SHAME.
WHAT IS?
HIS MEDICAL CONDITION. DOCTORS SAY HE HASN'T GOT MUCH TIME LEFT.
I'M VERY SORRY TO HEAR THAT.
YES, WELL, LET ME SHAKE A FEW MORE HANDS AND THEN WE'LL SEE ABOUT THAT BUSINESS OF YOURS.
I LOOK FORWARD TO IT.
"I WAITED ABOUT HALF AN HOUR FOR CRENSHAW TO RETURN. I WAS ABOUT TO LEAVE WHEN...
BLAM!
4

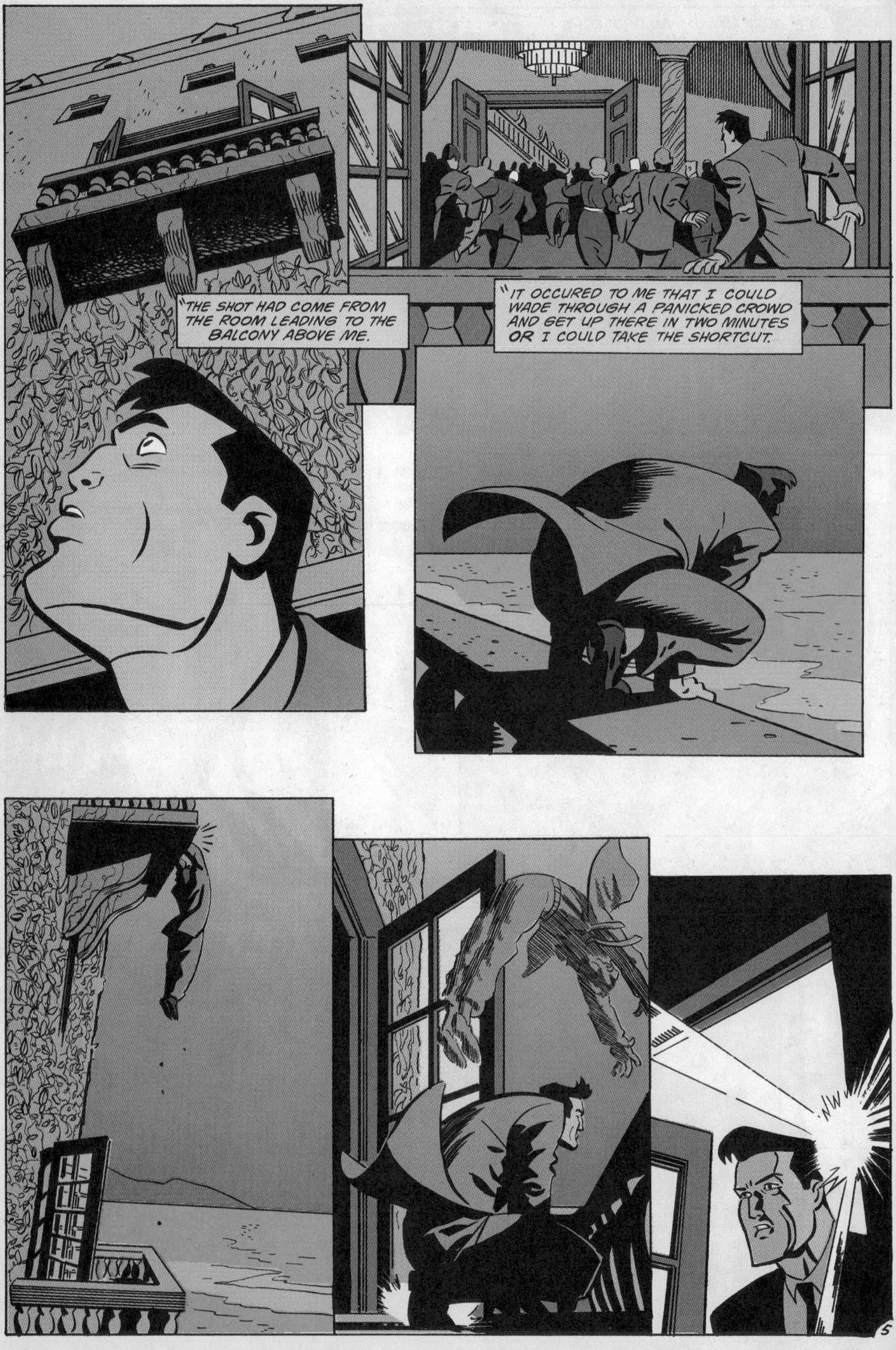
"THE SHOT HAD COME FROM THE ROOM LEADING TO THE BALCONY ABOVE ME.
"IT OCCURED TO ME THAT I COULD WADE THROUGH A PANICKED CROWD AND GET UP THERE IN TWO MINUTES OR I COULD TAKE THE SHORTCUT.
5

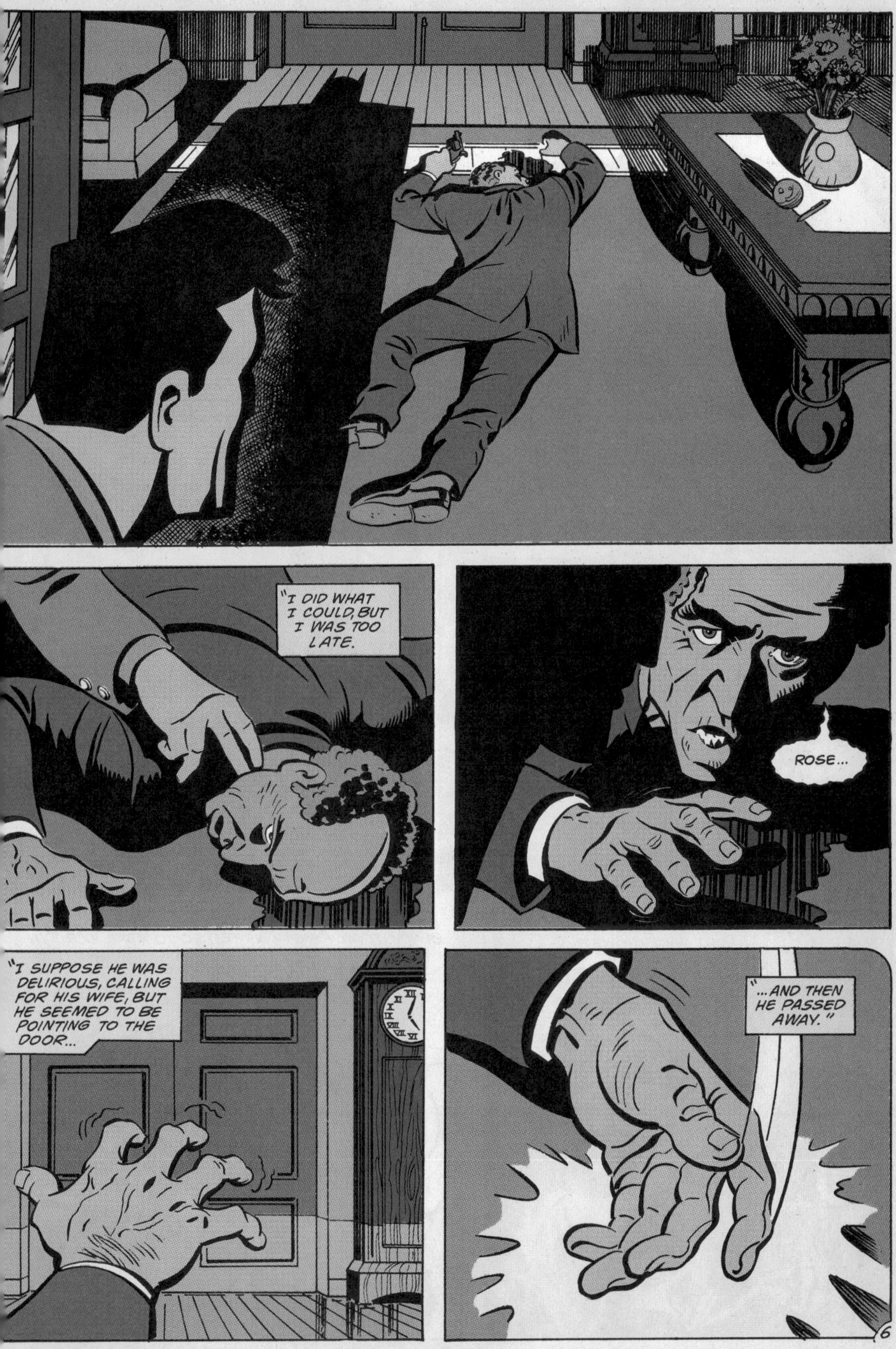
"I DID WHAT I COULD, BUT I WAS TOO LATE.
ROSE...
"I SUPPOSE HE WAS DELIRIOUS, CALLING FOR HIS WIFE, BUT HE SEEMED TO BE POINTING TO THE DOOR...
"...AND THEN HE PASSED AWAY."
6

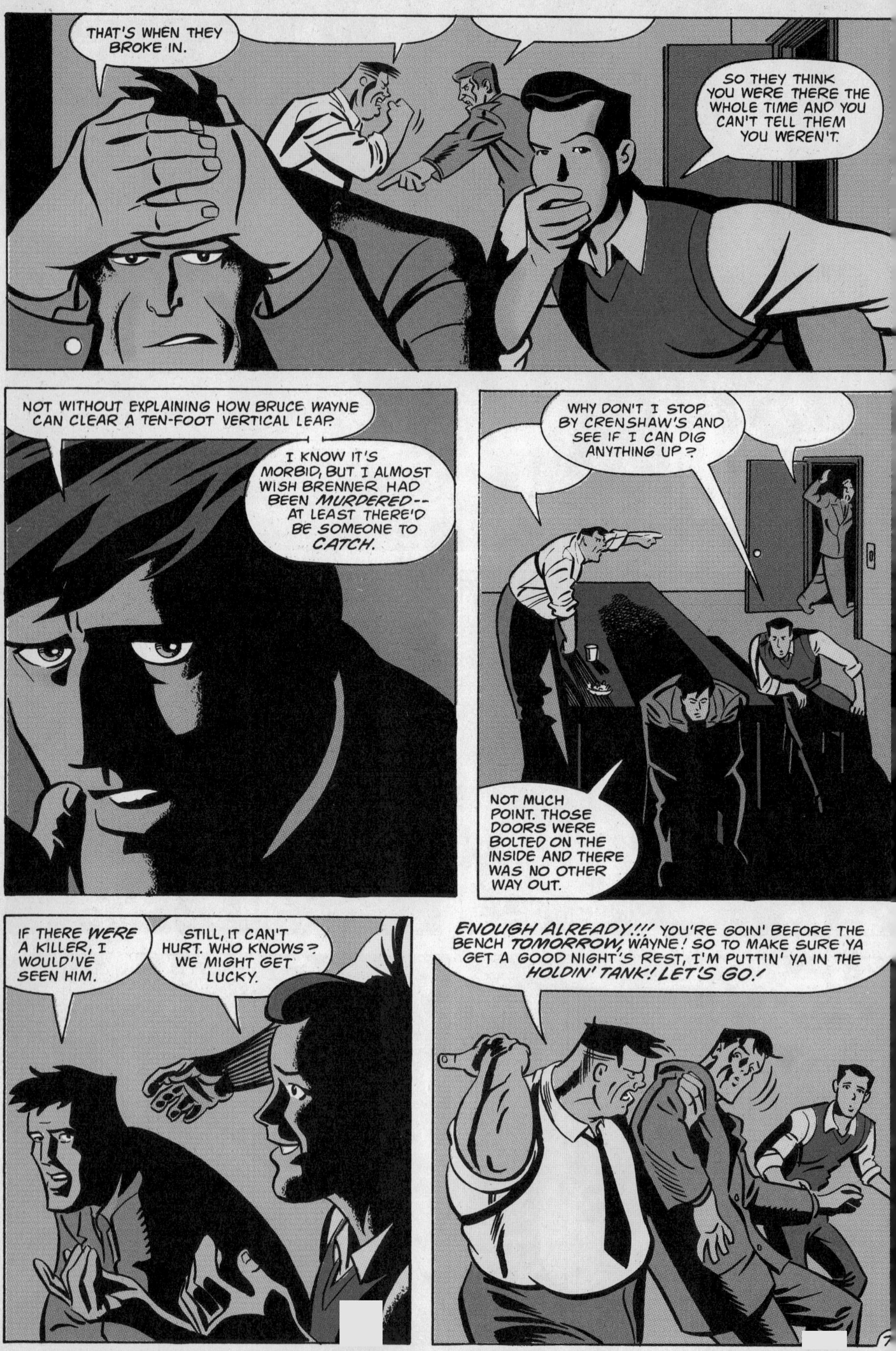
THAT'S WHEN THEY BROKE IN.
SO THEY THINK YOU WERE THERE THE WHOLE TIME AND YOU CAN'T TELL THEM YOU WEREN'T.
NOT WITHOUT EXPLAINING HOW BRUCE WAYNE CAN CLEAR A TEN-FOOT VERTICAL LEAP.
I KNOW IT'S MORBID, BUT I ALMOST WISH BRENNER HAD BEEN *MURDERED*-- AT LEAST THERE'D BE SOMEONE TO *CATCH*.
WHY DON'T I STOP BY CRENSHAW'S AND SEE IF I CAN DIG ANYTHING UP?
NOT MUCH POINT. THOSE DOORS WERE BOLTED ON THE INSIDE AND THERE WAS NO OTHER WAY OUT.
IF THERE *WERE* A KILLER, I WOULD'VE SEEN HIM.
STILL, IT CAN'T HURT. WHO KNOWS? WE MIGHT GET LUCKY.
ENOUGH ALREADY!!! YOU'RE GOIN' BEFORE THE BENCH *TOMORROW*, WAYNE! SO TO MAKE SURE YA GET A GOOD NIGHT'S REST, I'M PUTTIN' YA IN THE *HOLDIN' TANK! LET'S GO!*

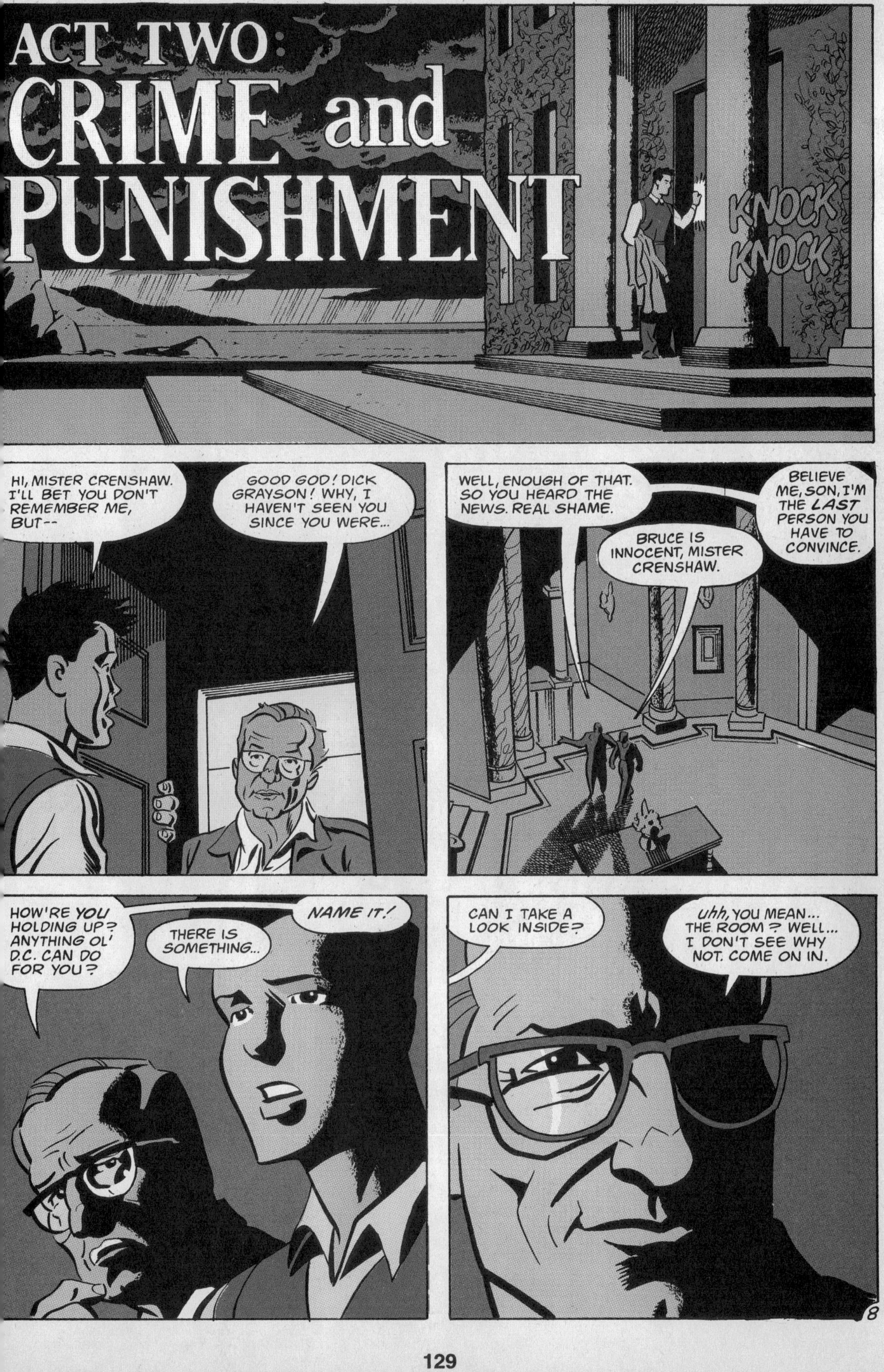
ACT TWO:
CRIME and PUNISHMENT
KNOCK KNOCK
HI, MISTER CRENSHAW. I'LL BET YOU DON'T REMEMBER ME, BUT--
GOOD GOD! DICK GRAYSON! WHY, I HAVEN'T SEEN YOU SINCE YOU WERE...
WELL, ENOUGH OF THAT. SO YOU HEARD THE NEWS. REAL SHAME.
BRUCE IS INNOCENT, MISTER CRENSHAW.
BELIEVE ME, SON, I'M THE LAST PERSON YOU HAVE TO CONVINCE.
HOW'RE YOU HOLDING UP? ANYTHING OL' D.C. CAN DO FOR YOU?
THERE IS SOMETHING...
NAME IT!
CAN I TAKE A LOOK INSIDE?
uhh, YOU MEAN... THE ROOM? WELL... I DON'T SEE WHY NOT. COME ON IN.
8

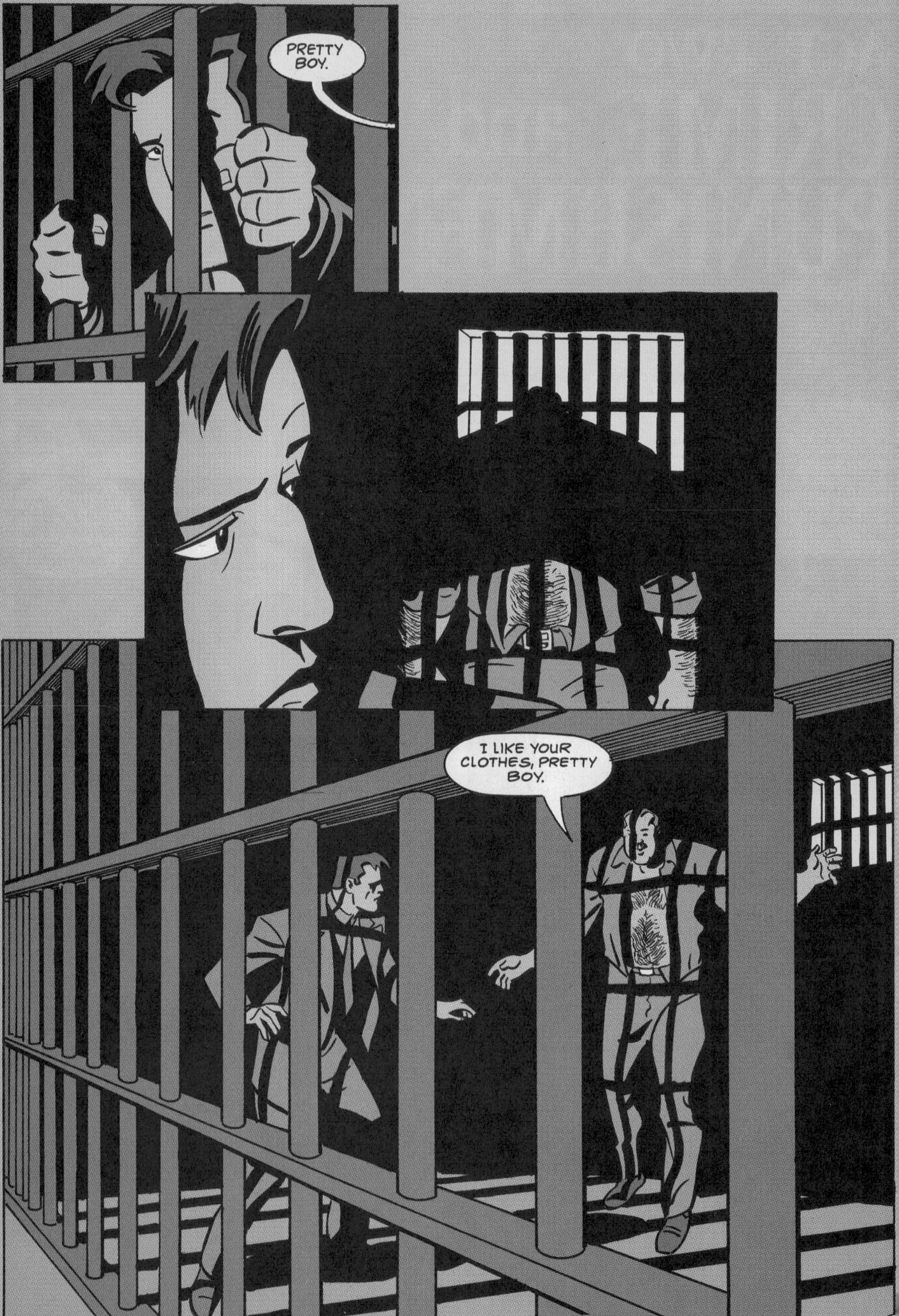
PRETTY BOY.
I LIKE YOUR CLOTHES, PRETTY BOY.

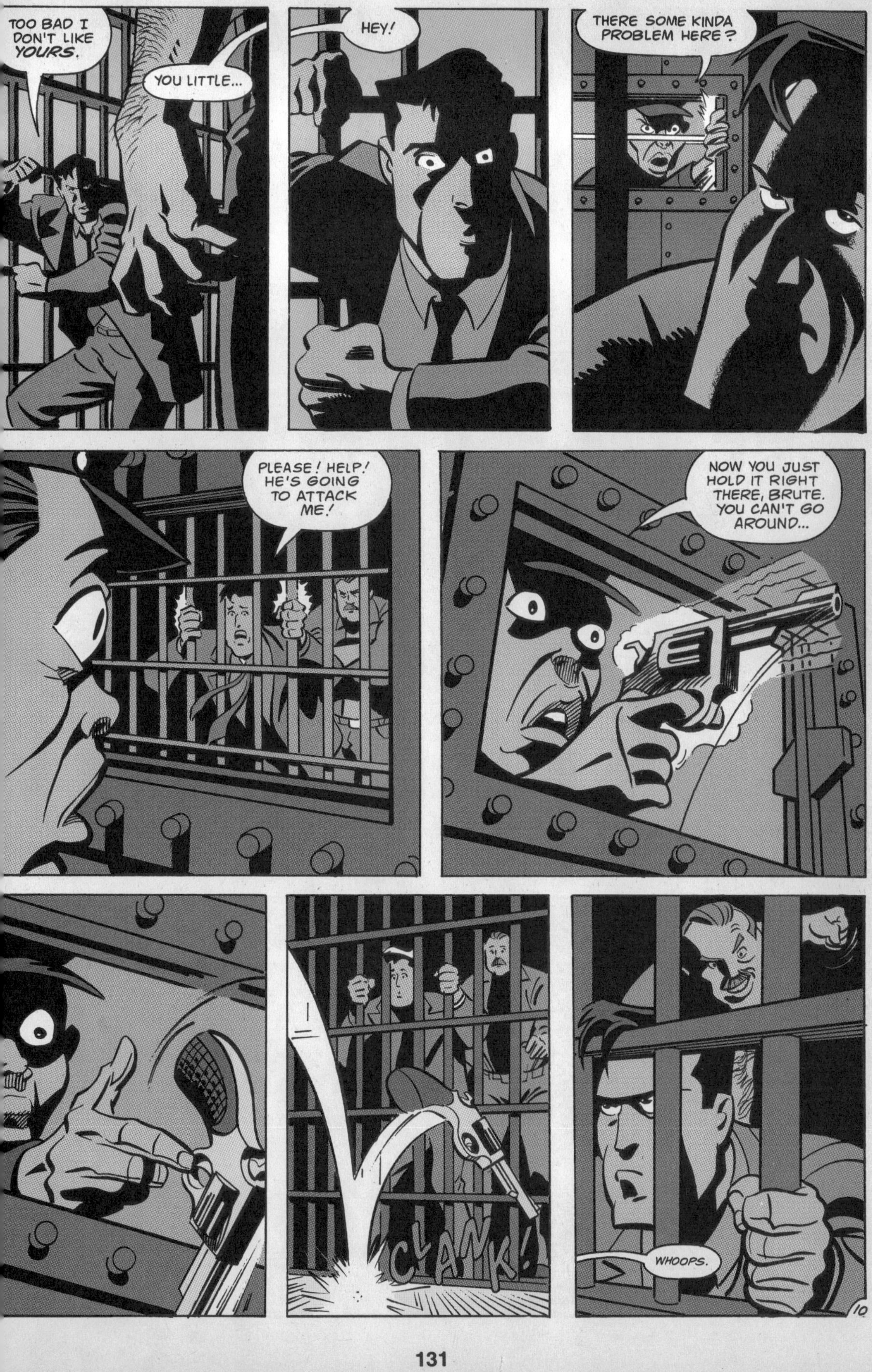
TOO BAD I DON'T LIKE *YOURS*.
YOU LITTLE...
HEY!
THERE SOME KINDA PROBLEM HERE?
PLEASE! HELP! HE'S GOING TO ATTACK ME!
NOW YOU JUST HOLD IT RIGHT THERE, BRUTE. YOU CAN'T GO AROUND...
CLANK!
WHOOPS.
10

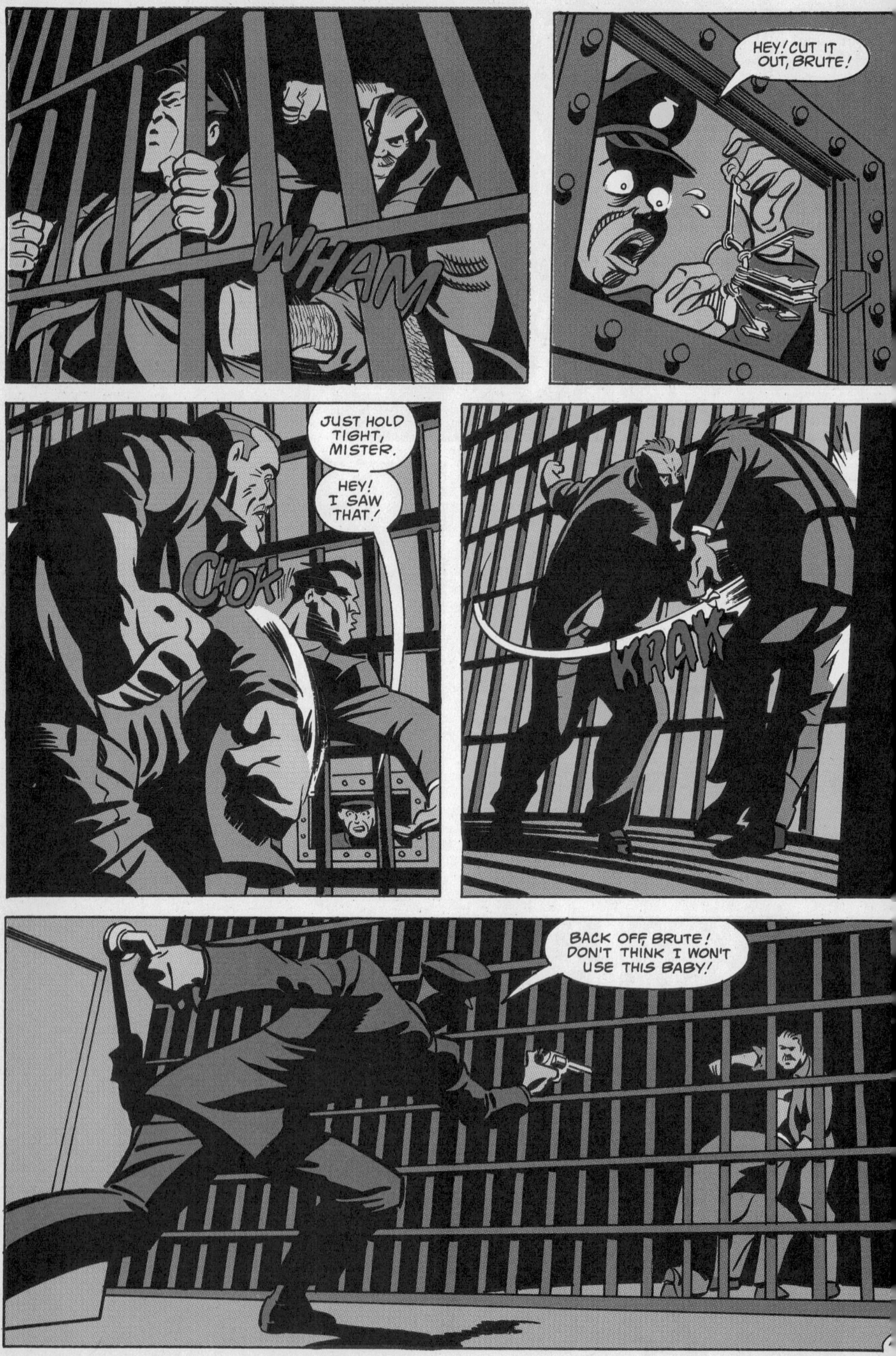
WHAM
HEY! CUT IT OUT, BRUTE!
JUST HOLD TIGHT, MISTER.
HEY! I SAW THAT!
CHOK
KRAK
BACK OFF, BRUTE! DON'T THINK I WON'T USE THIS BABY!

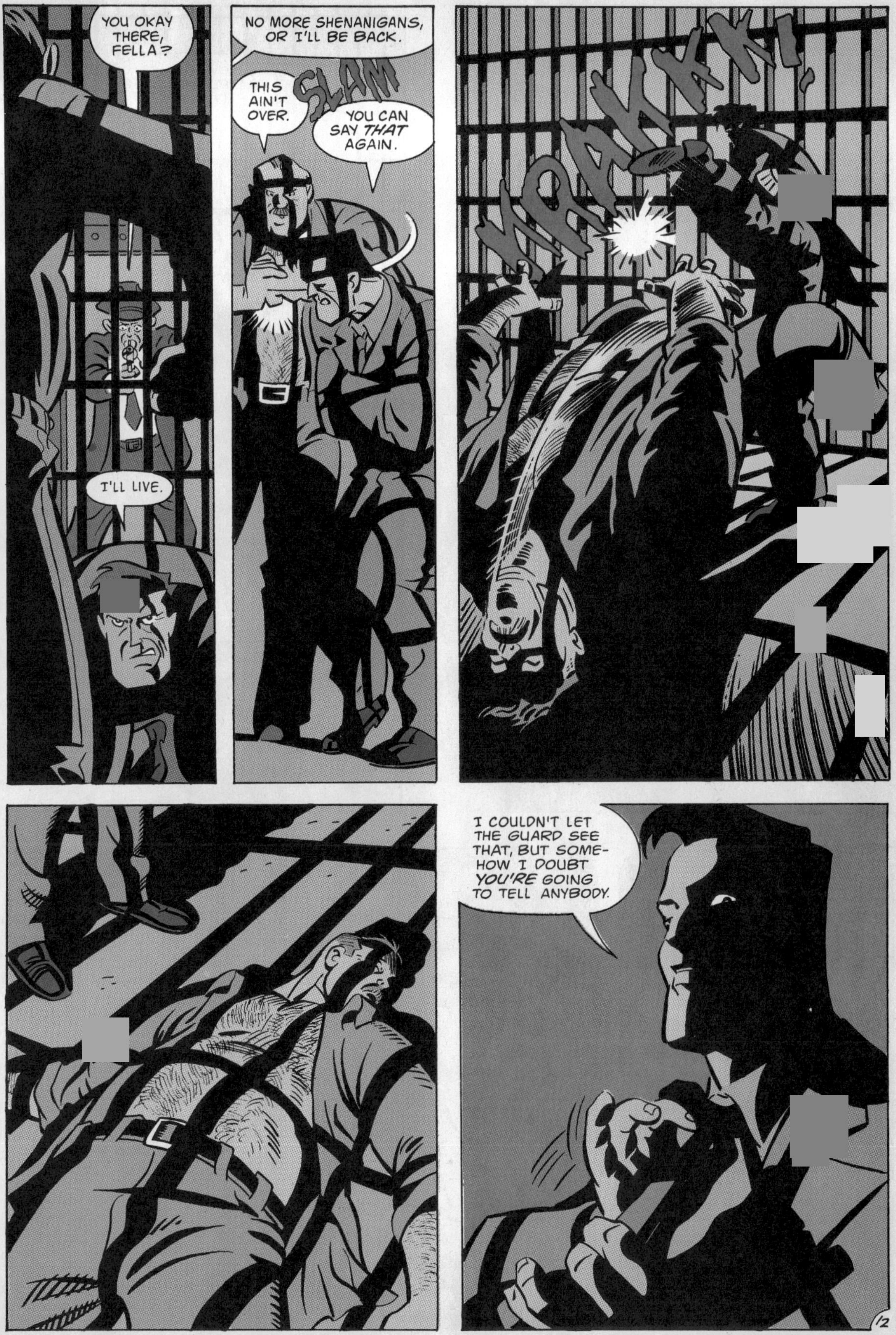
YOU OKAY THERE, FELLA?
I'LL LIVE.
NO MORE SHENANIGANS, OR I'LL BE BACK.
THIS AIN'T OVER.
SLAM
YOU CAN SAY THAT AGAIN.
I COULDN'T LET THE GUARD SEE THAT, BUT SOMEHOW I DOUBT YOU'RE GOING TO TELL ANYBODY.
12

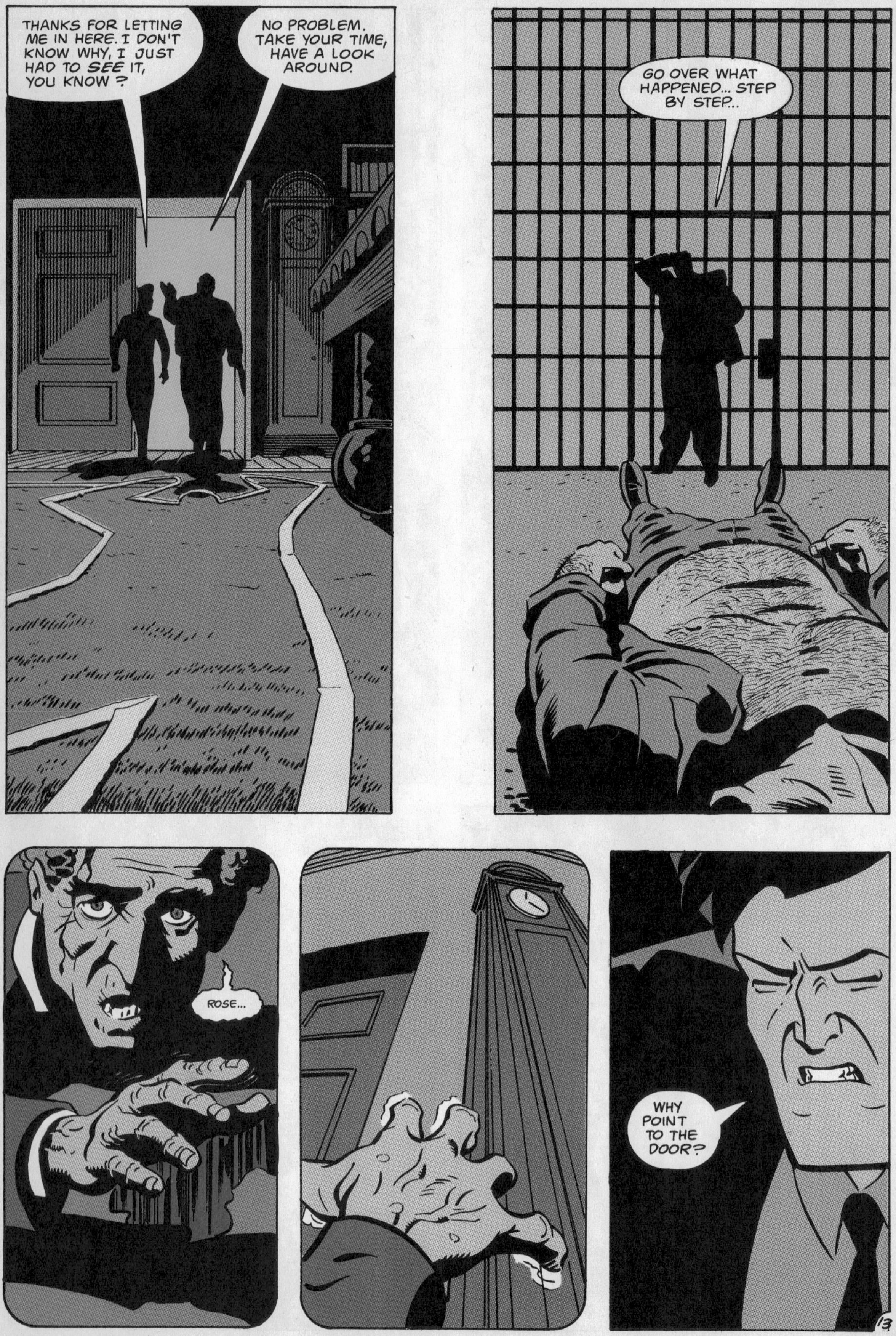
THANKS FOR LETTING ME IN HERE. I DON'T KNOW WHY, I JUST HAD TO SEE IT, YOU KNOW?
NO PROBLEM. TAKE YOUR TIME, HAVE A LOOK AROUND.
GO OVER WHAT HAPPENED... STEP BY STEP...
ROSE...
WHY POINT TO THE DOOR?
13

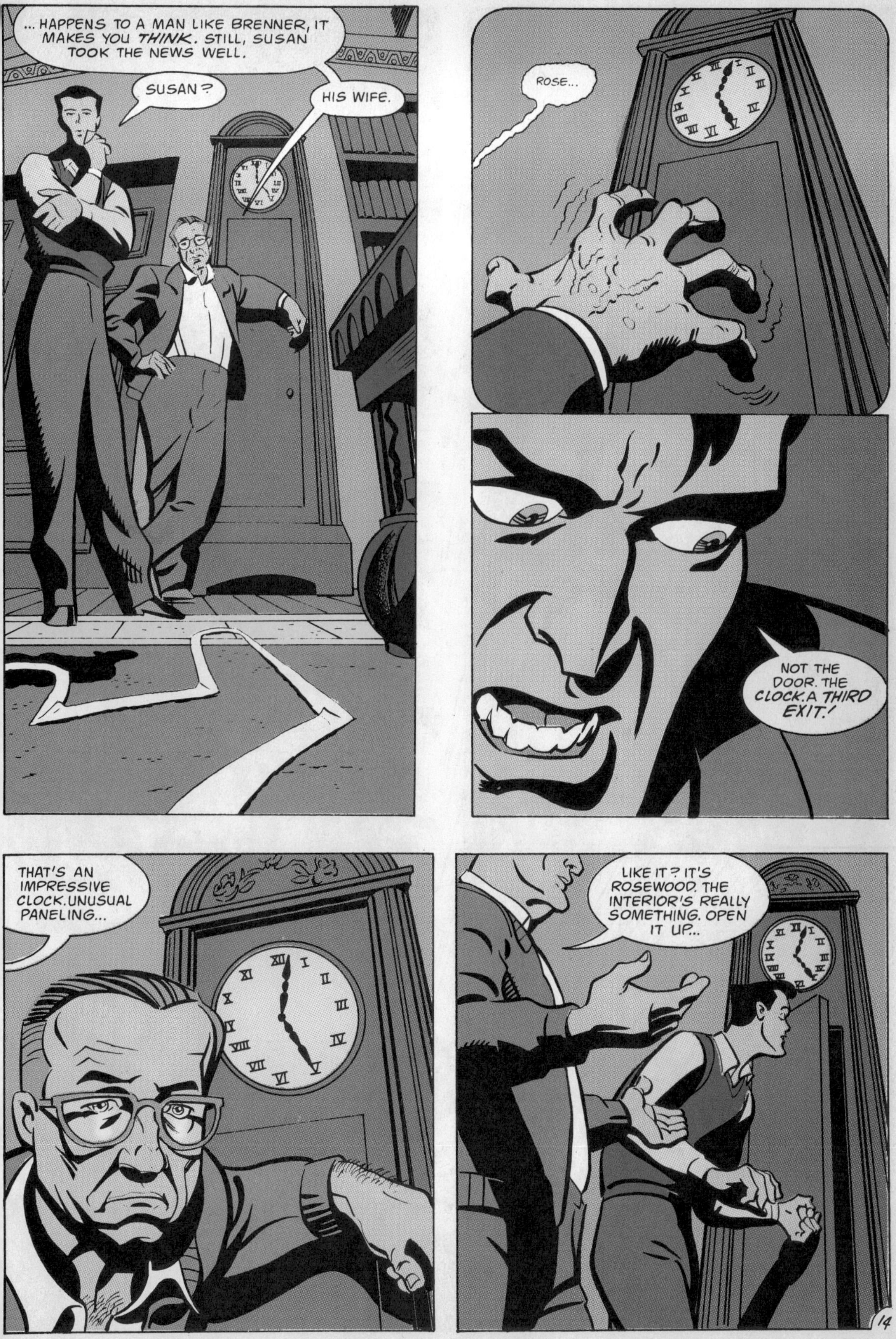
...HAPPENS TO A MAN LIKE BRENNER, IT MAKES YOU *THINK*. STILL, SUSAN TOOK THE NEWS WELL.
SUSAN?
HIS WIFE.
ROSE...
NOT THE DOOR. THE CLOCK. A *THIRD EXIT!*
THAT'S AN IMPRESSIVE CLOCK. UNUSUAL PANELING...
LIKE IT? IT'S ROSEWOOD. THE INTERIOR'S REALLY SOMETHING. OPEN IT UP...
14

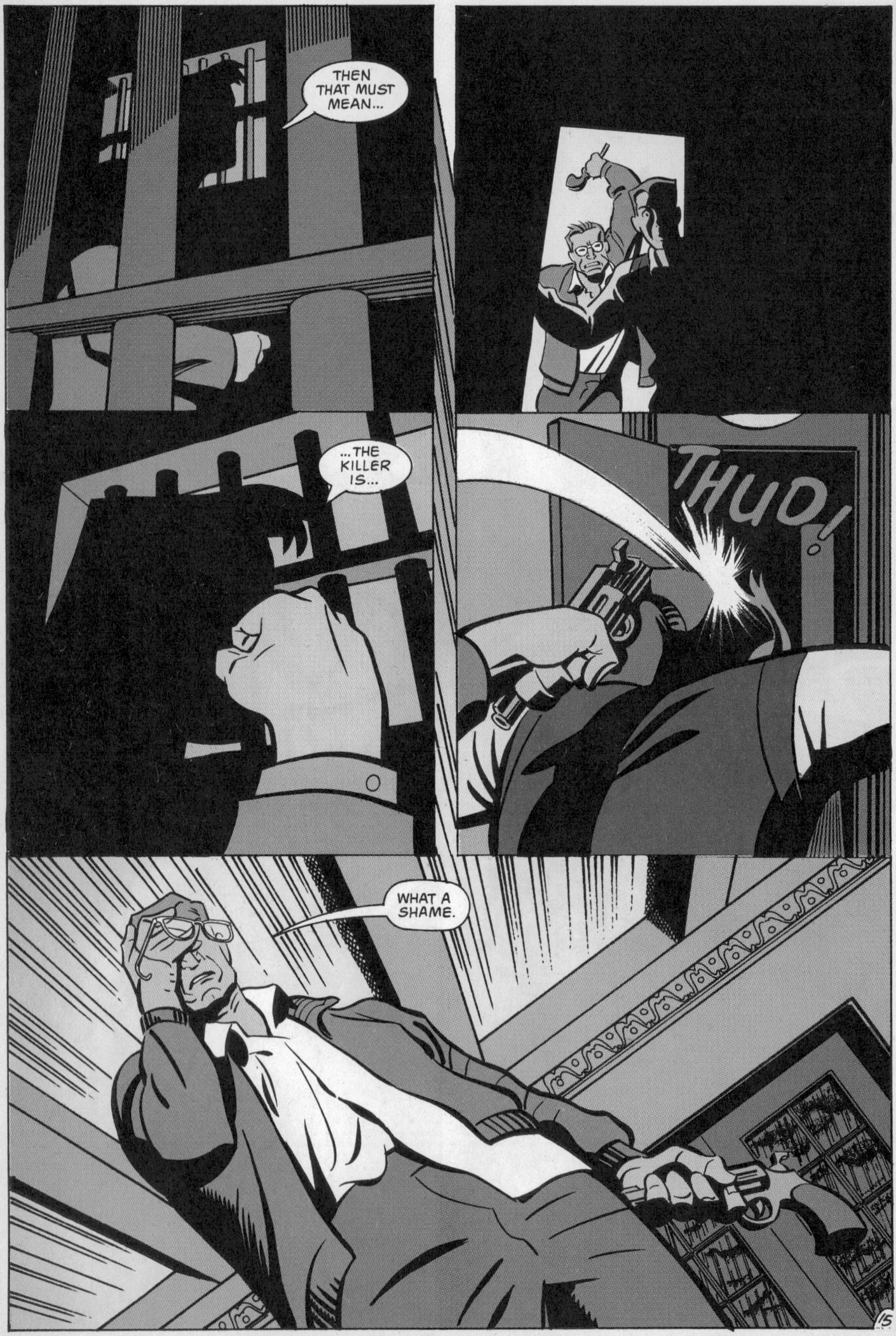
THEN THAT MUST MEAN...
...THE KILLER IS...
THUD!
WHAT A SHAME.
15

ACT THREE
WAR AND PEACE

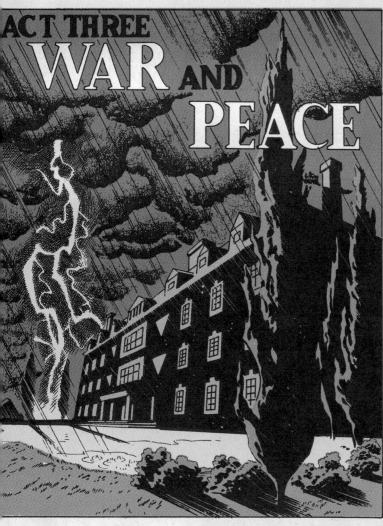

HAVE TO STAY *CALM.* THE DRIVER WILL BE HERE *SOON.*

I'LL FLY SOUTH, RELAX, REVIEW MY OPTIONS. GET RID OF THE... *LIABILITY* ALONG THE WAY. WHAT'S NEEDED NOW IS *PATIENCE.*

WHAT'S TAKING HIM SO LONG?!?

16

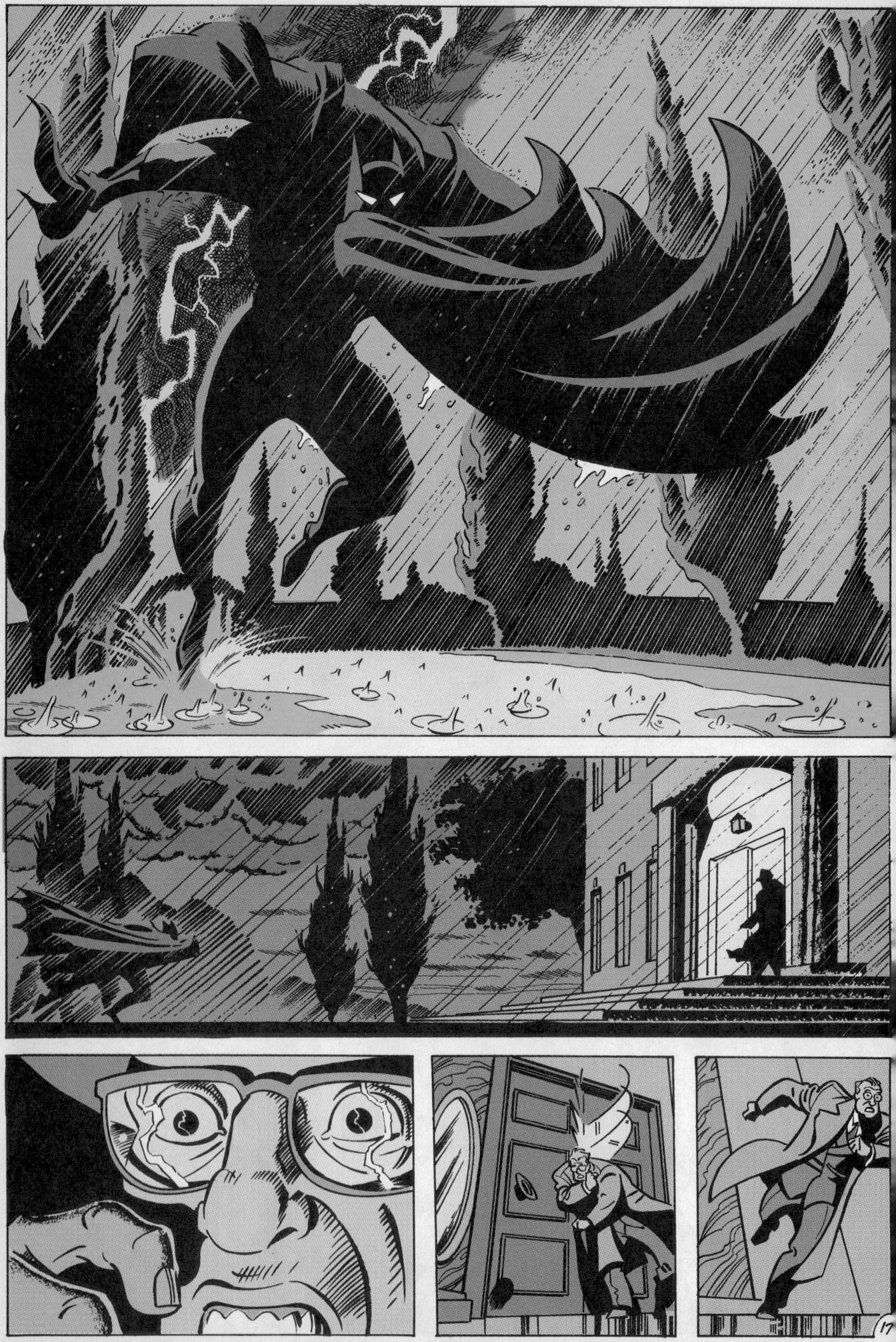

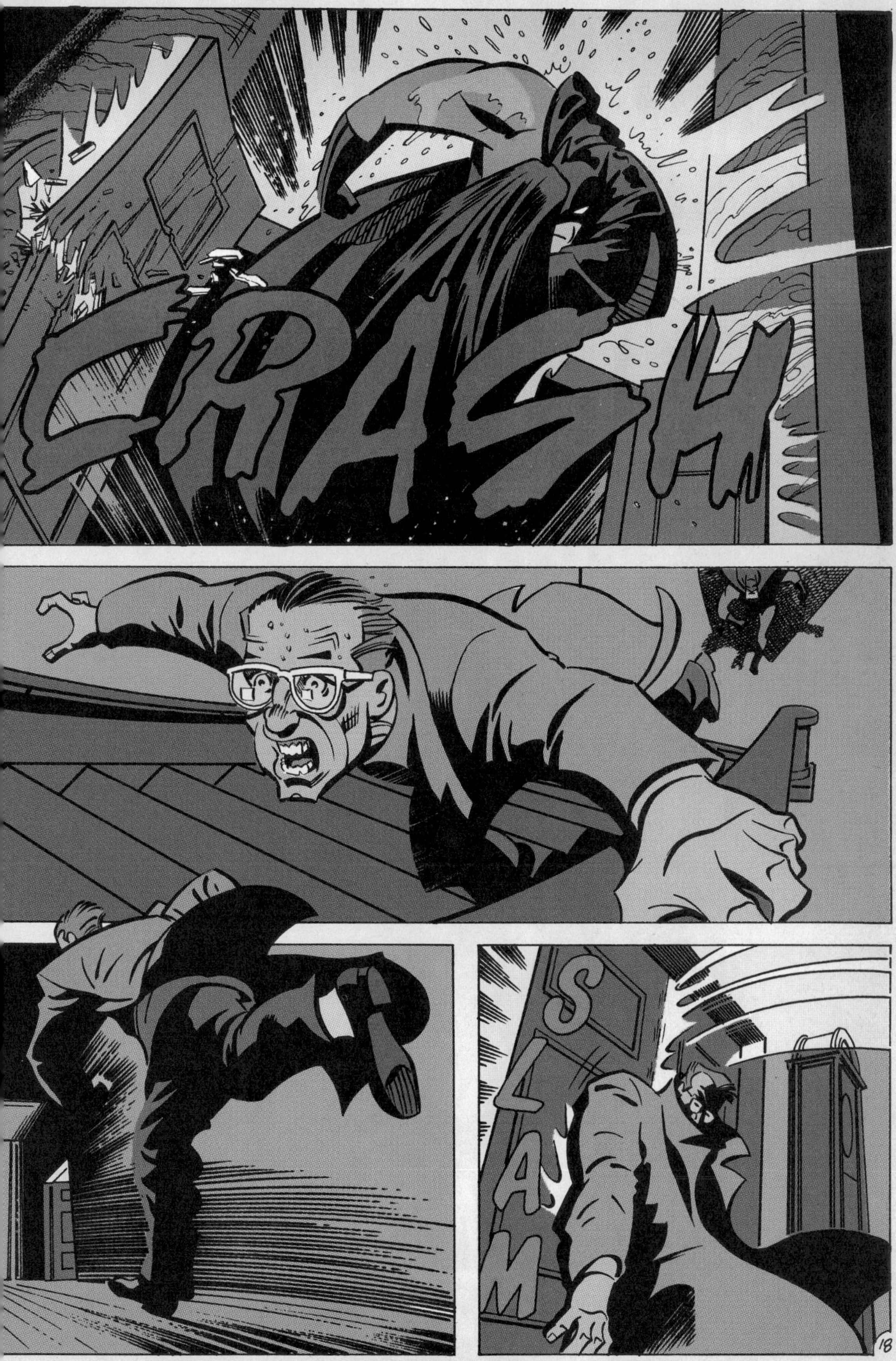
CRASH
SLAM
18

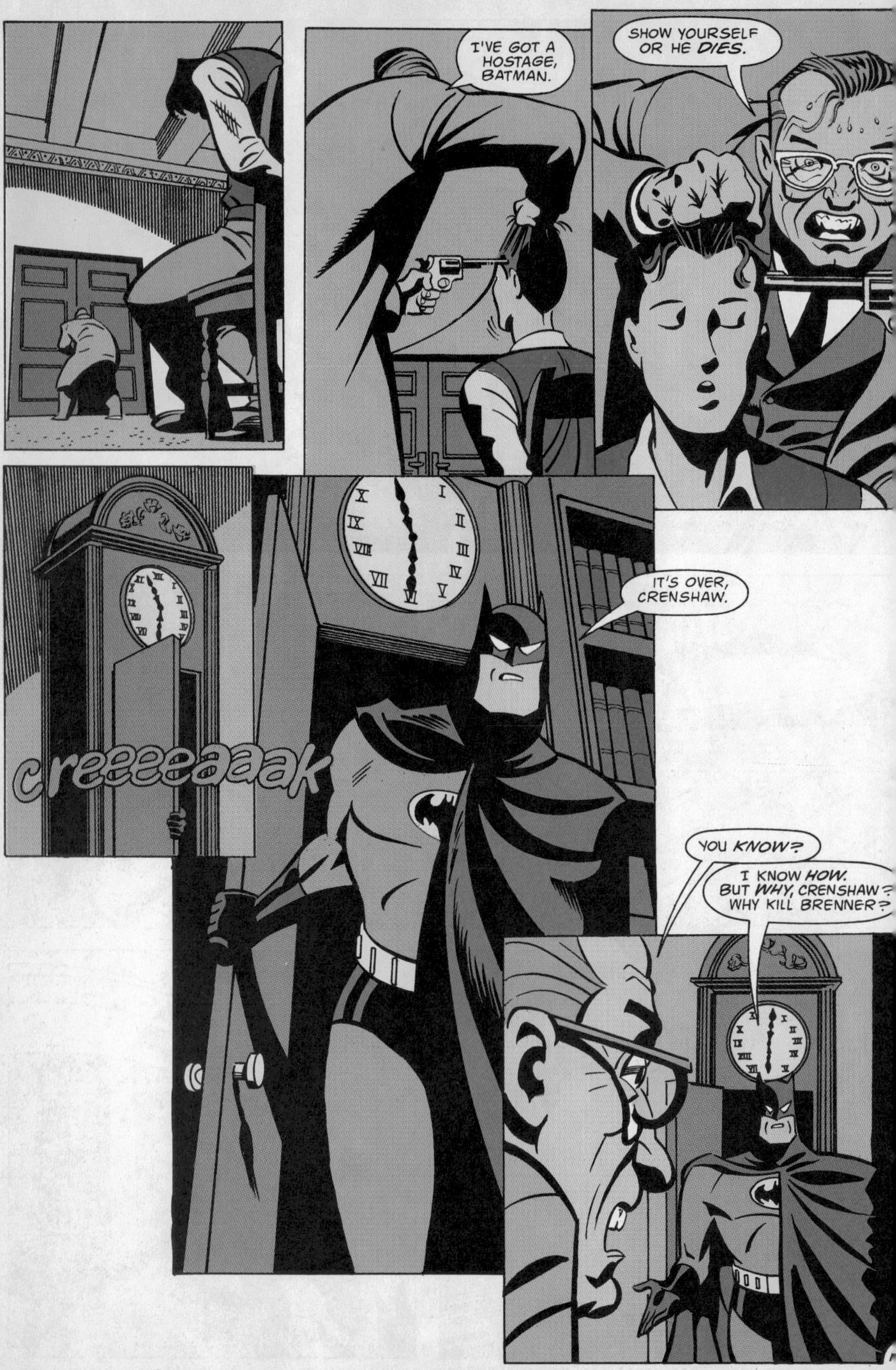
I'VE GOT A HOSTAGE, BATMAN.
SHOW YOURSELF OR HE DIES.
creeeeaaak
IT'S OVER, CRENSHAW.
YOU KNOW?
I KNOW HOW. BUT WHY, CRENSHAW? WHY KILL BRENNER?

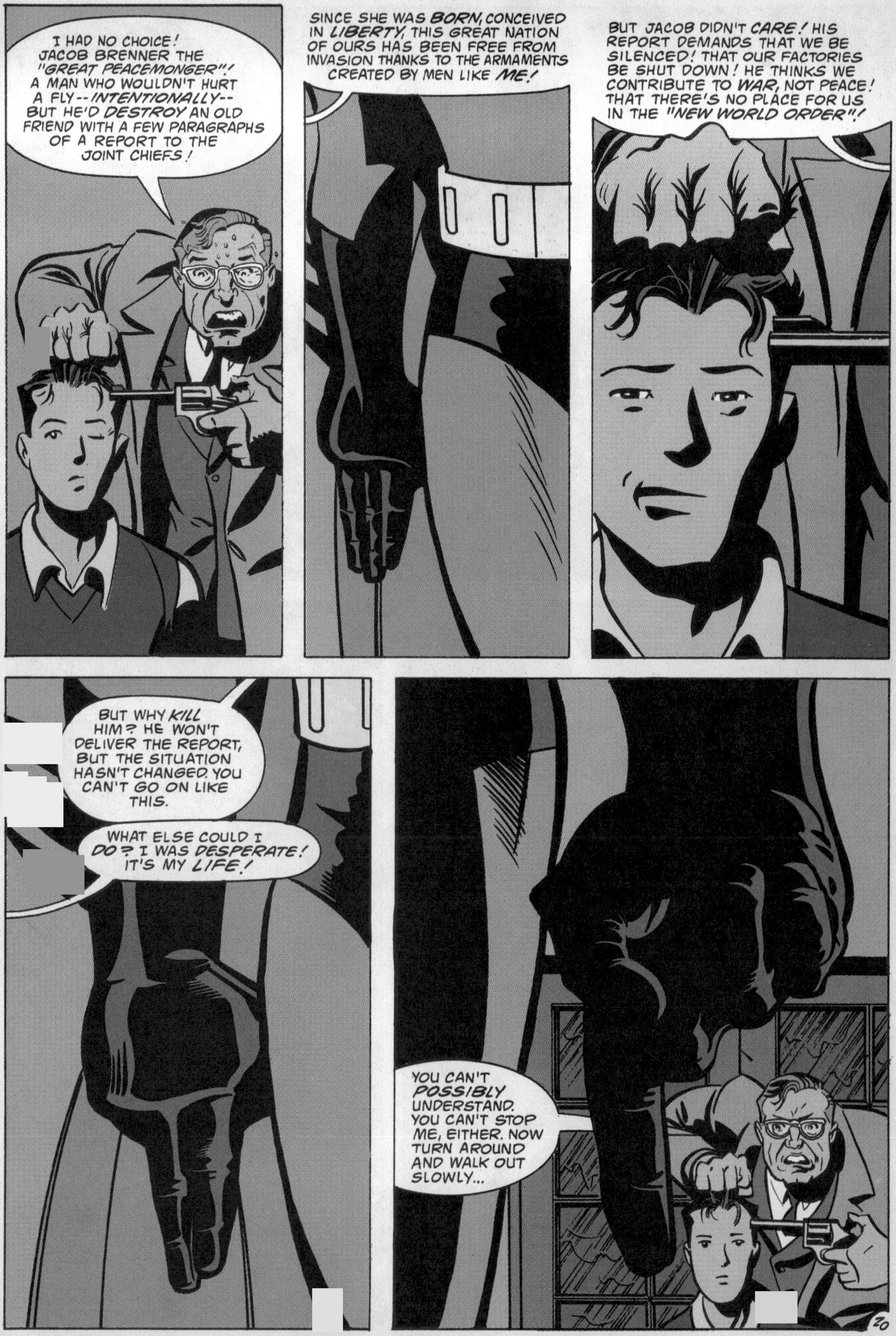
I HAD NO CHOICE! JACOB BRENNER THE "GREAT PEACEMONGER"! A MAN WHO WOULDN'T HURT A FLY--INTENTIONALLY--BUT HE'D DESTROY AN OLD FRIEND WITH A FEW PARAGRAPHS OF A REPORT TO THE JOINT CHIEFS!
SINCE SHE WAS BORN, CONCEIVED IN LIBERTY, THIS GREAT NATION OF OURS HAS BEEN FREE FROM INVASION THANKS TO THE ARMAMENTS CREATED BY MEN LIKE ME!
BUT JACOB DIDN'T CARE! HIS REPORT DEMANDS THAT WE BE SILENCED! THAT OUR FACTORIES BE SHUT DOWN! HE THINKS WE CONTRIBUTE TO WAR, NOT PEACE! THAT THERE'S NO PLACE FOR US IN THE "NEW WORLD ORDER"!
BUT WHY KILL HIM? HE WON'T DELIVER THE REPORT, BUT THE SITUATION HASN'T CHANGED. YOU CAN'T GO ON LIKE THIS.
WHAT ELSE COULD I DO? I WAS DESPERATE! IT'S MY LIFE!
YOU CAN'T POSSIBLY UNDERSTAND. YOU CAN'T STOP ME, EITHER. NOW TURN AROUND AND WALK OUT SLOWLY...
20

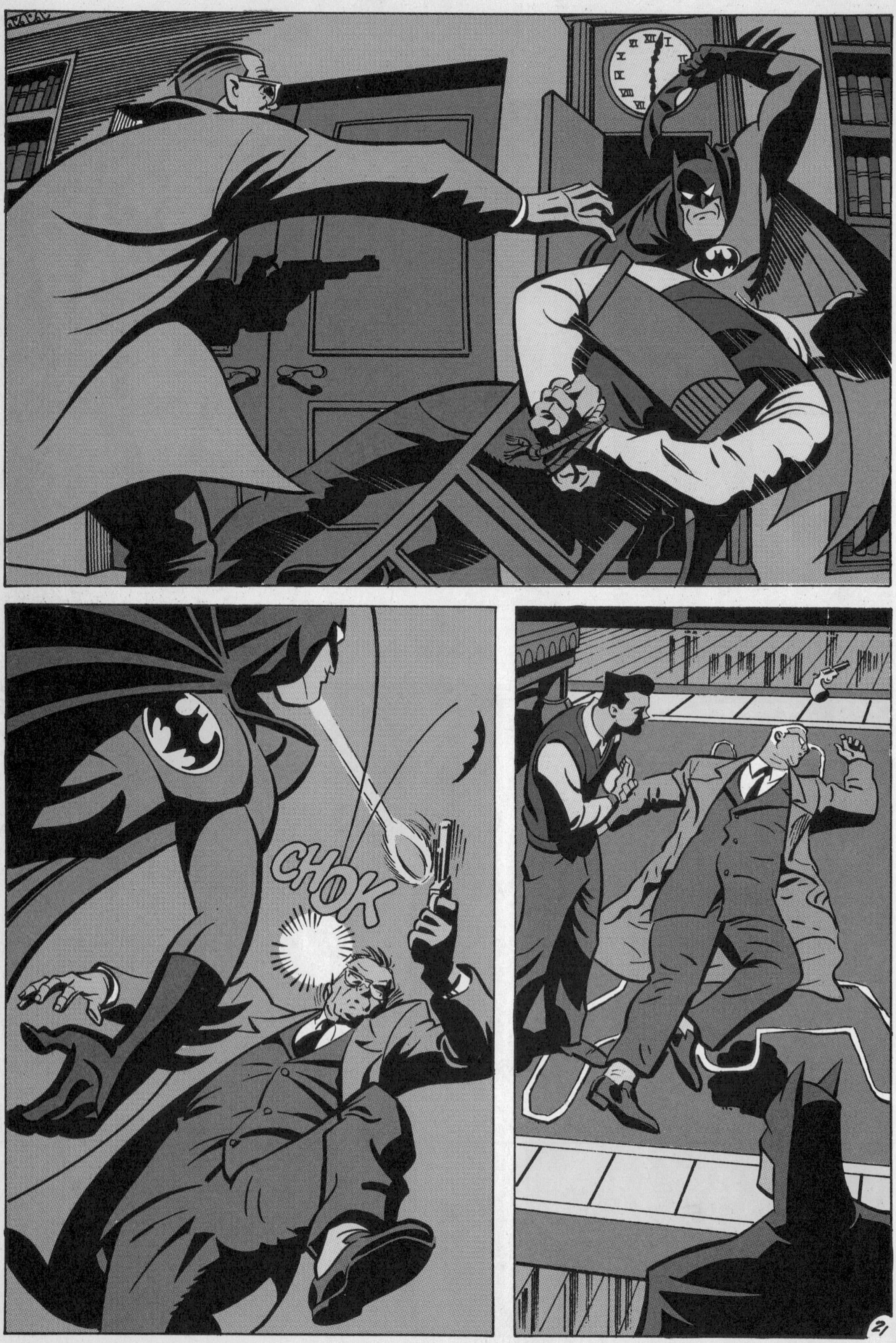
CHOK
21

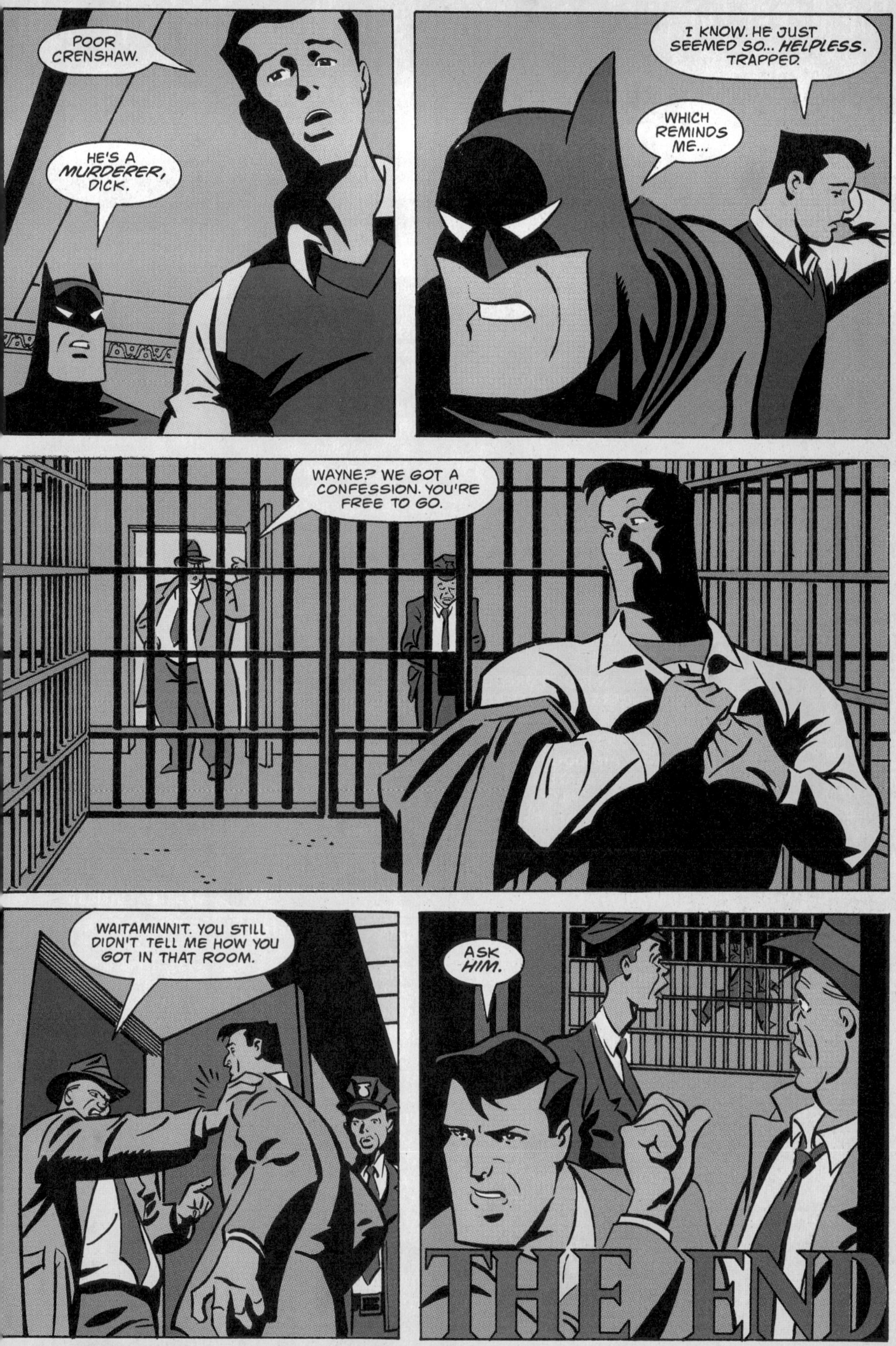
POOR CRENSHAW.
HE'S A MURDERER, DICK.
I KNOW. HE JUST SEEMED SO... HELPLESS. TRAPPED.
WHICH REMINDS ME...
WAYNE? WE GOT A CONFESSION. YOU'RE FREE TO GO.
WAITAMINNIT. YOU STILL DIDN'T TELL ME HOW YOU GOT IN THAT ROOM.
ASK HIM.
THE END

The Quest for Justice Continues in These Books from DC:

GRAPHIC NOVELS

AZRAEL/ASH
Dennis O'Neil/Joe Quesada/
Jimmy Palmiotti

THE BATMAN ADVENTURES: MAD LOVE
Paul Dini/Bruce Timm

BATMAN CHRONICLES: THE GAUNTLET
Bruce Canwell/Lee Weeks

BATMAN & DRACULA: RED RAIN
Doug Moench/Kelley
Jones/Malcolm Jones III

BATMAN & HOUDINI: THE DEVIL'S WORKSHOP
Howard Chaykin/John Francis
Moore/Mark Chiarello

BATMAN & SPIDER-MAN
J. M. DeMatteis/Graham
Nolan/Karl Kesel

BATMAN FOREVER MOVIE ADAPTATION
Dennis O'Neil/Michal
Dutkiewicz/Scott Hanna

BATMAN RETURNS MOVIE ADAPTATION
Dennis O'Neil/Steve Erwin/
Jose Luis Garcia-Lopez

BATMAN: ARKHAM ASYLUM
Suggested for mature readers
Grant Morrison/Dave McKean

BATMAN: BANE
Chuck Dixon/Rick Burchett

BATMAN: BIRTH OF THE DEMON
Dennis O'Neil/Norm Breyfogle

BATMAN: BLOODSTORM
Doug Moench/Kelley Jones/
John Beatty

BATMAN: CASTLE OF THE BAT
Jack C. Harris/Bo Hampton

BATMAN: DARK ALLEGIANCES
Howard Chaykin

BATMAN: FULL CIRCLE
Mike W. Barr/Alan Davis/
Mark Farmer

BATMAN: GOTHAM BY GASLIGHT
Brian Augustyn/Mike Mignola/
P. Craig Russell

BATMAN: HOLY TERROR
Alan Brennert/Norm Breyfogle

BATMAN: THE KILLING JOKE
Suggested for mature readers
Alan Moore/Brian Bolland/
John Higgins

BATMAN: MASQUE
Mike Grell

BATMAN: MASTER OF THE FUTURE
Brian Augustyn/Eduardo Barreto

BATMAN: MR. FREEZE
Paul Dini/Mark Buckingham/
Wayne Faucher

BATMAN: NIGHT CRIES
Archie Goodwin/Scott Hampton

BATMAN: SCAR OF THE BAT
Max Allan Collins/Eduardo Barreto

BATMAN: SON OF THE DEMON
Mike W. Barr/Jerry Bingham

BATMAN/DEADMAN: DEATH & GLORY
James Robinson/John Estes

BATMAN/DEMON
Alan Grant/David Roach

BATMAN/GREEN ARROW: THE POISON TOMORROW
Dennis O'Neil/Mike Netzer/
Josef Rubinstein

BATMAN/JUDGE DREDD: JUDGMENT ON GOTHAM
Alan Grant/John Wagner/
Simon Bisley

BATMAN/JUDGE DREDD: VENDETTA IN GOTHAM
Alan Grant/John Wagner/
Cam Kennedy

BATMAN/JUDGE DREDD: THE ULTIMATE RIDDLE
Alan Grant /Carl Critchlow

BATMAN/RIDDLER: THE RIDDLE FACTORY
Matt Wagner/Dave Taylor

BATMAN/SPAWN: WAR DEVIL
Doug Moench/Chuck Dixon/
Alan Grant/Klaus Janson

BATMAN/TWO-FACE: CRIME AND PUNISHMENT
J. M. DeMatteis/Scott McDaniel

CATWOMAN/VAMPIRELLA: THE FURIES
Chuck Dixon/Jim Balent/
Ray McCarthy

THE JOKER: DEVIL'S ADVOCATE
Chuck Dixon/John Ostrander
Graham Nolan/Scott Hanna

PENGUIN TRIUMPHANT
John Ostrander/Joe Staton/
Bob Smith

COLLECTIONS

BATMAN VS. PREDATOR: THE COLLECTED EDITION
Dave Gibbons/Andy Kubert/
Adam Kubert

BATMAN VS. PREDATOR II: BLOODMATCH
Doug Moench/Paul Gulacy/
Terry Austin

BATMAN: A DEATH IN THE FAMILY
Jim Starlin/Jim Aparo/
Mike DeCarlo

BATMAN: A LONELY PLACE OF DYING
Marv Wolfman/George Pérez/
various

BATMAN: COLLECTED LEGENDS OF THE DARK KNIGHT
Robinson/Moore/Grant/Sale/
Russell/O'Neil

BATMAN: CONTAGION
Various writers and artists

BATMAN: THE DARK KNIGHT RETURNS 10TH ANNIVERSARY EDITION
Frank Miller/Lynn Varley/
Klaus Janson

BATMAN: DARK LEGENDS
Various writers and artists

BATMAN: FACES
Matt Wagner

BATMAN: FEATURING TWO-FACE AND THE RIDDLER
Various writers and artists

BATMAN: HAUNTED KNIGHT
Jeph Loeb/Tim Sale

BATMAN: KNIGHTFALL Part 1: BROKEN BAT
Various writers and artists

BATMAN: KNIGHTFALL Part 2: WHO RULES THE NIGHT
Various writers and artists

BATMAN: KNIGHTSEND
Various writers and artists

BATMAN: THE LAST ARKHAM
Alan Grant/Norm Breyfogle

BATMAN: LEGACY
Various writers and artists

BATMAN: MANBAT
Jamie Delano/John Bolton

BATMAN: PRODIGAL
Various writers and artists

BATMAN: SHAMAN
Dennis O'Neil/Ed Hannigan/
John Beatty

BATMAN: SWORD OF AZRAEL
Dennis O'Neil/Joe Quesada/
Kevin Nowlan

BATMAN: TALES OF THE DEMON
Dennis O'Neil/Neal Adams/various

BATMAN: THE MOVIES
Dennis O'Neil/various artists

BATMAN: VENOM
Dennis O'Neil/Trevor
Von Eeden/various

BATMAN: YEAR ONE
Frank Miller/David Mazzucchelli

CATWOMAN: THE CATFILE
Chuck Dixon/Jim Balent/
Bob Smith

CATWOMAN: HER SISTER'S KEEPER
Mindy Newell/J. J. Birch/
Michael Bair

THE GREATEST BATMAN STORIES EVER TOLD Vol. 1
Various writers and artists

THE GREATEST JOKER STORIES EVER TOLD
Various writers and artists

LEGENDS OF THE WORLD'S FINEST
Walt Simonson/Dan Brereton

NIGHTWING: TIES THAT BIND
Dennis O'Neil/Alan Grant/
various artists

ROBIN: A HERO REBORN
Chuck Dixon/Tom Lyle/
Bob Smith

SUPERMAN/BATMAN: ALTERNATE HISTORIES
Various writers and artists

WORLD'S FINEST
Dave Gibbons/Steve Rude/
Karl Kesel

ARCHIVE EDITIONS

BATMAN ARCHIVES Vol. 1
(Batman's adventures from
DETECTIVE COMICS 27-50)
Bob Kane/Bill Finger/various

BATMAN ARCHIVES Vol. 2
(Batman's adventures from
DETECTIVE COMICS 51-70)
Bob Kane/Bill Finger/various

BATMAN ARCHIVES Vol. 3
(Batman's adventures from
DETECTIVE COMICS 71-86)
Bob Kane/Bill Finger/various

BATMAN: THE DARK KNIGHT ARCHIVES Vol. 2
(BATMAN 5-8)
Bob Kane/Bill Finger/various

For the nearest comics shop carrying collected editions and monthly titles from DC Comics, call 1-888-COMIC BOOK.

971030